The Lost Gods

Book 1: The Adventures of Tom Wolfe

First published in 2013 by Cherry House Publishing
The Lost Gods
Text Copyright © 2013 Peter Maley
Cover Copyright © 2013 Hannah Maley & Jamie Coull
Illustrations Copyright © 2013 Rachel Meehan

The rights of Peter Maley to be identified as the author of this work has
been asserted by him in accordance with the Copyright, Design and
Patents Act 1988

ISBN: 978-0-9575946-7-8
www.cherryhousepublishing.co.uk

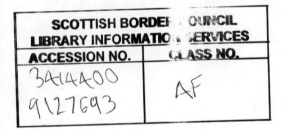

To my family

CONTENTS

PART ONE

1	Introducing Mr Locke	1
2	Bernard's Saga	13
3	There Be Giants	35
4	Caught In A Storm	45
5	Between A Roc And A Hard Place	63
6	The Court Of King Augeas	88
7	Cleaning The Augean Stables	104
8	When You're In A Hole, Keep Digging	119
9	Frost Giants Attack Asgard!	127
10	"Princess, Can You Swim?"	136
11	"The Floodgates Have Opened!"	138

PART TWO

12	Into The Furnace	157
13	Ice By The Bucket	177
14	Pilot's Licence	181
15	Dragon Naps	189
16	Everyone Plays Darts	219

PART THREE

17	Snow And Ice	233
18	Odd's Last Game Of Chess	247
19	Trial Without Jury	261
20	Danelaw High	281

PART I

1 Introducing Mr Locke

Tom Wolfe was wary and alert. He was sitting at the back of the class with his arms folded. He was looking straight ahead at the blackboard and doing his best not to catch the teacher's eye. It was a scary eye, flint-grey and blood-shot. The teacher stood like a hooded crow looking down on some road kill. With ragged black hair, nose pointing like a hooked yellow beak and that awful staring eye, he stood sideways looking at the pupils as if poised ready to pounce. Norman Porter was taking 3B for English. Tom checked his watch. It was the first period after Lunch. *Good!* Tom thought. *Only ten minutes left.* He had good reason to be wary of the teacher. Mr Porter turned away from the pupils and faced the blackboard.

"Copy down everything I write on the board," he said.

This is it! thought Tom, taking a deep breath. After lunch they always had to copy out pages of Porter's boring notes.

Picking up a stubby piece of chalk Mr Porter tried to write on the board. Nothing happened. The teacher's lips pursed in annoyance.

"Something wrong with the chalk," he said. "Pay attention while I find a new piece." He reached for another

1

chalk stick. Five pieces lay in the board gulley. He held the chalk in a pen-grip and began to write. The tip screeched on the board but no words appeared. Mr Porter tried all five pieces without success. He breathed out loudly in exasperation. Tom held his breath again. Porter would struggle to fill the board with notes today. Just before lunch break ended and before anyone else had returned to the classroom, Tom had slipped back early. He carefully dipped all the chalk sticks - both ends- in a small tub of quick-drying matt varnish he had smuggled into school earlier. Sealed in varnish the chalk could make no mark. No notes from Porter today!

The teacher studied the last chalk stick.

He was annoyed. "Someone has been tampering with the chalk!" he said through gritted teeth.

"Who was it?" He hovered menacingly by the front desks.

"Who?" And he peered along the pupil rows.

"You, Bainbridge?"

"Nossir!"

"How about you, Clarke?"

"Nossir!"

Porter had picked on the two tallest lads in the class. Bainbridge and Clarke played in the second row for the school rugby team. They were Ice Giants, thought Tom. Bainbridge and Clarke, only just turned fourteen and already almost six feet tall. Porter was one of those clever teachers who knew that a class could be intimidated if the biggest pupils were quelled first. Porter showed no fear for himself. He injected it in others.

"How about you, Wolfe?" Porter said, suddenly, swivelling on one heel and turning to face Tom whose face was pointing down at his desk.

"Nossir!" Tom said, parroting the words and tone of Bainbridge and Clarke perfectly.

"Thomas Wolfe. Or to name you in the grand style gifted to an unsuspecting world by your parents: Thomas

Storm Torsson Wolfe." Porter's words dripped with malice and sarcasm. He turned his head to one side and muttered, "'Storm? What were they thinking?" Barely audible, but loud enough that several pupils in the front row heard. It was almost a signal: Wolfe's the target today!

"It's just the kind of empty-headed prank you would carry out, boy!" Porter blazed.

"Not me, sir," Tom repeated, careful not to allow the grin that was threatening his carefully composed and firmly set chin from spreading.

"If I find you did this, Wolfe you'll be in very hot water indeed especially after the escapade with the dusters."

"Wasn't me either, sir," Tom said.

A week ago Tom had fitted some explosives from an illegal fireworks pack and some gunpowder into a paper envelope along with some intricate wiring and just the right mix of chemicals to make a simple detonator. He then packed the envelope with chalk dust he had gathered by scouring all the blackboard gutters in the school. He had carefully scooped up as much dust as he could find. He had placed the envelope inside one of the wooden handled, felt-covered dusters that were used to clean the school blackboards. He then repeated the trick with a second duster pad. The dusters were usually emptied by clapping two of them together so the dust fell into a waste bin.

"Clean the dusters, if you please, Vanbrugh," Mr Porter had said.

Maxwell Vanbrugh did as he was told. He stood over one of the waste bins and whacked both dusters together. They exploded with a report like a gun going off. A huge mushroom cloud of chalk dust erupted round the classroom, falling like ash from an Icelandic volcano. Porter had concluded that Tom Wolfe was the culprit without a shred of evidence. The conclusion was based solely on the fact that Tom had done that sort of thing before.

Tom thought he had got away with it.

Now he was certain his latest bit of mischief was about to spare the class ten minutes of note-scribbling.

He was about to find out instead what happens to *'the best laid plans'*. Mr Porter put a hand inside the tweed jacket that he always wore for teaching, retrieved a fresh piece of white chalk and wrote on the board -

"The Ancient Gods of Norse Mythology were known as:

    a). Norselings

    b). Frost Giants

    c). The Aesir. "

He placed the chalk back in his pocket and turned once again to face the class.

"Which of these statements is correct?" he asked.

The pond of faces that stared at him, sixteen girls and fourteen boys, was flat-calm and still. 3B occupied one of the pre-fabricated buildings on the edge of the school, overlooking the playing field. Outside the gardener was sweeping towards the pre-fab, cutting the grass on a small motor-mower. It looked like a Toytown tractor. It zipped along, slicing its way through the long, green grass, sending up a smell of pure summer. It buzzed louder as it approached. The gardener executed a flourished u-turn and headed off in the direction of the distant chestnut tree that marked the boundary of the school cross-country course. Porter waited until the noise of the tractor died away before continuing with his questions.

"Pilkington?" he addressed a slimy boy with lank, blonde hair near the front of the class. Pilkington's hair had strayed over the collar of his blazer, the black jacket with a blue-piping edge that was the foundation of the school uniform. The girls wore a variant of the same jacket with a nipped waist. "Any idea which of these statements might be correct, Pilkington?"

"No, sir!"

"'Nossir,'" Porter mimicked. "Do any of you

hypnotically-thick toads have any idea which statement might be true?"

"Oh, sir," Blaze Cinders protested. "'Toads' is *so* twentieth century. It's just *so* last week!" She was the only American in a class composed mainly of teenagers from the North of England.

"The twentieth century elapsed a lot more than a week ago, Cinders," Porter said. "I'll try again. Which statement is correct? Any idea at all?"

He waited and waited. And waited a bit more. The silence was trying his patience!

Tom knew the answer. It was easy. Porter had taught the class the Ancient Myths of Greece and Rome, the Legends of Ireland and Scotland, and the fabulous world of the Norse Gods less than a month ago. Now the teacher was doing revision. Tom was sure more than half the class knew the answer. He knew the answer too but he wasn't saying what it was.

It wasn't that he didn't like Porter. He kept his mouth shut because the teacher didn't like him. Tom had tried hard during English, History and Religious Studies, all subjects taught by Porter. He liked reading books, even though it wasn't cool for a boy to admit to liking books. He could get away with it because he had a really cool name and was very good at sport. He was really quite good at almost anything that involved a bat, ball or racquet. He had enjoyed reading about the Norse Gods but wasn't going to put his hand up and give the right answer. He was afraid that the teacher would poke fun at him. For reasons that Tom couldn't fully understand, the teacher had recently made it clear that he didn't like him, even though Tom had done his best throughout the term. He knew that Porter suspected him of carrying out the recent outbreak of practical jokes. Like all class jokers, in Tom's opinion, the teacher had to remain fair and impartial, unless he had evidence that Tom was the prankster. Those were the rules. The everlasting rules of school.

Porter seemed to have a special list of put-downs that he used only on Tom. Four weeks ago, Porter had asked the class out of the blue if anyone knew anything about Baldur the Beautiful. Tom knew the myth and had raised his hand immediately. "So what happened, Wolfe?" Porter had asked him innocently. "Enlighten the class."

"When Baldur was born" Tom said, obeying the teacher, "his mother, Fricka, the Queen of the Gods, saw that he was very handsome so she decided to ask all living things not to harm him. She asked everyone and everything - gods, giants, gnomes, toads, trees and plants – everything - you name it! - not to harm Baldur. Everyone and Everything agreed. Only she forgot to ask the mistletoe. She thought it was so small and harmless, she didn't bother.

"After that, when Baldur had grown up, the gods used to play games by throwing things at him: javelins made of oak and steel, swords with wooden pommels, branches of trees – and they all fell to the ground before they hit him, because of the promise that they had made to the Queen. Only she hadn't reckoned on Loki, the God of Mischief. He made a dart of mistletoe, used fire to harden a sharp point on it. Then he took it to Hodur, Baldur's blind brother and pretended to show Hodur how to join in.

"'I'll help you throw the dart,' Loki said, 'and you can hurl it at your brother. It will fall to the ground harmlessly before it reaches him. Why miss out on the fun because you can't see?'

"And Loki directed his arm and Hodur threw the dart. And because it was made of mistletoe and wasn't bound by any promise, it hit Baldur and pierced his heart. It killed him instantly. Hodur was guilty of murder and was executed."

"Very good, Wolfe," Porter had said, quietly. "Hodur was a bit of a wolf in sheep's clothing was he not?"

He then turned to look at Tom and said, "while you, Wolfe – what are you? Wolf in sheep's wardrobe or a lamb in a wolfish cardigan? Sheepish or dogged?"

Tom had been confused. He had no idea why Porter had turned on him like that. Not long after, Porter had asked if he was the 'Boy who cried wolf?' and the class laughed. Everyone laughed apart from his best friends Stella Cooke and Robert Saunders who would never dream of doing anything unfair or spiteful – unlike the other twenty-seven teenagers who hunted like a pack when the teacher offered up a victim.

So Tom didn't answer. And after Porter had poked fun at him four weeks earlier without any provocation Tom had retaliated by carrying out pranks. Now he watched and waited. It felt as though an age had crept by.

"Any idea which of these statements might be correct?" Porter asked again, this time in a louder voice, and then he repeated his own imitation of the class, "Nossir!"

It was important when the teacher got into this mood to avoid catching that bloodshot eye. Most of the class were looking at their desks or straight ahead, pretending to study the options on the blackboard. Bored, gazing into space, Tom glanced for a moment out of the classroom window. He was the only one who saw the gardener spin the Toytown tractor around the edge of the distant chestnut tree and then set off back in the direction of the school buildings. He was the only one who saw the gardener remove a long leather whip from inside his jerkin. He was the only one who saw him flick it in a vicious slash towards the high perimeter fence that ringed the school. He was the only one who saw the lash flicker out a tongue of bright red and yellow flame and scorch a thick stand of nettles so that they all fell over, burnt to the roots, eaten up in flames which then disappeared. There was a flourish of fire, black smoke and white vapour. Then all the smoke and vapour disappeared. All trace of the nettles, flame and the smoke had vanished.

Tom was astonished. He looked round the class. No one else had seen. Porter had been facing the blackboard.

He spun around now and caught Tom's startled face.

"Ah, Wolfe – you have been silent for some time now. Will you emerge from your woolly ways? You have something to say?" Porter asked. "I'll repeat the question that I've set out on the board: the Ancient Gods of Norse Mythology were known as-"

"The nettles!" Tom blurted.

"'The nettles'?" Porter repeated in a shrill voice. 3B collapsed in a heap of exaggerated laughs and snorts, whoops and yelps. The sportsmen among the boys whooped, "'The nettles!'"

Volleys of "'The nettles!'" rolled round the class. It was like listening to hounds bay and howl.

"'The Nettles'?" Porter said again. "Where on this blackboard do you see the word 'nettles'? Is that your half-witted attempt to pronounce the word, 'Norselings'? I'd have thought, Wolfe, that someone who knew as much about Baldur and Hodur as you would at least be able to pronounce the word 'Norselings'!" adding with a sneer, "Even though 'Norselings' is clearly wrong, I'd have thought you could have avoided mangling the word in your canines, Wolfe! How do you get Nettles from Norselings? When it comes to Norse mythology, you really have grasped the nettle!"

The class laughed as a mob. Everyone, apart from Rob and Stella, realised that they were safe from embarrassment for as long as Tom Wolfe was being hounded by the teacher.

"What on earth do you mean by shouting out 'nettles'?" Porter had walked from the front of the classroom, along the aisle between the rows of desks and was now standing directly in front of Tom's desk. "Explain yourself, Wolfe!"

"The gardener!" Tom began.

"Oh, 'the gardener!'" Porter interrupted. "We've had 'nettles' and now you're babbling on about gardeners!"

And again some of the boys bayed out, "'The gardener!'"

8

"'The gardener!'" echoed a chorus round the classroom.

Tom knew that he wouldn't be able to explain to Porter what had happened without landing in more trouble but he was determined to try.

"The gardener just blasted a thick bunch of nettles at the edge of the playing field using a flame gun, sir!" Tom said. "That's why I accidentally shouted out the word."

"There is a famous phrase, Wolfe, coined by one of our politicians in recent years: he said, 'when you're in a hole, you should stop digging.' You're in a hole…" Porter paused to grin at Tom and shared the grin with the rest of the class. His teeth glinted, sharp and pointed, like those of a fanged predator. "…and you're digging like fury. Well I've had enough of this. You've been disruptive all term. You've been gazing out of the window. I suspect you of being behind most of the practical jokes that have plagued the class this term. You yell things out uncontrollably in class. And to cap it all – you make up a complete fantasy. The gardener doesn't have a flame gun or anything even remotely resembling a flame gun. For disruptive behaviour and lying in class, Wolfe, you can take yourself off to the headmaster!"

Tom was astonished. He hadn't done anything that deserved being sent to the head for punishment. For a moment he was speechless.

Stella Cooke and Rob Saunders tried to help.

"Wolfe hasn't been disruptive, sir!" Rob said in a loud voice.

"He has answered lots of questions in class this term, sir!" Stella protested.

"Cooke and Saunders, do you wish to accompany Wolfe to the office?" Porter asked in a steely voice. Rob and Stella looked away from Porter's gaze and stared at the ground.

The teacher pointed to the door.

"Out, Wolfe – you know the way. A tongue-lashing from the Head might knock some manners into you.

Detention and lines – or worse - will almost certainly follow"

Tom got to his feet, looked round the classroom in confusion and walked slowly to the door.

"It's not fair, sir," Stella tried one more time but her voice froze when she saw how furious Porter had become.

Tom didn't want to get his two best friends into trouble so he hurried out of the classroom. He was tempted to slam the door but didn't. He knew he would only end up in more hot water. He stormed along the corridor.

Why hadn't Porter allowed him a chance to explain? He *had* seen something extraordinary. How had the gardener been able to scorch the plants? It hadn't looked like a flame-gun? Whatever it was, had to be against school rules? Why hadn't Porter listened to him?

The main corridor ran for what seemed like miles through the middle of the school with doors to classrooms, laboratories, including the "Language Lab", the Science Annex, the Art Room and the Music rooms.

This was so unfair!

Tom thought he was being victimised! He had been cheeky in an earlier lesson ages ago but he had paid the price for that. After that it was the unwritten law of school: once retribution had been exacted by the teacher, Law and Order were restored and from that point on the master was expected to be scrupulously fair in his treatment of each and every pupil. Porter had no evidence that Tom had carried out the pranks. It wasn't just unfair. It was unjust! Mr Porter hadn't allowed him the chance to explain that he *had* seen something extraordinary. Something he couldn't explain. At the end of the corridor, two flights of stairs led to the headmaster's office. By the time Tom reached the steps his temper was worse not better.

He knew that Porter had treated him badly. It was *so* unfair. He wouldn't have minded being reported to the Head if he had actually done something wrong, or at least he thought – being fair all round to everyone including

Porter and himself – if he had actually been *caught* doing something wrong.

"This is *so* unfair!" he yelled.

Without thinking, instead of turning left and striding up to the Headmaster's office, Tom swung right, through a set of double doors and stormed out onto the upper terrace that overlooked the schoolyard.

He didn't know where he was going. He had darted out to get some fresh air. He would clear his thoughts before going to see the Head.

He cut across the lawn to the left of the yard and found himself walking under the oak trees that separated the terraces and the yard from the gym. The gym was a big, old Victorian stone building with a barrel roof.

The sound of the motor mower's petrol-engine was loud in Tom's ears. The machine had cut a long swathe from round the base of the chestnut tree all the way back towards the prefab classroom. The gardener was new to the school and had only been in the job a couple of weeks. He kicked the mower into neutral, leapt from the machine and advanced on Tom in three easy strides. How had he covered the ground so quickly? Tom couldn't make out if the man was very big or very small. He had dark curly hair, and oak-coloured skin. He wore a leather waistcoat over a checked shirt and denim jeans tucked into calf-length biker boots with buckles. He wore a Robin Hood hat with a bright-green feather in it. Was he a cavalier sort of biker? Or was he a dandy highwayman gardener? It didn't add up. The gardener grinned at Tom. He extended his arm. Tom assumed that he was offering his hand to shake.

"Locke's the Pantomime Dame," said the gardener.

"'Pantomime Dame'?" Tom repeated uncertainly.

"Locke's the Pantomime Dame! It's rhyming slang! Pantomime Dame – Name. Locke's the name!"

"Wolfe," said Tom, again uncertainly, raising his own hand unable to shift his gaze. It was pad-locked on the gardener's face. Tom saw that Locke had scary, green eyes.

"I know who you are, Tom Wolfe," said the gardener, his grin growing wider and extending his arm further. "Or more accurately, Thomas Storm Torsson Wolfe, I know all about you!"

Tom reached out to shake hands, eyes locked on Locke, and realised that he had reached out and grasped the closed metal blades of the sharp set of hedge shears that Locke was pointing at him.

"Well done, Master Wolfe," said Locke with a nasty laugh. "That will do nicely, thank you!"

If he had been surprised by what had already happened, Tom was startled when he heard the gardener say, "You've really grasped the nettle now. Whether it hurts or helps you – only time will tell!"

And a brilliant, green light forked from the shears and coiled round Tom and the gardener like an emerald-coloured serpent. Tom looked down and saw that the shorn grass of the sports field, the chestnut tree, the terraces, the schoolyard, his classroom, Mr Porter, Stella, Rob, his classmates and all the rest of the school were already half-a mile below his feet.

He looked down again. He was flying immediately above a rainbow as wide as the Tyne Bridge. As wide and bigger, it was a rainbow-coloured bridge that seemed to stretch away forever. Tom closed his eyes.

2 Bernard's Saga

Tom was only half awake, snoozing comfortably in his bed. While he dozed he remembered: not long ago he had walked home with his friends, Stella and Rob to have lunch. They all agreed that Porter had been picking on Tom for ages though Stella also reminded Tom that he deserved some of the teacher's attentions: Tom had been cheeky in class, telling stories and playing practical jokes. You couldn't be the class joker and expect to be Teacher's Pet. One or the other. He mused over what they had said and done during lunch break while he dozed, wondering if he should wake up and get on with the day.

At least once a week, Stella and Rob went to Tom's for lunch. The rest of the time they ate in the school canteen. The canteen was foul and rarely had vegetarian food on the menu. Stella had been vegetarian for six months and Tom's Uncle Bernard made great aubergine dips, vegetable pakoras, samosas, veggie Cornish pasties, stir fries and omelettes. Tom had been brought up by his Uncle Bernard after his parents died in an accident at sea and his uncle had always encouraged him to bring friends round to visit. Uncle Bernard's house was less than half a mile from the school. Stella had been first to pick up the conversation once they were clear of the school gates. They all agreed that Porter had been in fiery form.

"He might as well hang a sign round your neck, Tom, saying, 'Pick on Me!'" she was clearly upset. "Just because

13

you stumbled over pronouncing 'triumvirate'!"

Tom winced. The day before they had been studying the Roman Civil War. Porter was covering the alliance between Caesar, Pompey and Crassus, the famous 'rule of three' or 'triumvirate'. Tom winced because he knew that he had deliberately stumbled over the pronunciation.

He had said in a loud voice that Caesar, Pompey and Crassus were part of the "'Try an' fart!"

The lads from the rugby team had howled with laughter.

"What was that, Wolfe?" Porter had said, his face purple with annoyance.

But Tom wasn't stupid: he pronounced the word 'triumvirate' correctly at the second attempt as the teacher hovered over him ready to strike.

Tom was bright. One of the brightest in the class, but he was also good at sport and it was a bad idea, among the boys anyway, to appear too bright. Most boys would do anything to avoid being called a *swot*. He and Rob had tried to explain this to Stella several times. It wasn't easy being a boy in a place like Danelaw. You had to show enough ability to keep the teachers off your back and do reasonably well at your studies. At the same time, you had to avoid giving the Locks and the Props the impression that you might know a thing or two. The Locks and the Props were two gangs of sporting gorillas that made up almost half the boys in the class. Rob and Tom had to get along with the gorillas – they played in the same rugby team - but otherwise they tried to avoid them. They didn't hang out with them during break or after school. At times Tom also behaved as if it was more important to be the Class Joker than a Star Pupil.

"I think Tom might have tripped himself up on purpose," Rob said, trying to help out. "'Triumvirate's not the kind of word you want to seem too comfortable with. Not if you want to keep your front teeth next time you're doing tackling practice with the Props."

Stella's hands made fists. She was furious!

"When are you both going to learn? You've been given brains that you should use. Why hide them from fear of the Morons from Outer Space you play ball games with?"

"You look gorgeous when you're angry, Stell," Rob said. "Your eyes burn like coals!"

Tom snorted. "What? They smoke and smell of rotten eggs?"

Stella laughed. She couldn't stand Rob's flattery and Tom's insults only amused her. Frankly they both got on her nerves at times. It was clear they both fancied her – a lot. Rob was obvious and flattered her several times a week. He would lay his overcoat in a puddle for her to walk on if the opportunity came along – or at least he *said* he would. He had never actually done it yet! Trouble was she did like Tom. She *really* liked him but he was an emotional dunce. The nearest he came to getting close was by poking fun at her or offering insults in poor taste. He thought he was being funny in the way that all class jokers thought they were funny but really the only person entertained by the Class Joker was the Class Joker.

Still, they were the closest friends she had. They had been friends since the day they arrived at Danelaw together to start First Year.

They had something else that had brought them together as friends. Danelaw was a private school. Most of the pupils' parents paid a treasure trove of funds each year so that their children could have the best education money could buy. Tom, Stella and Rob were scholarship students. To keep its status as a charity, Danelaw offered a handful of free places each year to youngsters with outstanding academic ability. Tom had passed the entrance exam with ease. But the school had also had him in its sights for a while. He was the first boy ever to have played for the county under-13 Rugby team while still at primary school. He had been ten years old at the time.

"'Triumvirate' - that could be us!" Tom said, offering an olive branch to Stella.

The 'eyes like coals that smoke and smell' gag had not gone down too well. "We've got to mix a bit of brawn with our brain that's all," Tom said quietly.

"That's just it – you two don't! You only do the brawn!" Stella protested. "Look at Dackett. Have you heard him say the word 'intellectual'? He's so dumb he thinks there's a creature called an 'Inner Lectural'."

"As distinct from an 'Outer Lectural'!" Tom said with a laugh.

"Exactly!" Rob and Stella chuckled with him.

"But Dackett's a great prop forward!" said Tom, opening the gate to his Uncle Bernard's house and walking up to the front door.

"My point exactly!" said Stella, as Tom opened the door with his key and stepped into the house.

"We're here, Uncle Bernard!" Tom shouted as they stood in the lobby. Blazers were quickly hung up on pegs. They saw Bernard Thompson's head appear in the kitchen doorway.

"Through here!" he called.

Tom's mother was Bernard's sister. Though he had last seen her when he was a baby, Tom thought he could remember his Mum as clearly as if she had been sitting next to him at school that morning. It was funny how unalike the brother and sister were. His mother had been slim and fair-haired. Bernard was a big roly-poly man with broad shoulders and an even broader stomach. He had bright gold and chestnut hair, a big, thick beard and a laugh loud enough to launch ships.

Bernard had laid the pine table in the dining room with a blue-and-white check tablecloth. There was fresh orange juice in a jug. Crisp-edged, juicy mushroom omelettes with a film of grilled cheese and some green beans were cooling on three plates. Toast, butter and a pot of tea were also arranged on the table.

"'Fraid it's only omelette today, kids. Didn't get a chance to get along to the Co-op."

"Don't worry, Uncle Bernard – it looks lovely," said Stella. "Much better than what they're serving at school today. Last year's lamb with tomorrow's potato."

"'Tomorrow's potato'?" Bernard said uncertainly.

"Tomorrow's potato," Stella repeated. "Spud from a packet! Not Jacket...Packet potato."

Although he was technically uncle only to Tom, Bernard was Rob and Stella's honorary uncle. They were both very fond of him. They weren't just Tom's classmates. They were his best friends. They were almost family.

The three teenagers sat down hungry, ready to begin eating. Stella picked up the conversation exactly where she had left off. Tom admired the way she could keep an argument going. There was no one like her. Stella Cooke: Beautiful, bright Stella. Hair fair as straw and with a voice as soft as smoke. Fourteen years old and in Tom's eyes she would rival Helen or Aphrodite in a challenge for the Golden Apples of the Hesperides.

"I was telling them off for dumbing down in class, Uncle Bernard."

"Were they at it again?" Bernard's voice rumbled through the serving hatch that opened into the kitchen.

He stepped into the room and set three mugs on the table along with a jug of milk.

"The old brain versus brawn argument? It isn't easy, y'know. It's an argument I used to have with Tom's mother, even though Tom was just a baby at the time. She was sharp as a razor, my sister, and very keen that one day Tom should go to University. But his father...well he thought it was more important that Tom should know how to take care of himself: learn to box, play football, rugby, hockey. Be able to run like the wind. To be an athlete. To fly - "

"Um, uncle – this is kind of embarrassin'," Tom said in a mock transatlantic accent. His uncle had spent some time in California and sometimes went a bit overboard in the Poetry of Life Department.

"Well if you find my reminiscence 'embarrassin' you can do something useful, young man. Get yourself into the garden and pick some lettuce, some fresh chives, chervil and parsley."

"Aw but Uncle Bernard-"

"No 'aw but Uncle' nonsense, Tom. Into the garden: lettuce, chives, chervil and parsley – Thank You."

A plain and unmistakable command. Tom curled his bottom lip but said nothing. He pushed the back door open and stepped outside onto the garden path. The garden area next to the house was a well-tended eruption of azalea, wisteria, peonies, fuchsia and penstemon. A broad stretch of lawn that would have graced Wimbledon's Centre Court stretched away from the shrubs and flowers to a broad strip of kitchen garden that Bernard had given over to vegetables, fruit trees, shrubs and fruit canes as well as herbs and useful plants.

Stella waited until her school chum had left the room and then spoke to Bernard Thompson.

"Will you tell us about Tom's parents, Uncle Bernard?" Stella asked. "Just while he's in the garden?"

Bernard hesitated at first.

"Please?" Stella pleaded.

"I'm not sure-" Bernard said. "Besides, I've told you the story before."

"And I'd like to hear it again," said Stella. "We might have missed something."

"'Missed something'?"

"Something that might explain the way that Tom is...why he behaves the way he does!"

Bernard gave in and told the story of the Great European Romance. He told of his sister, Freya and her university career, teaching Medieval History and Languages at Durham University. Of her beauty, matched only by her intellect. Great things were expected of her. Bernard was a librarian and had settled down to a steady career working in Newcastle's Central Library after spending a decade in California, long before Tom was born. Nowadays he took a long lunch break once or twice a week, sometimes more often, to prepare a meal for Tom and his two friends.

He carried on with the story.

Imagine how horrified everyone had been when Freya returned from a conference in Norway one day with a fair-haired giant on her arm and announced that she had married Tor Odinson-Wolfe in Oslo. They were happy together. As happy as a university lecturer could be with a man who moved from deep-sea fishing to working on oil rigs to doing steeple-jack work on Ely Cathedral in the space of six months.

Out in the garden Tom picked some chervil and some parsley, rubbing the leaves gently between finger and thumb before breathing in some of the fresh scent.

He loved the fact that someone as big, old and burly as his Uncle Bernard had such green fingers. Tom would never admit this to any of the thugs who made up half the rugger squad but he was almost as happy in Bernard's Veggie Patch as he was when playing rugby, making a vital kick out of defence, the ball zapping like a torpedo to the touchline and stopping the other team from scoring a certain try.

He stooped to look at the Webb's lettuce growing in a tidy row along from the parsley. The lettuce had bright, fresh, green leaves and was crisp and crunchy, ready to eat.

He studied the plants. The row was dry. He placed an index finger under a leaf that was half-drooped on the soil that supported it.

"Could do with some rain," he said to himself, but saying the words aloud and without thinking. He was lost in thought, studying the lettuce.

There was a rumble of thunder.

He squinted and cocked one eye at the sky. Clouds were rolling in from the north. Another thunder clap. He began to pick leaves and herbs quickly, determined to gather everything he needed for lunch before the weather closed in. And before his omelette got cold! Lightning crackled in the distance. Looked like a thunder storm was brewing.

You'd think I'd summoned a storm, Tom chuckled to himself.

"Tom's parents were a great couple," said Bernard as he continued to reminisce.

They had all gone to Norway on holiday when Tom was a baby. They had had a pleasant time, spending a week with Tor's Oslo friends. Tor and Freya had been so proud showing off their beautiful baby to Tor's old chums.

"'Beautiful baby!'" whispered Rob with a snigger. "Tom would be squirmin' in embarrassment if he was here now!"

"Shush, Rob! I'm listening!" Stella said.

"We had flown out to Norway and were planning to sail back on a fishing boat with some of Tor's old mates," Uncle Bernard ignored the interruption.

"Tor's chums were mainly from Oslo. He had sailed and fished with them off and on over the years. We didn't have to return in a boat. We weren't hard up. We could have flown back or taken the ferry. But Tor wanted us all to enjoy the experience of crossing the North Sea in a small boat.

"The night we were due to embark a foul storm blew in. I looked at the sea from the safety of my hotel window and said it was too treacherous. I refused to sail. I said that Freya and the baby should stay behind and fly back to England with me.

"But Tor along with my sister, carrying Tom in her arms, climbed aboard the fishing boat.

"I tried to persuade Freya to stay but she wouldn't leave Tor. He reassured her that it wasn't a *real* storm. He had sailed through much worse seas in the past. This was a minor squall. His last words to me were:

"'Tor Odinson-Wolfe isn't about to let some tiny white

tips in the North Sea scare him from a voyage!'

"Brave words but unwise given what followed. It was an incredibly violent storm..."

Uncle Bernard took a deep breath. Stella waited.

"It's OK, Uncle Bernard. We can wait. You can save it for another time if you'd prefer," she said.

"It's quite alright, Stella, thank you. I'd rather continue and finish the saga. I flew back to England unaware that anything had happened. I had unpacked and was in the kitchen here when I heard a report on the BBC News. A fishing boat had been lost in the North Sea. I dashed to the nearest police station. It was chaotic and confusing. Everyone on board the fishing boat had drowned apart from the skipper, one of the crew and young Tom. He was in hospital being looked after by nurses with a doctor in attendance. I spoke to the police and later tracked down the skipper. Tom had been rescued by a small helicopter which then mysteriously disappeared. A second helicopter appeared moments later and saved the skipper and one crew member. Everyone else died, including Tor and Freya."

"Wow! Tom's a baby 'plucked from the sea'!" said Rob.

"Born from water," Bernard murmured. "It was sad - horrible - his parents drowning but miraculously Tom survived. The strange thing is-" Bernard said, hesitating.

"Yes?" said Stella.

"The strange thing is that neither the skipper nor the crew member got a good view of the aircraft that saved Tom. When the smaller helicopter appeared the skipper was in the wheelhouse fighting to steer the boat and the crew were down below keeping the engines, the generators and the pumps going. At first the passengers were in a cabin below deck. The skipper said he heard the sound of the helicopter. Noisy enough. The sound of the craft and the hope of rescue brought the passengers on deck. In the chaos there must have been a panic. The crew deserted their stations and also clambered on deck. Only one man –

the other survivor - remained below, dealing with the engines.

"It must have been a mad panic. They were breaking all the rules of rescue at sea. There's a procedure to be followed for Air and Sea Rescue. You wait below until called. It was bad enough that a seasoned fisherman like Tor had panicked with his wife and baby but for the crew to ignore standing orders was a disgrace. What caused the panic? They'd been in storm conditions before.

"With all the spray hitting the wheelhouse visibility was poor. Nevertheless, the skipper could make out the shape of a small whirlybird. Too small to evacuate everyone on deck.

"The skipper was screaming at the watery shapes of the passengers and crew: 'Get back below deck! That helicopter can't take you all!' But the skipper couldn't leave the wheel. Ghostly in outline, its image washed by the rain the small helicopter flew in close. It was white or green, light-green. Hard to see in the storm. It hovered. At that moment a massive wave swamped the boat, sweeping everyone who was on deck into the sea. Just before the wave struck, the small helicopter rescued Tom but all the passengers including Freya and Tor were thrown overboard. The crew were hurled into the sea. Apart from the man who had stayed in the engine room.

"The helicopter was gone and so was Tom. The skipper didn't know the baby had been saved until he got back to dry land himself much later. A Sea King came along a few minutes later and flew over the boat. A really big whirlybird. Huge by comparison with the earlier one. And much louder. The skipper remained in the wheel house long enough to lash the wheel into position so the boat would point into the waves. Then he called on the last crew member to abandon ship. The skipper swung himself through the wheelhouse door and onto the deck.

"The winchman came down from the Sea King and rescued the last crew man. The fishing boat was shipping water fast then and the next big wave smashed over it, knocking the skipper off his feet and straight into the drink. The fishing boat sank like a stone. The Sea King picked up the skipper from the water soon after the boat sank. Then it quartered the area of sea where the boat went down, hoping to pick up more survivors. The helicopter hovered over huge waves for as long as it had fuel, searchlights panning over the sea, looking for the passengers and the rest of the crew. But found nothing. Only big waves and a cruel hungry sea.

"Some things remain a mystery though," said Bernard. "I have never been able to find the pilot or any of the crew from the small helicopter that was first on the scene. The one that saved my nephew. I've placed ads in the newspapers, even appeared on television asking for someone to come forward. Nothing. Even more bizarre - I made enquiries through the police and other authorities: there was no other, smaller helicopter on patrol that night. Only the Sea King that rescued the skipper. So who was flying the whirlybird that saved Tom? Who delivered him safely to the police on Tyneside? And more importantly-"

But Bernard had to interrupt the story then, unfinished and incomplete. For just as he said the words, 'more importantly', Tom shoved open the kitchen door and strolled in with a basket of salad vegetables and fresh herbs.

Bernard stood up from the table.

"Well done! Thank you, my lad," he said. "And the rest of the story will have to wait 'til next time!"

"'Story?'" said Tom.

"Nothing," Bernard repeated. "Time to crack on with lunch or you'll be late for school. The rest can wait for another day, another lunchbreak!"

Tom was still dozing. He wondered which story Uncle Bernard had been telling Stella and Rob. It was funny the way the day had turned out.

Funny – we had a great time during lunch, he thought to himself. He was still half asleep. *And then Porter's class turned out to be a real pain. Porter and the chalks and then being sent to the Headmaster's. After that weird gardener, Locke zapped the nettles with flames -*

Tom sat bolt upright in bed. He saw at once: it wasn't his bed. His dreamy memory of lunch with Uncle Bernard, Stella and Rob fizzled out of his head. Porter's class, the chalk duster bombs, Porter picking on him - it all faded away. It was replaced by the sudden, vivid memory of Locke's scary green eyes and the flash of light that wrapped itself around his feet. He remembered soaring into the heavens.

Tom wasn't dozing dreamily now. He was wide awake. His heart was pounding in his chest, thumping against his ribs.

A small, green dragon lay at the foot of the bed. It seemed to be asleep. Its scaly head was resting on its foreclaws, its hindlegs tucked up like a cat's. Its breathing was slow and regular.

Tom didn't know whether to chuckle in pleasure or howl in fear. The instant he moved on the bed, one of the dragon's eyes flicked open. Tom felt his own face freezing into a friendly smile. The serpent's other eye opened. Two, bright-red eyes, burning with the colour of rubies, seared his gaze. The dragon was about the same size as a Shetland pony. It had been sleeping like a cat. Now it moved like a cat. It stretched itself and moved from the foot of the bed.

Tom saw that he was in a big, circular room. The walls, floor and ceiling were of stone. The walls were hung with rich tapestries showing scenes from Old Norse legend. Battleaxes, shields and helmets dressed the walls in the gaps between the tapestries. A small fire burned in an enormous open fireplace. Halfway along the wall was a stout door. Between the fire and the door there was a large round window.

The dragon padded over to the window and thrust it

open. Then the creature aimed its nose at the sky. It fired a burst of smoke blasts through the open window and into the air outside. Again Tom didn't know whether to chuckle or howl in fear. The blasts of smoke formed horizontal lines and round dots. Perfect hyphens and full-stops.

Tom was intrigued. The slashes and spots formed a smoky pattern.

"Wait a minute," he said to himself. "I know this stuff. It's Morse code: Dash. Pause. Dot-dot-dot-dot. Pause. Dot. Break. Dot-dot-dot-dot. Pause. Dash-dash-dash."

He scanned the smoky pattern in the sky and said out loud, "T-h-e h-o-s-t-a-g-e i-s a-w-a-k-e."

Tom had had enough of being startled, surprised and confused. He decided that the only way to get through whatever was happening to him was to stay cool, calm and collected. Easier said than done of course when you've got a red-eyed, green-skinned, fire-breathing dragon sending smoke signals out of your bedroom window!

"'Hostage'? Tom said in a loud voice. "What do you mean: I'm a hostage? Ha! I don't know what's more surprising - a dragon that understands English or a dragon that does Morse code with its nostrils!"

"Norse code," the dragon said.

"What's that?" said Tom jumping at hearing the lizard speak. Its voice was warm but not warm in a *nice* way. *Warm* as in *Might get sizzling hot any minute!*

"Up here we prefer to call it Norse code. Not Morse Code."

Tom grinned and his sense of danger eased a tiny bit. Who would have believed that a fire-breathing dragon had a sense of humour, even if the humour in question was of the poor variety?

"Where's 'here'?" Tom asked.

"Asgard, of course," said the dragon. "What are they teaching you on Middle Earth these days?"

"Asgard – mythical home of the Norse Gods. The

Aesir," Tom intoned, reciting some of the homework that he had learnt for Mr Porter. "Worshipped by Norse, Normans and Danes alike-"

"'Mythical'?" The dragon said. "Just you be a bit more respectful, my lad, or you could end up as a freshly-seared kebab!"

"'Freshly-seared'?" Tom repeated in annoyance. For some reason the threat had made him angry rather than afraid. "How did you get the red eyes, Smaug?" he said, calling the dragon after one of the most famous serpents in literature. "Fond of a tipple?"

"You should be careful, young man!" The dragon hissed. "I don't like cheek!"

"Like a drop of the hard stuff, eh? Isn't a taste for whisky dangerous if you're a fire-breathing dragon? Or maybe that's where the fire comes from?"

"Cheeky pup!" The dragon said through tight lips. And the fact that he hadn't been seared like a kebab made Tom more certain that he had guessed what was happening. The dragon was under orders to guard but not harm him. So someone else must be due to make an appearance. He wondered who it might be.

"But you're right. You can't be mythical if we're both here and I'm having a conversation with a red-eyed dragon," Tom continued. "So this is Asgard – and I'm forgetting my manners." He had pushed things about as far as he dared. Winding up a fire-breathing dragon! This was one bit of cheek that not even Stella or Rob would have believed him capable of! He stood up and said to the dragon with as much good manners as he could muster, "Allow me introduce myself. Tom Wolfe's the name." He was about to offer his hand to shake when he remembered what had happened the last time he did that. He raised his hand and scratched the side of his neck instead.

"I'm glad to meet you, Master Wolfe," said the dragon. "Though I know your name already. Let me return the compliment. My name is Silversscalessnafﬂlingserpent the

Green. But you can call me Snaffler for short. It's easier to remember."

"Delighted to have met you, Mr Snaffler," Tom said, making it very clear what he thought of the name by the look on his face.

"I'm proud of the name 'Snaffler', you young scamp!" the dragon said. "I earned it."

"How did you earn it?"

"I'm partial to a bit of fish," said Snaffler. "Can't beat char-grilled sea bass or flame-frazzled halibut. Every now and then when I'm allowed to visit Earth, I fly over the Norwegian fishing fleet. I wait until the fishermen are dragging in the nets, then I swoop down and snaffle a belly-full of cod, pollack, or haddock. Flick a share of the catch up into the sky, flame-grill it in midair and then gulp it down before it falls back into the boat. That's the art of snaffling at its best. And no one does it better." The dragon stretched its claws and padded over the stone-flagged floor. It nodded at one of the brightly-coloured tapestries on the wall. It showed a fishing boat and fishermen hauling nets. And in the middle of all the sea and spray and fish and fury, a bright green dragon the size of a Shetland pony.

I wonder if that's Snaffler? Tom thought to himself.

"Yes. That's me," said Snaffler.

Tom was shocked.

"You can read my thoughts?" he said aloud.

"Yes, of course," said the dragon. "It's a useful skill, possessed by most dragons. I've found it comes in handy all the time. I use it to read the minds of fishermen so I can tell which way they're going to throw a basketful of fish."

"What a waste of skill!" Tom said.

"Cheeky pup!"

"But you could *really* use that skill. You could bring about World Peace!"

"World Peace isn't as interesting as a creelful of fish."

"Of course it is!"

"It might be to peace-making *people*. Not to a *Fish-eating dragon*. Maybe you need to search for a Peace Dragon?"

The dragon looked at the tapestry again and for a while seemed lost in its own thoughts.

"Most fishermen consider it an honour. No – more like a blessing – if I raid their nets. They love to see a master at work. None of the other dragons can snaffle fish like me."

"Is that so?" Tom said. It seemed the dragon liked to blow its own trumpet. Tom hoped the trumpet wouldn't melt!

Then Snaffler said, "Shouldn't brag too much. Even though bragging is an Art to the Vikings. Not a Vice, as I'm sure you know!"

The dragon padded over to the stout door.

"Anyway – can't spend all day talking to you, young Wolfe. I've chores to attend to and the Master is on his way to see you."

Snaffler flung the door open.

"Wait!" Tom said. "I've got loads of questions. How did I get here? What time is it? Does my Uncle Bernard know where I am? Do my friends know what's happened to me? Where on Asgard are we?" He stopped and thought about the last question just before Snaffler disappeared from view, closing the door behind him. "'Where on Asgard?'" Tom said to himself. "Better than that – where is Asgard when it's at home?"

"At the other end of the Rainbow Bridge from Midgard!" said a voice from behind the door just as it was flung wide open to reveal Locke the gardener. But it wasn't Locke. The person that stepped into Tom's room looked like Locke and even sounded like Locke – but this was someone or something completely different. He was dressed like a cross between a harlequin and the Pied Piper of Hamelin in olive, green, and brown, but even the brown cloth seemed to have more than a hint of green in it. He wore a waistcoat of green, khaki and gold and a dark

Homburg hat. His voice, manner and bearing were completely different to Locke's. The newcomer was proud and had the eyes of a serpent. Tom recognised at once that he was in the presence of an aristocrat. He looked into those hard eyes again. They were the brightest green he had ever seen. They were brighter than emerald.

There were many strange things about this person who looked like Locke and sounded like Locke. The strangest was that while he was quite tall, he seemed to have the potential to be a giant. As if there was a giant hidden inside the shape and size of a man.

"You've met Snaffler and swapped introductions, young Master Wolfe." That was even weirder, thought Tom. The stranger had just delivered a perfect imitation of Snaffler's voice and way of speaking. "Allow me to do the same.– I am Loki, though some prefer Lokke or Loge, Messenger of the Gods."

Not to mention - God of Mischief, Cheating and Lying, Tom thought to himself. *Murderer of Baldur and General Lord of Misrule.*

"You're quite right not to mention those things," said Loki, mischievously. "It would be almost suicidally cheeky if you were to mention such things!" Tom was startled and it showed. "All that stuff about Baldur and Mischief - You shouldn't believe everything in the old myths. I hope you had a good night's sleep as there is much to be done today.

"A night's sleep? How long have I been here? I have to get home. Now! My uncle will be sick with worry!" Tom was scared now. What would Uncle Bernard be thinking?

"That's quite out of the question, young Wolfe. Follow me! You have much to learn. And you'll have to learn quickly as you must leave before the day ends. The shower is there," Loki pointed to a door in the wall. "You'll find clean clothes in the wardrobe over there. The Danelaw High Third-Form uniform you're wearing stands out like a thumb that's been hit by Thor's hammer. Wash, get changed and then come down to join me at the bottom of the tower."

"'The tower'?" Tom repeated.

"Yes – the bottom of this tower. You spent the night in one of the many towers of Asgard's Royal Castle. I'll meet you at the bottom of the stairs in fifteen minutes. Don't dawdle!"

Loki walked to the door. Before leaving he turned to Tom and said, "Don't worry, young Wolfe, I can't read your thoughts. Years of watching people means that I can guess what they're likely to be thinking when they meet me for the first time. Especially if they have read some of the old stories. It's a trick."

Yeah, thought Tom. *It's a 'trick'. But you would say that, wouldn't you- if you want to read my mind without me realising that's what you're doing? And you'd put on that little performance about it just being a trick to knock me off balance so I won't know whether to trust my own thoughts?*

He stopped thinking and turned to stare at Loki, raising an eyebrow to emphasise the question he was thinking, hoping to catch the God of Mischief out but Loki had disappeared, leaving Tom blinking and pinching himself to prove that he was definitely awake.

The shower was in an alcove off the bedroom. It was inside a huge crystal cylinder with a carved granite floor. Hot water flowed from gargoyle-faced shower heads and a ship's wheel mounted below the bright silver pipes changed the temperature and flow of the water. After showering Tom inspected the clothes that had been left for him in the wardrobe. Thick woollen breeches, linen vests and undershirts and a heavy woollen tunic. Calfskin boots and a leather waistcoat. A scarf, woollen gloves and a woolly hat. A thick woollen cloak and a broad-brimmed leather hat, lined with wool. He began to realise that Asgard was not Florida. He pulled on the new clothes which had the wonderful scent of fresh linen and clean, wind-dried wool and stepped over to the mirror. He laughed at what he saw.

"All I need is a horned helmet and I can pass for a Viking!" he said to himself. Then he remembered things from Porter's homework and corrected himself. "Vikings didn't wear horns on their helmets, or feathers, or eagle wings come to that. Those are modern myths!" and he laughed. As if that sort of detail was relevant to his present predicament!

He stopped musing.

"What are you laughing at?" he asked himself, horrified. "You've been kidnapped by someone renowned for murder and treachery! Where does Uncle Bernard think you are? What does he think has happened? He'll have called the police! There's nothing funny in any of this. This is the most terrifying thing that's happened to you in your entire life! It's time to get back home. Now!"

He saw his face fall in the mirror. This was not funny. It was terrifying!

He didn't hang about in the bedroom after that. He had a thousand questions to ask Loki.

The door from the bedroom led onto a landing and then to a corridor. A few yards along the corridor, Tom came to a spiral staircase made from great sandstone slabs. He scuttled down the stairs, too excited to notice the paintings, plaques and portraits that lined the curved walls.

Loki was waiting for him at the bottom of the staircase.

"Come on – there isn't much time," the God of Mischief said to him. "You're going to have what I believe you mortals refer to as a Whistle-Stop Tour of Asgard and then we need to procure the things you require for your journey."

"Journey? No way! I want to go home. I have a barrel-load of questions I'd like to ask you and then I want to head home! When did I get here? How did I get here? Are you Locke or are you Loki and have you told the school and my uncle that I'm here?"

Loki shook his head.

"What have we here? Fourteen-year-old Tom Wolfe, a

Third Form pupil at Danelaw School. Lives with his Uncle Bernard. Best friends at school: Stella Cooke and Rob Saunders. Very fond of Miss Cooke though he has never had the guts to tell her precisely how fond he is of her. Good at games. Third-Year champion over two hundred and four hundred metres. Captains the school Third-Form rugby team. Also House captain at boxing and athletics. Reasonably competent at hockey, cricket, tennis, swimming, cross-country and football. Being good at games allows him to duck being labelled a 'swot'.

"With me so far?" Loki asked. "The only fly in the ointment: Mr Porter has been giving Master Wolfe a hard time lately. Caused our star pupil to clam up in class. Porter didn't know what he was doing. Over-reacted to a couple of practical jokes and then positively began to *pick on* the Wolfe cub. Oh, what a shame!" the God of Mischief said in the voice an adult might use to show sympathy to a toddler. It was a perfect imitation of Mr Porter's voice!

"He couldn't help himself," Loki confided. "Porter was under the spell of *Hard-Times-A-Giving*. One of my favourites and one I often inflict on teachers, High Court Judges and traffic wardens. Porter was bewitched into being horrible to you!"

"Under a spell? Why would you do that?" Tom asked.

"To test you."

"Why do I need to be tested?"

"That's enough questions from you for now," Loki said firmly. "But before you start to think I'm a harsh master, I'll answer all your questions at once and before you can put them to me. I'll put your thousand questions into a cauldron and boil them down to fewer than six." Loki's right hand performed a flourish under Tom's nose and he would have sworn that the hand held five fingers and a thumb. "I whisked you from Earth over the Rainbow Bridge to Asgard by magic so that you can undertake a quest. Time, as far as you are concerned, has frozen on Earth for as long as you are carrying out this quest. It froze the very instant that you turned right and went off towards the gym when you should have turned left and gone to the headmaster's office. Your Uncle Bernard, Mr Porter, the Head, Stella Cooke – none of them has missed you. Why? Because they're cruel and heartless? No! Because they aren't aware that you've gone. You're here to perform a service for the gods. And you won't be allowed to return home until you complete that service."

Tom could think of nothing to say. It was all very confusing. It was more than confusing. It was alarming. But he could control his fears. In spite of how extraordinary everything was – he felt calm and in control. That was good. He wouldn't quake and quail. *Be yourself*, he thought, *even if that lands you in hot water.*

"So nice of you to ask!" he said, sarcastically. Loki hadn't asked. He had simply assumed Tom would comply. "What service you want doin'? And what if I decide I don't want to play ball?"

"Oh you will!" Loki said. "Now – follow me. At the double! The guided tour. And remember -there isn't much time!"

Tom followed Loki to the main entrance, passing a stuffed polar bear standing by an oak table covered in empty drinking flagons. They stepped out into a wide courtyard, hurried over to a wooden tower and stood looking through a high double doorway in the tower wall. Inside the tower there was a narrow, iron, spiral staircase.

"Hurry, young Wolfe – follow me to the top. This is the North Wall Watch Tower. No talking. Save your breath for the steep climb ahead of you."

Not for the first time that day Tom was alarmed. He stepped back and looked up. The wooden tower rose high, higher and higher, far above the stone tower that he had slept in. The wooden tower seemed to hoist itself into the clouds.

"That looks like a long climb," Tom said nervously as he stepped through the doorway and stood at the bottom of the spiral staircase.

"I was having some fun at your expense," Loki laughed. "Asgard isn't stuck in the Middle Ages! Hang onto the railing, Master Wolfe. Hang on for dear life!"

Loki struck a metal handle at the bottom of the tower. It cranked round in a full circle. There was the sound of machinery firing into life, gears biting and shafts cranking. The staircase rumbled and began to move. It was like the rhythm of a steam locomotive pulling a long train of carriages. Slowly, slowly at first and then with a clanking and a thumping that sped up and gained momentum, the entire staircase began to move. It began to move quickly.

With a judder and coiling round the centre as it went, the staircase wound up and up and up. Faster and faster, hurtling Tom and the God of Mischief to the top of the tower in seconds. Tom was sick with dizziness.

3 There Be Giants

They stepped out onto a broad, wooden platform. Tom's head was spinning. He closed his eyes and waited for it to stop flying round like a gyroscope.

"Hold onto the edge of the turret," Loki said. "And don't look down."

Tom's tongue was frozen in terror. He couldn't speak. It wasn't just that he was higher than he had ever been before without actually being on an aeroplane. It wasn't the view across the fortress walls to a cold, frozen wasteland beyond. A terrifying land of vast, splintered mountains. A land of ice rivers and snow fields and broken rock and frost. A land of huge things that moved, with shapes like men but the size of trees. It wasn't the giant men carved from ice that he thought he could see in the distance. None of these things terrified him as much as when he glanced down from the tower. When he looked directly down from the turret he looked into space. Looking down had been instinctive. He had forgotten what the God had said. The impulse to check where he was had been too strong. He looked down at nothing. It was like looking at the Night Sky. Below his feet. Below the tower: blue-black space. Stars and constellations.

"I said 'Don't look down'!" Loki snarled.

In one sweeping movement of his arm, he caught Tom by the collar and cast him over the edge of the turret. Tom screamed. He was falling into space. He could see The Great Bear. The North Star. The Little Bear and there was

Orion's Belt. There were stars against a black background and nothing else but a deep infinite void. He plummeted. Then he caught a glimpse of the Earth below him. It was just like one of the photographs he had seen taken of the planet from a satellite. How could this be happening? How was he still breathing? He was falling towards Earth from space. He was falling from miles above the planet's surface.

At the very moment when he began to wonder why his blood hadn't boiled out through his skin and why all the air hadn't been sucked out from his lungs in the vacuum of space, his descent slowed. Like a boomerang, he felt himself suddenly starting to swing back in the opposite direction, back towards Asgard. He flew up from below deep black space, swinging high into the air. Light and blue sky, birds and clouds floated back into view. An irresistible force flung him back into the turret and he landed next to Loki, panting, breathless and shaking with exhilaration and fear.

"A practical demonstration," Loki said dryly. "The only way to leave Asgard is by the Rainbow Bridge. You can't fall from here through space. The bridge is the only way."

Loki paused, "That is true. It is also a lie," he said, "As you will shortly find out."

Tom tried to make his mouth form the words, "I don't understand," but could only stammer nonsense.

"You don't understand?" the God of Mischief said. "You were falling through space. You thought you were falling to your doom? Not from here. Asgard is Heaven. Look at the area contained within Asgard's walls." He pointed to the land that spread away from the palaces, halls and towers. Green, sugar-loaf hills grazed by lambs and sheep rolled down to meadows that were home to fat, contented cattle and buzzing bees. There were forests of ash and oak, and broad rivers and streams that ran with fresh, clear water. The mountains of rock and ice seemed many miles distant. Yet when Tom first clapped eyes on them he would have sworn that the mountains were nearer.

"Asgard. Home of the gods. Heaven - and everyone knows that Heaven is in the sky?" said Loki.

Tom nodded, still unable to form words and phrases. He wondered if he would ever regain the use of his tongue.

"Wrong!" Loki snapped out the words. "Asgard is both Heaven in the sky and part of Middle Earth! Connected by the Rainbow Bridge. Connected by Bifrost, to give its proper name. The only way to travel from Asgard to Midgard is over the Rainbow Bridge. It's the only way that it is physically possible to make that journey...apart that is from one other way...which you're about to find out-"

"Why?" Tom was at last able to frame a single word question.

"Because that's how Odin wills it. The Father of the Gods stops gods and godlings from wandering off among dull mortals without his say-so. And just as importantly it stops the Frost Giants from wandering down to your Planet and playing fast and loose with your weather systems! When I flew here with you earlier you'll remember I was very careful to hover directly above the surface of the Rainbow Bridge. As you discovered, if anyone is foolish enough to try and by-pass the Bridge they quickly find themselves returned whence they came courtesy of some very powerful magic brewed up by Odin, the All-Father himself."

Tom understood why he had whirled out into space and back again.

He wondered if he dared repeat the thrill? One look at the face of Loki was enough to convince him: the God of Mischief didn't necessarily approve of other mischief-makers. Tom wouldn't try the trick again. His breathing was almost back to normal. Without framing the thought consciously, in case Loki *could* read his mind, acting on instinct he played the cheeky teenager again.

"You should advertise this place to tourists," Tom said. "That's the biggest bungee jump in the universe!"

An eyebrow raised in disdain was the only sign that Loki might have heard him. The God of Mischief pointed again to the green hills that stretched away south from the watch tower, as far as the eye could see.

"Observe the beautiful land of Asgard."

He then turned and pointed beyond the high boundary wall, north to the land of mountains, ice and frost.

"Behold the terrifying world of the Frost Giants and Ice Demons, of Mountain Giants and Trolls. As a student of Norse lore and law, young Wolfe, I'm sure you'll know that the Giants are held at bay by the magic of Odin and by their fear of Thor, the God of Thunder and his deadly hammer, Mjolnir."

Tom nodded.

"A natural balance of power that has served us well for thousands of years. There's only one problem..." Loki's mouth had curled in sourness. "Odin and Thor are not here. They're trapped on Midgard. They can't get back. But don't tell him." Loki pointed far away in the direction of the Rainbow Bridge. Tom squinted and focused his eyes on the great warrior God who stood at the bridge. Though far away he recognised him immediately.

"Heimdal," Tom said, his voice hushed in awe. "Guardian of the bridge. The Norse Gods' own sentry. His sight is keener than an eagle's. His hearing? He can hear the grass grow on the hills and the fleece growing on sheep!"

"Ha!" said Loki. "If only that were true. He's as blind as a bat and deaf as a post. There's little chance he'll hear us!"

"I don't understand," Tom said. "The Norse stories were very clear- "

Loki interrupted. "Only when Odin is here. His power supports everything. If Odin were in his palace now we wouldn't be having this conversation. Not even in whispers. Old Heimdal would have caught every word. But with Odin gone – he needs a hearing aid."

"So why have you brought me here?" Tom asked at last. "What has any of this got to do with a-third-form pupil from Danelaw school?"

The God of Mischief gestured to the land beyond the tower.

"The reason I brought you to Asgard will be revealed shortly. The reason I brought you to this tower, you can see for yourself. Look."

Tom hesitated.

"You said I wasn't to look down!" he protested.

The God shot him an impatient look. "You should pay attention. I said you weren't to look *down*. Don't look directly below the tower. I am asking you to look across at what you can see beyond the walls of Asgard!" And Loki pointed in the direction of the outer walls and then his arm rose up to take in the wide sweeping landscape beyond the walls.

Tom squinted again. Three immense, concentric stone curtain walls protected the home of the gods. Beyond the outer wall to the north, he could see the dim shapes of giants, wrapped in mist.

"Giants are trying to scale the walls!" he said.

"Trying and failing. Odin's magic is strong enough to protect us for the time-being. But it weakens every day that he is away from his rightful home and throne. Look at the giants, boy, and be afraid. If they break through Asgard's walls, they will charge down the Rainbow Bridge and overwhelm Earth. The entire planet will be covered in an ice sheet! Forget about Global Warming. You are on the brink of a new Ice Age! Now follow me. You have seen why I brought you to the tower. Now you need to see why I brought you to Asgard!"

They crossed over to the stairs. Loki cranked the machinery again. An iron capsule shaped like a giant runner bean lowered itself onto a rail that ran round the edge of the tower. Loki opened the capsule and invited

Tom to step inside with him. The God pulled another lever. Cogs bit into place. The capsule moved slowly at first and then gained speed until it flew at lightning pace, flinging itself round and round the outer edge of the tower, riding on cup wheels down a metal rail track, travelling down to the ground in giddy acceleration.

Tom climbed out of the capsule and walked with knees wobbling across the great courtyard behind Loki. The boy was dizzy from the speedy descent. Loki looked as if he had stepped out of a taxi cab. The God reached inside his knapsack and pulled out a belt. It was a broad leather belt. He handed it to Tom.

"Here, put this on," he said.

"Why? I don't need it. I'm already wearing a belt," Tom protested. The belt was thick, old and scruffy. It looked as if it had been gnawed by an Irish Wolfhound. "And this one looks crap. Looks like it's been chewed by a dog!"

Loki stopped and pointed with his finger. When he spoke his voice was sizzling with impatience.

"Can you see your shadow?" the God asked.

"'Course I can. It's a sunny day. My shadow's as clear as yours!"

"Put the belt on, and no more silly protests. Then look at your shadow."

Tom did as he was told. He slipped the belt on and pulled the buckle tight. The moment that the buckle fastened, he gasped. His shadow had all but disappeared. There was only a vague, wispy outline of a boy's shape on the ground where before it had been clear and dark.

"The Belt of Invisibility," Loki explained in a quiet voice. "To the naked eye, you have completely disappeared – though you're still there and the belt isn't strong enough to completely fool all the light. You are left with a very slight shadow. Keep the belt on. I don't want any other gods knowing you're here.

Now follow me," Loki said and stepped towards the doorway.

Just before he reached the door, he shuddered as if in the grip of a seizure. His head lolled back and he staggered. At last the fit ended. When he was upright again he turned to face Tom. Loki had vanished. In his place was Locke the Gardener dressed in leather waistcoat, checked shirt, denim jeans and biker boots.

"Blimey! What 'ave we 'ere?" said Locke. "This is exactly what my Lord and Master, Loki was warning you about. Without Odin's magic to maintain Order, everything begins to run out of control. My Master's a Shape-Changer. He usually only transforms into good ole Locke 'ere when he wants to wander in the land of men unnoticed. With Odin gorn there are times when Loki 'morphs' into old Locke accidentally. I mean – *uncontrollably!*"

Locke glanced about nervously.

"But we can't wait for the shift to wear off. Foller me young Wolfe! Yer'll just have to follow in the footsteps of a peasant instead of a god!" With that, Locke tramped off across the courtyard.

They were walking towards a King's hall. It was a great hall set among several great halls and palaces. Tom couldn't calculate the size of the area enclosed in the courtyard. It was the biggest space surrounded by walls and buildings that he had ever set foot in.

Tom hurried after the gardener. Locke stopped in front of a great oaken door, barred and strapped and set with iron nails. The wall enclosing the door was made of soft, bright metal.

Suddenly the gardener's entire body went into a spasm, jerking and twisting as if suffering an electric shock. A moment later a tall, languid form stood where Locke had cowered. Loki stood proudly at the entrance to the great hall, wearing a black morning coat and breeches, with a long black cape spread over his shoulders. He looked every inch the honourable Victorian English gentleman.

Tom crept forward until he was directly behind Loki.

"Back again!" he said in a loud whisper. He had hoped to startle the God but Loki didn't flinch.

"I sensed that you were there, Wolfe. Did you really think you could sneak up on a God?"

Tom ignored the question and peered at the palace.

"The walls are bright as silver!" he said.

"That is because they *are* silver. This is one of Odin's palaces. Over there is Gladsheim where he usually sits with twelve Judges and rules over the affairs of Asgard. There is Valhalla, the fabled hall and home to all the dead heroes that have fallen in battle. This is Valaskjalf. Take a good look. It's the principal home of the King of the Gods."

Tom studied the palace. It was built in the style of an old Norse Great Hall, a broad and long, sturdy building with panels of pine and woven reeds laid over a timber frame, except that for Odin's Great Hall the pine and reeds had been replaced by panels of solid silver. The roof was of oak beam overlaid with thatch. Tom looked more closely. He could see the oak frame with its fine, hard grain and silver panels. Then he studied the thatch. Beautiful reeds like swan's quills were bundled and set over the roof beams. Only the roof was not covered in dried bundled reeds. The thatch was silver. Each quill a perfect mimic of natural thatch in beaten silver.

Silver thatch? thought Tom. *Maybe that could be this old geezer, Odin's nickname!* But he decided against sharing the joke with Loki.

"Admire the workmanship, whelp," said Loki. "Each piece of thatch is a miracle of craftsmanship, worked by Weyland, Smith of the Gods. You will bear witness to more of his work shortly. The walls, also Weyland's work, are of silver. A silver palace for the King of the Gods.

"Follow me."

With that, Loki heaved the door open and Tom stepped inside.

The roof was lofty and the oak beams holding the silver thatch soared high above Tom's head. A fire burned in a brazier placed directly on the floor in the middle of the hall and the smoke from the fire curled lazily up to an open roof window. Burning torches were held in silver brackets along the walls and the hall was well-lit. Safe inside the palace, Tom removed the belt that Loki had given him. He looked at his feet and saw his shadow restored.

A thought struck Tom. There was no one in the palace. They had not encountered a soul in the courtyard. From the watchtower they had seen giants in the distance but no people. And no gods. Apart from Snaffler, the dragon, Tom had seen and met no one other than Loki. No gods other than Heimdal, again seen only in the distance. The place was deserted.

"Where is everyone?" Tom said. "The place is like a morgue!"

"The gods have travelled to the outer walls. They are in counsel, asking how we should prepare to defend Asgard. The children are at school. There is no time for you to meet the young Aesir."

The God of Mischief beckoned and Tom followed him into another courtyard. Stone walls had been built inside the palace grounds and a large terrace garden laid out. Ash trees, hazel and alder had been planted. Water ran along a wide stone channel and a fountain cascaded into a broad pool. Set back from the channel and the fountain in another part of the terrace garden and partly shaded by ash trees was another large pool. Set in a broad circle of limestone, the round pool was still and deep. No fountain disturbed its still surface. No ripple, no sound blurred its mirror-like sheen.

Loki was standing by the water.

"This is the Pool of Mimir," he said to Tom. "Stand by the edge of the pool and look. Observe but say nothing."

And the Master of Mischief cast his hand over the water. He half-closed his eyes and muttered,

"By Odin's hand I now command
Mimir's pool become the tool

That Wolfe and I can use, your eye
And Odin's mind will Odin find."

Tom caught his breath but said nothing as the surface of the water shifted itself as if stirred from below by a big paddle. Then as quickly as it had been disturbed, the water lay flat, as clear as a sheet of polished glass and pictures formed.

"Watch," Loki said softly. "And listen. Think of the Mimir Pool as a Window on the World. It is a window to yours and to different worlds. You will see and hear everything you need to know."

Suddenly the pool was all that Tom could see. It was the biggest, clearest picture he had ever seen, and then sound rolled in.

4 Caught In A Storm

Overhead a pair of storm fronts fought their way across the City, two heavyweights slugging it out toe-to-toe, smashing hammer blows to granite jaws and cracking knuckles on cheek bones. The collision sent thunderbolts ricocheting off the sides of skyscrapers. The storm suddenly erupted like the crowd at a boxing match firing off a thunderclap of applause. Flashbulbs of lightning turned every sidewalk into front-row seats, right alongside the boxing ring. The two bruisers were frozen by the lightning for a second, picked out like Storm Giants caught in a winter blizzard and then they charged forward again, swinging club-like fists and the thunder rolled and rolled. And the rain poured and poured.

An old man and his younger companion had been caught out by the storm. They were picking their way along an alley, ducking in and out of doorways to avoid the worst of the weather. Making a break for it when the rain seemed to ease for a while, only to get drenched again as another surge of water fell from the heavens. The old man walked with a stoop. Over his shoulders he wore a thick, woollen cape that covered him to his ankles and he had a broad-brimmed hat jammed on his head. A moat had formed in the brim of the hat, deep enough to drown shrews, field mice and even the occasional brown rat. The overspill ran from the tip of the brim like sea water over a longboat. He wore a black eyepatch over one eye. The old man was briny, like sea and frost-rime. He was salty like a mariner and old enough to have flown a Zeppelin. Water ran in spills from the broad-brimmed hat and poured onto his cape. Even with his collar pulled up, driving rain found his brows and cheeks, filling up the deep lines and crevices of his face so that it ran with rills of cold water.

He was struggling to walk properly. His right hand clutched a tall, antique staff made from ashwood. The wooden pole was knotted and gnarled with a carved top. The old man used it as a crutch, leaning against it for support. Even with the ash pole he walked unsteadily, almost slipping on the wet pavement.

The younger man held the old man's left arm at the elbow and guided him along the alley. They were making slow progress but then the old man stopped again.

"It's no good, Bigger," he said. "I can't go on. I'm too tired."

"We have to keep moving, Odd," the man called Bigger said. "Otherwise you'll catch a cold. Look - the hostel isn't far. Just fifty yards beyond the end of this alley. Then you'll be indoors, somewhere dry and warm."

"Why do we call ourselves by these silly names?" the old man asked.

"'Odd' and 'Bigger'?" replied the younger man. "We have to have names to be allowed into the hostel for homeless people. These names do the job. They're all we have."

"Why are they all we have?"

"Because we can't remember our real names."

"Oh yes – of course – I'd forgotten!" said Odd. He said it without laughing. "So why are these invented names memorable?"

"I can't remember!"

"It's because they fit us like a glove. These are the names that the tramps gave us when we arrived at the hostel. The names have stuck."

The old man with the Odd name shook his head. He didn't like being homeless and on the streets. Bigger took his arm again. He would help him to the end of the alley. From there they would be able to see the hostel. He thought they were going to make it back safely. The alley was wet and dark. The storm sent waterspouts of rain splashing against the sides of the tall buildings that flanked the alley. This was no place for an old man. Bigger glanced ahead to the end of the alley and his heart sank.

Four young street thugs had stepped out of the shadows and into the light. The thugs walked towards them, slowly and menacingly, blocking the way to the hostel. Odd and Bigger were backed into the shadows of the alley.

The gang leader reached Odd first.

"Slicer is my name," he said, a fat leer splitting his face. "And slicing is the game. Meet my associates." He pointed to the three rough-looking types who had swarmed towards Odd and Bigger, "Ringtone, Jay-Q and Zee-Tab."

Slicer continued talking. "I really admire the fancy stick." He pointed at the ash staff. "I think I'll take it."

"No you won't," said Odd. "This is mine."

Ringtone stood at Slicer's shoulder while Jay-Q and Zee-Tab blocked Bigger. Four against two and one of the two was old and broken-down. The odds were not fair.

Slicer pulled a chunky bar of metal, five inches long and made of brass and steel, from his pocket. He flicked a stud on the side of the bar with this thumb and a bright, blue-grey metal blade flicked out from the side of the bar. It was a switchblade, very sharp, armed and ready to cut.

"I like slicin'," said Slicer. "Cheese, salami, cake – but nothin' slices as nice as skin! It's how I got my name. *Slicer*. Now are you going to behave like a nice old-timer and give me that stick? Or am I goin' to have to introduce you to the Slicer?"

Bigger moved to place himself between Slicer and the old man but Slicer was faster.

"My but you're a big 'un," he said, staring up at Bigger's face.

"You're a big 'un alright. But d'you think you're

47

bigger'n' this knife? Faster than this knife? Unless you're wearing some sort of body armour you'd best step back. This is between me and the old timer!"

Bigger hesitated.

Slicer took a step towards the old man and waved the blade under his nose.

"Give me the fancy stick!" Slicer commanded.

"Never!"

Slicer took another step towards the old man.

"Old man – you can't say I didn't warn you. This is going to hurt!" He plunged forward with the blade.

"You're right. I'm afraid it is," Odd agreed. He stepped back, moving quickly for an old man, grasped the staff two-handed and held it horizontally in front of his chest. He then thrust the staff towards the thugs and yelled out a dozen words in a language that came clearly through the Mimir Pool to Tom's ear. He recognised the words. They were familiar – but he could not translate them.

The moment the words left Odd's mouth, a blast of air stronger than the belch of a Rolls-Royce Jet Engine tore into Slicer and his gang. It scooped them up, lifted them high into the air, hurled them over several city blocks and dumped them in the East River. Seconds passed and at last four heads bobbed to the surface, gasping for breath and screaming in the cold river water. The thugs began to swim in desperate panic to the shore. Eventually they made it back to dry land. They were terrified, drenched and already developing a horrible stomach bug. All that remained of them at the scene of the incident was Slicer's knife. Odd reached down and picked it up. He folded away the blade and hid the flick-knife inside his cape.

"How did you do that?" Bigger asked.

"Oh I just folded back the blade with the heel of my hand and then it locks itself into place. You don't have to know how the button on the side works. It's fairly simple really."

"No – I didn't mean the blade!" said Bigger. "How did

you fling four big thugs through the air as if they were tissue paper?"

But Odd could only shake his head.

"I wish I knew the answer to that but I don't. I can't remember!"

He stood in the rain for some time and pondered, without moving, his chin tucked down inside his cloak. His face looked grim as the rain water ran down his nose. He shook his head.

"No, Bigger, it is no good. I cannot remember how I made that happen. But what do you expect when I can't even remember my own name? Come on." He started to walk in the direction of the hostel. "It's time we reacquainted ourselves with Hobble and our fellow travellers!"

And with that the two men set off, trudging through the rain in the direction of the shelter for homeless people and tramps.

The surface of the Mimir Pool misted then shimmered. It became opaque and then settled again and was clear. When Tom looked into the pool once more he only caught his own reflection.

"Wow! That was fantastic!" he said. "Better than anything I've seen at the flicks!" and then regretted what he had said. This was Asgard. The Mimir Pool wasn't a Hollywood movie. What he had seen was something that had not been staged.

"That was real, wasn't it?" he said. "The Pool is a window to different worlds. Which world is that? Who are those people?"

Loki's green eyes flickered like a snake's tongue.

"That world is your world, Wolfe. Midgard. New Jorvik. The present day. As for who they are? I will tell you shortly. The main thing you need to know is that they are lost. And - " Loki paused " – their memories have been blasted into atoms! Wiped clean like a pane of glass."

Loki stepped back from the Mimir Pool and sat on a stone bench away from the water.

"Take a seat and listen," he said to Tom. "You asked who those people were," Loki said. "To begin with, the two who were left standing together in the rain are not 'people' at all. They are gods."

Loki took a small knife from a pouch in his belt. He got up and walked round the pool until he came to a small yew tree. He reached up and pulled off a small, thick branch. He returned to where he had been sitting and began to whittle the branch.

"The gods are Odin, the King of the Gods and his son, Thor, the God of Thunder. They travelled to Earth some days ago. I know you've studied the old stories. They are called Myths and Legends on Middle-Earth, are they not?" Loki's laugh was a sneer. "Myths and Legends? They're Real History. Reuters' correspondence could not be more accurate than those so-called Myths and Legends.

"Odin has been griping for centuries about wanting to have an authentic travelling experience on earth. He knows Midgard from top to bottom. And so he should. He visits the place every year. Has done since time began. He calls those trips his Midgard-gadabouts. Think of the number of stories you have read about Odin in disguise on Earth. Odin disguised as a ferryman. Odin disguised as a mortal to visit his foster son, Geirrod, King of the Goths. Odin disguised as Gangngrad to visit Vafthrudnir. But all that time on all those visits, he still had his godly powers. So what happened?"

"I've no idea," Tom said, which was true. He didn't have a clue what could have happened.

"Every time he came back, Odin used to grizzle about not having got to know the 'Real Earth' because he always had his powers as a god to fall back on. He could always use magic to get him out of any scrapes.

"'I'd like to go there as a traveller. Not as a tourist!' he'd grumble. 'What would it be like to experience Middle-

Earth as a mortal?' And so I conceived a scheme – next time I'd help him to have a unique experience. He wouldn't go as a tourist god. He'd go as a mortal traveller. No magic to rely on. No godly powers to depend on. He would find The Real Earth."

"What did you do?"

Loki continued whittling the yew stick. Soft shavings of light, creamy wood fell at his feet.

"I made a concoction. Among other things I used some artemisia and some pure absinthe. Avoided rosemary, ginkgo and forget-me-not for obvious reasons. Uttered some select incantations and produced a liquor that caused complete memory loss. Delayed action. Takes effect after twenty-four hours. I added some to Odin and Thor's drinking flasks and waved them off as they strode down Bifrost towards Earth. Not nasty. Not vicious. Just a bit of honest mischief designed to improve the traveller's time on earth. Think about it. If you don't know that you're Odin – you can't work any magic. If you can't remember any spells or incantations - you'll have a Real Earth time on Earth. Supposed to wear off after a couple of days…but that's the problem. Several days have passed since Odin's departure."

Tom remembered everything he had seen in the Mimir Pool. It had been so vivid, so clear.

"The potion hasn't worn off," he said. "It hasn't even started to wear off! They're both suffering from total memory loss. They don't even know who they are!"

"A regular Junior Detective, aren't we?" said Loki sarcastically. "Well, investigator Wolfe…I've got a job for you."

"What's that?"

"It's very simple. Travel to earth and give Odin and Thor the antidote."

"Oh, right! If it's that simple why don't you do it? You're a god - why don't you just slip back down there and fix them?"

"For the same reason that I cannot hold my shape," Loki said, "Without Odin's influence my powers are waning too. I only had enough magic left to get back to Asgard with you. I must spend days inside Valaskjalf to rekindle my powers. Even then they will not return to what they were – without Odin. With Odin absent no one is gathering the magic apples of eternal youth, the apples that the gods must have to retain our vigour, our power. We need Odin to come home or Asgard will perish. Odin nourishes Asgard in every sense. Without him I am failing. We are all fading. Remember what I told you about Heimdal's hearing and sight?

"And I must also remind you, young Wolfe, if Odin and Thor fail to return, not only will Asgard perish, your world will perish. All the people you know and love will freeze to death...if they aren't clubbed to death by rampaging Frost Giants and Trolls first."

"Let's get goin' then," said Tom. "I'm keen to get back to see Uncle Bernard and old Porter will be wonderin' why I haven't been up to see the Headmaster. You give me the potion or pill or poultice, or whatever it is and I'll stroll back down the Rainbow Bridge - sorted!"

Loki gave a condescending laugh. "You're ahead of yourself, whelp! If only it were that simple."

The God was still whittling the yew stick, though he was more careful in making cuts and snicks now than when he first began hacking at the wood.

"For instance, Bifrost is closed to you. Heimdal would never let a mortal pass from Asgard to Earth."

"The Belt of Invisibility!" Tom began.

"Not possible," Loki interrupted. "His powers have slipped since Odin left, but even a failing Heimdal would hear you as you tried to slip by him. No, that wouldn't work."

"Then how on earth can I get back to Earth?" Tom asked, wondering for the umpteenth time that day how he could use an expression like that without his head exploding.

"You mean: how on Asgard can you get back to Earth?" Loki said pedantically. "There's another way." Even as he spoke the words, his face twisted and with a snarl he had morphed back into the shape of Locke the gardener. He looked bewildered for a moment or two before continuing as though nothing had happened. "Blimey you ask a load of questions. Can't you keep yer trap shut for half a mo' and just listen? Pin back your King Lears-"

"King Lears?"

"Ears! And listen." Locke-Loki had finished whittling. "And look!"

He held out a large dart, complete with pointed tip and a carved flight of four wings, fashioned from the freshly cut yew branch. It was slightly bigger than the sort of dart thrown at a modern darts board.

"Move your Brass Bands. Yer 'ands! And catch!"

The Trickster threw the dart towards Tom who stepped to one side and caught it in mid-flight. It hadn't been thrown hard enough to hurt him but it had still taken considerable skill and superb timing to catch the dart in mid air.

Tom twirled the dart in his fingers and lobbed it up. He caught it by the shaft before it hit the ground.

"Very good," said Locke. "Now the real Pint of Best. I mean, Test. Follow me."

Locke had begun to walk away from the pool but then he hesitated, reached under his leather waistcoat and withdrew a mirror. The mirror was in the shape of an oval with a band of gold framing its glass. A large locket mirror, it was hinged and with a clasp on one side.

The gardener flicked the clasp and the mirror opened up like an oyster. Locke ducked over, reached into the pool with the mirror and using it like a ladle scooped out a film of water onto the glass. Then without spilling a drop he flicked over the face and shut the mirror, firmly locking it once again.

"What did you do that for?" Tom asked.

"You'll find out soon enough. Now – follow me. At the double!"

As Tom had discovered more than once before, Locke could move very swiftly when he chose to. They hurried along silver halls, furnished with silver chairs and tables, silver bookcases holding books bound in leather and smothered in silver-leaf. They passed silver mirrors that reflected against silver mirrors, images that twinned with one another and went on forever. There was a tall birdcage with two large, silver perches and one, large, black bird. The birdcage looked sad, as if it were missing something.

"Odin's Ravens!" Locke said, pointing at the cage as he scurried along the hall.

Tom wondered what "Odin's Ravens" rhymed with, if it was rhyming slang. Then he realised that Locke was in fact referring to Huggin and Munnin, two giant ravens that belonged to the Father of the Gods. A thought wriggled like a little worm in Tom's brain. What was it? He tried to remember. Something about the names of the ravens. There was something special about the birds. Huggin meant "thought" and Munnin was...was what? But he could not remember. He wondered if he was missing something. Why should he trust the God of lying, cheating and theft? But before he could give the matter any further thought, Locke came to a halt. The gardener shape-shifted.

A tall man, elegant and dangerous in a long, black, Victorian morning coat once again stood before Tom. He looked almost as aristocratic and as cruel as the famous vampire, Count Dracula.

Loki opened another side door and Tom found himself in another part of the great courtyard.

Loki was standing in front of a high, silver gate.

"Now –follow me through the gate," Loki said. "But first your instructions. When we pass through the gate we will enter a courtyard that few gods ever see. This is the way to Weyland's forge. Weyland – blacksmith, engineer and armourer to the gods as well as keeper of our horde of magical weapons. From the moment we step through the gates, you must do exactly as I say. I will utter my instructions once and once only. It is imperative that you follow my words to the letter, if you wish to live."

If I wish to live? What's going on now?

The silver gate opened onto a narrow lane, set with cobbles. At the end of the lane an iron gate barred the way. Beyond it was a tall round tower, built of hard sandstone and with a conical, slate-tiled roof. Two yew trees grew on either side of the gate and beyond them two more were growing on either side of a stout door built from solid sheets of iron, set into the side of the tower.

Tom followed Loki as he walked up to the gate and almost leapt out of his skin as a wrinkled face appeared from deep in the heart of one of the yew trees. The face was living wood, old and gnarled and twisted.

"Halt!" the yew face snapped. "The boy must pass the test if you are both to enter!" said the yew.

"Test? What test?" Tom stammered.

Loki spoke slowly and deliberately. "Listen carefully. It is a test of skill and accuracy. You must stand on this side of the barred iron gate. You must throw the yew dart through a gap in the gate. You must throw the dart so that it flies straight and true to the door at the end of the yard. The dart must fly straight through the large keyhole in the door. You cannot miss. You are only allowed one throw. The keyhole is in the middle of the carved yew target in the centre of the iron door."

Tom weighed up everything Loki had said to him. He walked up to the iron gate and looked at the door. It was eight feet or so beyond the gate. This would be quite a throw! He stepped over the yard so that he stood in front of the talking yew. The face was old and gnarled and sour-looking. It would be so easy to poke fun at an ugly old face like that!

He would shove his nose right up close to the face in the tree and say, "Yew lookin' at me?"

He was on the point of delivering just such a pointless splash of verbal acid when he caught himself. What was he playing at? This was Asgard! The fate of everyone he knew and held dear was in the balance. He suddenly knew what it must feel like at times to be Mr Porter dealing with a cheeky pest who just could not stop himself from playing the fool. He abandoned the list of insults that had sprung into his mind and started to speak.

"Excuse me, sir," he said in the most polite and well-mannered voice he could muster. "May I borrow some of your needles?"

"Of course you can," said the yew. "Good manners will always gain some sort of advantage. Most young whipper-snappers who try to pass the ordeal simply barge up here, throw the dart without so much as a "By-your-leave", and of course they miss the target. Then we have to hurl them over the walls and they are chopped up into tiny bits by the Frost Giants and fed to the wolves."

Tom struggled to swallow. He hoped that the tree simply had a dark sense of humour. He picked a handful of twigs from the yew and scuffed some of the needles into his hand. He flung them in the air and watched them fall. He repeated the exercise.

"No magic allowed!" the yew warned.

Tom grinned. As if he could work magic.

If only!

"No magic involved," he said. "I'm testing the wind."

He measured the distance. He balanced the dart. He chucked it from one hand to the other. He threw it straight up in the air and caught it, watching carefully all the while, making mental notes.

He walked up to the tree again. No harm in keeping up the charm offensive.

"Do I have your permission to attempt the test?"

"You do, indeed, young man." Then the yew spoke to

its companion tree. "I actually hope that this one succeeds. I'm really going to regret having to hurl him to the wolves!"

"It's all the same to me," said the other yew. "Wolves have nary done me harm. This lot think they can just clip off our branches any time that suits them. Bows, arrows, darts – I dunno where will it all end? I'm quite happy to chuck 'im to the wolves to tell yer the honest truth!"

With that threat ringing in his ears, Tom stepped between the trees and stood in front of the gate. He measured the distance again. He flung one more handful of yew needles in the air and watched them fall. He balanced his feet carefully and steadied himself. He took a deep breath and half breathed it out again. He lifted his forearm and sighted along the dart, the flight just beyond his nose. He looked along the shaft to the point, settled himself and then flung the dart with a brisk flick of his fingers and thumb. The yew dart sizzled between the iron bars. It flew in a shallow arc and soared above the cobbles. It flew straight and true at the yew shield, straight at the face set in the door and straight through the keyhole. Three of the yew trees whistled in appreciation, shook hands and reached forward and back, waving branches, twigs and needles. The fourth simply looked glum. The gate rolled open and at the same time, the heavy iron door in the round tower opened, swinging back inside the tower.

"You have passed the ordeal, young man," said the kinder of the yew trees. "You may both enter!"

"Dunno what the poor wolves are goin' to do for dinner tonight," the other tree grumbled. "It'll be terrible if the poor, lonesome creatures 'ave to go 'ungry!"

Loki quickly ushered Tom along to the tower. As he stepped inside, he muttered, "Just as well I was able to whittle a morsel of magic into that yew dart for you. You should pick it up and carry it with you. It may come in handy!"

Tom did as he was told and picked up the dart.

Nothing could have prepared him for what lay inside the tower. It was an echoing, cavernous space with high beams of stout oak supporting the roof. One section of the tower wall opened onto a broad four-sided, three-walled workshop with another iron gate set in a high, spiked, metal fence in one of the sides where a wall should have been. Beyond the metal fence was yet another courtyard, though this one was more like a big farm steading than a palace court. The walls of the tower were hung with all manner of different swords: broad swords, two-handed swords, scimitars, stabbing swords, daggers and knives. There were axes – fighting axes, two-headed axes, smaller throwing axes, single-headed battleaxes and axes for chopping wood and building ships. There were hammers of all sorts, shapes and sizes, javelins, spears, bows, arrows, scabbards, shields, armour, including breastplates and ankle guards. There were helmets covered in studs and helmets with strip iron nose guards. Helmets with pin-hammered motifs traced on the metal. Helmets with leather skull caps inside. Plain round helms and conical head guards. Not a single helmet to be seen anywhere with horns, wings or feathers. Plain helmets only - too many to count. In the workshop Tom could see all the gear a smith could need: furnace, anvil, hammers, tongs, charcoal, pliers, chisels, a forming wheel, screwdrivers, spanners, gauges, callipers, compasses, tongs – his eyes could not take it all in.

He saw a massive bronze breastplate emblazoned with a bright gold-and-orange serpent. The serpent seemed to twist and glower in front of his eyes, breathing fire.

"Felmir – Odin's armour," Loki said, and he began to point. "And there is Gungnir – his spear which never misses its target. Your dart may well be a distant cousin," the God of Mischief said with a sly smile. "Draupnir, the ring which is a spawner of rings. I could go on. The tower overflows with magic spears and swords, shields and scabbards.

"This is all the work of Weyland, the Gods' blacksmith," Loki explained. "As was the machine in which we travelled to the top of the watch tower. He designed and built it."

"Weyland made that? Wow! It's like something out of Jules Verne or HG Wells." Tom was thinking of two of his favourite authors, the fathers of science-fiction.

"Never heard of them," said Loki dismissively. "Of course we could have travelled to the top the old-fashioned way," he continued.

"'The old-fashioned way'?" Tom asked.

"I could have flown us there by magic but we have to use the machine in order to humour Weyland – otherwise he sulks. When he sulks, he refuses to make swords and axes and shields, the things we really need. We should call his armour Blackmail! So we use his machines from time to time.

"Weyland thinks Asgard should move into the Modern World. Weyland knows how to use coal and steam and pumps. He is at home in a world of cogs and gears and pistons. He wants Asgard to move from the Dark Ages and into the Industrial Revolution."

Loki shook his head. "It will never catch on," the God of Mischief said. "When you are Immortal all you need is Art and Poetry, War and Romance, Virtue and Valour or in my case, Vice and Power. We don't need Progress!" he spat the last word like poison.

"We don't have time for a guided tour. We must simply get the key that opens the gate that will set you down again on earth."

Loki looked through the metal fence. His eyes narrowed as they fell on two dark objects that lay just beyond the gate. He peered at an anvil and a broad two-headed sledgehammer that lay on top of the anvil.

"Go through the gate and bring me that hammer, Wolfe," he said casually.

Tom's eyes were still snared by the weapons and the armour. Bedazzled by the wealth of skill and artistry set out in iron and steel, bronze, gold and silver, he nevertheless did as he was told. He pushed open the gate and stepped into the smallest yard that he had seen in Asgard so far. It was tiny. There was only space for the anvil and the hammer. Not even room to work properly. Though it was heavy in his grasp, he picked up the hammer easily enough and balanced the handle over his shoulder, the hammer head behind his back. He was unaware that Loki had been studying him closely and that the God had not breathed out from the moment Tom first touched the hammer.

"Good," said Loki, making an effort to stay calm. "Now we must act swiftly. We don't have much time. Weyland is three leagues from here, working on the outer walls, accompanied by the other gods who are deliberating how best we are to defend ourselves. Here is what you must do."

Loki joined Tom in the yard and pointed at another door set in the wall. Next to it a big brass key lay inside a stout metal cradle that was fixed to the wall.

"You must swing the hammer once and crack open the cradle. Take the key from the cradle and fit it into the door. The door will swing open. Put the hammer back on the anvil where you found it along with the key and step through the door. Don't look back.

"Once through the door you will land on Midgard. This is a secret portal from Asgard to earth, known to no one other than Weyland and myself. Once On Midgard you will embark on the first of three quests. If successful you will find Odin and Thor and restore their mind and their memory. Did you understand everything I said?"

Tom hesitated.

"Why do you hesitate, boy? The task is simple enough!"

"If it's that easy, why don't you do it? What do you need me for?"

Something didn't feel right. Tom had been feeling a growing sense of unease. He had been uneasy from the time of his first encounter with Locke the Gardener, but this was something different.

"You dare to question my instructions, boy?" Loki's voice echoed round the workshop, booming like a howitzer. His green eyes had narrowed and were hard and threatening.

"No, sir!" Tom blurted, seeing the look in Loki's eyes. It was a look that wielded a knife, stabbed ribs and cut throats.

"Then deliver back to me the instructions I gave you!"

Tom nodded and did as he was told, carefully repeating Loki's instructions, parrot-fashion. When he had finished, the God reached under his coat and pulled out a knapsack made from soft leather.

"This is all you need – the potion for Odin and some magic trinkets, including two more belts and three more of the magic yew darts that I have whittled for you as well as a couple of small pets to keep you company and help you along the way. All the instructions you are ever likely to need are inside the rucksack. Put it on your back and then swing that hammer."

"But how am I supposed to save Odin? I don't understand!" Tom was confused. "I thought you were going to tell me step-by-step what I need to do!"

"I've placed scrolls inside the knapsack. Everything you need to know is in the scrolls!" Loki said. "Now break the cradle, take down the key and open the door!"

Tom pulled the rucksack strap over his shoulder. He hefted the hammer. He was completely and utterly confused. How was opening this door going to help get him back to earth? Earth was miles below Asgard and set apart by deep space and time as well as being just around the corner over the Rainbow Bridge! But he realised that in spite of his reputation for mischief, everything Loki had said so far had been correct. He had not misled him. And it was clear that Asgard was in peril. The Lord of Tricksters wouldn't lie about this. Why would he? His own survival depended on Tom succeeding! He swung the hammer and the metal cradle shattered as soon as the hammer head touched it. He recovered the brass key, turned and replaced the hammer on the anvil where he had found it, tightened the strap of the rucksack over his shoulder one last time and then jamming the key into the lock, he turned it. Immediately the door swung open, out and away from him and he teetered on the edge of a horrible, yawing, black sky of distant stars and cold and frost. He stood frozen, petrified, in the doorway. He hesitated.

Too late! With a deft shove from his boot, Loki heaved Tom over the edge and the door swung shut. Tom closed his eyes as he fell; shooting headlong once again through deep, black space.

Loki stood back inside the yard. The key had returned to the cradle. Light and heat fused metal and the cradle reformed as if it had never been damaged. Loki bent down as if he was going to lift the hammer from the anvil. He squeezed his fingers round the handle and tried to lift it. He strained and heaved. The bottom edge rose about a finger nail's gap from the solid iron block and he was forced to free his fingers and jump back before the handle thumped back down. He shook his head. He thought as much. He had never seen anyone other than Thor, the God of Thunder, lift the hammer. It was called Mjolnir, Hammer of the Gods and slayer of Frost Giants. Just as well he had booted the boy through the door before the young Wolfe had a chance to raise the hammer a second time!

5 Between A Roc And A Hard Place

Tom opened his eyes. It was very hot. He looked up. The sun blazed down on him. There was no sign of Asgard. No sign of the door that he had fallen through. The deep, black void had disappeared. Above him was a bright, blue sky, lit up by a dazzling golden discus. He was kneeling on a sandy beach.

He had fallen through space and survived. But where had he landed? A clear blue sea washed up the sloping sand and lapped back. He heard voices, distant voices. He couldn't see where the people were. He thought they must be screened by the trees that he could see beyond the beach. He couldn't work out what they were saying. They were speaking Greek. While he recognised Greek because he had been to Greece on holiday, he couldn't speak the language. He spotted the soft leather knapsack that Loki had given to him. It was lying in the sand. He picked it up and opened it. As soon as he pulled back the satchel flap, a large insect, half the size of his hand flew out.

Crap! That's a big moth! thought Tom.

"I'm not a moth!" the creature said angrily, in a loud voice for something so small. "I'm a dragon! And you shouldn't say words like 'crap!'"

Tom looked more closely. The creature shimmered mistily. It wasn't an insect at all. It was a beautiful, milky-white, miniature model of Snaffler, the fish-eating dragon. This dragon resembled Snaffler but the image imprinted in Tom's mind's eye also showed differences. Snaffler was green-skinned with red eyes. This dragon had white scales and blue-green eyes.

Who are you? What are you? Tom wondered to himself. Once again speechless in this strange world of magic and mysteries. The words formed in his mind but he was unable to utter them.

"You may call me Snow," the dragon replied. "Loki, the God of Mischief, has commanded me to act as your companion on this quest and to assist you in every way that I can. He has given me a number of detailed instructions. This will not be an easy set of tasks, young Wolfe. And it will be very dangerous.

"And as to what am I? It should come as no surprise to you to learn that I'm a snow dragon, a close cousin of Snaffler, who is a common or garden fire dragon. Everything he does with heat, I do with cold. Where he breathes fire and steam, I make snow and ice. What we have in common is the ability to read thoughts."

That explains it! thought Tom. *I wondered how-*

"Exactly," said Snow, interrupting Tom's train of thought.

Tom looked along the shore and gazed into the distance. He looked one way and then the other. Sand stretched as far as his eyes could see along the shoreline and the sea was calm and deep, deep blue. Beyond the sand, over a slight rise in the land, he could see Acacia and Cypress trees growing. The voices that he could only just make out were coming from the trees. He listened carefully. There was no change in the sound or tone. No one had spotted him yet. But it wouldn't be long before they did!

Time to get moving, he thought.

"OK, Snow, you've told me what you were doin' in the satchel and why you are here. Now do you mind telling me where 'here' is?"

"Slow down, Wolfe," said the dragon. "Though at times you're more like a cub or a pup than a he-wolf. I'd suggest you gather up the knapsack and all your belongings and hide behind that conveniently placed large rock so that you're out of sight. Then we can confer."

Tom knew that the dragon was talking sense, even if that sentence made him wince.

Dragon talking sense? he thought to himself, shaking his head. *Whatever next?*

Tom ducked behind the rock. He noticed it was a strange oval shape with a rough, sandy-cream-coloured surface. When he was safely positioned behind the boulder, he opened out the satchel. *There's something about having a thought-reading dragon as a companion. Makes you very efficient and avoids time-wasting on idle conjecture*, he thought.

"Well – yes indeed!" confirmed Snow.

Tom reached inside the satchel and pulled out a handful of objects. There were two belts, one of which looked suspiciously like the Belt of Invisibility that Loki had made him wear to avoid being spotted by the gods on Asgard. There was a miniature drinking-horn. There was a flask, sealed with a cork stopper and the gold locket mirror he had seen Loki place in the bag. There were things wrapped in cloth and others wrapped in leather. He saw the flights of three darts, very similar to the one that Loki had whittled, sticking out from a cotton bag. Tom was about to start unwrapping some of the cloth-bound gear when he noticed that Snow had fluttered down from his shoulder and was looking at the things that had fallen out of the satchel.

"The flask contains water drawn from the pool of Mimir. It's to be added to the water in the mirror– if you are clumsy enough to spill any. Be very careful not to spill a drop."

"And the drinking-horn? The potion to cure the lost Gods?" Tom said.

"*Possibly*," the dragon answered with an unmistakable note of doubt in its voice.

"You seem to know a lot about what's in this bag,"

Tom said suspiciously.

"Of course. As I said, Loki gave me a thorough briefing about your quest before inviting me to climb inside the bag. I am here to act as your companion and help if you should get into any scrapes.

"What have we here?" the insect said. "A scroll. *The* scroll? I'd suggest you unroll it and read what it says."

Tom laid the scroll out as flat as he could without spilling too much sand onto the surface.

He began to read aloud,

"By Weyland's key you were set free,

To roam in Greece and find the piece,

That kills the rock and picks the lock,

To turn the tables, clean the stables.

Earn the key and Odin's glee,

A low door's key sets Odin free.

The key's the thing you must win

On hero's wing, win from a king.

Win this quest and then fly West

Try the wolf with another proof.

Three quests to prove that you're the best,

On a ship, in a chest, pass each test,

And on the third, free the bird,

Release the cage, earn Odin's wage,

The bird unbind, free Odin's mind."

Tom puzzled over the words. What did the rhyme mean? It didn't make any sense to him.

"What the -?" Tom uttered a very loud and crude expletive.

"You shouldn't swear like that!" said the dragon.

"Why the - not?" and Tom said the word again.

"You shouldn't swear," repeated Snow.

"But Vikings cussed!" Tom protested. "Swearing was an art form for the Vikings!"

"It's not fitting for a hero to swear and 'cuss' as you so crudely put it."

"I'm not a hero!"

"You will either become a hero or- "

"Or?"

"Or be yet another dead boy."

Tom winced. The dragon continued, ignoring the boy's discomfort.

"If you succeed in this quest you will become a hero. Your words will be written down and read by youngsters. You should act and speak like a hero... or at least someone who hopes to live long enough to become a hero. Not like some thug from the streets! Don't say that word. Say 'Fang' instead."

Tom laughed out loud.

"'Fang'?" he snickered. "Ridiculous!" Then he saw that the dragon was regarding him with a particularly cold, frosty, almost freezing look. Tom shivered. "'Fang'?" he said with another shiver, pretending that he was laughing. "It is funny though. And you'll know what I mean. So what the Fang? I'll say Fang, Ship, Crab and Bollards from now on. You'll catch my drift!

"Anyway, this stuff about my swearin' isn't helpin' with the scroll. What's it mean?"

"It's a riddle," Snow said at last.

"Oh really?" Tom said sarcastically. "Thank Fang for talking reptiles. I wouldn't have known where to begin. So it's a riddle, is it?

"I think I'd have spotted that it was a riddle, dragon," he said.

Snow was not unsettled by a cheeky teenager.

"Very good, Master Big Brain," the dragon said, paying him back in his own currency: sarcasm, "you'd have spotted that it was a riddle. Very good. Tell me: now you know it's a riddle, how would you go about solving it?"

"Solvin' it?" Tom said. "I haven't a clue. It's a riddle!"

"Lucky I'm here to unravel it for you then," the dragon said, showing that it had the patience of a school-teacher. Loki has set you three quests. For the first quest we must travel to the palace of King Augeas and find another key.

It will resemble the key you just used to open the portal from Asgard."

"'Portal'?"

"Loki has discovered a number of portals - windows in and out of the universe of Order and Chaos. The portals are points where the world opens onto holes in Space and Time. You fell safely to this place and this time on Earth directly from Asgard, by-passing the Rainbow Bridge. That has never happened before. Now you need to find another portal to take you 'to the West' as the riddle puts it. The key is located inside a drain in one of King Augeas' stables. And that's the catch."

"'The catch'?"

"King Augeas' stables have not been cleaned - "

"I know the myth," Tom said, beginning to remember. It was something he had studied with Mr Porter. King Augeas' stables figured in one of the Ancient Greek Legends, the Labours of Hercules. "It's not that the cowsheds haven't been cleaned for a while. It's that they've never been cleaned, full stop."

"That's right. They've never been cleaned. Never."

Tom pulled a face. That was a load of Crab... in more ways than one. He remembered the rest of the myth: to atone for earlier sins, Hercules had to carry out a series of tasks or labours for King Eurystheus: kill the Lernaean Hydra, steal the Golden Apples of the Hesperides and clean the stables of King Augeas in a single day. There were six or more other tasks, later rounded up to twelve in total. All myths. A thought struck him.

"Wait a minute. The story of King Augeas' stables is a myth. So that means we're in the Greece of -"

"Myths and Legends. Loki has explained to me the nature of your three quests, young Wolfe," the dragon repeated.

"*Three* quests?" Tom groaned. "I'd hoped I'd only need to get that drinkin' horn to Odin and Thor and get them to drink it. Job done! Sorted! Memory back!"

"I'm not sure the drinking horn does contain the potion for restoring memory," said Snow."

"And what's with this business of *three* quests anyway?" Tom stormed, not listening to the dragon. "Why are myths and legends, fairytales and nursery rhymes so hung up on things happenin' in threes?" he grumbled. "What a load of Bollards! Loki said time was of the essence. The Ice Giants are at the gates of Asgard. They will tumble down the Rainbow Bridge to Middle Earth and bring a new Ice Age, killing my Uncle Bernard, Stella, Rob and everyone at Danelaw School – not to mention the rest of the planet – if we don't stop them. And he's lined up *three* quests for me? Why not arrange one quest, let me find the portal after one quest. Find the portal that takes me directly to Odin and Thor? Three is a complete waste of time. What a load of Crabby Bollards!" Tom was in mid-rant when the dragon raised a hand to quiet him. Or at least it raised what would have passed for a hand if it had been human. Raising its right upper leg and foreclaw had the desired effect anyway. Tom's rant spluttered to an end.

"When you have quite finished," the dragon said. "I told you that the portals were fashioned at the point where Odin's world of Order and the universe of Chaos meet. The chute of space-time that you travelled through brought you through Order and Chaos to here, this place and this time in Ancient and Legendary Greece. There isn't a single portal anywhere in Chaos that would take you directly to Odin. You have to find two more gateways through Order and Chaos and the last one will take you to Odin. So - three quests.

"In fulfilling each quest you should recover a key. Each key will open a door that takes you to the next part of your quest. The final part of the quest, the final key will open the lock on Odin's memory. It will return Odin and Thor to Asgard."

"'Open a lock'?" He told me I was to supply them with a potion!"

"Trust me," the dragon said. "You'll free Odin's memory with a key. Now we should press on. The Norse Gods are depending on you. It is in your hands – the fate of Asgard, Midgard, the world as you know it, exactly as you said, past, present and future. It all depends on a fourteen-year-old boy from Danelaw High School. Worried? You should be!" The dragonfly paused, allowing the full weight of the words to sink in. Tom felt his temples beginning to throb.

"And as I was saying before I was so rudely interrupted," the dragon continued, "the first one is to be faced here in Ancient Greece.

Snow stopped speaking and listened intently. The faint murmuring that could be heard coming from the fringe of trees beyond the beach was growing louder.

"The rest of the contents of the satchel will have to wait for the time being, young Wolfe. If we are to avoid you being mobbed to death inside the first hour of your quest I really do need to acquaint you with this small friend of mine."

To Tom's astonishment, Snow began to talk softly to the open satchel.

"Come on, little one," said the dragon. "He won't hurt you. As long as you promise not to hurt him."

A faint buzzing noise came from the bag.

"Help him get out," the dragon ordered testily. "Quickly! You don't have much time! He needs air!"

Tom opened up the mouth of the knapsack a bit wider. The smallest bee that he had ever seen crept out. As soon as daylight fell upon it, the bee stretched its wings and immediately, before he had a chance to react, flew straight up into the air, skipped on Tom's shoulder and shot straight inside his ear. For a brief moment he panicked and all he could hear was the loudest, scariest buzzing sound he had ever heard. Then the panic subsided. The bee was silent.

"What the heck is going on?" Tom shouted. He looked

up from the shore and peered into the distance, looking inland. A group of people had left the shelter of the trees and was walking towards him.

"Relax," said Snow. "I've trained an Interpreter bee to set up its home in your ear."

"'Interpreter bee'?" said Tom.

"Yes – they can turn any language into Modern English and vice-versa. This is going to prove useful in less than a minute. It's going to keep you out of an awful lot of trouble."

"'Interpreter bee'?" Tom said again, doubtfully.

"Yes!" said Snow testily. "*Interpreter bees*. Sometimes called Undrones."

"'Undrones'?"

"Yes! 'Undrones' because they aren't drones and they turn droning sounds into perfectly good sense! They're cousins of Spelling bees and Word bees. They've all got a famous grandmother!"

"'Grandmother'?"

"Grammar Bee – she's the grandest mother bee of them all. Now be very careful. You're going to get a chance to utilise some new skills!"

"But first: don't move. I must hide!"

To Tom's astonishment, Snow shape-shifted in an instant. The dragon turned into a small dragonfly and flew up and hid behind his ear.

Tom grabbed up the contents of his satchel, jammed them back in the bag and turned just in time to see three boys and a girl walking warily over the crest of the sand ridge towards him. They seemed to be about the same age as Tom. They were wearing linen tunics and their skin was tanned bronze. The girl stood at the back of the group. Tom wished he could see more of her but a broad-shouldered, burly youth had marched forward and blocked his view.

"Name yourself, stranger, and explain what you are doing in our kingdom!"

It was a strong, voice, accustomed to command and Tom was grateful that the Undrone was translating the words for him. He framed his response in English, wondering if any of the group would be able to understand him and was astonished to find that the Undrone was able to translate his thoughts into Greek so that he could pronounce them perfectly out loud as spoken Greek sentences.

"Was that 'Name yourself, stranger' or 'Name yourself stranger'?" Tom asked aggressively.

The broad-shouldered youth's beetling brow betrayed the fact that he didn't have a clue what the interloper had just asked him.

Tom took a step forward. During boxing practice, especially sparring with boys bigger than himself, he had learnt that sometimes if you feinted a step back only to then move quickly forward it wrong-footed the opponent in front of you. The bigger boy faltered.

"Was the command for me to tell you my name or were you telling me to change my name to something more bizarre? Telling me to make my name stranger means you think I already have a strange name. That's an insult." He took another step forward and now his nose was very near the bigger boy's although lower down as the big boy was two or three inches taller than Tom.

"Are you saying I've got a strange name, stranger?" Tom said.

It was a classic schoolyard stand-off. In Tom's experience these things only went one of two ways. A fist fight broke out in seconds or the nearest pupils grabbed both opponents and dragged them away to separate parts of the schoolyard.

Something else happened.

"That's very witty!" The girl said, stepping forward so that she stood alongside the broad-shouldered youth. "Sharp rather than funny. And I have to say that kind of wit is completely lost on Theron here. He does his heavy thinking with his arms. A bit like heavy-lifting. So let me ask you, politely as befits one who is perhaps visiting our shores for the first time: what is your name?"

She was very pretty and asked the question with such an open and honest friendly smile that Tom answered her at once and without any cheek or irony. She had long, dark hair and big brown eyes. She was beautiful.

No doubt about it, thought Tom. *If this girl was at Danelaw High, she would be one of the Popular Set.*

"My name is Tom," he said with growing confidence, "a name you probably haven't heard before. As for what I'm doing in your land – that's a long story. First you'll have to tell me where I am. I had no control over how I got here. I was..." and not for the first time that day he hesitated. How could he explain his arrival on the sandy beach? He could hardly say that he fell from the sky. Dropped from the stars. What reaction would he get if he started jabbering away about Asgard and Midgard, Rainbow bridges, Magic Portals and Loki?

"I was..." He couldn't think of an explanation. The hulking youth in front of him was becoming impatient.

"You were what?" he said in a threatening tone.

"Shipwrecked?" whispered a voice close to his ear.

"Shipwrecked!" Tom said and at the same time thought, *Thank You, Snow.*

"Don't mention it," came back the whisper.

"So - where's your boat?"

"That's enough, Theron," the girl said in a bright, brisk voice. She was as tall as anyone in the group and Tom was surprised to see that all three boys at once deferred to her, though the bigger boy, the one she had called Theron, was still bristling with aggression.

"Can't you see that Tom is confused. Wouldn't you be if you'd been shipwrecked?"

"Well, she's pretty as a picture, isn't she?" came Snow's whisper. "In any self-respecting myth or legend she'd be described as having the deep, dark eyes of a water nymph and black hair the colour of a raven's wing!"

Quiet! thought Tom. *I'm trying to concentrate on what the bee is telling me!*

The girl was still talking, "It's obvious that he has lain unconscious in the sun, long enough to have dried off after swimming ashore. He will be confused from the shipwreck and the heat of the sun. You'll recall it is why we were taking our lessons among the trees. To avoid the mid-day heat? The wreckage of his boat is doubtless out in the bay somewhere!"

"Apollonia, you are too ready to trust this boy," the youth called Theron warned. "Look at his clothes. What is that stuff he's wearing? He *is* strange. And his name *is* stranger A crazed-looking stranger who is probably up to no good. I say we call the guards and have him slammed in the dungeon."

It was the girl's turn to become annoyed. She looked at Tom again.

"Ignore Theron, Tom," she said. "He must have drunk too much bull's blood for breakfast. His name means 'Hunter' and there are times when he seems to think that everything unfamiliar is prey for him. My name is Apollonia. Let me welcome you to the lands of King Augeas.

"Theron you are already becoming acquainted with and the other two fine, charming lads are Pamphilos and Hilarion."

"I just have to express my sincere admiration for your dress sense!" Hilarion said to Tom. Pamphilos started sniggering and Tom realised that Hilarion was the joker in the pack. Before he had a chance to say or do anything and before Apollonia could respond, Theron erupted.

"Why do you trust this crazed stranger?" Theron blurted, his face bright red with anger.

"Because he is obviously an innocent abroad, Theron," the girl explained patiently. "Why else would he have put himself in such grave danger by hiding out of sight behind the egg of a Roc?"

"I don't think you need the bit about 'egg of a' in that sentence, Apollonia," Tom said with a gentle laugh. "Just plain 'rock' will do – though in my opinion it's more a darn', great boulder than a rock!"

"Learn to hold your tongue and listen, boy!" hissed Snow. "It's a useful lesson for life! You are in grave danger! Listen!"

"No – I do indeed mean 'Roc'!" insisted Apollonia, who then turned back to the youth named Theron. "What greater proof could we need? 'An innocent abroad'. He has no idea that this is from a Roc!" She pointed at the large, ovoid boulder.

"No, honestly, Apollonia," Tom protested. "I do know what that is. We have rocks where I come from. And pebbles and boulders too!"

Just how dumb-ass are these Ancient Greeks anyway? She may be beautiful but you have to admit for someone with dark hair she's bein' more than a bit...well...blonde!

"Look and listen," Snow whispered. "In fact – watch out!"

Tom was unable to tell whether it was coincidence or magic but at the very moment that Apollonia pointed at the rock, an extraordinary thing happened. The top of the boulder cracked open and the head of a giant chick poked out. It wasn't a huge boulder after all. It was a huge, rock-like, gigantically-big egg. It very quickly became clear that the young bird was no giant duckling or titanic baby chicken either. It had a large vicious beak and evil eyes. Luckily its neck was held by the thick, broken edge of the eggshell as its first instinct on bursting out into the world of air and sun and sand and sky was to bend over suddenly and peck at Apollonia. Tom pulled her away and out of harm's reach just in time.

I thought birds were supposed to think "Mama" when they clapped eyes on the first living thing they saw. Maybe this species doesn't like their Mums? He thought.

"No – it's a Roc! They're instinctive carnivores and killers!" whispered Snow.

"*Gives a whole new meaning to the term 'Rock Chick'!*" thought Tom.

"This isn't the time for teenage quips!" hissed Snow.

"Unhand the princess, foul barbarian!" Theron fumed and then as he dived at Tom, yelled, "Guards!"

Theron was fast and strong and in the next instant, had his arm round Tom's neck in a wrestling grip. Tom was stuck. His throat was being crushed and he was choking. Just as he was on the point of blacking out, Tom was startled to see another giant chick's head bump its way out of the egg shell. It stretched its neck and pecked viciously at Theron's shoulder. The youth cried out and lost his grip on Tom. Then Theron jumped away from the egg. It had cracked in two more places but was still strong enough to imprison its lively contents.

"*Twin chicks in one egg? That's something I've never seen before!*" thought Tom.

"'Twin chicks?' It's a two-headed bird, you clot! I'd have thought the fact that the chicks are six-feet tall would have been clue enough, setting aside the two-headedness for a moment! Haven't you read about the Roc?" whispered Snow.

I know all about the Roc, Tom thought. *Just didn't want to miss a chance to wind you up*.

"You're the one that's going to be wound up – wound up all the way to the gallows. Look lively! Haven't you seen the armed warriors hurtling this way from the trees?"

Behind him the ferocious, baby monster bird was battering against its shell. Theron was dragging Apollonia away from Tom and the hatchling monster. As Snow had observed, four Greek warriors clad in breastplate, kilt and cloak and armed with shields, javelins and wearing dark bronze helmets were charging over the sand towards them.

Now what? thought Tom.

"Don't say it!" hissed Snow.

Can't help it, thought Tom. *I'm caught between a Roc and a hard place!*

"Seize the barbarian!" yelled Theron. "He laid hands on the Royal Princess! The penalty is death!"

The guards were built for combat not initiative. They were used to obeying orders. Two seized Tom by the arms.

"He laid hands on the Royal Princess, did he?" said Apollonia, her cheeks burning. "Then what exactly are you doing, Theron?"

The youth had wrapped his arm round her waist when he dragged her away from the baleful bird. His arm was still in place. Theron blushed and began to stammer. Then taking command with regal authority Apollonia glared at the soldiers.

"Sergeant Plodalonganon? While you're 'seizing' this young stranger what, may I ask, are you proposing to do about the killer two-headed monster bird that is hatching less than ten yards away from the Royal Princess?"

The sergeant stood to attention and saluted.

"Beg, pardon, miss! Respectfully ask permission to unhand young stranger and begin butchering young monster bird wot will otherwise grow into a Gi-normous Great Monster and be a plague and pestilence in all the lands of His Majesty, King Augeas?"

Apollonia almost screamed in frustration. At that moment a solitary, dark cloud passed overhead, putting the beach in shadow and causing a noticeable drop in air temperature.

"The gods give me strength! Do I have to do all the thinking around here? In the interests of state security and to protect the royal personage, I'd suggest!-" She had been about to suggest that the sergeant and the three other guards should escort the entire party back to the safety of the woods, but the rest of Apollonia's words were cut off by the scream that issued from her lips instead.

She screamed as a giant two-headed bird swooped down from the sky, landed clumsily on the sand and grabbed the cloth of her tunic in one set of talons. It bunched the cloth to hold the girl steady while one head drew back ready to strike with its vicious, curved beak. The bird dwarfed the chick that was struggling to free itself from its shell. Reacting faster than anyone, Tom grabbed a javelin from one of the guards and jammed the sharp tip into the giant bird's leg inches above the talons that held Apollonia. With a shriek the bird released the princess but moving faster than Tom could ever have imagined possible, its other claws flashed out and grabbed him round the chest. He felt pain then. It felt as if the walls of his chest were about to collapse. The Roc was bigger than a rock. It was the size of an elephant. Its feathers were tawny, and the hideous yellow of its talons matched the ugly colour in its four eyes.

The guards were slow to react but at last they did. Two of them dragged the princess away from the chaotic struggle. Hilarion and Pamphilos took charge of the retreat. The sergeant and remaining guard along with Theron were stabbing at the gigantic mother bird with javelins. Tom couldn't tell if Theron was trying to save or skewer him. The Greek youth didn't seem to care where he jabbed or stabbed and a spear point struck dangerously near Tom.

The soldiers were jabbing towards the bird's chest. They inflicted no damage but they were distracting both of the birds' heads. It couldn't sit down and rip out Tom's intestines.

The noise made by the Roc was enough to awaken the dead. It screeched and screamed, darting at Theron who stabbed two-handed with the javelin towards a flailing neck. The monster was distracted and Tom felt its grip slacken but only enough for him to free one hand. He fumbled in the satchel. It was piy oned by his side under one of the bird's claws. The fury vented by its mother had a dramatic effect on the six-foot tall hatchling. In a dreadful wailing rage the two-headed chick burst from its shell and attacked Theron, the sergeant and the remaining guard.

Knowing that Snow was 'listening,' Tom thought, *Any advice what to do next?*

Too late! The chick wasn't powerful enough to kill or maim the soldiers but it was big enough to deliver a nasty nip. With Theron and the guards distracted, the mother bird hopped back and flung itself into the air. With three heavy wing-sweeps it rose high into the sky. Tom took a deep breath as he saw the beach fall away beneath his feet.

Now I'm for it! He thought. *The Roc will have all the time it needs to pick me apart limb by limb!*

"No – you're in luck! This is the mother bird remember. Hold tight!"

Just then, as if it had been listening to Snow, the two-headed bird swooped back towards the shore. Tom felt the wind whistle past his ears as the Roc dived. It was dive-bombing the warriors, doing everything it could to protect its chick. It flew in a steep dive and lashed out with its free talons. It sent one of the guards tumbling, before it swung out to sea again, gaining height as it went. The smitten guard rolled head over heels, his armoured breast plate torn open by the blow and then lay still, dazed.

"This bird must have been to Dragon Training School!" hissed Snow. "This is classic dive-bomb and strafe tactics. See how it gets to the ideal height, just high enough to gain speed from the downward swoop but not so long a climb that the Greeks can finish off its chick. It's keeping them on the hop, while picking them off one-by-one!"!

And when it finishes them off, it will turn its attentions to me, thought Tom.

Exactly as Snow had predicted, the Roc took little time to achieve dive-height. It came plunging down like a runaway train and caught Plodalonganon a glancing blow on the helmet, leaving the sergeant stunned. Only Theron was left standing defiantly on the beach, javelin in hand, balancing bravely but uncertainly on his feet, not sure whether he should attack the freshly-hatched Roc Monster or look out for the Mother Bird.

In a panic, rummaging in the satchel, Tom' felt his hand grasp the dart of whittled and hardened yew wood that Loki had given him.

I've got the dart!

"Now's our chance for Immortality and Fame," said Snow as the Roc flew into the air, heading out to sea. "Wait until the Monster is about to strike Theron and prepare to jump! Then once you're free and the bird comes flying back – aim the dart at the ice circle on its breast! It's the bull's eye!"

What do you mean? The Bull's eye? Why must everything be in riddles?

"Shush! It's dive-bombing again. Wait. Watch. Get ready to strike!"

Tom watched with gritted teeth as Snow flew out from behind his ear. No longer an insect, he saw that the creature had assumed its real shape in miniature. The tiny, insect-size dragon flew up from behind his ear and as Tom twisted in the grip of the Roc's claws, he was horrified to see that Snow was flying straight at one of the great, gaping beaks. Tom squirmed around, convinced that he was going to collide with Theron as the Roc hurtled down towards the youth who was being attacked at the same time by the vicious chick. It was all going to end now, a horrible death for Tom and Theron - he knew it!

Swooping very close to the ground, the giant mother bird suddenly convulsed, sneezed loudly and broke its dive. In the first sneeze the bird's talons shuddered, and the spasm weakened its grip on Tom. He stabbed into the talons with the dart. The monster shrieked in pain. He broke free and dived headlong into the sand. Sneezing like a geyser with a stutter, the Roc lofted into the air once more before diving back to fly straight at Tom who had scrambled to his feet.

Armed only with the wooden dart, Tom knew any

second now he was going to become bird food. Snow had disappeared. The enraged, sneezing Roc was crazed with anger. Wings flapping as big as the sails of a galleon, the bird dived for the last time. The vast, two-headed monster flew straight at Tom. Talons and beaks lashed at him! Just then he saw that a bull's eye, a perfect ice circle bull's eye, had formed in the middle of its breast feathers. With all his might he hurled the wooden dart. It flew straight and true and thudded into the middle of the ice circle, straight through thick feathers. Straight through skin. Straight through the Roc's heart. The monster screamed once and fell dead in a heap. One of its wings collapsed on Tom.

Theron didn't waste a moment. He spun on his heel, aimed and plunged his javelin through the heart of the monster chick which squawked once and perished.

"Well done, young Wolfe!" whispered Snow, dragonfly-size and shape once again and resting on Tom's shoulder. "That was quite a throw. Where did you learn to play darts?"

Tom didn't reply. He could only groan. Firstly, he had a hunch that Snow knew about the origins and nature of the wooden dart. He could only make such an uncanny throw with the help of Loki's magic. Secondly, the wing of the dead Roc was gargantuan, heavy enough to keep him pinned to the ground, making his bruised ribs ache even more. He couldn't breathe!

Apollonia was running back to the beach. Running with her were dozens of guards as well as the boys, many more guards than had first appeared with the sergeant.

"Tom!" she yelled in a frightened voice. "Sergeant Plodalonganon! Bring your men and lift him out from under this – this hideous thing!"

Six guards lifted the Roc's wing while another two dragged Tom free. A stretcher was set down on the sand and Tom was carefully lifted onto it.

Apollonia knelt down and placed her hand on Tom's cheek.

"Are you hurt?"

Tom groaned again.

"Where does it hurt?" the princess asked.

"All over!" said Tom who realised with relief that Undrone had survived the Monster Bird attack unharmed.

Theron dragged himself over to where Apollonia and the guards had gathered round Tom.

"Why don't you ask if I'm hurt?" Theron said in a sulky voice.

"Because he just killed a Roc!" Apollonia said.

"I killed a Roc too! Shoved my javelin straight into its chest!"

"But he killed a fully-grown Roc Monster which then proceeded to collapse on top of him, not a one-hour- old chick that you could fit on a single spear!"

Tom opened one bruised eye and looked over at the six-foot tall chick, skewered on Theron's javelin.

"Nicely done, Theron," he said. "I think you just invented fast food. Look: it's instant chicken kebab!"

Apollonia looked at him anxiously.

"I think Tom may have been hurt. He's gibbering. We should get him to the infirmary!"

"You're more interested in this barbarian than you are in me! I'm a Royal Greek Prince!" Theron complained.

"Then start behaving like one!" said Apollonia and she turned her back on Theron to examine Tom. "I think he's only bruised with some bad scratches," she said to the sergeant. "He will live if we can get him back to the palace quickly. Plodalonganon – order two of your men to form a stretcher party."

"Sergeant!" Tom said, remembering something he needed to do. "What are you planning to do with the Roc?"

"Butcher and serve it up in the barracks, sir! Sergeant Plodalonganon is the name, though the men tend to call me 'Sergeant Plod', a sort of term of affection, young sir. That was a fine bit of work wiv the mini javelin if I may say so!" The sergeant said and then knuckled his forelock in the direction of Apollonia. "Pardon the interruption, miss!"

"Oh no apology needed, sergeant. Do carry on!"

The sergeant needed no second bidding. He continued with relish and enthusiasm, "Served up in the barracks, young sir. Wiv some of the meat going to the townsfolk. Roc meat is very rare and on the rare occasion that a hero gets to kill a Roc, we feasts on Roc fillets for days. Especially rare when we doesn't 'ave to bury the body of the poor hero wot died in the process of killin' the Monster Bird in the first place. Which we usually 'ave to do. Mixes a lot of sadness in wiv' the hilarity of the feastin' when you 'as to bury the dead hero. Make a nice change to 'ave the 'ero alive and joining us for some Roc souvlaki. It'll make it more of a feast than a wake...which as I jus' said is what it usually is."

"Which we may yet have to organise if we don't get him to the palace soon!" said Apollonia between gritted teeth.

"One request, please, Princess, if I may beg a favour!" said Tom as the guards stooped down to take the wooden handles of his stretcher.

"Of course. You need only ask – you saved our lives!"

She ignored the loud snort of frustration from Theron.

"Could the sergeant ask some of his men to cut out the Roc's heart and keep it for me, along with the little wooden javelin they'll find there or in its chest?"

"What? 'Cut out its heart'? Barbarian! Told you he was a barbarian!" Theron thundered.

Apollonia thought this *was* a strange request but royal breeding enabled her to remain cool and gracious. She nodded to Plodalonganon that the request should be carried out.

"Now – no more delay and haggling over choice cuts of meat or other bits of butchery. Back to the palace and my father's physician immediately!"

Tom wondered how he was going to maintain "jolly

hockey sticks" conversation with a royal princess while his ribs ached worse than if he had been used for tackling practice by the entire pack of the Danelaw First Fifteen. He needn't have worried. Apollonia told Plodalonganon that he should send eight men to run along with the stretcher bearers. They would rotate carrying the stretcher, making faster progress. She would follow along with the boys and the remainder of the guard later.

"She's clever and practical, that one," Snow whispered in Tom's ear when the guards had picked up speed and were jogging briskly away from the beach.

"*I was wondering where you'd got to!*" thought Tom. "*What happened? Why did you run off when the Roc made its final dive?*"

"'Run off?'" spluttered the dragonfly which then buzzed round and hovered angrily in front of Tom's nose. Tom thought that if the fly had had different anatomy it would have made a fist with its right hand and would be waving it directly under that same nose.

"'Run off? Foolish, boy! You didn't follow what happened? I'd reverted to dragon form, though still in miniature. I flew up to the Roc's right head, darted inside one of the nostrils in its beak and breathed a snow storm inside the nostril. It had to sneeze. Couldn't stop itself. I did the same to its left head and nostrils. No creature on earth can maintain a consistent dive while sneezing its heads off! And that's why it loosed its grip on you too!"

You filled its nostrils with snow?

"And ice crystals! As I said, it's almost impossible to sustain a deadly dive when your nasal passages are blocked off! Then after you broke free and the Roc was making her final dive to kill you all on the beach I searched my memory for all those lessons I attended at Dragon School on the anatomy of legendary monsters. I remembered where its heart was. I flew up to its chest and marked the spot with an ice circle. The bull's eye – just as I told you! It might have two heads, but the Roc only has one heart. I suppose there's some credit due to dragonkind for our role in this."

Tom knew that he had played the part of the cheeky, sardonic teenager for too long with the flying serpent.

I'm grateful to you, Snow! he thought, warmly. *You saved my life, and Theron and probably the princess and everyone else on the beach!*

"Teamwork, Tom," said the dragonfly. "It was a fine example of teamwork. The way you hit the target with that wooden dart took skill and courage. And don't forget the Greek youth, Theron, or whatever he's called. He showed courage. He played his part well."

Killing a baby bird. Don't think that gets much applause. But I'd be happy to drink a toast to Tom and Snow. Roc Slayers!

The dragonfly disagreed but chose only to say, "You've a lot to learn, young Wolfe. A lot to learn. Now lie back and rest and enjoy the scenery."

Tom thought that was a good idea. He set his head back on the stretcher and looked at the landscape through half-closed eyes. The guards were jogging along at a fair old lick. Their armour jingled as they ran reflecting sparks of sunlight.

Inland the road wound its way over a broad level plain, lined with trees separating fields that sprouted abundant crops. Vineyards were scored with vine stems, luxuriant with bright green leaves and budding grapes. Olive groves offered shade from the sun as well as the promise of good health. Green hills curled away to the east and tall mountains rose to the south. Oak and elm gave way to cypress here and there and thick stands of pine could be made out on the higher ground. Tom thought the place looked warm and comfortable. He wondered if mythical lands ever suffered economic hardship. Only if they had a mythical problem the size of a Hydra or a Sphinx, a Grendel or an Ice Giant? Otherwise they were almost always prosperous. The cattle were always fat and produced good beef and superb milk. Apples were golden and grapes were full and ripe.

Lying on the stretcher was like being on a hammock. The rocking rhythm lulled bruised senses. Tom began to doze.

The guards entered Elis through a fortified gate in the centre of the city walls. Elis was the main town in the lands of King Augeas. Sandals clattered over limestone pavements as the guards made their way to the centre of town. The houses were built of mud brick, baked in the sun and covered with skimmed mud or plastered. Terracotta roof tiles glowed orange in the heat of the sun. Few windows looked out onto the street. Homes faced inwards viewing hidden, cool and secure courtyards. There weren't many people on the streets as they sheltered from the sun and those that were out and about shrank back and stooped in doorways as the Royal Guard barged unceremoniously through town. They jogged all the way to the King's Palace.

"To the Royal Guest rooms!" barked Plodalonganon and the guards jog-marched through the palace. Tom tried to look around but the guards were hurtling along. Rooms and corridors blurred by. He travelled through an arcade of clean, white stone with broad arched windows. At the end of the arcade, the guards barrelled along a corridor with a marble and granite floor. Deep alcoves sported marble sculptures of athletes and warriors, discus-throwers, sprinters and wrestlers as well as figures of the gods and goddesses of Ancient Greece.

The guards clattered through the palace until they reached a quiet corner along yet another corridor near the Royal Chambers.

"Guest Room, Royal Chambers!" the sergeant announced in a loud voice as the stretcher was lowered to the ground. "Thank you, Sergeant Plod," Tom said brightly as he clambered to his feet.

"Don't mention it, sir. Hope to see you again soon. Always a pleasure to carry a Hero. 'Specially when he's likely to live to see Apollo riding his golden chariot into the heavens again and not about to breathe his last. Not about to be whisked away by Hades to...well...Hades if you see wot I mean!"

Tom smiled. He understood only too well.

The sergeant was pointing.

"This is yours, young sir. The princess told us we should leave you here and tell you to make yourself at home. She will be along to join you shortly."

Tom drew back a curtain and entered the room. It was enormous. There were three beds, enough chairs and tables for a conference and wardrobes to accommodate a theatre company.

Tom jumped onto one of the beds and yawned. It was a huge yawn. The yawn tested the hinges of his jaw!

"I'm bushed!" he said. "This hero-ing Mullarkey is knackerin'!

"The princess gave strict instructions. I'm to make myself at home," he added for good measure.

And before Snow could protest or say anything at all, Tom Wolfe lay down on the bed and fell into a deep, deep sleep.

6 The Court Of King Augeas

He awoke to the sound of voices whispering. They were talking gobbledygook whoever they were. He had no idea how long he had been asleep. He half opened his eyes. Apollonia was hovering over him. He couldn't tell whether she was talking to him or Hilarion or Pamphilos who were standing alongside. Luckily Snow and the Undrone woke at the same time and while Tom stretched and made a loud yawning noise, the Interpreter Bee crept from behind his ear lobe where it had been taking a nap alongside mini-size Snow and crawled unseen back inside his ear.

"Can you hear me, Tom?" the princess was asking. "Has your hearing been damaged?"

"I think he's more entertaining like this," said Hilarion. "Maybe he's one of those simpletons whose brain improves after a bang on the head!" Pamphilos sniggered.

"Not funny, Hilarion. I hardly think he's a simpleton," Apollonia said with some force.

"Most heroes or would-be heroes are nine parts simpleton and one part foolhardy lout," countered Hilarion. "Just look at Theron!"

"Not funny," said the princess. "Did it ever occur to you that when your parents named you, they were also trying to be funny? They succeeded and were. You don't and aren't!"

"I don't have any of the qualifications to be a simpleton, Hilarion," said Tom, sitting up suddenly and grateful that Undrone was doing its job, "though I bet you could give lessons!"

Tom was glad to see that Hilarion and Pamphilos both laughed.

"Ouch – it's like being stung by a bee!" said Pamphilos.

If you only knew, thought Tom.

"Stung by an eel," said Hilarion, "or a jelly fish. Slimy but with a stinger!"

"Not funny, Hilarion. And that's enough!" Apollonia said firmly. "I don't have time for any of this chaff." And then she suddenly called out, "Matron! The patient is awake!"

A large, buxom woman appeared. Apollonia stood up and ushered Hilarion and Pamphilos away from the bed.

"Clear off, you two. Keep out of my hair. This is work for experts, not chattering boys."

"Matron," the princess turned to the woman and gave instructions, "we need to look this one over for broken bones."

Tom wondered how they would cope with his thick, woollen Norse clothes but on looking down was horrified to see that he was wearing a dress.

"What's this?" he yelled, pointing.

"It's a chiton.

"But I don't want a 'Kite-on'! I want clothes! Where're my clothes?"

"Don't be silly, Tom. This type of tunic – called a chiton – it's standard in this part of Greece."

"What happened to the clothes I was wearing?" Tom asked, horrified now by a sea of possibilities.

"You've been bathed and dressed as befits a hero in Greece," Apollonia explained, on seeing his confusion. "Matron gave you a powerful sleeping draught and you slept through it all. Missed all the fun!"

"Bathed? Dressed? Fun?...Who...?" he stammered, feeling his cheeks burning red.

"By slaves, of course. Who else?" the princess said, teasing him.

"Oh, of course, slaves," Tom muttered. "You lot haven't heard of William Wilberforce or Abraham Lincoln then?"

"Who are they?" Apollonia asked, uncertainly. "Fellow heroes?"

"You can say that again," Tom said.

"You have slept a long time. From yesterday afternoon through evening and night. It's early in the morning now. We have to prepare you for your audience with my father," Apollonia was talking to him while the woman she had referred to as Matron patiently held out Tom's arms one after the other and tugged and poked at them before bending over and prodding him in the ribs.

"We don't have long before you are to appear before the King, Tom," Apollonia said. She was gazing at him very intensely. "Please tell me – where you are from? Your clothes? We have nothing like them in Greece. What were those things you wore on your feet? What are you doing here? Were you really shipwrecked? You were dry as a bone when we found you!"

"Told you he hadn't floated ashore!" Hilarion bellowed. "Even though he looks like driftwood!"

"Not funny," said the princess.

"Might be a good time to start talking like a mythical hero," Snow whispered in his ear and not for the first time, Tom was glad that he had the dragon along as a companion.

"I come from a land far, far away," said Tom, wincing as the matron pummelled his bruised ribs. "Far, far away to the north. If you were to sail west far out beyond the Ionian Sea and then north for hundreds of leagues, you would come to a land wreathed in mist and cloud, inhabited by sheep and goats, bears and wolves. Nothing to mark it out from the other misty islands that lie to the north, except that one day it will invent cricket, football and rugby."

"'Cricket'? That's an insect. Looks like a grasshopper,"

The princess said, uncertainly. "But what are the other things?"

"Sorry, Apollonia, I was being playful," said Tom. "There is no such thing as football. Where was I? Oh yes, I flew here from the land of mist and cloud and sheep and goats. I flew on the back of my fine steed, a winged, fire-breathing dragon who had his stomach ripped open by the very Roc I later slew. The dragon lived long enough to deliver me safely to the fair land of Elis before tumbling back into the sea. If you dredge the waters between here and Zakynthos, you'll find a huge lump of charcoal or solid ash."

"Solid ash?"

"Yes. Solid ash – or charcoal. It's what fire-breathing dragons turn into when they fall into salt water. It made a heck of a sizzle!"

Apollonia's eyes opened wide in wonder.

"You rode here on a fire-breathing dragon?"

"'Flew'," he corrected her and then it was his turn to open his eyes wide in wonder, though he was pretending to be astonished, "Isn't it standard practice for heroes on a quest? I thought dragons were the steed of choice!" and then he grunted as the Matron dug a thumb between two of his ribs.

"I've never seen a dragon," said Apollonia.

"He's being pummelled by one right now!" said Hilarion in a voice low enough that only Pamphilos could hear and he was rewarded by another snigger.

Tom watched Apollonia as she digested the explanation. He had been ribbing her, just as he had when talking about sports that had yet to be invented. He could not believe that she was taking him seriously.

"This is the land of Greek Myths and Legends," Snow whispered. "Your explanation might seem fairly normal to her. Remember: she has seen a Roc and probably knows about hydras and gorgons. A dragon steed might not be as exotic to her as you think."

"'Dragons, heroes on a quest'? What is your quest? Might it be to win a fair maiden?" Apollonia asked with a shy smile.

"Now that," said Tom, "Would be telling. It's something reserved for your father to hear first!" He could not resist a merry grin, realising too late that he might be misunderstood. Apollonia blushed crimson from ear to ear.

"I think you have just complicated things enormously, young Wolfe," Snow whispered from behind Tom's ear, noticing the girl's rosy complexion.

Tom flinched.

"Then we must present you to my father forthwith," said the princess with increased urgency. "How is he, Matron?"

"He'll live," said the woman who had fingers like steel spanners. "He has strong muscles for one so young. A bit scrawny for a hero though. Even the ones we've buried – most of 'em have been twice his size!"

"I know," said the princess, "It's what makes him so endearing!"

Endearing? And with alarm bells ringing in his ears, Tom found himself marching behind Apollonia, flanked by half a dozen Elian warriors, on his way to the throne room. He tried to breathe slowly and to remain calm and relaxed. Snow was whispering in his ear once again.

"Think before you speak," whispered the dragon masquerading once again as a dragonfly. "I'll whisper a few choice words in your ear. Whatever you do, don't dive in feet first and whatever else you do, do not try your infantile cheek nor your juvenile sense of humour on this man. Augeas is a king. One doesn't get to be a king and then remain a king in Ancient Greece without being quite happy putting people to death, especially the odd commoner. And in his eyes you're an especially odd commoner!"

Tom gritted his teeth and walked on.

He picked up the pace and tried to catch up with Apollonia. She was a friend, an ally, he was sure of it and he had tons of questions he wanted to ask her before he met her father. He was about to step alongside the princess when Sergeant Plod pulled him back, gently tugging on his shoulder.

"Bad idea to join ranks wiv a Royal personage when on your way to an audience wiv 'is Royal Highness, young sir," Plod said quietly. "Miss Apollonia wouldn't mind but 'er father might take it as an insult. That would be a very bad idea!" And the sergeant mimed the act of drawing a very sharp dagger across his throat. "No one is allowed to touch members of the Royal Household without first being given permission! Penalty, if the king is in the wrong mood: Death!"

Tom saw that he was entering the throne room. It was as big as a Viking great hall with high walls covered in stucco. Frescoes lined the side walls and the wall behind the high throne which Tom could just make out at the end of the room. The frescos depicted scenes of battle: infantrymen hurling javelins at shield walls and at brave cavalrymen mounted on mad-eyed plunging horses. Heroes rescued maidens from all manner of monsters. There were lions, basilisks, salamanders, sphinxes and, of course dragons. One fresco in particular caught Tom's eye: a green-and-grey-scaled fire-breather was being lanced by a heavily-armoured hero on horseback.

Don't look, Snow! he thought. *Too late!*

"What a shame," said Snow quietly, glancing out from behind Tom's ear. "That's Grubbsbinkaadwammedup the Grey from Sandnessjoen. We called him Gordon for short. Didn't know he'd ever flown this far south. So that's how he met his end! I wouldn't have thought Gordon was the type to go around menacing maidens. Not like him at all. There must have been some funny business involved. A king who wanted to remove a wife or unwanted daughter. The promise of gold or silver. Never could resist gold.

Poor Gordon!"

The dragon was about to say more but they had reached the first group of royal attendants.

A host of courtiers thronged about the King but the Elian aristocrats parted before the armed escort. The Throne Room was big enough to hold hundreds of people. The King's Throne stood on top of a raised dais from where he could survey the entire room. Apollonia turned and smiled at Tom as they approached the throne.

"Not long now! I'm sure Daddy is going to like you!"

Tom caught his first glimpse of Augeas and wasn't so sure. His heart sank. The King was a big, fat man. His belly stretched his tunic which was made of bright red and purple cloth. He had a scything beak of a nose and his eyes, like his nose, were sharp and hard. His mouth was soft like grapes. Laurel leaves covered with gold leaf had been woven into his black curly hair and he looked for all the world the very picture of a fat, pampered and mean-spirited tyrant.

Tom was surprised to hear the King utter a rumbling belly laugh when the court crier announced in a loud voice, "Please, your majesty, allow to be admitted to the Royal Presence: the Princess Apollonia and Tom from the Misty Isles Far Away to the North, erm...Hero and Roc-Slayer!"

The King's belly laugh turned into a raucous guffaw.

"'Tom from the Misty Isles'?" he said. "I'm sure we can do better than that!"

Wonder what he means by that, thought Tom.

"You'll soon find out," whispered Snow.

"Apollonia, my dear!" the King hailed his daughter. "Always a pleasure to see you especially when you bring a new, fresh, young Hero to my court."

The King half-rose from his throne as his daughter approached and kissed him on both cheeks. He smiled at her and then in an instant his face froze the smile. Still smiling, he said in a very business-like voice, "A delight to see you my dear, now run along and join your mother and your sisters while I talk to Tom from the Misty Isles. This is men's business."

Tom was surprised to see that Apollonia didn't protest. If Stella had been in her place, she would have been stroppy and argued with her father that there was no such thing as 'men's business' but Apollonia meekly did as she was told. She turned around long enough to give Tom another smile of encouragement and then stepped down from the dais and left the Throne Room.

"This is Ancient Greece, young Wolfe," whispered Snow. "Thousands of years will pass before they hear about equal rights!"

The King turned his shark's smile on Tom.

"Tom from the Misty Isles. Welcome to Elis. Apollonia has told me all about you and your wonderful exploits. Take a seat. You may have the Queen's throne. She isn't using it!" the King laughed and pointed to the smaller high-backed chair that stood next to his own. "You saved my daughter's life and a handful of young nobles today. That makes you a hero throughout the land of Elis and puts me in your debt. I have ordered a feast in your honour this evening."

"Thank him and tell him that is most gracious," whispered Snow. Tom did as he was told without any questions – or cheek - for once.

The King made an imperious gesture with his right hand and Tom watched impressed as the King's advisers and those courtiers who had been clustered round the throne stepped back and drew away out of earshot. Four members of the Royal Bodyguard stood on either side of Tom and Augeas but otherwise they were alone for the moment.

"That was solely for public consumption," said the King in a quiet voice. "I *have* ordered a feast. I hope you like the food. You may be spending a lot of time with us. My daughter wants you to remain here in court. The trouble is I think she has taken a fancy to you, young man from the

Misty Isles. It's an inevitable complication following the old Saving the Maiden from the Vicious Monster routine."

"Complication?" Tom said, without any prompting from Snow.

"It's a complication all right. She doesn't know it yet but I've arranged for her to be betrothed to young Cadmus, the son of Cleon of Crete. I can't have you jeopardising that political alliance. It's worth a wagon train of gold now. Not to mention mountains of gold and an enormous parcel of land for me sometime in the future. A very lively young man, Prince Cadmus. Loves horse-riding and racing in his chariot. Dangerous sports and he is certain to continue pursuing those sports even after he marries my daughter when his property becomes tied to her. And so to me. Accidents are almost inevitable especially when gold and parcels of land are concerned...and when it comes to horses and chariots, accidents are so often fatal - but you don't need hear about that. As I said, I can't have you jeopardising that alliance. Now listen to this. Here's my proposition."

King Augeas had been addressing the walls, the guards' sandals, the ceiling in his quiet low voice. He had looked everywhere other than at Tom. Little flecks of spittle had gathered at the corners of his mouth as he spoke, words spilling like froth from his fleshy lips. Suddenly the King looked Tom directly in the eye and said, "You look as poor as a beggar to me. Wherever you're from I don't believe the 'arrived here by dragon' story. You don't look the Dragon-taming type. Believe me. I know. I've met one or two in my time."

"But!" Tom began to protest.

"Quiet!" *whispered* Snow, in a voice so soft that only Tom could hear.

"Silence!" flashed Augeas. "Never interrupt a King!" His eyes blazed red with fury but the shark smile floated back onto his face as he recovered his composure. "You need a lesson in royal etiquette, young man. You must never interrupt a King. It can be very dangerous. Fatal even-though not this time as you have recently saved my daughter. That buys you a small amount of indulgence."

Oh Fangin' Crab! – thought Tom – *this is worse than being in class with Mr Porter*!

"A lot worse!" confirmed Snow. "Now shut up and listen!"

"As I was saying," Augeas continued, his eyes fixed on Tom's, like a snake hypnotising its prey. "I have a proposal to make. In order to remain in court, you need to be a Greek noble. This 'Tom of the Misty Isles' title won't do. Won't do at all. At the same time, I don't want you to...um...distract Apollonia.

"I'm proposing to make you the Duke of Eleum. It's a mountainous region south of Olympia. I'll marry you to the Earl of Olympia's daughter. The marriage can be arranged for the end of the month. You'll be rich beyond your wildest imagining. What do you think of that? Is it not true that King Augeas is a generous and noble-hearted king who knows how to reward a lusty young Hero?"

"Tell him it is indeed a wonderful and generous offer and you will be only too glad, nay, indeed, humble to accept," whispered Snow in Tom's ear. "It will buy us some time and I'll think of a way out of this mess later. Go on. Say it!"

Tom was horrified. He had no plans to marry at fourteen! Completely ignoring the dragon, he said,

"But I'm only fourteen! How old is the earl's daughter?"

"She's old enough for marriage! She's the same age as Apollonia."

"And how old is your daughter?"

"She's fourteen!" the King said angrily.

"Fourteen? That's far too young!"

"'Far too young'? At fourteen?" It was the King's turn to protest. "She's almost past it. On the shelf. Almost old enough to be a grandmother"

"We do these things differently in the Misty Isles," said

Tom. "At fourteen we're still at school. Getting married at fourteen is against the law!"

The King was so shocked by what he was hearing that he had even forgotten his instruction about not interrupting a king.

"Besides," said Tom thinking on his feet. "I thought it was custom and practice for the Hero to be allowed to name his prize after slaying the Monster and saving a princess!"

The King's eyes narrowed. The shark smile had all but faded.

"Be very careful what you would wish for, boy. If you have designs on Apollonia, you can forget that idea altogether. I have said that I intend her to become betrothed to Cadmus, son of Cleon."

"Oh no, sire, most noble and generous King, I have no designs on Apollonia," Tom was at last giving half an ear to Snow's whispered words of advice. "In fact I'd rather not marry anyone. Not for a while anyway!

"I only wish is to serve you. My first wish is to be allowed to clean your stables for a small fee." One part of his brain was listening to Snow and saying the words that the dragonfly wanted to hear, translated by the Undrone. At the same time, another part of his brain was racing. Apollonia promised to someone called Cadmus, someone she probably had not even met? An arranged marriage? It didn't bear thinking about. He had to avert the princess being forced into a miserable life. She was a chum. He had to save her from misery and her father's greedy plotting.

The King's face froze. He was uncertain whether the youth was joking or not. Then he began to laugh. His laughter rolled round the Throne room and boomed against the walls like cannon fire. He clutched his sides. Even one of the guards had to stifle a snigger.

"You don't wish for the hand of an Earl's daughter. You don't want land, a palace, gold tribute for life. As a reward for saving my daughter, you wish to clean my stables?" The king was laughing again. "In return for what?"

"Whatever I find left lying around in them once they've been cleaned."

"Oh, you're welcome to that!" The King guffawed. "Once the horses, bulls and cattle have been moved out to pasture you can have whatever you find there. It might even fill a bucket or two!" and once again the King roared with laughter.

He gestured for the courtiers and attendants to approach him once again and Tom felt the presence of Greek aristocracy close in about him.

"My noble lords, friends, members of court, listen to this. The young hero from the Misty Isles has just turned down an offer to marry the daughter of the Earl of Olympia. He wishes instead -" the King waited until all eyes were on him and Tom "– wishes instead to clean out my stables!"

Loud, laughter rolled round the throne room like a herd of donkeys braying.

"Anything else?" King Augeas asked when the sycophantic laughter finally subsided.

"Three things," Tom said, before Snow could whisper anything in his ear.

"Three?"

"Firstly, you allow me to have as many spades, shovels, hammers, stakes, rope and pick-axes from the Royal stores as I choose to take. Anything I need."

The King thought about Tom's request, but only for a moment or two.

"You only have two hands, two arms and two legs. I agree to your request. Secondly?"

"You allow Sergeant Plodalonganon and a company of his men, say twenty in total to assist me."

"That I shall think about," said the King. "What is the third thing?"

"If I complete the task within one full day, you must

grant me any wish that I make."

Not for the first time that morning, the King roared with laughter.

"Within a day? Young man, you are hilarious!" he said. "You obviously have no idea of the size of the challenge. My stables have not been cleaned in years. The buildings are spread over several acres! The amount of muck in the stables would fill the royal palaces many times over!"

"Twenty men and a boy?" the King muttered. "If you laboured for a year you would not complete the task. The sergeant and a company of his men shall assist you – you will fail anyway!"

"So...we have an agreement, my lord?" Tom asked politely. "All the tools I want, the sergeant and a company of men and if the stables are cleaned in a day I can name my wish?"

Augeas sneered.

"Agreed, boy. And I can assure you of this. By this evening, when you have failed, your only wish will be for a hot bath and some clean clothes!"

"But if I succeed I could, for example, ask to marry Apollonia after all!"

"CAREFUL BOY! You try my patience!" the King snarled.

"The word of a King? You've agreed. I can name my wish. In theory I could ask for the hand of your daughter."

The King's face turned bright purple. It was the sort of lurid mix you'd get if someone was to fill a bath tub with five-dozen tins of tomatoes and added five bottles of red wine, stirred it up and then ground in the skins of eighty-four aubergines just for fun. His jaw clenched in fury. Just when Augeas was on the point of commanding one of the guard to take Tom away and throttle him, a courtier who had been standing nearby leaned forward and whispered something in the King's ear. After listening for a little while, the colour subsided from the King's cheeks. His breathing slowed. His chest ceased to heave and he was master of his temper once again.

"In theory – you're right, young Prince of the Misty Isles, as you say, 'in theory'. But you wouldn't want to marry my daughter. She is very fond of you. You're a hero – but I've already agreed to marry her off to someone else," the King said. He had been thinking for a little while and his demeanour had brightened. "– but anyway, the idea that you can clean the stables in a single day is preposterous. It's worse than preposterous...It's stark, staring mad!"

His humour fully restored, he chortled. "Clean my stables in a day!" he sniggered. "The very idea of it! It's absolutely ridiculous! So yes – if you succeed, you may name your wish!"

Tom bowed and prepared to leave.

"Wait!" the King commanded. "You have left me with a problem, particularly where the land of Eleum is concerned. Balance should be introduced. We shall allow the arrangement to have more of the nature of a wager.

"You win and the stables are cleared in a day, you may indeed name your wish."

The King paused for effect.

"You lose and I dispose of you as I wish."

"But!"

"Silence! This is the King's decision. You may not negotiate!"

"But - 'dispose'?"

"A useful verb with many meanings...not all of which are fatal!" and the King gave a horrible, sinister grin.

Tom climbed down from the throne and bowed.

"May I borrow the services of Sergeant Plodalonganon to escort me through your fair city and show me the way?"

"Of course! For all the good it will do you. Take Plodalonganon and anyone else prepared to lend you a hand!" the King snorted.

Got you! Thought Tom.

Tom bowed again and began to retreat from the Throne

Room.

Walking back through the throng of courtiers was not as easy as it had been when he first arrived.

Details of the wager were spreading fast.

The laughter that swept round the court wasn't so much a ripple, more like a bunch of Rollers sweeping in from the Atlantic after a storm off the Cornish Coast. Guffaws greeted Tom as he walked briskly back through the room. One or two earls and dukes even slapped him on the back. He smiled as he walked and waved in response to the cheers. So much of this Hero-ing business was about putting on a front.

They think I'm Mad as a Hatter!

"They aren't the only ones," said Snow when they at last got out of the Throne Room and Tom was striding down another long corridor.

"Are you sure you know what you're doing?"

I've got a pretty good idea.

"Wouldn't it have been easier to go along with the King's wishes? Agree to marry the earl's daughter. Then, while you're enjoying all that royal favour, ask Augeas to have the stables cleared for you? We find the key without having to get our hands dirty and we leave in the middle of the night, vanish without a trace and no one gets hurt. Almost as important, we don't have to wade knee-deep in horse muck!"

A couple of problems with your plan, Tom thought. *It would take a long time to find the right moment to ask Augeas to clean the stables. Time is not on our side. I wouldn't want to embarrass the earl's daughter. More importantly, Apollonia must be saved from a forced marriage.*

"You're concerned about the reputation of a girl you haven't even met and the fate of another girl you met only yesterday?"

It's what Heroes do! thought Tom, using a very loud thinking voice.

"I was wrong to agree with you earlier," whispered

Snow. "You aren't Mad as a Hatter."

No?

"No. Hatters are reasonably sound, well-balanced creatures with Masters Degrees in Reason and Rational Behaviour when compared to the lunacy of Tom Wolfe! What on earth to do you hope to achieve? Hercules himself only just managed to clean the stables in a day! He was part-god and the strongest man on earth. You're only a boy!"

Only partly correct!

"How might I be only partly correct?"

I'm part boy, part Hero! The Boy Hero from the Misty Isles. Ask the King!

"I give up!" said Snow. "I just give up!"

It's time to whisper again, thought Tom. *Here comes the sergeant right on time. He's our escort to the stables.*

7 Cleaning The Augean Stables

It was early morning and the rising sun was low in the sky. The King's stables were near one of the main bridges over the River Alpheus not too far from the city. The road between the city gates and the bridge was busy. Merchants and tradesmen travelled in both directions, going about their business. A train of pack horses laden with amphora, some filled with wine, others with olive oil, had to pull up suddenly to avoid colliding with a company of heavily-armoured palace guards. The soldiers were marching at a juddering pace. They were a strange sight. Instead of swords and shields, they carried spades and shovels. Bringing up the rear were two large, four-wheeled carts, drawn by oxen and piled to the side rails with tools for digging. As well as spades and shovels there were hammers and chisels for breaking rock, mattocks, trenching tools, buckets and pick axes. Tom was marching at the front of the company alongside Sergeant Plod.

The city was built on a hill with the Royal Palace commanding the highest ground near the centre. Outside the city walls, the land fell away gently to the river. The stables, spread over several acres, had been built on the flood plain. Tom had been confident of his scheme when he had spoken to the King. As he gazed down at the stables, his face fell. There seemed to be no end to the horse blocks and cow sheds. Inside a fenced compound, the mud brick buildings that housed the animals stretched away for what looked like miles but was probably only one or two hundred yards at most. Although they were still some distance from the stables, Tom could already hear the sound of horses whinnying and cattle lowing.

"Permission to speak, young sir?" Sergeant Plod said, out of the blue.

"Permission granted, sergeant," said Tom, "And no need to keep calling me 'sir'. I'm young enough to be best mates with your son, if you have one!"

"Oh I've got one all right. A right little tearaway. Raskalion by name and rapscallion by nature. His heart's in the right place but he's a tearaway and no mistake!"

The sergeant paused and then out of the corner of his mouth said, "That was a handy bit of Hero work – the way you dealt wiv the Roc, young sir. Good soldiering, if you don't mind me saying so. Very acc'rate delivery of the old dart. I might get you to give some throwing lessons to my men later if it's awright wiv you!"

"Come off it, sergeant! Your men couldn't learn much from me!"

"Sure you're not just being modest?"

The sergeant's eyes were now fixed on the stables and cowsheds as they drew nearer.

"Just as well the sun's not up yet and the wind is blowing from behind us," he said.

"Why's that?"

"The pong, sir! His Majesty wasn't kiddin' when he said the stables haven't been cleaned in years an' years. They haven't been cleaned ever. Not never! They hum! Oh, how they reek! Thing is – when the wind's blowin' from the other direction, you can find your way here in the dark – if you know what I mean!"

"I think we do!" Snow whispered into Tom's ear. He had taken up his usual station just behind Tom's ear as soon as they had set off from the palace. "I think I'm going to meet quite a few cousins any minute now."

Cousins? thought Tom.

"Yes – 'cousins'," Snow said, reading his thoughts as

usual. "I'm in dragonfly shape – remember? Cousins as in flies. They swarm over the stuff – and there must be tons of the stuff in there. Do you have any idea about the size of this challenge?"

Oh yes, thought Tom. *Somewhere in the middle of the stables there is a trapdoor. Under the trapdoor there is a small compartment containing a key. The key will unlock the door of the portal that takes me to the next quest. The second of three quests. Unfortunately, the trapdoor is under piles and piles of horse and cow crap and I don't even know which stable contains the trapdoor! I might have to clean all of them – with my luck it will be in the last one!*

But maybe not! Tom was confident his idea would work. It had arrived welling up from somewhere while he was talking to the King. It was more than just the germ of an idea. This was a complete plague of ideas. Big enough to be an epidemic.

I think I may have thought of a way to do this. And in the time set, he thought, knowing that Snow was 'listening'. *Cleaning Augeas' stables is one of the legendary Twelve Labours that Hercules had to complete. I say 'had to' but he hasn't done it yet. The myth I read ages ago is in the future if you see what I mean?*

Hercules didn't do any muck-shovelling in the stables. Instead he dug channels from the two rivers, Alpheus and Peneus, that flow round the city and diverted them through the sheds. The river water washed the stables clean.

"Well remembered," said Snow.

Tom muttered, "Thank you, Hercules!"

"Who's 'Hercules' when he's at home?" asked Plod.

"Oh someone who'll drop by here one day," Tom answered. "I must stop calling him by his Roman name."

"'Roamin' name', young sir? So he's a gypsy then? A travellin' man this Hercules?"

"Sort of, sergeant, and his name is really Herakles - but if he appears around these parts: give him a wide berth. He's one of those heroes who disembowels first and then asks questions later. I'm going to make him quite upset!"

"What on earth are you blethering about, young

Wolfe?" whispered Snow. "Hercules was the strongest mortal ever to walk the earth. He was the son of a god. He dug two canals single-handedly in a day to scour out the stables. You're a teenage boy and on your own. What on earth can you hope to do?"

Wait and see!

Tom and Plod had reached the wooden gate that barred off the stable yard. The first whiff of what lay inside the stables was just starting to reach Tom's nostrils. He felt them twitch. He'd have to get used to the smell or his nose would twitch itself off his face! He unbolted the gate.

"Let's have a quick look round the place, sergeant!"

Plod's face wrinkled.

"Ordinarily I'd say that time spent on reconnaissance is seldom wasted, young sir...but on this occasion," and it was the turn of the sergeant's nose to wrinkle. "But...oh alright then," Plod raised his face to the heavens. "Can't deny me military trainin'. Reconnaissance is never wasted. Come along. Great Zeus give me strength!"

The rest of the guard waited beyond the gate while the sergeant and Tom entered the compound.

"We're in luck in one way," Plod said. "The cows have been milked and are off grazing in the fields on the other bank of the River Alpheus. The bulls are on the other side of the River Peneus. Most of the horses are in a field beyond the stables and as for the blood-drinking, Mad Horses of Eli the Corruptible – they're in another stable block on the other side of the city. Thank the gods you didn't volunteer to clean those stables out!"

Holding his nose, Tom peered in over the stable door. There wasn't much light in the first cow shed but it was enough to confirm his worst fears. The shed was knee-high in cow muck. The manure had been there for years. He checked two more to make sure that he hadn't just been looking at a particularly bad example. No. Not a bad example. If anything the first shed was a bit cleaner than the others.

Then suddenly Tom grinned. There was so much crap. This was going to make the feat all the more astonishing. Definitely turn him into hero material. The germ of the idea that was going to grow into an epidemic might even get the Hero from the Misty Isles his own special mention in the Myths and Legends of the Ancient Greeks!

"Happy, young sir?" Plod said, puzzled.

"Happy as a pig in..." Tom began.

"That's not the language of a hero!" whispered Snow in alarm.

"Happy as a horse with a clean cow shed!" Tom said instead and turned back towards the gate, walking with a spring in his step. The spring in his step was not prompted by the cleverness of his idea. No. The spring-in-the-step technique was the best way to avoid stepping in some of the stuff that had spilled from the cow sheds and into the yard.

Outside the gate again, Tom turned to Plod.

"Sergeant, please take your men and the wagons and set up camp on the high ground beyond the fence furthest from the river? And send one of your men over with two each of the tools in the wagons?"

"Two each?"

"That's right. Two spades, two shovels and so on-"

"Beg pardon, sir, but you're going to need more than two of everything if me an' all the men are goin' to help wiv the diggin!"

"Oh but that's it, sergeant. You aren't."

"Aren't what, young sir?"

"Aren't going to help with the digging. I insist on doing this on my own – at least to begin with!"

"But it would be an honour and a privilege to help the Young Roc-Slayer!"

"No – at least not yet - but thanks, anyway, sergeant."

"But one of my men overheard what you said to the King. There's no way you'll get all that...all that...well if you can pardon the expression, all that crap dug out of there in one day!"

"Just watch me, sergeant!"

"But you'd need muscles the size of Mount Olympus to shovel all that lot out. In a day. On your own!"

The sergeant walked away, following instructions as a good soldier should.

When Plod returned with the tools and another of the men he was even more mystified. Tom had wandered away from the stables and was on the edge of the Alpheus, looking over the river bank.

"Um the stables is over there, sir," Plod said gesturing in the direction of the buildings, away from the river.

"Thank you, sergeant. I'm aware of that. Now: one more favour?"

"You only have to ask, sir"

"Get three or four of your men. Gather up planks of wood and hammers and nails, carpentry tools, bars of iron, some chains and big hinges – as much as they can filch from the royal stores? I'll give you a list of what's needed. Then can you – and I'd prefer if you were to do this in person – can you go back into Elis and find Theron and those other bums he hangs about with – Hilarion and the other joker, and tell Theron that the Roc-Slayer is digging the stables clean and refusing all help! Stress this. Stress that the Hero will not under any circumstances allow anyone to help him dig! Not only that. Tell him that the Hero thinks the task is so easy he is going to start by doing some digging-practice in the field next to the stables. Have you got all that?"

"Planks, nails, hammers from the stores. Check list you give me. Find young Theron, them other two ...erm...bums. Impress on them. Roc-Slayer working alone. Refusing all help. Digging-practice etc."

"That should do it, sergeant. Thank you!...Oh and sergeant!"

Plod half-turned on his heel. He had only taken three steps when Tom called him again.

"When you come back with Theron, don't be upset by any of the things that I say."

"What's that, young sir?"

Tom scratched his chin. This could be tricky. He had to put it in a way that the soldier would be happy with, or he could end up being spit on a javelin before he had even begun to tackle Theron. He had seen how handy the sergeant was with a spear.

"Have you heard of 'Black Watch Rules'?"

"No, sir?"

"The Black Watch. Famous regiment of fighting men in the Misty Isles. Their officers have a set of rules they use in the mess. Innocent fun among soldiers, sergeant. Black Watch Rules are: the opposite of what you say is what you mean!"

"No – you've gorn and lost me there, young sir. Run that by me again-"

"You mean the opposite of what you say and say the opposite of what you mean. Say you had a Captain Chickenheartenes in the guard-"

"Just so happens we do, sir!"

"And he was the meanest, tight-fisted son of a...son of a..."

"'Son of a cur', sir?"

"Tight-fisted son of a cur that never bought anyone a drink and never paid his way."

"You've met him, sir?"

"In Black Watch Rules, you'd say, 'That Captain Chickenheartenes is the most generous, big-hearted son of a god that ever bestrode the land of Elis. Always first to the bar, it's almost embarrassin' the way he treats the entire regiment to a round of drinks, even when it isn't his turn!"

For the first time since they met, Tom thought he caught a twinkle in the sergeant's eye.

"The very opposite of what you mean...like you say. Black Watch Rules!" The sergeant went away chuckling. "The *Black Watch*, eh? Wouldn't mind a few of them in my own platoon!"

Tom grinned. He'd played rugby with Charlie Dackett for years and though Dackett was a Prop and had the Prop's general lack of wit and wisdom, his father had been a Captain in the Black Watch. Dackett had inherited some good stories about life in the regiment from his father. For a while the entire First Fifteen had observed Black Watch Rules until it led to three full-blooded fist-fights, two black eyes and a bloody nose. Black Watch Rules were dropped by the rugby team after that. Forever.

Standing alone inside the field that separated the river from the stables, Tom spat on his hands, rubbed them together and lifted the spade. He dug into the earth. He was less than ten feet from the river. He heaved a thick clod of earth over. A march of a thousand miles begins with a single step. The Grand Union Canal, Suez and Panama all lay in the future, but the Great Canal System of Elis had just taken its first spadestep.

"You can't seriously believe you're going to imitate Hercules and dig a pair of canals in a single day?" said Snow in a loud voice, now that Tom was on his own.

"No."

"No?"

"'Course not. Hercules hasn't been here yet. In the future – when he gets round to doing it - they'll say he imitated me!"

"This is madness," Snow said. "I'm off to get some breakfast."

"'Breakfast'?" Tom echoed.

"Some nymph larvae but mainly mosquitoes. Standard dragonfly diet. We're very useful creatures, dragonflies. Do our bit to keep malaria and yellow fever at bay. I'll catch up with you later!"

Snow turned in mid-hover and flew straight back to Tom's ear.

"I'll take Undrone with me," he said. "He could do with

some exercise...and food. Even an Undrone can't live forever using your words for food – no matter how sustaining you might think they are. Bees need nectar and fresh air and a view not coloured by ear wax!"

Before Tom could protest, he heard a buzzing in his ear followed by a gentle popping sound, as of a wine cork being eased from a bottle, and then his ear felt unblocked for the first time in a while. He only hoped that the Greeks passing by on the main road above him were not great conversationalists.

Tom smiled. Just as well dragonflies didn't feed off the germs of ideas or his latest brainwave would never reach the epidemic stage. He wondered how much Snow had "overheard". The dragon probably knew more than he was admitting. When Snow was out of sight, Tom reached down and picked up the leather knapsack that Loki had given to him. He ignored the Belt of Invisibility and pulled out another wide leather belt and fastened it loosely. He would cinch the belt up and tighten it when he started lifting really heavy loads. He would use it like a weightlifter's belt.

He excavated an area the width of a narrow country lane and dug down until he had cut out a deep trench. He had been digging for quite some time when he first heard and then saw Sergeant Plodalonganon with a number of his men, coming back along the lane, accompanied by Theron with Hilarion and Pamphilos. It was still early in the morning but Tom felt his brow warm with sweat. He cleared his forehead with the back of his hand. The sergeant was waving enthusiastically. Tom couldn't tell if it was a friendly wave or a warning. Watch out! Even at this distance he could tell that Theron was angry. Angry already? Good. That was just what he wanted.

Tom ignored the approaching group and returned to digging, pretending to be calm when he wasn't. Where were Snow and the Undrone?

Theron was yelling at Tom.

Waste of time, sunshine. Can't understand a word you're screamin' at me! I'll have to pretend I've lost my voice!

Two insects, a large dragonfly and a tiny bee hovered in front of Tom's nose and in the nick of time the Undrone buzzed past the dragonfly and flew into Tom's ear.

A few seconds later, Theron was at Tom's shoulder, bristling with anger but mindful that the royal guard had been commanded to defend "the Boy from the Misty Isles", the Greek youth held his temper in check.

"What's this I hear, barbarian?" Theron's voice was doing its best to smother a snarl. "You have spurned the hand of a Greek beauty in favour of digging out the King's cow sheds? What's more – you say you're going to enjoy a spot of exercise, practise your digging before you start on the stables? And then you have the gall to refuse the help of twenty of the King's finest palace guards?"

"I'm sure the Earl of Olympia's daughter is a royal beauty," Tom said. "I just prefer a bit of honest toil...it's what heroes do."

Theron bristled even more at that.

"Digging out cow's muck? What's heroic about that?"

"Cleaning King Augeas' stables single-handed...in a day..." Tom mused. "Oh I think that the poets and troubadours, the balladeers and songsmiths will be given something to work with! Something along the lines of -"

He began to hum quietly to the tune of *Those Magnificent men in their Flying Machines,*

"The hero he came from the Great Misty Isles,
And he cleaned out the cowsheds, the yards and the aisles.
He swept away cow's muck and all the pat piles
And he piled up the piles with the greatest of styles..."

"Needs a bit of work and the rhythm ain't quite right in Ancient Greek, but you can see what I'm gettin' at, Theron? Besides – it's quite good fun!"

And he set about ignoring Theron while patiently digging over another clod.

"Spurned an earl's daughter – and now you insult the palace guard!"

"Oh, I don't think I could do that," said Tom and half-turned to where Sergeant Plodalonganon was standing carefully watching everything. He half-turned his head and winked at Plod. Theron and the other two boys couldn't see his face and missed the wink. "The palace guard are too dim to know when they've been insulted!"

Plod silently mouthed the words, "Black Watch Rules! I've told the men!"

"Insolent barbarian!" Theron thundered. "You insult their intelligence – but why refuse their help in doing this base, labouring work?"

"You mean why don't I accept help from a bunch of limp-wristed, lily-livered milksops whose muscles suggest they've lived on a diet of strained dandelion and gooseberry soup and who aren't fit enough to lift a grain of earth with a teaspoon? A bunch of feeble-forearmed, footlin' vagabonds with all the force of a stewed dumpling lying in a bath of milk pudding?" Tom waited until Plod's stifled chuckling subsided before saying, "No thanks, Theron. This is one hero who'd rather do his heroism solo. There's no one in Greece can match me!"

Before you say I'm over-doing this – remember: bragging was regarded by the Vikings as being as much of an art as cussing and swearing! The thought was for Snow's benefit. *I'm braggin' with purpose!*

Theron's face turned Imperial Purple with rage and he grabbed a shovel and spade from where the guard had set them down.

"We'll see about that!" Theron roared. "'Digging-practice'! I'll show you digging-practice. This is one Greek who will more than match you at digging. Pamphilos, count time. Give me two thousand."

Pamphilos jumped to it, doing as he was told. Hilarion seemed to understand that this was deadly serious and didn't trouble them with any of his usual prattle.

"Barbarian, on this mark. We'll see who digs the most! I'll teach you to mock Greek women and Greek warriors!"

"Well, I'd really rather you didn't. I'd be much happier digging the storage area myself."

"'Storage area'?" Theron stuttered.

"Where else do you think I'm goin' to put all the crap that I get from cleanin' out the stables?"

"That does it!" Theron snarled. "Pamphilos – ignore the barbarian. These are delaying tactics. Begin the count."

"Hang on, Pamphie ole chum!" Tom yelled and then issued his challenge to Theron.

"OK, chicken-slayer," he said. "To the same depth as the small trench that I've already dug. I'll bet you can't dig more than me in a count of two thousand. Sergeant Plod – you check the depth. Wouldn't want the slayer of baby birds to get away with a shallower trench!"

Purple-faced, Theron snarled: "Pamphilos!"

And the youth began to count:"One By Zeus. Two By Zeus. Three By Zeus."

Tom had only been digging at a casual pace before Theron arrived. Now he put his back into it. He was confident that he would be able to keep ahead of the Greek youth. Theron was fit and muscular, a natural athlete. But he was of noble blood and had trained as a warrior. He hadn't done a day's hard work in his life. Tom was sure of it. Tom was fit and strong, a natural athlete but had spent hours digging over the vegetable garden and the allotment patch for his Uncle Bernard. The skin on the palm of his hands was tough and he knew how to use a spade.

Let your legs and back do the work.

Theron threw himself at the earth, jabbing furiously with both hands, punching the spade's blade into the ground and ripping out clumps of mud, silt and stone. For the first five hundred counts he dug and dug. His arms were a blur. That was the problem. He wasn't using his feet and legs to place the bite of the spade. He wasn't levering the earth away, wasn't using the spade to best effect. He was lifting the earth bodily and dumping it. He had no rhythm. Though Theron had stormed into a slight early lead, Tom knew that he would reel him in, using economy of movement. Tom could dig all day at this pace but the Greek youth would start to tire. Or so he hoped!

Just before the halfway point, Tom began to increase his efforts. He dug the spade in deeper and lifted bigger lumps and clumps. He didn't want to risk getting a sore back so he at last tightened up by one notch the belt that he had taken from the satchel.

That was strange – he felt a weird tingling course through his body. It was as if his muscles were being filled with the fuel that sends rockets to the moon. Suddenly even the biggest shovelfuls of earth felt no heavier than a sugar cube. It was then that Tom understood: Loki must have put some sort of charm into the belt. Something that increased his strength to an extent greater than he could imagine or measure.

This will come in handy, thought Tom. *No need to show off though. This is something to use another day. I'd have beaten Theron without the use of a magic belt!*

"Good thinking," whispered Snow. "Keep your powder dry, as my old friend Oliver Cromwell used to say. And I think you'll find that the belt, one of several that Loki has loaned to you, is Meginjoro, Thor's belt of strength."

After a thousand counts passed, Tom had drawn level. He eased into the lead and by the time Pamphilos called, "One thousand nine hundred and ninety-nine By Zeus, Two thousand By Zeus!" Tom had comfortably dug out more rows of trench than Theron.

The Greek boy's face ran through several different colours, all at the hot end of the spectrum. He was straining to suck air into his lungs and was bent at the knees.

"Tell you what," Tom said. "I know you weren't really trying just then. Why don't we make a wager? We'll measure out how much I dug in that time and I'll bet you a bagful of drachmas that no one individual – not you, Theron, Hilarion, Pamphilos, not even a soldier from the sergeant's bunch of limp-wristed lilies – can dig out more in the same time."

"Done!" said Theron before Pamphilos or the sergeant had time to say anything in reply.

"Sergeant – let's go and fetch your men," said Tom. I'll ask you to leave a reliable man – and I don't mean Black Watch Rules reliable! – to count off the time, three men to compete alongside the Posh Lads - " here he pointed at Theron, Pamphilos and Hilarion – "and lastly two of your best men can wait with me by the tool wagons."

Snow shifted nervously behind Tom's ear.

"I hope you know what you're doing, young man!" the dragonfly whispered.

Nope – Haven't got a clue. Can't you see I'm just wingin' it? Tom thought in return. He chuckled. It really was too easy to wind up a dragon!

People were beginning to dawdle on the main road, taking time to glance over to where Theron and Tom had been digging. They slowed down, stopped, watched for a while and then continued on their way.

That's exactly what I need, thought Tom, *just a little bit of curiosity.*

He walked up the gentle slope to the bottom of the hill that rolled easily towards Elis. He reached the wagons, still brim-full with tools.

I'm going to need more tools, he thought.

"What?" whispered Snow. "You've got enough to go - round this lot thirty times over!"

Tom didn't answer. Instead he explained to Plod that there had been a change of plan. The guards would stay with Tom at the wagons. Tom asked the sergeant if he would ask his son and any of his pals who happened to be out and about in Elis at the time to meet him by the wagons. Finally he instructed the sergeant to give his compliments to Princess Apollonia and could she and her maid servants gather up as much Royal Ribbon or bunting as they could lay their hands on and bring that along to the wagons too.

Plod saluted and said, "Permission to utter a compliment, sir! Master Theron doesn't understand Black Watch Rules, does he? 'Limp-wristed lilies'! 'Course that means we've got iron bands for muscles, and-"

"A handshake that would frighten a hydra!"! said Tom with a grin.

Satisfied that he *really had* grasped what was meant by Black Watch Rules, the sergeant set off down the road again with fifteen or sixteen of his men, laden with shovels and spades going in the direction of the river and the stables. As they marched, the sergeant chanted under his breath, "Take the men to the digging. Get 'em started. Fetch the princess. Ribbon and Bunting. Bring that rascal son of mine and any of his mates...gather up. Got that. Men to the digging. Princess. Bunting. Son and mates...plain and simple! Simple as that!"

8 When You're In A Hole, Keep Digging

The Princess was first to respond. She arrived with a caravan of maidservants, hand maidens, courtly maidens, and just plain ordinary maidens. The fair maids of Elis were carrying baskets full of ribbon and bunting, exactly as Tom had asked.

"Tom!" Apollonia called out, when she was near the wagons. Her face lit up with a lopsided smile. Tom realised that she was smiling because she was glad to see him but also trying desperately hard not to laugh.

"You have a novel way of cleaning out stables," the princess called out. "Do you honestly think you'll do it by lounging about against a wooden cart all day?"

She had caught him with his guard down and before Tom had a chance to reply, she ran up and gave him a smacking kiss on the cheek.

"That's better!" she said brightly. "I've been meaning to do that ever since you saved my life!"

Tom felt a deep crimson-red blush start somewhere near his ankles and spread up his rib-cage towards his neck. He hoped he could head it off at the pass. Staunch the flow before it reached his cheeks. Think about rugby practice on cold winter afternoons. Think about cross-country races through ankle-deep snow. Think about cold, cold exercise and head off the blush - before the crimson tide could spread to his neck and face.

"Apollonia-" he stammered.

"I'd have done that a lot earlier," she said, interrupting

him, "but Royal protocol forbids it. If I'd hugged you on the beach or in the palace, you'd have been pin-cushioned by a thousand javelins wielded by the Royal Bodyguard, Commoners not being allowed to lay hands on the royal personage and all that. So thank you, dear Tom. You're my hero!"

She was beautiful. One of the most beautiful creatures he had ever clapped eyes on. She was a heart-tangler alright, the beauty of her eyes hypnotic! Then Tom thought of home and Stella, his girlfriend, or if not his girlfriend then at least his best friend who happened to be a girl and one day surely would be his real, proper girlfriend! How could he break the princess' heart? She would have to know about Stella. But could he allow this beautiful young girl to be handed over to some lout called Cadmus whom she had never met? Allow her to be ensnared in a marriage arranged with a stranger? And she was only fourteen! Tom really was in a dilemma. If he succeeded in his task, surely as a Hero he would have to marry Apollonia if only to save her from the oaf?

And I'm only fourteen too! What on earth am I supposed to do? Why isn't Uncle Bernard about when I need him? I really could do with his good advice right now.

The princess moved closer to him.

"I wonder?" she said in a very quiet, low voice.

"What?" Tom said nervously.

"If you could do something else for me?"

"Oh no!" whispered Snow. "Here it comes. Expression of undying Royal Love for a commoner. Proposal of marriage. Royal scandal. Death by a thousand cuts!"

But Tom's heart and thoughts were too scrambled to say anything.

"Wh-what's that?"

"Try to get Theron to propose to me!"

"WHAT?" Tom couldn't believe his ears. The relief he felt at that moment was overwhelming. The explosive display that would have been delivered if Guy Fawkes had succeeded in detonating thirty-six barrels of gunpowder under the Houses of Parliament would have been a damp squib compared to the fireworks that went off in Tom's heart just then. What a relief! Apollonia didn't fancy him after all. Nevertheless, male pride insisted that he appear to be disappointed.

"But I thought – you and me..."

Apollonia smiled, "You thought you and I would make a Royal 'We'?"

"Well – that was what I thought - "

"Oh, Tom! I'm sorry to have to hurt you like this. You must be broken-hearted! I understand."

The girl was so kind, so considerate.

If you only knew! You've just got me out of the worst pickle...

"But I thought – Theron's a brute and a bully..."

"Oh you two just got off on the wrong foot. He envies you and the fact you killed the Roc, a fully-grown monster while he only despatched the chick. He was blustering because he sees you as a threat. He thinks I've fallen in love with you. And I haven't – sorry! I know it must hurt. It will be hard for you. Honestly, Tom, Theron can be really sweet."

"Theron 'sweet'?" Tom said, incredulity making him raise his voice.

"Oh! He can be. Don't let anyone know that I told you this but he writes poetry to me and sends love letters!"

"'Poetry'? Are we talking about the same Theron?"

"Poetry. It isn't very good but it does at least rhyme and it's the fact that he is trying so hard to be romantic. That's what counts."

"You could knock me down with an oak leaf," Tom muttered.

"I've always loved Theron. Have done for as long as I can remember. If only that pig-headed, stubborn, obstinate mule would realise that the gods mean us to be together!"

"I'm more than disappointed," Tom said with a grim look on his face, hoping that he was giving every impression of being heart-broken. "But I would only ever want you to be happy."

And I mean that, he thought so Snow could hear. *She's a pal!*

"So when it comes to nudging Theron in the right direction – well, I'll do what I can. In the meantime, there's a special favour I need you to carry out for me in return!"

Before Tom could begin to describe what he wanted the princess to do, the sergeant returned from Elis with more armed guards. Armed that is with spades, shovels and picks. Following some distance behind the well-ordered, soldiers was a straggling crew of teenage boys. Tom asked the sergeant to command the boys to wait by the tool wagons. He then led the princess, her maids, the sergeant and most of the guards to a point on the road where they could see the river, the spot where Theron was digging and the lie of the land all the way to the stables. Tom spoke to the princess and the sergeant, quickly giving instructions. The sergeant had spent some time in the Royal Engineers and knew at once what was required. Apollonia hesitated.

"Tom, I'm not sure this is activity fit for a member of the royal household," she said uncertainly.

"Theron is digging down there in the field next to the river. Think about it. You'll be helping him to win his goal!"

That was enough for Apollonia and she ordered her servants to follow her to the field. The sergeant followed and ordered some of his men to drive stakes and poles into the ground. and using the ribbon he marked off three parallel lines of bright cloth. The royal maids streamed the ribbon so that it stretched tightly, setting out tramlines that ran from the river all the way to the stables with a central dividing band. In a very short while, the edges of Tom's plan had been set out.

Satisfied, Tom walked back to the wagons where a large gang of boys was milling about, impatient and edgy. One of the boys was picking his nose and flicking bogeys in the general direction of the guards protecting the tool wagons. Near enough to annoy them but not so close that they were going to rush over and arrest him. Another was making fart noises erupt from his armpit by clapping a greasy hand over it and squeezing. They told jokes, poked fun at one another, swore and belched. Getting them to do what he wanted was not going to be easy.

They need a leader.

When Tom reached the edge of the jostling, milling crew he called out,

"Which one of you horrible lot is Raskalion?"

A skinny youth who looked slightly younger than Tom pushed his way through to the front of the crowd.

"That's me!" he piped up. "'Oo's askin'?"

Tom wondered what the boy's mother looked like. He bore little resemblance to the sergeant. Where Plod was medium height and built like a bear, Raskalion was tall for his age and skinny, with a rabbit chin.

"Got something I'd like you and your mates to do for me!" Tom said, brightly.

"Oh yeah?" Raskalion said defiantly. "Wotcher want and wha's in it for us?"

"What would you say to earning a barrel of loot?"

"How much loot and for doin' wha'?"

Tom put his arm round Raskalion's shoulder and in a conspiratorial whisper said to the sergeant's son.

"I want you to divide your gang into three groups."

"'Three groups'," Raskalion repeated. Tom realised that there might be a resemblance between father and son after all.

"The first group splits up and wanders along the road between Elis and the river. Any aristocrats – princes, dukes, earls or even bog standard Right Honourables, they go up to them and say – 'do you see that bunch of men and youths digging away down by the river?'"

"'Men and youths digging away by the river'-"

"A band of intrepid nobles have been challenged by a gang of commoners. Some scruffy low-lifes are claiming the nobles have gone to pot and can't do a hard day's work to save their lives. Couldn't even dig part of a ditch. The nobles are proving the virtue of the old families of Elis. They're digging away in the right hand trench, down by the river. Got that?"

"Intrepid nobles wot's been challenged...low-lifes...day's work...prove virtue...right hand trench. Yep. Goddit!"

Tom listened while Raskalion repeated it. Ah yes. He was Plodalonganon's son all right!

"Good – the second group splits up and wanders along the same road. Any tradesmen, farmhands, labourers, craftsmen, builders, any ordinary bog standard Common Folk, they go up to them and say – 'do you see that bunch of men and youths digging away down by the river?'"

"'Digging away by the river...' – sounds a bit familiar already, matey."

"Pay attention. This is important. Your pals say to the Common Folk – 'there's a band of hard-working ordinary people that have been insulted by the aristocrats. The Nobs have said the Common People of Elis aren't worth a candle. Can't do a hard day's work to save their lives. They've challenged them to a contest to see who can dig out the most earth in a day. The Common Folk are digging in the left hand trench'."

A crafty light began to glow in Raskalion's eyes.

"Think I'm beginning to see what you're drivin' at," he said in a low voice. "What do you want the third bunch to do?"

"I want you to lead them," Tom said. "I can tell you're a natural born leader."

Raskalion's scrawny chest puffed out like a pigeon's.

"Yeah?" he said keenly. "'Natural born leader'? Wait 'til my old man hears this!"

"I want you to lead the third group into the

countryside. Visit farms, olive groves, vineyards – and tell the farmers – Come to Elis, bring the biggest ox-drawn cart you have. There's a once-in-a-lifetime chance to buy extraordinarily ripe, well-rotted farmyard manure at a bargain price. Ten drachmas per cart filled."

"Come an' get some lovely manure! 'Fill your own bag'! Think it'll catch on as a slogan? – sor' of cowpoo equivalent of 'Pick your own strawberries'?"

"'Fill your own bag'?" Tom said aloud, "Manure? Could cause confusion if it caught on?"

But Raskalion looked baffled.

"Those aren't strawberries they're going to be picking," Tom said. There wasn't time to explain the joke. "And listen, Raskalion – this is important." The farmers must approach the stables from the other side. Not this end where the people are digging. Get two of your lads to direct them to the rear gates."

"Waitaminute!" Raskalion said in an irritated voice. "You still 'aven't told me what we're going to earn from this!"

"Fifteen per cent of all the money we take from the farmers."

"Twenty?"

"It's a deal!"

Tom made the youth repeat everything he had said one more time and then left the young gang leader to organise his troops.

"That seemed to work reasonably well," Snow said when Raskalion was out of earshot. It was so long since Tom had heard Snow speak he almost jumped out of his skin. "It would appear that you might actually have a plan after all! And I'm glad to see you're using this-" the dragonfly tapped him on the head-" rather than straining your muscles!"

Maybe I've been listening to a dragon-mentor, Tom thought.

"Very good," said the dragonfly. "Now I'd suggest that if you've got everyone busily employed that we find a quiet spot to find out what's happening to Odin and Thor."

"Good idea," said Tom. He made sure the guards who remained by the tool wagon had their orders. He then found a spot where he was out of sight behind some large rocks in a shaded area under the city walls.

9 Frost Giants Attack Asgard!

Hidden from view, Tom reached inside the satchel and withdrew the mirror containing Mimir water. The gold frame and glass would reflect bright sunlight, giving away his hiding place, so Tom was careful to hold it flat on the ground in the shade. He waited and watched as the mirror began to writhe and ripple with moving shapes and images.

The dragonfly flew out from behind his ear and settled on the rim of the mirror.

"Careful!" hissed Snow. "Keep the mirror flat. Don't spill any water. We don't have much in reserve!" Snow flew up again and swooped over the glass.

The dragonfly hovered over the image that had begun to form and dropped a small snowflake onto the mirror.

"What's that?" Tom asked.

"A charm to change the timing. I want to see what has happened to them recently. Not just what's happening to them now. Make sure they're safe."

The image moved swiftly. Tom watched spellbound as he saw the Gods, Odin and Thor, still dressed as hoboes, secure their beds in the tramps' hostel for another week. Hobble, one of the tramps, was looking after them. He saw them eating breakfast and lunch and finding places where they could get free, clean drinking water. Tom listened as he heard Thor announce that he was going out to get a job.

"Looks as if they're survived for a few days using one of

New Jorvik's hostels for the homeless! Let's see what they're doing now." Snow took another tiny droplet of Mimir water from the flask, froze it into the shape of an arrowhead and stirred the droplet onto the mirror. The image blurred, speeded up and then settled down again.

"What's that?"

"Fast Forward? I've sprinted to Now – or at least 'Now' where Odin and Thor are at present. Their present. Our future."

The image grew sharper. Tom watched as Thor stepped through a gate onto a big construction site in the middle of New York. Tom wasn't going to think of it as 'New Jorvik'. He didn't feel restricted to calling everywhere on earth by the eccentric names used by Norse Gods and dragons.

The God of Thunder was alone. Odin had remained at the hostel. Though he appeared to be entirely human in form, Tom could see that Thor would stand out in any crowd: a broad-shouldered giant with piercing blue eyes and a jaw that a blacksmith could use as an anvil. He had fair hair, cropped short like a Norman warrior and streaked with zig-zag bolts of ginger, like red lightning. He watched as Thor entered a portakabin office on the edge of the site. Thor shook hands with a burly man wearing a jacket and tie as well as stout steel-capped boots and a safety helmet. The man pointed overhead to the steelwork that was going up all around them. There were cranes and cables, chains and girders. Men scurried about the site heaving steel into place. They were building a skyscraper. The man, who was obviously the site manager or supervisor, was pointing to the highest point of the steel skeleton that had been erected.

Thor, still clad in his tramp's wardrobe, peered up at the top of the tower. He grinned. The supervisor gestured in the direction of a bucket that was being set down on the ground for Thor to climb into, but the God who didn't know he was a God, ran towards the nearest steel upright, picked up a riveting gun on his way, slung it over his back and then climbed up the H-sectioned steelwork. Grasping the flanges with his hands he climbed spider-monkey style and as fast as an orang-utan swinging through the trees, to the top of the skeleton building. The supervisor was open-mouthed. Men all around the site had stopped working while they watched. On top of the highest girder, Thor drove home some rivets with the gun, put on a pair of leather gloves, grabbed a long hawser that ran from the highest girder to ground level and slid down the cable, using his gloves and boots as brakes.

When he reached the ground, men began to cheer. The supervisor frowned and shook his head in disbelief. He had never seen anything like it in his life. Health-and-safety rules meant that he should have the man thrown off site and told never to come back. Such flagrant disregard for his own well-being and that of everyone else on the site! Then he saw the keen, eager look on Thor's face and the manager grinned. He was looking at the best skyscraper steel man he was ever going to have working for him. He simply had to explain to him some of the rules. He reached up to put his arm round the shoulder of the tall, fair and red-haired giant who had just slid down to earth from the heavens and began to describe the wages he could offer.

"That's all we need!" muttered Snow.

"What's wrong?" Thor was offered a job! They'll be able to buy food and move to a decent hotel-"

"What's wrong? The God of Thunder working as a steel jockey in Vinland? If they stay much longer they'll start to become used to that way of life. Loki warned me about this. The more they become accustomed to normal Life on Earth, the more difficult it will be for us to restore their memory and return them to Asgard."

"What is happening on Asgard?" said Snow, one claw making a pattern above the water. The picture on the mirror changed.

Tom thought he was looking at another gargantuan

Viking Hall. If anything, this one was even bigger than the main hall in Odin's palace, Valaskjalf. It was full of sleeping and dozing warriors with dozens of Viking kids milling about.

"That's Thorkel!" said Snow, pointing at a boy in the middle of the picture. "And that is Grettir the Strong!" the dragon pointed to a big warrior, slouched in a chair near the log-fire.

"Who's Thorkel when he's at home?" asked Tom.

"A lad about your age. His home is on Asgard. Watch and listen! We can learn how much Odin's absence is affecting the home of the gods!"

Tom concentrated on the screen.

Thorkel was sitting at the feet of Grettir the Strong. Grettir was one of hundreds of dead Norse heroes who had died in battle and now "lived" in Valhalla. The Valkyrie, legendary beautiful maidens rode on flying horses over battlefields in ancient times and decided who should live and who should die. They also decided which of the slain were heroes and should live again as living, breathing heroes on Asgard until the Day of Judgement. Living in Valhalla, Odin's fabled long hut, a palace with a huge log fire in the middle of the hall where warriors drank mead and ale and sang old drinking songs and songs of heroism and battle. The male children of the gods were allowed to visit Valhalla where they listened to the heroes tell their sagas of strength and battle, of outlaws and trolls, and ghosts and dragons. The dead heroes taught the boys how to use sword and buckler and bow and axe, how to hurl a throwing axe and how to thread a javelin past a giant's guard. The heroes talked of strategy and tactics and fighting styles. They schooled the boys in battle drill: how to make a charge against a shield wall and how to close ranks and repel a charge.

Sadly heroes such as Grettir and Njall and Thorgir and Nialfel knew they had a captive audience and at times their bragging and their tall stories rambled on for what felt like centuries.

Earlier that morning Grettir had asked Thorkel what he wanted to do when he grew up.

"Grow up?" Thorkel protested. "I *am* grown up!"

Grettir swats him with the back of his hand and Thorkel tumbles head over heels for three paces before springing to his feet, both feet planted firmly on the ground. He lands as Grettir has taught him, feet planted, ready for battle. A warrior's stance.

"Whelp!" says Grettir. "How old are you?"

"Fourteen winters," Thorkel says, a fat grin already replacing the sulk that had been smudging its way across his features.

"Let me put this another way then," says Grettir.

Snow whispered to Tom:

"Vikings do not regard childhood as a special or privileged condition. Children once they can hold an axe or sword or hoe or sickle, are viewed as small adults and expected to carry out their share of toil and be prepared to face danger. Listen to what Grettir is telling Thorkel."

Grettir spoke to the young would-be warrior. "What do you plan to do when you have seen the snow of eighteen or twenty winters come and go?"

"That's simple," said Thorkel. "When I am old enough to leave Asgard, I shall join the Varangian guard."

Grettir stifled a slow-burning smile. Ever since he had been old enough to pay heed to the dead warriors' stories, Thorkel had been fascinated by tales of the Varangian guard, the Viking warriors who had served as the Emperor of Byzantium's personal bodyguard. When the boys gathered in Valhalla, under the tutelage of the dead heroes, to practise combat and feats of arms, Thorkel had drilled two dozen of the tougher boys and drilled them into a squad that could manoeuvre and wheel and charge and retreat and form a shield wall with prefect precision. It wasn't the Viking way but Thorkel had studied the history of warfare and the boys had responded well to his leadership. He was a natural, Grettir recognised it. Valhalla had its own cohort of Varangians, aged fourteen years, most of whom had not yet begun to shave.

"Then after I have learned all that there is to learn of arms and war, of attack and defence, of armour and archery, I shall return to Asgard and offer my services to Odin as the next God of Thunder."

Grettir laughed aloud.

"It's good to have ambition, boy, but Thor is immortal!" Grettir chuckled. He found Thorkel's presumption and arrogance very entertaining. These qualities were not failings or faults but virtues in a Viking. "From what I know he has no intention of taking early retirement...And if he did, rumour has it that the Thunder God has a long lost son!"

Thorkel smirked.

"Thor's long lost son? That's a legend. Stuff and nonsense. There's no such boy!"

Grettir decided to interrupt the young whelp. Warriors had to have confidence, self-belief, and ambition but there were times when Thorkel was too full of himself! Grettir decided to change the subject. He was about to tell for the umpteenth time of how he had wrestled with the undead spirit of the spook, Glam, before killing him with his short sword when one of the youngest of the boy warriors, Gylfi, burst in through the main entrance door.

"Grab your weapons! To the main walls! The Frost Giants have broken out of Jotunheim!"

Thorkel stood up and bowed before Grettir.

"What are you waiting for?" Grettir asked as Thorkel hovered in mid-bow.

"Waiting for you to don your armour, grab an axe and join us!" Thorkel said brightly.

Grettir grinned a cruel warrior grin.

"Believe me when I say, young Thorkel – nothing would make me happier than to be given the chance to clasp a battle-axe and hurl into a mob of mountain giants."

"Why do you sit there and wait then?"

Grettir laughed a dark, hollow laugh.

"We are the dead heroes of Valhalla, boy," he said. "We are tied to this place until the day of the Last Battle. We are doomed to remain in this hall drinking mead, bragging and swapping stories of the great old days until Ragnarock. Until Judgment Day. Until Golden Crow sings. Until Jormundgander, the Midgard serpent makes its appearance. Until Fenrir the wolf and Surt the giant burst across the sky, we are held here as securely as if we were tied with hempen chords by the Thunder God himself.

"I'm sorry, Thorkel," Grettir said at last, "But you and the rest of the lads, the few gods that are in Asgard presently... you're on your own."

"What about Uncle Bernard, Stella and Rob?" Tom said to the dragon.

"There isn't time. There's a limit to how much we can use the Mimir water."

"We have to make time," Tom said. "I'm risking my neck for my uncle and my friends first and your two wayward and lost Gods second!"

The dragonfly frowned.

"It will have to be swift and without speech this time for haste."

Snow and Tom looked at the mirror glass as a new set of images appeared.

Uncle Bernard stood at the back door that led from his kitchen to the garden. He was gazing in the direction of the vegetable patch and seemed concerned. Rob and Stella were picking herbs from the same spot where Tom had gathered chervil and parsley earlier. Stella pointed at the lettuce plants. Many of them had wilted, their leaves scorched by frost. Rob tried to put his arm round Stella but she brushed him off angrily and stormed along the garden path towards Bernard, speaking as she walked.

Bernard looked on and listened sorrowfully.

"What happened?" Tom snapped. "Get the sound back on!"

"We have to take a break from the mirror," Snow said. "Get back to the quest!"

"What happened?" Tom repeated angrily. "Why did Rob put his arm round Stella?"

"To console her. The lettuce had been frosted. She was upset."

"Upset over some *lettuce*? Stella? You don't know Stella if you think she'd be upset over some wilted salad!" Tom snapped. "Why was it frosted? At this time of year? We haven't had a frost in weeks!"

"Exactly. 'Frost in May' or however the saying goes – even though it's June! All the more reason for us to make haste. I fear Odin's protection is fading faster than Loki had supposed. Ice on lettuce might be trivial to you and to Stella Cooke. I believe it is more serious than you suppose! I fear it means that a Frost Giant has slipped past Heimdal and is already at work on Midgard! We should get a move on!"

The images on the mirror were fading. Tom jammed the cork back into the flask of Mimir water, clasped the mirror firmly shut, placed everything back in the knapsack and stood up.

"At least they're all safe from harm, as far as we can make out," he whispered to Snow. "Time to get back to the stables. If we don't complete the task and find the key it won't matter how much Thor gets used to climbing about on girders. They'll be stuck on earth forever if we can't get away from Ancient Greece!"

"And there are at least two more quests to complete even if you succeed with this one!"

"All the more reason to get a move on!"

"That's what I've been trying to tell you, boy!" Snow said, in a voice rich in exasperation.

Tom slung the satchel strap back over his shoulder,

waited until Snow had settled behind his ear once more and crept out from behind the rock. He edged slowly along the face of the city wall until he was back on the road running from Elis to the river. In his absence, the place had been transformed.

The road thronged with people spilling out of the city.

Noblemen and Commoners mingled on the highway, jostling one another in their eagerness to get to the tools that were being distributed by Plod's men.

Looking at the wagons, Tom saw the stock of spades and shovels had dwindled.

Raskalion's mates were doing a good job. A steady stream of nobility picked up shovels and spades and flowed down the field to join their peers who were digging for all they were worth. Almost alongside, another stream of the common folk also gathered up tools and marched down to join their comrades. They too pitched in and made ready to dig all day if necessary. Whatever it takes to beat the gentry!

As the pile of tools was being depleted, Tom had another idea. He sent two soldiers off to buy more tools from Elis and instructed the guard to begin charging a hire fee: so many drachmas to the Nobles and a tenth of that amount to the Commoners. Money up front!

"And if anyone asks – those are the King's orders."

"What if the King happens by?" asked the remaining guards.

"Then you can say that they're my orders. By then they'll be queuing up for the chance to start digging."

10 "Princess, Can You Swim?"

Satisfied everything was going to plan, Tom made his way back to the riverside. He spotted Apollonia on a patch of higher ground. She was looking down at Theron digging. The youth was soaked in sweat. His face was red and his hands were blistered. Tom heard Pamphilos counting.

"Ninety-eight by Zeus, Ninety-Nine by Zeus, Two thousand by Zeus...Sorry, Theron, but you still haven't dug as much as-"

"Then let's start again, by Zeus! Find me another patch of ground and get ready to begin the count," Theron's voice boomed back. "I'll beat that stripling from the Misty Isles if it's the last thing I do!"

Tom grinned but then grew serious as he realised that Theron wasn't going to quit. Maybe there was more to the youth than the hectoring and bullying character he met on the beach. Catching Apollonia's attention, Tom asked for a word in private. They walked to a point where they wouldn't be seen by the men and boys digging.

Tom explained that he had thought of a ruse that would deliver everything Apollonia had wished for.

"How will you do all that, Tom?"

"You will have to trust me, Apollonia. You won't regret it! But before I go – can you swim?"

"Yes."

"Does Theron know?"

"I don't think so. Why?"

"Can Theron swim?

"Like a fish? Why, Tom? Please explain – I don't understand!"

"No matter – it will all become clear. Now I really must dash!" And as he hurried away from her he pointed to the sun. "The god you're named after – he won't slow that darned chariot of his down for anyone. I'm running out of time."

Tom left Apollonia struggling in a stew of puzzlement and jogged over to where Sergeant Plod was working with his men.

"Everything shipshape and going to plan, young sir?" the sergeant said by way of greeting while mopping his brow. Digging was warm work.

"As well as can be expected, sergeant!" Tom said confidently. "Now I have another mission for you and your men. A vital part of the exercise. Essential to our objectives."

The sergeant's eyebrows behaved like hairy caterpillars tensing before a bird strike as he concentrated on what Tom had to say:

"Find half a dozen carpenters and men from the Royal Engineer corps.

"March 'em down to where we first started digging!"

11 "The Floodgates Have Opened!"

Hours had passed. Apollo in his bright golden chariot pulled by a team of beautiful flying horses had completely ignored all the laws of flight and most of the laws of physics by soaring high in the heavens up and up until noon was reached and then he had begun his slow, gentle arc of descent, though only the gods knew what he used for brakes.

Apollonia looked over the plain that led from the rivers Alpheus and Peneus to her father's stable block. It had been transformed. Sturdy lock gates had been built into the river banks. Hordes of people were busy digging on the plain. It seemed as if the entire population of Elis, rich and poor, wealthy and slave, were toiling as Navvies. Two deep canals had been excavated and ran like tramlines from the lock gates all the way to the stables and out the other side.

She looked on in amazement. It was most unusual for a royal princess to be lost for words.

Tom grinned. He decided to help her out.

"Aren't you going to ask me how I did it?" he said, his grin growing broader with each word.

"I'll ignore your impertinence in addressing a member of the Royal Family before being spoken to," Apollonia said. "Besides," she added with a smile, "Roc-slaying heroes must be allowed some extra leeway. And I must admit- curiosity has the better of me – How did you do it?"

Tom paused long enough to pique the royal curiosity even more and then said.

"First credit goes to Sergeant Plodalonganon and his men. They're all trained engineers as well as fighting men. They constructed the lock gates – those wonderful stout wooden gates that you see holding back the river waters. Then helped by your maids they marked out the boundaries of the new canals using the bright royal ribbon provided by you! After that it was all thanks to Theron!"

"'Theron'?"

"Yep – Theron!"

"I don't understand! I thought you two were mortal enemies! Why would he help you?"

"Easy. After I'd whipped him in a digging contest, I challenged him and the young aristocrats and then the soldiers to the same competition. If you want to get the male of the species working flat out for absolutely nothin' - No reward whatever - there's nothin' compares with sporting competition. You can't beat a contest. We do stuff for free when it's called sport that we'd never do as work. Not for money. Not for all the gold in your father's palace.

"The young nobles were digging between one set of ribbons. The soldiers were digging in the other.

"Then the really clever part - I sent for Sergeant Plod's son, Raskalion and all his young chums."

Tom described what Raskalion had done.

"People queued to see what was happening. At first they came to peer. Some even came to jeer. They stayed to dig."

"Astonishing."

The princess peered into the distance. "Why are all those carts jamming the highway on the other side of my father's stables?"

"Even cleverer! Raskalion himself led a third group of youngsters into the countryside and spread the word to the farmers – 'Come to Elis and buy farmyard manure at a bargain price."

"You got Raskalion and those louts he calls his friends to work...for nothing?

"Oh no...teenagers aren't stupid. They were the only ones who insisted on being paid! Twenty per cent of all the money we took from the farmers."

Once again Apollonia looked puzzled.

"What's a 'teenager?'"

Tom scratched his head.

"I'm sorry," he said. "I forgot: they haven't been invented yet!"

Most of Elis was at work in the trenches, working either side of the ribbon line that separated the aristocrats from the ordinary people.

Initially the commoners had forged ahead. There were a lot more of them to begin with. The nobility reacted by summoning their slaves and ordering them to pick up a spade and also dig. The nobles paid the hire fee without complaining.

As the final clods of earth were hewn out and dropped into buckets, it was neck and neck. In a matter of minutes, one of the groups – it was too close to say which one – would clear a channel right up to the stable doors. Tom began to understand how the pyramids had been achieved. The canals were almost complete. They had been excavated to a depth well below that of the river that ran nearby. Earth dug from the trenches had been piled up in long mounds along the edge forming levees. The trenches had reached the outer gate of the stables. The lock gates built by Plod and the King's engineers were set in massive timber piles. The timbers had been driven deep into the river bank. The lock gate was firmly closed and secured with bronze bands. Plod had detailed more of his men to work on the other side, chest deep in water to clear the face of the gate.

To the rear of the stables, wagons were removing the last of the manure and were leaving. All day the traffic had moved relentlessly up and down the road. The farmers were making their way home as the sun sank lower in the sky. Clouds of flies followed the straggling wagons. The air in the vicinity of Augeas' stables was already more tolerable than it had been a few short hours ago. Raskalion's chums had done such a good job in goading aristocrats and commoners alike that Tom had been forced to start other trenches sooner than he had planned, linking the rear of the stable yard to the nearby Peneus. The Alpheus was straining against lock gates that held back its surging waters from two pairs of canals that met at the entrance to the stables. The channels on the exit side were lower than those that entered the stables and ran all the way down to the Peneus.

Although late in the afternoon it was still a bright, warm day and Apollo was still doing his best to illuminate Elis, King Augeas' stables, the rivers and the labouring men and boys. Women and children mingled on the plain, safe behind the levees and drank lemonade and chatted and watched. Small children played mud pies while those big enough to play rougher games played "Prince from the Misty Isles, Roc-Killer" and threw twigs at bundles of feathers pinned to a youngster's tunic.

Tom was standing alone on top of one of the empty tool wagons gazing down at the trenches. It would, in fact, have been incorrect to describe the tool wagon as empty. It had been emptied of tools and as such was no longer, technically a tool wagon. Now it was the Ancient Greek equivalent of a bullion van. Thousands of drachmas had been piled up inside the wagon and covered by a broad canvas sheet. This partly explained why a dozen of Plod's company, armed once again with javelins and swords rather than shovels and spades, were guarding the cart.

Tom focused on the men and older boys at work in the trenches. Wasn't human nature a funny thing? At first the nobles and commoners had laboured with spade and bucket in spite and hatred. It had been about pride and status. Now that they were nearing the end, though thousands of men were still digging in competitive gusto, laughter could be heard coming from either side of the dividing ribbon. Funny insults were traded, insults that were signs of grudging respect. It was like the banter that sportsmen and women traded during and after a contest. Respect? He would never have believed it. A cheer went up as the gates were reached. Tom couldn't see which group had won. He saw handshakes being offered and accepted all along the line.

"Looks like this hare-brained scheme of yours might work?" Snow whispered.

Never had any doubts, thought Tom with his hands behind his back and his fingers crossed.

"Just as well. The lives of everyone on Earth and Asgard depend on it!" said Snow.

Tom beckoned to Sergeant Plod who had been waiting for a signal since the cheer had gone up. Plod almost charged up the slope to reach Tom.

"Ready to open the lock gates, young sir?"

Tom had given up trying to correct the sergeant's deference. It was ingrained. It had been drummed into him after years of military service. He wondered if it was possible to change something that had almost become instinctive in Plod. He hoped that it *was* possible, that it was never too late to learn new skills. He hoped you *could* teach an old dog new tricks. Things were about to change mightily for Plod if Tom's plans came to fruition.

"You have your instructions, sergeant," Tom said.

I could get used to this imperial manner, he thought. *It's second nature now!*

"Not a good idea to become accustomed to the imperial manner," Snow said, behind his ear. "If this works we're going to go home soon and then you'll fall back to earth with a bump. Literally!"

Tom, not for the first time since he landed in Ancient

Greece, ignored the dragonfly.

"And I have more instructions, sergeant," Tom said. "We've got thousands of drachmas and a sack full of solid gold coins stacked away in the wagon here. I've been thinking about what to do with it."

"You have, sir?"

"A thousand drachmas goes to whoever won the digging contest."

"Erm, no one dug more in two thousand counts than wot you did, young sir!"

"In that case the prize goes to whoever came second. Who was that, Plod?"

"That would be the young nobleman, Theron."

"A thousand drachmas to Theron then, sergeant."

"As you say, sir."

"Now let me ask: in Elis how much does it cost for a young nobleman to publish his intention to marry a princess?"

"About a thousand drachmas, sir."

"Very good, sergeant. See to it that he gets the money."

"Yes, sir."

"Five thousand drachmas to fund a centre so Raskalion and the young people of Elis can hang out together."

"'Hang out', sir?"

"Impossible to explain, sergeant. You find the centre. They'll do the hanging out. You'll see how it works."

"I see, sir." Plod said doubtfully.

"No, sergeant, you don't. Not yet. But you will."

"Finally five thousand drachmas to Sir Henry Plodalonganon, recently created Knight of the Realm of the Misty Isles and Lord Lieutenant of Northumbria, with the operational rank of Major in King Augeas' army."

"Sir Henry...Knight of the realm...Lord Lieutenant...Major? Ain't no-one of that name and rank in the whole of Elis, sir!"

"You're right, sergeant. But there soon will be. Kneel sergeant – but first lend me your sword."

The sergeant handed over his bronze broad sword. Tom took it by the handle and pointed it at the soldier's collarbone.

"Sergeant Plodalonganon, by the powers vested in me by Loki the Cautelous I hereby invest you as a Knight of the Realm of the Misty Isles. Arise, Sir Henry Plodalonganon!"

"Erm but I don't understand how I'm supposed to become a Major, sir!"

"How much does it cost to buy a senior commission in King Augeas' army, Plod?"

"About five thousand drachmas or thereabouts, sir – almost the same as building a centre for the youths to um...hang out in," said Plod and then as Tom counted out a pile of gold coins, a light ignited in his eyes. "Ah I see, sir!"

"And as a major-to-be, Sir Henry what can we now dispense with?"

"Ah – the def'rential use of 'sir', si-....Tom."

"Thank you, sergeant. And apart from a small sack of gold pieces which I am claiming as my own reward for this little scheme, all the money left over can be distributed among the common people and the poor of Elis. Now, Sir Henry, please undertake the lowly duties of sergeant one last time. Get your men ready to open the lock gates. Remember: you open them on my signal. Synchronise opening front and rear. Make sure everyone gets moved onto the high ground behind the levees."

"Permission to deliver one last, salute, young sir? It's been a pleasure to serve with you!"

And before Tom had a chance to protest, the sergeant fired off a precise military salute and then marched back to the trenches. He summoned more soldiers and cleared the trenches. He then climbed on top of the levee by the Alpheus and caught the attention of his men who were standing ready by the lock gates.

This is it, thought Tom. The lock gates had been

strengthened and lined with stout, diagonal, wooden battens. They were lashed with bronze and stiffened with cross-straps. The hinges were strong and well-oiled. The lock gates were closed by chains that winding on a capstan fixed to a pile driven into the river bank. The gates were barred shut against the water flow. The capstan was capable of pulling a lock gate closed against colossal pressure. As soon as the digging was complete, the chains would be unlocked and allowed to run free. Tom hoped the river would burst through the gap like a dam bursting.

He hoped.

What if it doesn't work?

"No time for cold feet," said Snow. "Give the signal!"

Tom picked up a hammer and began to swing it in a big circle above his head. This was the signal he had agreed with the recently-knighted Sir Henry Plodalonganon, Lord Lieutenant of Northumbria in the Misty Isles.

Hope I've thought of everything!

"Too late to worry!" said Snow. "Sir Henry is giving the signal! Here goes!"

With a loud cheer from the people crowding the levee on the Elis side of the canals, Plod's men bent over the capstan and the gates and removed locking pins and bolts. With the chains screaming as they slid round the capstan, the gates were heaved open by the river water. Great waves surged through the gap as the lock gates swung open. A herd of wild horses, with manes flying in the wind, rearing up like crazed stallions, the first waves raced against the sides of the canal, lapping up, trying to bolt over the levee banks before swilling back down into the channels and racing in a mad, foaming, frothing, careering tidal surge, gouging, scouring and sweeping everything before it. The first waves raced along the canals and up to the open stable gates. Some water lapped up and over the sides but only swirled around the perimeter wall. The rest of the gargling sea flooded through the entrance to the stables and surged on through the blocks, the furious water boiling along and through every building in the compound, boiling, scouring and washing before sweeping out through the open rear doors.

"The floodgates have opened!" Tom yelled.

Care to carry out some observation, Snow? Tom thought.

"I'm ahead of you, young man!" said the dragonfly who was already flying off in the direction where the flood water would exit.

Tom waited patiently until the dragonfly returned.

"It's working better than you could ever have imagined. Water from the Alpheus running through each and every one of the stable buildings before sweeping into the channels on the other side taking the water...and what remains of the, erm, well, muck, into the Peneus. It's all flowing away downstream."

Excellent, thought Tom. *Not long to go now before we close the floodgates. First it's time to honour my obligation to Apollonia.*

Tom slipped a few fistfuls of gold coins into a leather pouch that he had removed from his rucksack.

"Keeping some of the loot?" said Snow.

We might need some funds for the next quest, thought Tom. *It's called planning! I'm giving almost all of the money away. Good idea to have a small reserve in hand. No idea where we'll end up next.*

Tom removed from his knapsack the three sharp-pointed wooden darts that had been whittled with magic by Loki and also placed them in the leather money pouch. He then fastened the pouch onto his waist belt. Tom had his knapsack slung loosely over one shoulder as he walked over to where Apollonia stood with her maidservants. Theron stood nearby as well as Hilarion and Pamphilos on one of the raised levee banks, admiring the mad surging waters. Tom was standing very close to Apollonia. The courtiers and attendants were too ensnared by the irresistible wonder of the raging flood to have noticed the boy from the Misty Isles sneak up alongside the princess. Before anyone could challenge him. He edged closer to her and whispered in her ear.

"Apollonia, you're about to fall in the water," he said. "Don't say a word until Theron sweeps you off your feet!"

"What?" Are you mad?" said Apollonia, not for the first time, completely baffled by the riddling words uttered by this so-called Prince of the Misty Isles.

"Goodbye, princess. You're a pal!"

And at that moment, Tom used an old rugby trick to nudge Apollonia with his shoulder so that she slipped and fell straight into the racing turbid waters of the canal. She sank under the water and was swept along in the surging tide.

"Apollonia!" yelled Theron.

"She can't swim!" Tom shouted. "What are you waiting for, Theron? I thought you were a hero!"

The Greek youth scowled at Tom's goading but didn't hesitate. He kicked off his sandals and dived straight into the giddy canal. Tom saw Apollonia's head appear above the water and at that moment he gave the second signal to the sergeant. The soldiers heaved on the capstan handles and the lock gates began to swing back to form a watertight gate. The Alpheus returned to its normal channel and the canals at once began to lose their fury. The lock gates at the stables exit closed more slowly and for a while a swimming pool formed in the lower part of the compound. In the slower waters of the pool, Theron swam up to Apollonia and lifted her chin above the water. He then swam with her back to dry land. The young Greek picked up the princess in his arms and carried her to a flat stretch of riverside turf that was dappled in sunlight. At that point, Tom signalled again to Plod and the lower gates were opened to allow the last of the water to flow away and into the Peneus.

Tom spoke to the princess' throng of attendants. He nodded to where Theron had carried Apollonia to dry land and safety.

"I think you lot should run quickly over there and help

your mistress. She'll need some towels and a warm fire for starters... and then chaperones and someone to carry the good news to the King," he said to the maidservants. They needed no further bidding and bolted along the bank to rejoin the princess.

"'Good news to the King'?" Pamphilos asked.

"Theron just asked Apollonia to marry him," said Tom. "Though hopefully they'll wait a good few years before tying the knot if Misty Isles customs start to catch on round here."

"How can you hear what he said all the way from here?" asked Hilarion.

"I don't need to," said Tom. "It's what heroes do. It's in the blood. Hero saves beautiful young princess from drowning. Hero plights his troth or in Plain Greek, just before she gets a chance to catch her breath, Hero asks princess for her hand."

Pamphilos was already running over to where the young couple sat in the setting sunlight. Apollo was retiring in a glorious, blazed, romantic sunset.

"No last minute quip, Hilarion?" Tom said.

"You're the first one I've seen who uses water to make matches!" blurted Hilarion before he too darted away, following Pamphilos.

That's the first half-decent joke I've heard him tell...even though matches haven't been invented yet, thought Tom.

"It's Undrone," said Snow. "Translation becomes more liberal after a hard day's work"

Thanks, Snow. And double thanks for checking that Theron had actually popped the question...Now...time to look for that key.

Tom made sure that the satchel was secure on his back, checked that the money pouch was secured to his belt then climbed down from the levee and walked over to the twin canals. He followed the bank until he reached the entrance to the stables.

He stepped inside. Out of sight of the crowds, Snow flew out from behind Tom's ear and hovered near the leather money pouch. The dragonfly's shape seemed to flicker and shapes that resembled dandelion seed heads in yellow, red and blue fizzed around the fly's wings. From the centre of the apparition a miniature version of Snow the ice dragon emerged.

"Quick!" the dragon said. "Hold up the money pouch!"

"Why?" Tom asked.

"Don't question. Just do it! And hold it by the very top with the tips of your fingers!"

"I don't understand!" said Tom.

"Just watch!" said Snow. The dragon pursed its lips and a spiral of icy vapour hit the middle of the leather bag with the force and rhythm of a drum roll.

"Ah!" Tom dropped the pouch. It had suddenly become very cold.

"Don't just stand there!" hissed Snow. "Pick it up!"

"What have you done?"

"Look at the pouch."

Tom picked up the pouch, carefully using only the tips of his fingers. Etched into the middle part of the pouch in Gothic script were letters that read, 'Property of Tom Wolfe, Prince of the Misty Isles?'

"Very funny. Very handsome," said Tom. "How did you do that? I thought you were an Ice dragon. Those letters look as though they were scorched in place."

"In a way they were," said Snow. "I used super-freezing vapour. I froze the leather in the shape of the letters to scores of degrees below zero. The leather was so cold it cracked and dropped out to form the script. Looks rather fine if you ask me!"

"But why did you do it?"

"You'll see," said the dragon, cryptically. "Come on – we don't have time to stand around blathering. We've got to find the portal!"

Tom tied the pouch securely to his belt once again and looked around. The canal channels leading to the stables were sloppy, full of churned up mud but the floor of the stables was clean. A thin film of silt had formed in places on the flagstones and cobbles and a tide mark was visible along some of the walls but the compound smelt clean and fresh. It had been scoured spick and span. Tom began his search. He looked round the first stable block, sifting along the floor but found nothing. He turned over mangers and baskets, sacks and occasional bits of flotsam and jetsam but could not find a key. This could take longer than digging the canal!

Think, Tom! he thought.

The key has been here since the stables were built; it will be in the oldest building! and he quickly ran round the compound until he found what he was looking for. It was at the rear of the yard, its brickwork cruder than that used in the more modern blocks and one wall and a section of the roof were sagging. Tom got on his knees and crawled along the flagstones. They had been polished clean by the river water. Clean as a pin. In the middle of the stable floor he found a metal drain cover. Once covered in years of filth it had been rinsed and shone like a new coin. Peering through the mesh of the cover, Tom saw that a bright golden key was hanging by a slender silver chain from the drain cover. He pulled the chain up through the grill with his fingers and the key lay snug in the palm of his hand. He peered around the stable. No one looking – and he yanked the silver chain so that it snapped and the key was free in his fist. He stood up and looked round again, examining the cowshed more carefully now. It was not much different from the other stable sheds. Older and with fewer windows. But with the same two-door front and rear entrance as the others. But there was something different about this one. What was it?

And then he noticed a small, ancient, wooden door, halfway down one of the side walls. It was too low to admit a man standing. Bent double, Tom thought he might just be able to stoop through the frame. It must have been buried for decades under cow muck and now stood revealed. Tom thought he could see a keyhole. He wondered...

Tom turned in time to see King Augeas and a host of guards, nobles, courtiers, servants, slaves as well as several dozen plain ordinary, hangers-on emerge from the city gates and promenade down the road to the stables. They were joined by Apollonia and Theron. Tom was glad to see that the princess had been wrapped in warm woollen blankets and seemed quite happy. She had her arm hooked through Theron's.

And now the King's going to pretend that this is all new to him. That he hasn't been watching us all afternoon from one of the towers overlooking the river!

"I think you may be right in your surmise, young Wolfe," said Snow, hiding behind Tom's ear once again. "Now – take care. Don't upset the King. We have the key. We simply need to find the correct door and its keyhole and we're free from Elis and its problems!"

The King stood on the bank and looked into the stable. Tom walked to the stable door and stood blinking into the evening sunlight. Apollo was working overtime. It was time he had the chariot in its garage and the horses out to pasture.

"Well done, young Hero from the Misty Isles," the King declared in a loud, swelling voice, "you have indeed cleaned my stables and earned enough to allow Sergeant Plodalonganon to buy a commission as Major in the Royal Bodyguard, a recommendation I shall honour."

Tom bowed with a broad grin.

"Permission to speak, sire?" Tom yelled so that Augeas, and more importantly the gathered crowd, could hear him clearly.

The King waved, signalling that Tom should continue.

"I claim as my reward the gift that your daughter, the Princess Apollonia, should be allowed to marry her childhood sweetheart, young Duke Theron!"

The crowd roared its approval.

"For cleaning out the stables, I am eternally grateful!" the king said, carrying on where he had left off and speaking as if Tom had said nothing.

A cheer erupted from the crowd that had gathered along the banks nearest to the stable door where Tom now stood. The crowd expected more good news. A reward for the young hero perhaps?

"However, because you did not complete the labour alone, you have forfeited the right to earn an extra wish."

The crowd's cheer subsided into a disgruntled murmur.

"Furthermore, I have evidence that you touched a royal person without permission, namely that you laid hands on the Princess Apollonia. Chief Justice read out the charges!"

Tom didn't like the sound of this. A tall, wizened man with long white hair and wine stains on his chiton and cloak pulled out a papyrus scroll and began to read,

"On the something day of the such-and-such inst. – these details will be completed later, I King Augeas find that Tom of the Misty Isles did lay hands, and violence on a royal person, to wit, by pushing my daughter, Princess Apollonia into the raging waters of the Alpheus and Peneus which the same Tom had illegally and without planning permission diverted through the Royal Stables. For violating town and country planning regulations, the sentence is a fine of five hundred drachmas and a prison sentence of six months. For violating the Royal Person the sentence is Death. Both sentences to run concurrently and to be carried out immediately."

Concurrently? thought Tom. *But I'll be dead!*

Tom heard a shriek from Apollonia and a howl of protest from the crowd, quickly stifled when hundreds of the King's bodyguards charged through the throng and swept towards the cowshed. Sergeant Plod tried to restrain some of his men but he was bowled aside by scores of soldiers whose instinct, drummed into them by years of training, was to obey the King's command without pause to question whether it was right or wrong.

No time to think! Tom thought.

"Then stop thinking. Start doing!" shouted Snow.

Tom turned. Again it was too good an opportunity to waste. He had been waiting to say it since the princess declared her affection for Theron. He only had seconds to act before the guards would be upon him. He yelled at the top of his voice, "Goodbye, *Apple-onia*. You and Theron will make a good *pair*!"

He saw Apollonia raise a hand and wave. Once again she hadn't understood a word which was probably just as well. Then he turned on a sixpence and bolted. He was running for his life.

Hanging onto the straps of his leather knapsack, Tom pinned back his ears and sprinted through the shed, his metal-studded leather sandals ringing on the flagstones. He reached the dwarf-sized door in the sidewall just as the first of the guards reached the entrance to the stable. He hesitated but only for a moment. This was bewildering! There was a picture of a Mississippi steam boat on the dwarf-sized door. Hundreds and hundreds of years out of time! But he didn't have time to ponder the strange picture. Tom ducked down and slid the golden key into the lock. It was a perfect fit. Instantly he turned the key and the door swung open. He plunged his head into the doorway and immediately began to fall into a fathomless black hole. The door swung and closed behind him as he fell, noiselessly, falling forever. The door swung shut with a bang and the first guard clattered into its solid timbers, splitting his nose on impact. The guard hesitated. Then he clasped his bloody nose with one hand and grasped the door handle with the other. The door promptly disappeared. It vanished into thin air leaving a solid brick wall in its place.

Acting Major Plodalonganon was a happy man. It was his last day as Sergeant Plod. Today he was in charge of a squad of ten men guarding the main bridge over the

Alpheus. Apollo was up there in his chariot. Though the Sun God was riding much lower in the heavens now, nevertheless, Plod could have sworn that the golden sun beams from the chariot were aimed straight at him. He felt warm and he felt good. Last day as a sergeant. Tomorrow, Sir Henry Plodalonganon would be formally commissioned Major in the Royal Guard by King Augeas himself. There had been such an outcry following young Prince Tom, the hero's strange disappearance that the King had been obliged to honour all of his promises to the boy from the strange land overseas. Augeas had decided to be generous, once the upstart from the Misty Isles was out of the way, though how he had come to be "out of the way" he could not say. The nobles and the common people had become rebellious at losing their hero – in mysterious circumstances - and the King had decided that it would be wise to honour the boy's pledges. Augeas was being decidedly cautious. He had never seen the nobility and the commoners show so much mutual respect. It was troubling. To calm some of the unrest, the poor got their drachmas and Raskalion and his young chums had their centre. They were practising 'hanging out', whatever that meant. And Theron's proposal of marriage to Apollonia had been allowed by the King. It turned out that Theron's family was wealthier than Cleon of Crete and that Theron's fortune would be greater than that of Cadmus anyway. Theron's father owned a goldmine that he had kept hidden from the King's tax inspectors but which he was proud to advertise and admit to owning now his son's prospects involved marrying into the Royal Family. And Theron's proposal had been accepted by Apollonia, though the princess had described young Tom as an 'oafish lout' and he hadn't needed to push her into the water for Theron to realise that he had loved her all along. Plod grinned at that, since that was exactly what the young Misty Isles man had predicted would happen. And exactly what the princess would say. And it looked as though his final prediction was about to come true sooner than he might have guessed.

A big brute of a man was striding purposefully towards the bridge. He was big as a brute and as brutal as he was big.

He had a broken nose and bright curly hair. In his right fist he carried a studded club the size of a pine tree. The pelt of a gigantic lion had been flayed and stretched across his shoulders. Plod had never seen shoulders like these before. The shoulders had shoulders on them. Shoulders like boulders. Boulders thrown up by an avalanche.

"Halt! Erm...if you don't mind me asking you to halt, that is, sir!" Sir Henry said. For a brief moment or two he wondered if he should quickly thump the brute and command his men to pile in and try to overwhelm him, using the advantage of surprise. This character had to be the Hercules or Herakles that Prince Tom had warned him about. How had the youngster described this Herakles geezer again? Ah yes: "one of those heroes who disembowels first and then asks questions later." Try a quick biff to the bonce perhaps? But Plod looked at the muscles that were like boulders upon boulders and thought about the way the young prince from the Misty Isles would have conducted himself.

'E woul'n't jus' pile in wivvout finkin' would he? Nah, he'd use his noggin and get to know what he was dealin' wiv first.

A useful way of doin' things, thought Plod or Sir-Henry-to-be as he really was. It might not be the military way but it was definitely the intelligent way and then he smiled to himself. He just realised he'd done his first bit of independent thinking in some time. Maybe that was the difference between majors and plain, ordinary squaddies and sergeants. He looked at the advancing brute who towered over him and rewarded the stranger with a big, beaming smile.

"Come a long way, have we, sir?" he asked, sympathetically.

The head nodded and the shoulders rippled.

"From Mt. Erymanthos – but I started out in Nemea where I met up with a Giant Lion," said the man-mountain.

"That would be the fabled Nemean Lion, would it, sir? Biggest lion ever seen in the whole of Greece?"

"The very same. The lion wasn't happy to have met me though," the man with the shoulders said with a grin that was very grim and with a meaningful glance at the lionskin.

"And if it isn't too much trouble, could you please state what business you might have in Elis, sir?" Sir Henry asked.

"I've come to clean King Augeas' stables. It's one of a fistful of mighty labours I've been given-"

"Herakles the name, is it, sir?"

The hero nodded, momentarily dumb-founded that his fame had reached this gods-forsaken bit of Greece already.

"'Fraid I've got a bit of bad news for you, sir."

Sir Henry was learning how to be diplomatic. He would have to be diplomatic from time to time in his new role as an army officer and knight of the Misty Isles Realm and he could see that this was a thorny problem. He was going to have to explain to a Hero of Greek Legend that one of his Mighty Labours - to wit, Cleaning King Augeas' Stables - had already been completed... by a fourteen-year-old boy.

Major Sir Henry Plodalonganon, Knight of the Realm of the Misty Isles and Lord Lieutenant of Northumbria put his arm round the shoulder of the hero, or at least that bit of his shoulder that he could reach and said in a gentle, sympathetic voice, "You should prepare yourself for some bad news, sir. Not sure if it's tragedy or comedy, Master Heracles...but you see it's all about timing..." he began.

PART II

12 Into The Furnace

First it was very, very dark. Then the stars came out for a while. Bright astral fireworks lit up the darkness. Then the stars disappeared. It was dark again, apart from one corner of the room that was lit up by a hot, bright, ruddy glow. It looked as if a furnace was burning there. Where on earth was he? A room with a furnace in it? As Tom's scrambled senses gained their balance he realised that he was no longer falling through space and chaos. He was in a room. A room with a corner. A building then? But what sort of building and where and when? Then Tom felt the floor move under his feet with a slow, deep, rolling heave. Perhaps he wasn't *on earth* at all? Perhaps he was *on water*.

He checked his arms, legs and ribs. He couldn't feel any broken bones. He still had his knapsack, strapped over one shoulder and the leather pouch tied to his belt. What else should he check?

"Snow?" he said, in a quiet voice.

"Still here, safe behind your ear," the dragonfly whispered.

"Undrone?"

He felt a gentle buzzing inside his head.

"Still there," said Snow quietly, "safe inside your ear!"

157

Tom felt the floor lurch.

"Now do you begin to understand Loki's riddle?" Snow asked.

"Which riddle?"

"The riddle of the scroll:

"Forgotten all about it! Didn't make any sense to me!" The riddle ran,

"'...roam in Greece and find the piece,
That kills the rock and picks the lock,
Turn the tables, clean the stables.
Earn the key and Odin's glee,
A low door's key sets Odin free.
The key's the thing you must win
On hero's wing, win from a king.
Win this quest and then fly West.'"

"West? Where in the West?"

Further conversation was denied. Dragonfly, bee and schoolboy were rudely interrupted.

Figures loomed out from the hot, ruddy glow. Stout, firm hands were placed on Tom's shoulders.

"You jes' best stay where y'are, youngster," said a deep, quiet voice. "We'all jes' called for the mate."

Where am I? Thought Tom.

"I've no idea," whispered Snow, "though from the rolling motion under your feet, I'd suspect we're on a ship of some sort! Watch out – I think we're about to find out!"

A door swung open, admitting bright light into the dark space. A voice swooped in, followed by its owner. It was a loud, confident and hostile voice:

"Whooo-ooop! Well blow me over and knock me down sideways. What has the cat fetched in? Set whar you are, young sprout! Don't stir about. Stir and I'll have at you with this club, or my name ain't Septimus T. Bargefly!"

A big face hove into view, illuminated by a storm lamp. The lamp was held by the same self-styled Septimus T. Bargefly. His other hand held a big, grizzly belaying pin. It was a big face, bristling with whiskers. Bargefly's bald head was running with sweat.

"Where'd 'you find 'im, Chief Stoker?" Bargefly roared.

The biggest of the men gathered by the flames stepped forward.

"He was over in the corner, behind the coal pile," said the Chief Stoker.

"Looks like I ketched me a stowaway!" Bargefly said, loud and proud.

"'Stowaway'?" Tom repeated the word. "I'm no stowaway! Where am I? Which ship is this?"

"This ain't no ship! This here's a finer vessel than any mere ship that ever sailed the Seven Seas!"

Bargefly was angry.

"Y'are on board the Paddle Steamer Velocity, the finest steamboat to sail the Mississippi from Natchez to New Orleans - The PS Velocity on which I am proud to serve as Mate!"

"And where exactly on the PS Velocity might I be standing?"

"You taken a blow to the head, young ankle-biter? Why it's obvious, ain't it? You're on the main deck, in the boiler room and over there where it's hotter'n' the fires of hell, where ole Bee-el-zee-bub himself would feel right at home, those are the ship's boilers!"

Bargefly drew closer.

"Here!" he yelled. "Start hauling your carcase over to the door over thar. You lead. And don't consarn yourself with thoughts of fleein', young feller. I'll be right behind you with the belaying pin!" And Bargefly roared with grim laughter.

"Why? Where are we going?" Tom asked.

"I'm takin' you to see the Captain," Bargefly said. "He knows what to do with stowaways. I 'spect he'll have you flung overboard!"

As Tom's eyes became accustomed to the light, he saw that there were three men standing next to the boilers, shovelling coal. Just as he reached the steps, he heard

Bargefly yell, "I don' 'spect any slackin' just because there's been some enn'ertainment. Keep shovelin' or you'll feel my knuckles on your dentures when I get back!"

Tom stepped out of the boiler room and continued along the main deck of the steamboat. In places the deck was wedged full of cotton bales. There were piles of cordwood and some barrels of molasses as well as sacks of grain but most of the cargo he could see was cotton. He guessed that there was a lot more down in the hold below the main deck. The Mate shoved open a cabin door and Tom stepped onto an open deck splashed in sunlight. He blinked while adjusting to the new explosion of brightness. Bargefly stared at Tom as he stood in the light of a Mississippi morning.

"Lord Almighty and all the Christian Saints! May my mother be a rattler and my dear old Daddy hatch from the egg of a' Eagle – what on this earth are you wearing, boy? Is that a dress?"

Tom was still attired in the Greek chiton that Apollonia had provided as a gift. Resembling the tunic popular in Ancient Rome, the chiton worn by Greek youths in antiquity did bear a passing resemblance to a short dress.

Tom began to feel his cheeks burn red in embarrassment.

"Beware the Greeks-" Snow began.

I know that one, Tom thought angrily. *This isn't the time to start remembering phrases from the Classics! I need to be able to explain how I got here and why I'm wearing this get-up!*

"I've got an idea," said Snow, who then began to whisper very quickly. "Tell them you were with ..." and his last words were whipped away by the river's breeze.

"Get on up!" commanded the Mate, interrupting Snow so that Tom only had time to listen to part of the dragon's idea before he was forced to climb two sets of steps.

"Where am I now?" asked Tom.

"You're on the hurricane deck just by the saloon," said Bargefly.

Tom looked quickly out at the view beyond the boat.

He glanced out over the big, broad, swollen river. It spread and rolled before his eyes, the biggest river he had ever seen. Away in the distance he could see growing beyond the far-away shore, oak trees covered in Spanish moss as well as hickory and shacks and cabins, and in the water, boats and skiffs, rafts and ketches. The far shore seemed miles away.

The Mate was standing in front of Tom on an open deck that was edged with a metal handrail. The mate stood arms akimbo, blocking any movement forwards. To Tom's left, the open deck gave way to a mixture of cabins, barrooms and saloons, built of oak cladding and interrupted by open windows and swinging saloon doors. The saloon had broad gallery windows all round and walkways to the open deck. Inside it looked like the biggest barroom that Tom had ever seen. Men milled about with glasses of whisky in their hands. They did not look happy. There were broad pedestal tables set up for card games and gambling. A piano was being played and somewhere someone with a loud voice was singing a song about the Tombigbee River.

Bargefly swung open a saloon door and hailed inside.

"C'mon and have a good look at this, gen'l'men. You ain't seen nothin' like it in your lives!"

"I was about to explain, Mr Bargefly," Tom began. Too late – a crowd had started to gather in the doorway. There were Southern Gentlemen in Planter hats, New York dudes in bowlers and suits complete with waistcoats and fob watches. Cowboys in ten gallon hats sporting six-guns in holsters and wearing buckskin jackets jostled with gambling men in starched cotton shirts with their sleeves rolled back and held in place by silver bands.

"C'mon and look, gentlemen. I've ketched a mos' unusual catfish. A stowaway. A young feller fresh from the Mississippi. Only he's wearin' a dress!"

A loud guffaw greeted Bargefly's words.

"Aw, ain't she cute?" howled one of the cowboys, a mean-looking skinny man with the face of a famished coyote.

"I can explain!" Tom protested.

"I wonder if I should get out my trusty Colt revolver and see if she can dance to the tune of the hot lead hornpipe!" the coyote-faced cowboy said.

"I can explain!" Tom yelled louder as the cowboy reached for his gun.

"You leave your piece in its holster, Mr Daid," a voice said very quietly. The words were quieter than autumn leaves rustling but everyone calmed down and listened. "The boy said he can explain," the quiet voice continued.

"Oh, yes sir, Mr Hickory!" said the cowboy called Daid, suddenly looking as if he were swallowing a golfball wrapped in barbed wire.

"Explain away, boy!" said Bargefly. "Now you've got the attention of Wild Will Hickory!"

Tom looked round the deck. More than two dozen men had spilled out onto the flying deck. Others stood in the open saloon doorway and yet more were hanging out over open window frames, straining their ears to catch what was being said.

"I've got money," Tom began. He pointed to the leather pouch that he had stuffed in his belt. "Enough gold to pay my fare."

"You're gonna have to show that to the Captain," said Bargefly.

"And if you don' mind me sayin' it, youngster," said Wild Will Hickory, "having some gold is one thing – I wouldn't go paradin' that fact on this or any other boat – and it still don't explain how you came to be on board and wearing a dress for that matter!"

"I was with a theatre company from England, touring in the Southern States of America..." Tom began. He had decided to use Snow's idea.

"Name of said theatre company?" interrupted Wild Will

Hickory from his position at the front of the crowd in the saloon doorway.

"The Lord Chamberlain and Jarvis Z. Brakespeare's Touring Repertory Company, Shakespeare: Our Speciality!"

"So how did you happen to find yourself swallowin' some Mississippi river water, young 'un?"

"We were playing a small town outside of Memphis" Tom continued. "I forget the name. We played so many small towns along the Mississippi – I can't remember the names of all of them. We were performing William Shakespeare's *Romeo and Juliet*."

"'William Shakespeare's *Romeo and Juliet*'?" said Wild Will. "Is there another's *Romeo and Juliet*?"

"Point taken," said Tom. "I was playing the part of Tybalt. We'd just got to the part where I'd stabbed Mercutio-"

"One of Romeo's best pals if I recall-" interrupted Wild Will Hickory, stroking the edge of his moustache and gaining a murmur of appreciation from the crowd in the saloon door. Gunslinger, Ace shot, quick-on-the-draw... and knows some Shakespeare!

"Exactly," said Tom. "Only the townsfolk didn't perceive that I was acting. That I was *acting* the part of Mercutio. They seemed to think the drama was for real. That Mercutio was real and I was a scoundrel! The front rows, who had consumed a mighty amount of corn liquor, yelled out that I was a 'Dirty, Rotten Backstabber' and other things besides – much worse! Someone proposed I should be tarred and feathered. The proposal was seconded. Gained general agreement. Became a policy. Then they tried to storm the stage."

Tom looked around the deck. They were still listening. Undrone was helping him to speak some of the local vernacular. Undrone had also read a lot of American literature.

"I lit out of there, still wearing my stage duds. In my

case - this tunic. It ain't *a dress*!" I lit out of there fast as my legs would carry me and dived into the river. Next thing I knew I was on the boat."

"To get from the Mississippi onto the deck of a steamboat without help from someone on deck is nothing short of a miracle. But the bigger miracle is to tell that story and 'spect us to believe you...while you're standing there bold as brass and dry as a parson's sermon," said Hickory.

"Oh I dunno, Will," said a voice from behind him. "I once saw a New Orleans deckhand miss his boat one day so he snuck upriver some ways and gathered up armfuls of alligators like bushels of wheat. Stacked them up in a row from the shore and then built a pile of them leathery varmints to the side of the deck rail and climbed aboard?"

"Is that so, Wyatt Herb?" said another voice. "Well ah once saw a Missouri pilot miss his boat and he jest filled his pipe with enough tobacco and smoked it so's he built a cloud the size of Mount Everest, hooked himself to the underside of that very same cloud and floated onto the hurricane desk. Didn't miss a day's pay."

"Buffalo Bill Croney, that's a bit tame!" Herb returned. "I once saw a Steam Packet Captain miss his boat right near Memphis and he jest pulled out a tin whistle, played a tune and all the town rats of Memphis piled into a rowing boat, took an oar each and rowed that pilot out to his boat. Didn't miss more'n' half a mile of the trip. The head rat led the crew back to Memphis and later stood for election as Town sheriff."

"Sheriff?" said Hickory, wrinkling an eyebrow.

"I guess, sheriff is stretchin' it some," said Herb. "Though he did post a bill stating he would stand for constable."

As the telling of Tall Tales grew and spread, becoming a competition on deck, the Mate said in a voice that was a little less certain than before, "'F' you c'n excuse me, I'll leave you gentlemen to your diversions. This youngster has an appointment with Captain Hardfleet."

"You take care of that youngster, Bargefly!" Wild Will Hickory said. "I found his conversation mighty enn'ertainin' and I wouldn't want to find that he was swimmin' in the Mississippi again *before* he had a chance to speak to the Captain!"

Bargefly took Tom by the shoulder and pushed him away from the saloon door and towards another stair rail running up from the hurricane deck.

"Take care, youngster!" called out Hickory. "We might see you later. I'd like to hear some of Tybalt's lines again! Oh and Mr Mate, be so good as to ask the Captain when he intends to solve the ice problem!"

A murmur of approval greeted Hickory's words. It was approval and it was angry. It was growing louder.

The Mate nodded to show that he had heard Wild Will Hickory's words and then he shoved Tom again towards the steps.

"G'on up to the Texas deck. I'm taking you to the Captain's stateroom!"

Tom looked on in awe as the full beauty of the Mississippi steamboat filled his gaze. From where he was standing on the Texas deck at the very top of the paddleboat, he could see the two broad steel funnels that belched black and white smoke and steam. He studied the fine ironwork deckrails that ran the length of the boat in a riot of metal scrolls and curls and leaves. Cabins lined the deck, painted blue and red and white and yellow. The paddle steamer was gaily painted and even from the top deck Tom could see the great rotating paddle wheels churning the waters of the Mississippi as the boat ploughed its course along the river.

The mate opened a door and pushed Tom roughly along a passageway. At the end of the corridor, the door to the Captain's stateroom was open. Voices could be heard. Raised voices.

"Wait here!" hissed Bargefly. The Mate walked quietly

along the passageway until he was just outside the Captain's cabin. He knocked on the door.

"Mind if I have a word, Cap'n?" said Bargefly respectfully.

"Wait there a minute, Mr Mate," said the Captain. "Be good enough to attend outside the door while I deal with this problem first."

Tom crept up to the door and looked past Bargefly into the Captain's stateroom. Bargefly was furious but expelling Tom would have made too much noise. He was allowed to remain where he was.

A young man with a head of wild black wavy hair and wearing a long, black tailcoat stood before an older man who was as broad as a cave. The latter had a mane of long curly white hair and wore a bright blue jacket with solid gold buttons. The older man, who was clearly the Captain, had fine white mustachios, curled either side of his nose, flowing along his cheeks like the scrolls on a Greek pillar. They were the most impressive mustachios that Tom had ever seen. Captain Hardfleet sat behind a large mahogany desk. He tussled with some papers while looking up from time to time over a thin set of wire spectacles that he had perched on the edge of his nose like a set of pince-nez.

"Remind me. What did you say your name was?" The Captain asked brusquely.

"Anatole Prince, citizen of France," He pronounced 'Prince' so that it rhymed with 'manse' and 'France' rhymed with 'jaws'.

"And your problem again?"

"When we put in at the last port a message was waiting for me. The buyer for my cargo has dropped out. I no longer have a deal."

"And your stock is?"

"Absinthe. The finest drink of spirits in the world. Add a chunk or two of ice and some water and voila: the finest aperitif in the world! I have two thousand bottles on board, bound for New Orleans. If I can't sell any of it – I am ruined. My mother, my sisters and my fiancée would all be ruined."

"So remind me what you'd like me to permit you to do on my boat?"

"Sell the absinthe in the saloons!"

"But that's jest the problem!" The Captain roared suddenly. "As I've been trying to explain to you, Mr Anatole Prince, Citizen of France. We have run out of ice. I can't get the bars and saloons to sell any booze, other than straight whisky. Wine, beer, cocktails – they're all off the menu on account of the fact we've run out of ice."

The Captain pushed his chair back from the mahogany desk and got to his feet.

"Do you realise how scratcherous those gentlemen in the saloons and bars become when all they have to drink is whisky? When every hour from eight in the morning, the mercury rises in the thermometer announcing that the day is going to be another scorcher and all they have to drink is fire water?

"This time of year, the only thing makes the passage tolerable is some ice in your potion whether that potion be rye whisky or rum, or even if you've taken the Pledge and nothin' stronger than a mint julep is your poison. No ice makes the crew miserable. Worse than that – as I was saying – it makes the passengers scratcherous. Aside from the usual blend of cowpokes, river traders, gamblers and sons of southern chivalry that I have on board, for this trip I'm also carrying Wyatt Herb, Wild Will Hickory and Buffalo Bill Croney, three of the fastest gun-slinging sharpshooters in the US of A."

Captain Hardfleet scratched his head in bafflement.

"Do you have any idea how incendiary that mixture is?"

"But I must be able to sell my bottles of absinthe!" Prince persisted. "If I could only show you the picture of my old mother, *mon capitaine*, you would have a change of heart. It will break her heart to be ruined!"

"Break mine even more to be in the same condition.

That is - ruined...Which I will be if I can't solve the Ice Problem!"

Captain Hardfleet shook his head.

"I'm sorry, Mr Prince. I'd like to be able to help you but the plain truth is I can't. I have enough wild yellowjackets of my own to attend to without opening up your own hornet's nest as well."

And the Captain, who was clearly a sympathetic man, troubled by the fact he couldn't help the young Frenchman, led him to the door. He set a friendly hand on his shoulder and steered him in the direction of the passageway to the deck.

"My mother, my family, my fiancée!" the Frenchman groaned as he eased by Tom and began to make his way along the passageway. Tom exchanged anxious glances with Monsieur Prince and tried to look sympathetic.

"What have we here, Mr Mate?" said the Captain when the Frenchman was out of sight.

"Come along thar, you thieving landlubber. Look lively! Look lively! In here and stand up straight before the cap'n'."

Bargefly turned to face Captain Hardfleet.

"Sorry to report we appear to have dragged up a stowaway, cap'n. Chief Stoker reported him and I ketched 'im less than a quarter-hour ago."

"I'm no stowaway!" Tom protested in a loud voice. "I have gold to pay for my passage!"

He reached down to retrieve the pouch of gold coins that he had recovered from Elis and instead received a horrible shock. The pouch had gone!

"No gold?" the Captain said grimly, reading Tom's face like a book.

"It's gone! It's been stolen!"

"Of course it has been stolen," said Captain Hardfleet. "Do you think this is Savannah or Charlotte where you could leave a pile of gold doubloons on your front porch and it never get touched? A place where ladies are invariably referred to as "The Flower of the South" and chivalry prevails? This is the middle of the Mississippi river, sonny. We're a packet boat carrying goods and passengers. Some of my passengers are no better than they should be."

The Captain looked Tom up and down and frowned.

"Must say you present a curious picture for a savage stowaway on the run. A youth in a dress..." Hardfleet let the sentence hang in mid-air.

"Stowaway says he's a' actor, Cap'n," interjected Bargefly. "Says he's bin playing Tibbles in something called 'Rome he owned what Julie ate.' An' that's why he's wearin' a Tune-Hick. It ain't a dress, 'pparently"

"Ah, that would be Tybalt, Mr Bargefly in that wonderful romantic tragedy, Romeo and Juliet, penned by the Swan of Avon. That makes this young man a thespian and a member of the Capulet Clan. That explains the dress or tunic as you put it. What about your satchel, young man? No funds in there?"

Tom marvelled at the knowledge of Shakespeare's work manifesting itself on the Mississippi that day but then shook his head. He had a small crockful of drachmas in his satchel but they were made of base metal and worthless in nineteenth century America. The money pouch had contained solid gold coins, valuable regardless of the date when they were struck.

"There's nothing of any value in the satchel, sir," Tom said. "A drinking flask, a mirror, a belt or two, some odds and sods. Northing of any real worth. But for what it is worth I was playing Mercutio, technically neither a Montague nor a Capulet..." Tom ended lamely, not sure why he had mentioned that to the Captain.

The Captain clawed at his head.

"Now you've given me another problem to scratch over," said Hardfleet. He tugged at one of his magnificent mustachios.

"Technically I ought to throw you overboard," said

Hardfleet.

"Masterful suggestion, Cap'n, if I may say so," said Bargefly.

"There's a long and honourable tradition of throwing stowaways overboard. On some ships it's an art form. Planks get to be walked. Chamber music is played. The passengers have some fun and everyone is taught a lesson about paying a fare price for a fair service."

The Captain looked Tom square in the eye.

"And while that might afford a moment of entertainment, it would be a shame to drown a youngster who already knows the difference between Mercutio and Tybalt and that the play in which they both most properly belong is not called 'Rome he owned what Julie ate.'

"What say you to the idea of stepping off a gangplank into the swelling waters of Old Glory, sonny?" Captain Hardfleet asked suddenly.

"I don't think I'd like it one bit!" said Tom, with a gulp. He didn't know much about the Mississippi or 'Old Glory' as she was popularly known all along her banks. He knew that it was the biggest river in North America. He knew it flowed all the way from Lake Itasca in Minnesota to the Gulf of Mexico. The stretch of river on which the Velocity was steaming was clearly big, wide and deep. It was not the best place for a fourteen year-old boy to practise swimming. He would drown...or worse: end up providing lunch for a man-eating alligator!

But then again, he remembered with a jolt: he had to find the next Portal if he was to save Odin and Thor, not to mention Stella, Uncle Bernard, Rob and the entire human race! What if the Portal wasn't on the steamboat? What if it was ashore somewhere along the banks of the river? He had to narrow down the possible range of locations. He had to find out if the portal could be onboard the Velocity. Who better to ask than the Captain? He would know the steamboat inside-out! Since landing in the boiler room Tom had been swept along by what was happening to him and what was happening round him. He had not been able to get away from Bargefly and had been a victim of events ever since. He had to regain the initiative or he would never find the next Portal.

"Do you mind if I ask, Captain – while you're making up your mind what to do with me as it were – do you have a key on board this steamboat that hasn't been used since the boat's first voyage?"

Captain Hardfleet blinked and started back. His eyebrows went up and he grabbed at one of his splendid scrolled mustachios and tugged mightily.

"Why yes, sonny...but how could you possibly have known?"

"No matter – for now," said Tom. "But it does mean that I'd rather not walk the plank. In fact I'd rather not leave the boat." If the spirit of Impudence was to swell itself into the shape of an orange-skinned imp with big bulging eyes and tongue permanently sticking out blowing a raspberry like the cheekiest gargoyle carved by the cheekiest stone mason in the whole of England that Imp was the tone in Tom's voice at that moment. The spirit of accidental impertinence.

The Mate's quick intake of breath confirmed at once to Tom that he had made a mistake.

"It ain't a matter of what you'd rather do or not do!" roared the Captain. "I can have you clapped in irons. Or thrown overboard. I can have you scrub the decks. Or heave coal in the boiler-room all day and all night. Have you any idea how long you'd last if I put you in the boiler-room? You'd shrivel like a prune in less than an hour. Your last thoughts would be a reverie about ice, water and then ice all over again." The Captain paused, allowing the threat to sink in. "On reflection, I think it might have to be the boiler-room!"

"Say - where are you from again, sonny?"

"England!"

"Well it's clear to me that you English just don't

understand, Sonny Jim. On a Mississippi paddle steamer the skipper isn't just like a god. He *is* Lord God Almighty – or the next best thing! What I say goes. And if that means I say you go overboard... overboard you go!"

The moment Hardfleet mentioned 'ice', Snow whispered quickly in Tom's ear and Tom nodded slowly to let Snow know that he had heard and understood what the dragon had said.

"One thing, Captain," Tom said quickly. "I'm not quite sure what the problem is concerning ice on your boat. Why don't you just pull into the nearest, big riverside town and buy up a load?"

The Captain laughed at that, some of the heat simmering out of his fury.

"Just haul up to a town and buy some? Let me ask you, sonny – how long have you been along the Mississippi."

"Not very long, I guess-"

"I don't guess – I know. Anyone that's spent more than a couple of weeks south of Chicago will know that it gets powerful hot along the Mississippi in summer and there's almost nowhere you can get ice other than along the coast and one or two places that have ice-making machines."

"But this is America!" protested Tom. "Don't all the towns have fridges?"

"'Fridges'?" repeated the Captain. "I'm afraid I don't follow your lingo, sonny. What might be meant by the term 'fridges'?"

"It's the middle of the nineteenth century!" hissed Snow into Tom's ear. "They don't have electricity yet, let alone fridges! Ice-making is in its infancy. There are only a handful of ice-making machines in the entire continent. They are mechanical and use steam and volatile liquids. They are about the size of a small bungalow!"

"'Fridge' is a slang term for an ice-making machine where I come from, sir," Tom explained, lamely, but at least thinking on his feet.

"Well the nearest ice-maker that I'm aware of is

hundreds of miles away. It might as well be along the Zambezi for all the good it will do me." The Captain went into what seemed like a reverie. "Years ago – when I wasn't much older than you, sonny, I sailed on ships that took ice as cargo from just south of the Arctic circle to the southern ports of the United States of America. From Charleston to Savannah and on to New Orleans. We towed miniature icebergs and loaded the hold with boulders of the stuff. Used to be a great trade in blocks of ice. People paid a fortune in summer for the crystal jewels. We'd lose a third of our cargo to melting during the voyage but it was worth it. Worth it? Why it was worth its weight in gold almost."

"But where would it be stored once you got it on land?"

"Deep underground in icehouses," said Hardfleet. "I enjoyed the old ice trade. Got to see a polar bear once. Now that's a critter to respect."

He came out of his reverie. "Nope – there isn't an ice-making machine within two hundred miles of me now. I can hear those rascals in the saloon checking their shooting irons already.

"Having no ice makes the crew miserable. As I said when Bargefly first dredged you in here, worse than that, it makes the passengers *scratcherous* and *itchy-vescent*. And when you've got a saloon that includes Wild Will Hickory, Buffalo Bill Croney and Wyatt Herb...well the last thing you want is those particular gentlemen becoming *itchiversiferous*. When things go wrong on a boat, the Captain always gets the blame. I don't mind. I'm big enough and old enough and ugly enough to take whatever gets thrown at me. That's what Captains do."

"This man is a model of stoicism," said Snow quietly. "We should help him and help ourselves into the bargain."

"So you see, sonny – much as it may pain me. I'm afraid I am going to have to set you to working in the boiler house. Probably alongside that darned Frenchie, Anatole Prince!"

"I'm sorry for any disrespect I might have shown earlier, sir," Tom said in a brighter voice than might have been expected from one about to be fed into the fires of Hell. "But I have an idea, Captain Hardfleet. I think I might be able to help."

"How can that be? How can a young whippersnapper like you help with a problem as big and as man-sized as this?"

"In return for full board and lodgings – and I mean three square meals a day – and a decent bunk in a stateroom – I'll provide you with all the ice your saloons and bars can handle between here and your next port-of-call. Price of ice is five dollars a bucket over and above my free board and lodgings."

"But that can't be so!" The Captain protested. "As I just explained to you. There isn't an ice house ashore for hundreds of miles!"

"That might be true...but I don't need an ice house."

"And pray tell me how do you propose to produce ice without access to an ice house?" Captain Hardfleet said, with a particular twist and tug on the end of a wispy white mustachio.

"I have with me a machine for making ice!"

The Captain guffawed and slapped his thigh.

"I'm almost tempted to let you have a stateroom just on account of your sass', young 'un. I've heard some whoppers in all my time on the Mississippi but that just about takes the biscuit. Did you hear those stretchers earlier when the passengers were sassing? One of 'em told that old chestnut about the steamboat Captain who got a passel of rats to row him over to his boat from the shore using only a tin whistle to tame the rats. Remember that one? Well: 'a machine for making ice'? That is the biggest stretcher I've heard anyone tell all year! Hee-hah! If that were true, you'd have the means to buy my boat and half the steam packets plying their trade up'n'down the Mississippi!"

"Just wait and see," said Tom. "I need a dark, quiet stateroom, no prying eyes – my machine is secret – it hasn't been patented yet. And then you'll have all the ice you need – by the bucketload!"

The Captain beckoned the Mate over to the desk.

"This might be hoss manure," he said. "But I'm in dire straits. I'll try anything. No matter how much of a long shot. Give the lad all he wants, Bargefly," said Captain Hardfleet. "But get one of the watch to keep a weather eye on his cabin door. He can keep the door locked and the curtains closed but no escaping. I don't want him sneaking overboard on one of the lifeboats!"

"An Englishman never breaks his word, Cap'n!" Tom protested.

"That may or may not be true, lad," said the Captain. "But it's also true that a *gentleman* never pledges his word lightly." And after he had allowed that apothegm to sink in, he added, "Besides... you're only an English *boy*!"

Tom allowed Bargefly to lead him to the door out of the Captain's stateroom. Just as they were on the point of leaving, Tom turned and said, "I meant to add, Captain Hardfleet – I'll need a couple of outfits of gentlemen's clothes before I set to work, as a down payment! I need to get out of this chiton as soon as possible."

"'Kite on'?" repeated the Captain. Tom had pronounced the word "chiton" properly with a hard "k" at the start and a long "i" as in "tie" or "flight". "'Kite on'? With all due respect, I'd have to say it's more like a dress than a kite, young 'un."

"Um, it's Greek," said Tom with some degree of embarrassment. "The Romans called these things tunics. Whatever it's called – I want out of it and back into breeches."

"See to it, Bargefly," Hardfleet commanded. "Have a word with the young pup who's training to be a pilot. That young peacock is bound to have some spare duds!"

"Yes, sir, cap'n! Consider it done!" said Bargefly and he

ushered Tom away from the Captain's quarters.

Back on deck and out of sight and hearing of the Captain, Bargefly seized Tom by the arm once more.

"Set where y'are, young spit!" the Mate snarled, his yellow teeth very close to Tom's ear. "I know when ah've ketched me a stowaway, and that's what y'are. You may have fooled the Cap'n into believing you've got some fancy-fangled ice machine but I smell a rat...and you're it. Make no mistake – I'll be keeping an eye on you."

Tom shook his arm free angrily.

"That's just where you're a mile wrong, Mister Mate!" he said confidently, some of the sap returning to his blood after the awful fright he had had in the boiler room and the Captain's cabin when he thought he was going to have to work in that blasted inferno. "You won't be keeping an eye on me at all. The Captain has agreed that I am to produce the ice in the confines of a locked and shuttered cabin. My machine is a secret and it hasn't been patented yet. I need silence and secrecy!"

The Mate scowled but then with a great show of reluctance led Tom down a set of steps and then steered him to the staterooms on the hurricane deck.

13 Ice By The Bucket

Tom had been given a cabin in a stateroom all to himself. There was a large, cosy bed, a wardrobe, a chest of drawers, a table and desk and several chairs as well as a wash basin and towels. He had two sets of clothes, which although a poor fit, were comfortable enough. He changed out of the chiton and into a white shirt and a suit made from black cotton cloth. He then methodically set about closing and fixing down blinds and curtains so that he couldn't be seen by prying eyes. He made sure that he was able to lock and secure the cabin door. Then he went back out to ask Bargefly if he could arrange the delivery of ten buckets of pure, clean drinking water. As soon as the buckets had been set down in a corner of the stateroom, Tom locked the door again, double-checked that the window was secured and then sat down on a chair at the table.

"It's OK, Snow," he said in a quiet voice. "You can come out from behind my ear now!"

"At last," said the dragonfly as it flew up into the air and performed a loop-the-loop and then a lazy Victory Roll in mid-flight before landing on the desk. "I was beginning to suffer from cramp!"

The shape of the dragonfly shifted and shook. Mistily it shimmered and then solidified back into the form of the Ice Dragon, Snow. The dragon stretched, and stretched again. It literally stretched, as its limbs extended and wings folded out. It was now the size of a small cat.

"That's better. We don't have much time. Bring a bucket of water to the table."

Tom obeyed and heaved the first of the buckets onto the oak tabletop. The cat-size dragon extended its talons once more, stretched and stood up on the table. Its leathery wings uncurled and flapped lazily up and down. It padded twice round the bucket, snow-white scales glimmering on its belly. The dragon then looked directly at Tom, its clear blue eyes piercing his thoughts.

"You should never look a dragon directly in the eye, Tom," Snow said.

"Why's that? Are dragons shy?" Tom asked, before looking to one side.

"Always got a cheeky answer," Snow murmured. "When will you learn to accept a friendly warning at face value? If you look a dragon directly in the eye, it can hypnotise you and capture your soul. You're lucky I'm a Good Dragon, and not in the mood for soul-stealing anyway. Now, let's have a look at this bucket, shall we?"

Snow padded once more round the bucket and said, "Yes, I think less than half a breath should do!"

The dragon stepped back and pursed its lips. A thin reed of air issued from its mouth and hit the bucket like a crossbow bolt. At once a chill mist formed round the bucket and beads of ice formed along its sides.

Tom peered into the bucket. The surface of the water had frozen completely. He lifted up the bucket and then dropped it down again.

"That's cold like fire!" he yelped. "It hurt!"

"That's fast-cooling, for you!" said Snow. "Another reason I told you not to look a dragon in the eye. Imagine if I was to give you a frosty look?"

Tom pulled the cuff and the sleeve of his shirt down over his hand, doubled the material back and used it as a glove to lift the handle of the bucket. He swung it upside down. Nothing moved inside. The water had been turned into a solid block of ice.

"Captain Hardfleet," Tom murmured. "Your redemption is at hand... and we're another step nearer the Portal."

"Don't just stand there swinging ice!" hissed Snow. "Bring the other buckets!"

Tom obeyed the cat-sized dragon and heaved the buckets one at a time onto the table. He watched as Snow repeated the magic. One incredibly brief puff of breath was all it took and a whole bucket of water glazed over into solid ice.

When Snow had finished freezing all ten buckets, Tom lugged them over to the stateroom door, unlocked it and asked the watchman to call for Bargefly. Meanwhile Snow flew up and landed out of sight on top of the wardrobe.

When the First Mate arrived, his face was a picture. His shoulders swung with the rhythm of a prize-fighter. His big, fat face beamed with a merry grin.

"Ready to admit defeat, young sprout?" Bargefly said with a horrible laugh. "It's a shame y'all got dressed up in those fancy duds, with a bright white shirt and a waistcoat....going to be a mite overdressed for working in the boiler room!"

The Mate roared at his own joke. Tom replied by reaching forward and dropping the heavy handle of an iced bucket straight onto the Mate's palm. The Mate yelped.

"Lord Almighty and all the Christian Saints...that's cold!"

"Look inside the bucket, Mr Bargefly," Tom said calmly. "Present this to Captain Hardfleet with my compliments and advise him that the first consignment of ice has been delivered. Oh – and don't forget. I am now owed fifty dollars!"

Bargefly turned mutely and walked away, the bucket swinging like dead weight from the end of his arm.

Tom returned to the cabin and locked the door. The grin he wore was as broad as the mouth of the River Tyne. Fishing boats would have been swamped by the grin and

Apollo would have had to swerve his golden chariot to avoid bumping into it.

"Thank you, Snow. Once again you have saved my bacon! Are you going to join me for a 'turn around the deck' as they say in nautical circles?"

"No thank you," the dragon replied. "Though given that we're on a river boat I hardly think that 'nautical' is the term you mean. But no, thank you, young man. Thank you for asking. As I haven't slept since the day we dispatched the Roc I think I'll catch forty winks."

"Go for it!" Tom said. "I'm going for a wander. I need to clear my brain and think of a way to get that money bag back."

"Let the bag go, Tom," Snow said. "It's only money."

"Not quite," said Tom. "Before leaving Elis, I transferred the magic darts to the bag so that I could reach them easily in the event of more trouble."

"Ah," said Snow with meaning. "In that case you certainly do need to recover the pouch."

Tom withdrew the key and prepared to open the cabin door. Snow looked down sleepily from on top of the wardrobe.

"Remember to wake me in an hour and whatever you do, do not allow me to sleep all the way through to sunset."

"Why what happens? Do you turn into a pumpkin?" Tom laughed.

"No," said Snow sleepily. "The same law applies to all dragons. I can catch a dragon-size nap lasting an hour or two during daylight without consequence. If I'm asleep when the sun goes down, however, I have no choice but to sleep for a hundred years."

"Aren't you just an exceptionally heavy sleeper?"

"Not exceptionally - No," snorted Snow. "It's dragon lore. I can't do anything about it."

"I'll remember to set my alarm!"

14 Pilot's Licence

Tom waited until Snow had curled up and was out of sight on top of the wardrobe. Then he unlocked the door and stepped out onto the deck, locking the door behind him as he went.

Almost immediately, he ran into Captain Hardfleet. The Captain was in a merry mood. He was twirling his mustachios in glee. He caught up with Tom on the hurricane deck and shook his hand warmly.

"Well done, young man!" said Hardfleet. "I'm glad you came up trumps! They're serving ice again in the saloon even as we speak and I can feel the warm glow of approval...or should that be the chilly glow of approval?...spreading to every corner of my boat!"

The Captain handed over a wad of dollar bills and a small bag full of coins .

"There's a couple of hundred dollars, youngster. I know we agreed five dollars a bucket and you're only due fifty – and in fact you will only get five dollars a bucket from me – but the passengers were so delighted with the sudden and unexpected eruption of ice that they had a whip round and raised an extra hundred and fifty dollars just as a show of goodwill!"

Tom grinned. This was good news. He decided to chance his luck a bit more.

"Well – given I've broken the ice in more ways than one, I was wondering, Captain, if you might do me the favour of allowing me to see the door or hatchcover that has been locked since the Velocity's maiden voyage? Employing that key you mentioned that has never been used since the boat first left harbour?"

Storm clouds gathered on the Captain's brow and he scowled as he made his reply.

"Sorry, young man. There are many favours and services I'd be prepared to render you at the present time, on account of your epic ice-making, but viewing that particular locked door is not one of them!"

"Are you sure?"

The Captain simply scowled and shook his head. Clearly not a man to languish for any length of time in poor spirits, the Captain's demeanour quickly brightened.

"So what are you up to now, sonny?" Hardfleet asked, changing the subject with all the subtlety of an elephant tearing up an acacia tree. His smile returned and began bouncing sunbeams off the deck.

"Just about to take a quick tour of the deck before getting back to working my ice-machine, Captain Hardfleet, sir," Tom said respectfully. Which was true for the next few minutes but as soon as he had looked up on deck, Tom planned to return to his cabin and open the Mimir mirror.

"Good idea! Great idea! But before you take a turn round the deck, take a step up to the Texas and say hello to the cub pilot."

Tom hesitated.

"Beggin' your pardon, Cap'n. Why would I want to introduce myself to the trainee pilot?"

"He's the young' un that loaned you two sets of clothes," the Captain explained.

"Ah, I see," said Tom who needed no further explanation. Grabbing the nearest stair-rail he dashed up from the hurricane deck to the Texas. A further short climb took him to the very top of the boat where he stood on a narrow deck next to the pilot's cabin.

The moment Tom reached the pilot's cabin, a young

man a few years older than he was but short in stature for his age and with a shock of red-brown hair stepped out to meet him.

They shook hands and introduced themselves.

"Thomas Storm Torsson Wolfe," said Tom. Undrone was encouraging him to use a flowery style of speech, much favoured in the Southern States - or so Undrone thought.

"That's enough names for a platoon, young 'un. I hope you aren't plannin' on dying any time soon. It'd cost your parents a fortune just to have your name in the obituary columns – if they charge by the line!" and the trainee pilot guffawed loudly at his own wisecrack.

"And you are?" Tom asked, dispensing with Undrone's chivalrous style.

"Sammy. Plain old Sammy will do," came the answer. "No need for surnames when a First name will do. For me it's a case of 'ne'er the twain shall meet!' Tom's a good, honest name. Forget the other guff!"

Tom didn't know what to make of all this.

Fangin' bollards! A geezer that's cheekier'n me!

Tom decided on a change of tack.

"Thanks for lendin' me the clothes. Let me give you some cash-," he began.

"Are you pulling my leg, youngster?" Sammy interrupted him. "Humour may be mankind's greatest gift but I fear you're stretchin' it some."

Tom looked puzzled.

"I'm a trainee Mississippi riverboat pilot. In less than a year I'll be earning hundreds and hundreds of dollars a month. I'll be rich beyond your wildest imagining so I won't deprive you of any of your hard-earned cash. Do you need anything else? A pair of shoes, say?"

"I'm doing just fine in the shoe line," Tom answered carefully. "What I do need though is information."

The trainee pilot sat down on a narrow bench next to the pilothouse and beckoned to Tom to do the same.

"So – what is this information you're so keen to acquire?" Sammy asked.

Tom then explained his predicament. He was a "Student of Life", travelling through America learning about its people, industries and culture. He was especially keen to learn more about the construction and fittings of the Mississippi steamboat. He wondered for instance if there was a porthole or cabin door or chest, casement or frame, window or minor hatch cover even that had been locked for as long as anyone could remember.

The cub pilot reflected for a while then said, "I can think of something that has been locked and undisturbed for years. Don't see how it can help you though."

"Doesn't matter!" Tom almost yelped. "Tell me what it is anyway!"

"Captain Hardfleet is enamoured of the memory of the Fair Shirley Shoretree,"

"Who the heck is the Fair Shirley Shoretree when she's at home?" said Tom bluntly, his bluntness prompted by exasperation.

"The Finest, the Most Elegant, the Most Beautiful Actress ever to step out of Charlotte, North Carolina."

"So what's the most beautiful actress ever to step out of Charlotte got to do with locked doors and hatch covers?" Tom asked, completely baffled by the turn the conversation had taken.

"Captain has a full-length portrait of the beautiful Miss Shoretree, dressed for the role of Shakespeare's Cleopatra, set in a locked and sealed, slim-line, airtight, wooden frame on the wall of his stateroom. Curtains conceal the casement from general view, and to protect the painting from sunlight. He opens the cabinet doors from time to time to bathe in the radiance of Miss Shoretree's portrayed beauty but the case has not been opened since the picture was installed over ten years ago."

"Why has he gone to all that trouble over a portrait? Why didn't he marry the beautiful Miss Shoretree?" This was an area in which Tom would be first to admit that he didn't have a great deal of experience, but the solution seemed obvious enough to him.

"Oh he was gonna," said the cub. "They were engaged and so on. All fair set for their nuptials when Shirley Shoretree was drowned along with just about everyone else on board the Paddle Steamer Exuberance when her boilers blew up two hours out of Natchez. Captain Hardfleet was skipper that day. The explosion blew him thirty yards away from the boat and he swam about that river for an hour searching for Miss Shoretree but her drowned body was washed ashore later that same day."

The cub pilot fell silent, acknowledging the sad moment and Tom waited, also in silence, holding his tongue out of respect for what he had just heard even though he was itching to get back to the quest. Eventually Sammy took up the story once more.

"The Captain had already had a full-length portrait of Shirley Shoretree painted in Charlotte over twelve, maybe thirteen years ago. Years before she drowned. Strange artist the feller that executed the painting-"

"In what way?" Tom interrupted.

"Dressed like a strolling minstrel, in a coloured vest, mainly in green, with a long pointed hat. A bit like the one of Robin Hood's Merry Men!"

Tom's thoughts were racing. A perfect description of one of Loki's favourite guises! If Loki had painted the portrait then twisted magic had to be involved...The Captain's portrait of Shirley Shoretree must be another Portal!

"I have to see the portrait," Tom said.

"Fat chance! There is no way that the Captain is going to allow a callow youth to see the celebrated portrait of Shirley Shoretree."

"There must be a way," Tom considered. "Does Captain Hardfleet have other interests?"

"Oh the Captain is a sportsman. He likes to compete.

He shoots, hunts, fishes, rides horses. He races. He's a crack shot and will take on all-comers at rifle-shooting, archery, darts, pistol-shooting-"

"Hold on a second," said Tom, "did you say 'darts'?"

"Sure did!"

Tom scrambled to his feet.

"And he likes to compete?"

"Likes nothing better! Say – where are you off to now, young Tom?"

"I'm off to find my darts!" said Tom. "So long, Sammy and thanks again for the duds. I have to fly. I've got fish to fry!"

He left the trainee pilot scratching his chin in bafflement.

Tom hurled himself down the steps that led from the Texas to the hurricane deck. Flinging himself onto the lower deck he almost landed directly on top of the young Frenchman who had left the Captain's quarters earlier that day under his own personal cloud of disappointment. Anatole Prince leapt back.

"Very sorry, M'sieur!" Tom said. "I didn't see you!"

"Ah, don't worry!" said the Frenchman. "Nothing could add more to my troubles just now. Better that you had accidentally knocked me overboard and then my troubles would be at an end!"

Anatole Prince was a man filled from his brows to his boots with the black ink of despair. Stepping back to give him room to pass by on the deck, Tom thought that he had not seen anyone look so miserable in a very long while. The last face he had seen showing such a picture of misery, he realised, was his own, when he looked in the mirror in Asgard after waking up as Loki's prisoner. Sympathy prompted him to bar the Frenchman's path once again.

"What – if you don't mind me asking, M'sieur Prince – is the nature of your troubles?"

"Please – it's Anatole – and my troubles are exactly as I

described to Capitaine 'Ardflit!'"

The Frenchman gestured that Tom should join him as he took a turn strolling on the hurricane deck. Tom fell in alongside Anatole and the latter resumed his story. It was indeed just as he had explained to the Captain.

Anatole Prince had sailed from France with his precious cargo of two thousand bottles of absinthe and landed in New Orleans. He had signed a deal with an American businessman who had agreed to sell his bottles all along the Mississippi -

"From Vicksburg through Natchez to Dubuque!" said Anatole.

The deal had fallen through, however, as the buyer had dropped out. Anatole's two thousand bottles were lying useless in the steamer's hold. His elderly mother, his lovely sisters Annabelle and Clara and his beautiful fiancée, Mademoiselle Claire de Belleflorette would all be ruined. Claire would have to break off their engagement or be dragged down into poverty along with Anatole and his family.

"Is there nothing you can do?" Tom asked. "Why not sell some of it on the boat? I'm sure the Captain wouldn't object if you were to try again to persuade him-"

Anatole interrupted him again.

"I'm afraid you don't understand, jeune Anglais. Absinthe is nothing without ice in a hot climate. The drink served with lukewarm water tastes like medicine!"

He shook his head and stared down at the deck, lost in thought, studying it as if he might find some inspiration in the grain of the wooden planks.

"But with ice," he mused out loud. "To see my pure green spirits, like a pool of translucent emerald with its superb aroma of aniseed and then when you add ice and a measure of cold water...et voila! See it turn a beautiful milky mint colour! There's nothing like it!"

"So all you need is ice!" Tom spluttered.

"Oui, d'accord," said Anatole, "But there is no ice on

board and no ice to be had anywhere for at least two hundred miles!"

Tom set off at a run again.

"I'll catch up with you again, Anatole!" he said in a loud voice. "Don't despair! There will be ice – or my name's Jack Frost! And it isn't." Then he added, "though it could be!"

15 Dragon Naps

Back in his state room, Tom locked the door behind him, reached up to the top of the wardrobe and gently woke Snow. The dragon flew down and landed on top of the desk.

"Ahhhhhh – that was a good snooze," said the lizard. "How long was I asleep?"

"Only a couple of hours," Tom said, "and we've still lots of time until sunset.

"Then why did you wake me?" yawned Snow. "I'm only able to have some shut-eye once every few years. Every hour gained helps!"

"Ah yes – but we have urgent business to carry out. I've got so much to tell you-"

"Yes - yes!" said Snow, tetchy at finding out that he could have slumbered for half a day or more. "But first we need to use the Mimir water to see how Odin and Thor are faring!" The dragon began to pace impatiently along the top of the state room table. "Fetch the knapsack. It's time to look in the mirror once more!

"Yeah!" Tom agreed. "But before that – listen - I think I've found the second portal!"

That stopped Snow in his tracks.

"Quite right. The portal. Pray continue, young Master Wolfe. I'm all ears!"

More like 'all scales', thought Tom with a grin.

"And *I* can hear that too!" said Snow.

-I know! Thought Tom, and he told the Ice Dragon what

had happened since he had left Snow slumbering on top of the wardrobe. He described his conversation with Sammy, the latter's account of the portrait of Shirley Shoretree and the artist who had produced the painting. Snow agreed it sounded very much like one of Loki's favourite guises when on Earth. Tom described Captain Hardfleet's fondness for games and competitions, for rifle practice, marksmanship, darts and pistol-shooting.

"But you can't fire pistols!" Snow said.

"No – but I can play a mean hand of darts...when I have the right set of darts!" Tom said. "If only there was a way of getting the pouch back along with my magic darts and the gold!"

Snow shook his head.

"I have no ice-bright ideas as yet, young Wolfe," said the dragon.

Tom then went on to describe his encounter with Anatole Prince and the Frenchman's predicament: that he faced certain ruin.

"No concern of ours," said Snow testily. "And this is no time to become sentimental. Our quest is to rescue Odin and Thor. We can't afford distractions. We simply must find a way of reaching the portal. No time to try and rescue forlorn Frenchmen and their mothers, sisters and girlfriends!"

"It's a shame," said Tom. "I'd have liked to help M'sieur Prince. You should have heard him describe his absinthe. It was like poetry. 'The pure green glass of spirits, like a pool of something emerald with its something of aniseed and when you add ice and something it turns to milky mint'! There's nothing like it apparently!"

Tom caught himself and stopped speaking. He repeated the words to himself in a whisper. A firebrand had burst into flame in his brain.

I've had an idea, he thought.

"I know. I heard it. I like it," said Snow.

"Let's get on with it then," said Tom. "You know what

you have to do?"

"Of course!" said the dragon.

"It's clever," Tom repeated to himself. "I think it could work!" he added excitedly. "And it could help Anatole!"

"That would only be an accidental side effect," said Snow. "My concern is Odin, Thor and Asgard! Now – fetch the Mirror. It's time we found out what is happening to the gods on Midgard!"

Tom retrieved his leather satchel from inside the wardrobe and lifted out the oval mirror and the flask of enchanted water. He set the mirror down on the bed, opened it, unstoppered the flask and held the lip over the mirror.

"This ought to do the trick!" he said.

"Careful! Remember – you only need a drop!" said Snow. "Only enough to refresh the Mimir water that Loki put there originally."

Tom patiently allowed a single drop of Mimir water to fall onto the mirror. The surface of the water rippled and flashed light. Then it became still and a clear picture formed. Snow hunkered down next to him and they watched the water as pictures began to form.

Thor was standing on a steel skeleton in New York. He was on the highest level of a new skyscraper being built not far from the river. He was pleased with himself. Although he and the old man, Odd, still had no idea who they really were and remained registered in the hostel for homeless people as "Odd" and "Bigger", they were going places. He had been hired to work on the construction site as a high-flying Steel man. The wages were generous and later that week he and Odd were planning to say goodbye to Hobble and the tramps at the hostel and head over to a decent hotel on the other side of the city. Bigger's name had stuck. He'd been called "Bigger" from the moment he first arrived on the building site and scaled the steel frame without a safety rope or harness. His name appeared in the logbook as Bigger and it was as Bigger that he would be paid. He was the biggest man on the site. On ground level he stood head and shoulders above the tallest man in any of the crews and the muscles that bulged under his chequered work shirt rolled like footballs. He could carry four times the load of even the strongest among the workforce and when he wielded a hammer, the ground shook and thundered.

"Watch out, Bigger! Here comes the steel!" shouted one of the two men he was working with.

"Don't worry, Thumper! I've got it covered. Stand back, Barney!" Thor yelled to the other man.

"Gawsh, it's cold!" said Barney as he looked out over the city skyline. "It's a heckuva lot colder'n it usually is for this time of year!"

A gigantic crane was lowering a long, thick, steel joist onto two upright sections. Like a colossal praying mantis with a flat bug caught between its jaws, the crane dipped the joist inch by inch towards its target.

"Slowly does it," said Thumper, quietly between his teeth, but at the last moment the shackles that held the joist slipped a fraction and the joist landed unevenly on the upright sections. One end was lying where it was intended to go but the other was balanced at an angle on top of the other upright.

"We'll have to start again," muttered Thumper and he thumped the side of the joist with his fist. Whether the day was going well or badly, Thumper would thump the side of his fist against the steel. In play or anger he was always making fists and slapping the fleshy side of his hand against the metal. "Jumpin' Jackrabbits! We're going to have to start all over again. It's cold as fury and we're going to have to start again. Stand back, boys, I'll give the signal to the crane driver!"

"Hang on, Thumper," said Thor. "It's less than half an inch out. I can fix that with the big hammer!"

"That isn't a good idea, Bigger!" said Barney. "I don't

doubt that you can swing that hammer but the boss doesn't want you using the hammer up here after what happened the other day."

"Stuff and nonsense!" said Thor. "You aren't going to pay any attention to that rubbish, Thumper! That's just superstition! Just you stall signalling to the crane. I'll have the steel in place faster than a salmon leaping!"

Before Thumper and Barney could do or say anything, the man they knew as Bigger had taken a huge post hammer from where it lay secured to a scaffolding pole and swung it at the joist. The jolly giant swung the hammer with the smooth rhythm of an Olympic athlete and Boom! The joist screeched nearer its proper slot. Thor turned to grin at his workmates but they were nowhere to be seen. As soon as he began to swing the hammer, they had fled from the platform and were now hurtling down the safety ladders to the floors below. A day or so earlier, the man they all called Bigger had been wielding a hammer working high up on the steel skeleton of the new building. After two strikes with the hammer, big black clouds had loomed over the city skyline and thunder and lightning erupted within minutes of the hammer-strikes.

"Stuff and nonsense!" said Thor. "Two more strikes from the hammer will do it!"

He had failed to see that as soon as he struck the steel beam the first time, an ominous thick black cloud had formed over the building site.

Thor raised the hammer and struck for a second time. The sound of the hammer smiting the joist rang out like Big Ben's bell and the steel moved again, sliding closer to home. On the second strike, the black cloud expanded like a mammoth set of lungs and formed the shape of a gigantic black anvil, lowering over New York and plunging the building site into gloomy twilight.

"Stuff and nonsense!" yelled Thor.

He swung the hammer for a third time and smashed it against the steel joist. In a galaxy of sparks and fireworks the hammer smote the beam and it dropped snugly into place. But before Thor could complete an imaginary bow for the benefit of the crane driver and Thumper and Barney who were looking up from three floors below, the black cloud erupted. The anvil shape swirled in fury and rolled. It boiled like molten black lava. It fired a single jagged bolt of lightning that cracked across the sky and struck the top floor of the steel building frame. The joist and the hammer sizzled like an X-Ray. Thor was hurled over the side of the scaffolding, falling headlong through the sky. In half a heartbeat he flung out his right arm and snatched onto the safety barrier on the next floor and his momentum carried him over the rail. He landed safely on the scaffolding planks.

He thought he heard the word, "Jotunheim!" roar from the centre of the cloud.

"I think I know that place," the words ran through his mind and then he passed out.

As soon as the Thunder God's eyes closed, the storm cloud shrank like a mirage losing light, halved in size, quartered and then disappeared altogether.

The sun came out and lit up the day.

The Mimir water rippled. Time sped along. Thor had been carried down to the manager's office. He was sitting in a chair.

"Here are your wages, Bigger," the boss was saying. "I'm letting you go!"

"What?" Thor said, groggily

"I'm paying you off. Here's your wages. I've paid you up to date."

The boss shook his head in sorrow. "I'm very sad having to sack you, Bigger. You're the biggest, strongest steel worker I've ever seen and fearless on high buildings – but you're too much of a risk. Too much of a risk to yourself, to my men and to my building site."

"Give me another chance!" Thor whispered.

The boss looked over his shoulder to where Thumper and Barney stood looking into the office. They both shook their heads.

"Sorry, Bigger – I warned you. Twice at the start of the week you swung the big hammer to nudge some steel in place. Each time we had storm clouds and rainstorms that halted work for the day. I told you not to use the hammer"

"Superstition and nonsense!" Thor muttered. "It was coincidence!"

"That may be. I don't care," said the boss. "You disobeyed my instructions. You swung the hammer today and the top section of the building got hit by rogue lightning. Look!"

The boss' finger was pointing up at the building. The top section was charred and twisted. Thor stood up gingerly and looked out of the door, over the shoulders of Barney and Thumper. He could see where he had been standing. It looked as if the spot had been hit by a meteorite. The steel joist had bowed like a banana and the rest of the steel girders and beams of the topmost section were tangled and welded in strange, manic shapes.

"Going to take days to get the top storey sorted out," Barney muttered to Thumper.

"Just sit down again, Bigger," said the boss. "I've phoned for an ambulance. Should be here any minute. We need to get you checked over. Don't want any claims for negligence..."

But Thor was walking away from the door.

"Farvel," he said to Barney and Thumper and trudged away from the site.

"Bigger, come back!" the boss yelled. "The ambulance-"

But the God of Thunder who didn't know that he was the God of Thunder merely waved in farewell and without looking back walked off the building site.

"What happened there?" Tom asked. "Was Thor attacked by an Ice Giant?"

"No," said Snow. "Another example of Odin's weakening grip. Thor fired up a lightning storm and hit himself with a thunderbolt, without knowing what he was doing!"

"But we heard the word 'Jotunheim'- that's the Frost Giants' home!"

"Thor's own storm magic is trying to warn him of the threat on Asgard. He is too addled to understand."

The dragon shifted anxiously.

"Did you see how cold the city looked? It's *June*. We are running out of time. What is happening to Odin? What is happening on Asgard?"

Snow cast a claw over the Mimir water and the picture changed.

Thorkel looked out over the plain of Flattjord and clenched the muscles in his jaw so that he would look grim and stern. He had to be warrior-like and ready for battle instead of dismayed and terrified which was how he felt. He clenched his jaw so that he would look firm and resolute, showing a warrior's example to the boy warriors who stood drawn up in ranks immediately on both sides and behind him. Clenched his jaw like a heroic leader ready to fight tooth and nail to defend Asgard rather than a young boy petrified and shaking like a rabbit on an ice floe. The thing that had terrified him was the sight that was looming ever nearer in his vision.

A horde of Ice Giants was breaking out of Jotunheim and marching with furlong-strides towards the home of the Gods.

The Ice Giants really were giants. When Tom had looked out from the watchtower on Asgard, the giants that he had seen then were far away in the distance. They hadn't seemed too big then. This was the first time he had seen them close-up them and they terrified him. He wondered how he would describe them if ever he returned to his old life, how he would describe them if he returned to Danelaw school...

If you want to know how big the Ice Giants are, leave your house and look at the nearest electricity pylons. If you live in the country it's easy. There will be a row of pylons in a field somewhere near where you live. If you live in a town or city you may have to take a trip. The journey will be worth it. Think of it as a pilgrimage to give you an idea of how big the creatures are that Thorkel and his fellow junior warriors are about to face.

Take a long hard look at an electricity pylon. Now imagine a creature with a head and arms and legs that would stand as tall as that pylon. Imagine a creature that resembles a man as tall as the pylon but with arms and legs made of granite and marble and ice with a jaw the size of a grand piano and rows of teeth like a mixture of broken stalagmites and icicles as thick as your arm. Imagine a creature with arms and legs covered in leather gauntlets and greaves and with chest and shoulders encased in wool with a chain-mail coat of armour draped over the wool. Imagine that creature, tall as a pylon gobbling up the ground to close with you where you stood with your fellows ready to defend your homeland. Now look at the great spike-studded club or the blue-grey glinted war axe that each giant wielded in its great clubbing fist and you might begin to feel and understand why Thorkel clenched his jaw so that he could look brave and hide his fear.

Tom blinked and woke from his terrified reverie. He concentrated on what he could see in the mirror screen.

"Stand firm, Varangians!" Thorkel shouted in as loud a voice as he could muster.

Thorkel waited. And almost couldn't believe his ears as he said, "And on my command, get ready to charge them!

"It's the last thing they expect and surprise is half the battle!"

The fear was draining from him. This was what they had trained for. This was why they had studied with the fallen warriors in Valhalla. They were the children of the gods. They were the next generation of Aesir. They would serve Asgard well and die bravely if they had to. Thorkel felt his heart pounding but the rhythm had steadied. This wasn't fear running through his veins. It was the thrill of battle.

Three Ice Giants stood two heads taller than all the rest. The biggest of their brood, Rock-Smiter, Evil-Fang and Iceberg-Grinner led the raging gang as it burst out of Jotunheim and swept over the plain of Flattjord. Rock-Smiter roared a cold, hard roar. It was the sound of a glacier sliding and sending an avalanche grinding and screaming and bellowing down a mountain side. It was the sound of ice grinding and mincing rock. It was a violent, chill roar. It was the Ice Giants' war cry.

"Can't wait to wrap my club roun' the brains of a scared rabbit Aesir!" Rock-Smiter said with a lusty laugh.

"Nor me!" yelled Evil-Fang. "After we've broke through the main wall, the yards of Asgard will drip with the blood of the gods!"

The giants' vast stride swallowed up the plains of Flattjord. They were very close to the walls now.

And at that moment, having worked out when would be the perfect time to give the command, Thorkel yelled, "Chaaaaaaaaaaaaaaaaaaaaarge!"

Rock-Smiter, Evil-Fang and Iceberg-Grinner laughed when they saw the company of boys charge towards them. Luck was with Thorkel at that moment. He did not see the leading giants chuckling at the thought of slaughtering a company of boys and baby gods. So intent was he on inspiring the Varangians to make a perfect axe-charge that he did not see the amused reaction on the faces of the three giants at the front of the gang. Even luckier for Thorkel when he did look up to check the enemy's position he saw only panic and confusion in their eyes. The reason for their fright became apparent moments later. Heimdal's throwing axe sliced through the air and tore Rock-biter's shield from his arm. The next instant, Heimdal's sword, Huvud, was cutting in a fierce slashing arc at the first wave of giants and their charge stalled.

Evil-Fang snarled at Iceberg-Grinner, "You said the

gods were either away from Asgard or lying feeble on a hospital bed with a nurse in attendance!"

Grinner belied his name and scowled. This was not how it was meant to be. Loki had visited him days ago and set out the plan. Heimdal was supposed to be weakened to the point of death. He could hear the giant's war cries behind him begin to fall in volume. He could hear the timbre of uncertainty in their voices as their mine-deep yells begin to fade. The sight of Heimdal armed and ready for them was sucking the fight out of the monsters. Any moment and they would turn tail and flee. Iceberg-Grinner brought his shield up and felt Huvud bounce off the metal boss and clang onto his mail armour. Iceberg-Grinner remembered his name then as an earthquake-wide cracking grin split his face. A blow from Huvud should have burst his shield and shattered his shield arm. He would have lost the use of that arm and turned and fled, a one-armed warrior cannot last long in combat. The blow had bounced like a snowball thrown by an Ice Giantess' nipper. The enemy with the sword looked like Heimdal and sounded like Heimdal but this was not the Heimdal of old. Grinner shoved forward with his shield and barged Heimdal so that the sentry of the guards staggered back two paces.

The front rank of giants saw Heimdal stagger and they cheered. And at that moment the throwing axes hurled by the Varangian guard clattered into them and the front rank fell, skulls split by well-placed axes. But behind the front wave there was another and another and another again beyond that. Grinner, Splitter and Fang survived as they were shielded by Heimdal who was using all his warrior skill to keep them at bay with Huvud. But that was all he could do. On a normal day Heimdal would have cut off their heads for their impertinence in approaching Asgard let alone trying to break through the walls. The heads would have been set on poles and displayed along the Flattjord Plains to deter other Giants from repeating their folly. This was not a normal day and Heimdal had to draw on all that he knew of swordsmanship and shield-work to keep the three giant leaders pressed in a tight group and away from the youngsters who were now fighting pell-mell with the main might of the giant army. Heimdal despaired. Not long now and Asgard would lose an entire generation of young gods.

Snow passed a clawed talon over the surface of the mirror. The Mimir water rippled. Time sped along again.

The mirror had returned to show the Day Room in the hostel for tramps and homeless people.

The old man who had taken the name "Odd" was frowning. Deep grooves furrowed his brow. He pursed his lips in concentration. He was sitting in the Day Room of the hostel at a pine coffee table opposite Hobble, the small, dwarf-like tramp who had been given a supervisor's job in the hostel for hoboes and tramps. The table was stained and chipped and one of its legs was cracked. In the middle of the table was an antiquated chess board with a set of eccentric pieces laid out on the chequered board. Odd peered at the chessboard. Hobble had backed Odd's king into a corner.

"I'm going to miss our games, Odd, old fellow," Hobble said as Odd pondered his next move.

"Can't be helped, my friend," said Odd. "You know the rules as well as I. Bigger has found work. He is earning good money, enough for us to rent rooms in a modest hotel. He may even be earning enough that we could pay for a room for you too! The rules of this place mean we can't stay. Besides – we'd be depriving some unfortunate "knight of the road" of a bed!"

"I'm about to deprive you of a knight of your own!" Hobble said cheerfully, looking at the board once more and removing one of Odd's pieces.

Odd smiled. He had seen a way to take the fight back to Hobble. Before he had time to move a piece the door to the Day Room was flung open and in strode Bigger.

"We're going to be staying with you a little while longer, Hobble!" Bigger announced. "I've been sacked. We're homeless again but that's not all. Come outside!"

Odd sighed. Typical young man – bursting in on a game of chess without so much as a 'by your leave'. Delivers terrible news and then declares that there's more to come.

Odd and Hobble slowly made their way to the door. A blast of cold air greeted them. Bigger was pointing to the East River.

"Look!" he said.

And they looked where Thor was pointing. Odd shivered. It was very, very cold. The air seemed to carry tiny specks of ice in it. A cold mist was rising from the river. Odd peered in the direction of the East River. No. There was nothing unusual – he could only see rows of tall buildings, cars and people.

"Look!" Bigger insisted, pointing.

They followed the line of his index finger and Odd and Hobble stared in amazement as, slowly drifting in the current in the middle of the river, a small iceberg floated by.

"An iceberg?" said Snow incredulously. "But Heimdal and the young gods were holding the Giants at bay! What has happened?"

Again a scaly talon passed over the surface of the mirror.

The picture in the Mimir water changed once more. Tom looked on as the outer walls of Asgard hove into view yet again. The Frost Giants and Storm Giants continued to lay siege to the walls. They were attacking one of the gates where the timbers had buckled and cracked but not yet broken. Ice-knuckled fists wielded iron swords. Wooden clubs frosted and studded with icicles bludgeoned the warriors who had been summoned to defend the fortress of the gods. The warriors were hurled back. A company of Frost Giants charged the buckled but unbroken gate. Thorkel led his young warriors in one last despairing charge. Suddenly Heimdal leapt down from the walls. He had hurled back Fang, Splitter and Grinner but only for as long as it would take them to draw breath. Heimdal's sword and shield cut through the air, carving through the giants' ranks. Heimdal slew any giant rash enough to press towards the gate and while he held the throng at bay, Viking warriors heaved the stout oak gates back into place and barred them with fresh timber and iron spars. The gate was flung open long enough for Thorkel and the Varangian guard and then finally for Heimdal himself to slip back inside the fortress. Then the warriors heaved the gate back into place and locked it and barred it once again. Heimdal turned from the walls and walked slowly back to the Rainbow Bridge. A trail of melting snowy footprints led from the gates to the bridge.

"I was too late," Heimdal reproached himself bitterly. "My hearing is failing. My sight is dimming. I was too late when I heard the giants attacking the gate."

He peered down the Rainbow Bridge. The footprints disappeared from sight just at the point where the bridge met the Earth.

"An Ice Giant has broken through to Midgard!" Heimdal said aloud.

"We must get back on deck and get to the portal, young Wolfe!" Snow hissed. "An Ice Giant on earth! There's no time to waste!"

"All the more reason for me to see what's happening to my uncle and my friends!" Tom said impatiently.

Snow began to protest.

"Show me what's happenin' now on earth or you can complete the quest alone!" Tom said.

The dragon's gaze would have frozen the heart of a stone. Luckily for Tom he was staring at the surface of the Mimir mirror and so failed to observe the chill look.

The Mimir water image shimmered and shifted. Tom saw a

clear picture of Stella, storming down the long, school corridor, hair flying, and her eyes a red flame of torment. Vanbrugh, one of the Fifth Form's good-looking tough guys and a member of the Props gang was trying to grab her wrist. Tom knew that Vanbrugh's nickname among the props was "Vamp" and was surprised to see him chasing and pawing at Stella like this.

A dark red surge of protective fury sizzled through Tom's blood. He felt hot and angry.

"What are you doing, Vamp?" he said aloud without thinking.

"Stop running and talk, Stella!" Vamp roared. "Wolfe isn't coming back. He has run away. You aren't going to see him again so you might as well agree to come to the gig with me. Snake Venom are playing at the Guildhall. I've got my brother's car and once we're at the gig I'll get us into the Mosh Pit!"

Stella stopped running and turned in fury on Vamp.

"Not that you'd have the sense to work this out for yourself, Maxwell Vanbrugh, otherwise known as 'Vamp' among the rugger thugs but really known as 'Peabrain' to those who really know you!" she snapped. "But I'll tell you anyway. Tom has not run away. He never runs away from anything. He has more backbone in his little finger than you have in your entire spine! The fact that he is missing can only mean that he has been abducted. That's the line of enquiry being pursued by the Police!"

"Woah! Back off, scary Ice Queen! If you don't want to go to the gig with me just say. You'll regret it – my brother's car is a Porsche!"

"Then he's as stupid as you if he lets you borrow it!"

"Why's that?"

"It's called being party to a crime."

"Eh?"

"You're only sixteen. You aren't old enough to drive anything legally in this country – let alone a high-performance sports car! In your hands it might as well be a flying coffin, you oaf! Now shove off and leave me alone!"

Stella pushed past the angry teenager and into the cloakroom. She sat on a bench and buried her face in her arms.

"Oh, Tom, where are you?" she whispered to herself. "We're all missing you and Uncle Bernard is worried to death. I hope you aren't sleeping rough. It's so cold just now. It's like the Arctic at night!"

The images faded and disappeared. Tom sat back in an armchair and rolled his eyes.

"What do you make of that, Snow?"

The dragon scowled.

"Odd and Thor still have no memory of who they are," Snow replied after reflecting for a few moments. "At least being homeless should keep them intent on survival, which will slow down the loss of their godly powers. The really bad news is that an Ice Giant has broken through to Midgard. This is calamitous. As Odin's powers wane that of the giants grows. I warned you that the Earth is not about to perish in Fire but in Ice! We're on the brink of another Ice Age! We must finish the Quest. Swiftly."

"What about, Stella?" Tom said, unable to keep the anger from his voice.

"What about Stella?"

"She is worried about me. Uncle Bernard is worried sick!"

"These are trivial matters compared to reviving Odin's memory and defeating the Ice Giants, young Wolfe!" Snow said with more than a hint of condescension.

"And you don't understand!" Tom hissed, remembering that he couldn't yell in the cabin as someone might be listening at the door.

"Stella is missing me. That means that Loki has lied to me. He said Time would stand still while I was on the Quest. That obviously isn't true. If he lied about that he may have lied about other things. How do we know the

Quest is genuine? What if it's all a Wild Goose chase!"

"It isn't," said Snow shortly.

"How do you know it isn't?"

"I simply know, and for you, for now, that's all you need to know! We have to save Odin and Thor. That's our priority!"

"It may be for you," said Tom. "My priority is my uncle and Stella! I've got to get back to save her from Vamp. Vamp's a slimy thug!"

"By saving the lost Gods you save your uncle and the girl. You must see that?" the dragon whispered. "Even if you could go back to Newcastle in the present day – which you can't – saving Stella and Bernard would be futile-"

"Why?" Tom interrupted.

"Because they along with you and Rob and everyone else at Danelaw High and along with everyone else on Middle Earth will freeze to death. The Frost Giants will rule the world unless Odin and Thor can be revived to stop them! You must find and save the lost Gods first!"

Frustrating though it was, Tom knew that the dragon was right. He couldn't believe though that he had to spend so much time helping out the adults – and adults didn't come any more "grown-up" than a god – he had enough problems of his own to sort out. If Loki had lied about time standing still then Uncle Bernard would worry about him and what about Stella? She was being stalked by Vamp. Why couldn't the gods look after themselves? Weren't they big enough? They were certainly *old* enough! It was madness expecting a teenage boy from the North of England to solve their problems for them! But he wasn't stupid. He had followed Snow's explanation. The only way to save Stella, Uncle Bernard – everyone - was to restore Odin and Thor.

"So we need to get to the portal," he said finally.

"Exactly," said Snow. "At last!"

"I dunno...you dragons, always draggin' your heels," said Tom. "Wonder if that's how you got your name: draggin'!"

Then after waiting for his cheeky joke to be digested by the Frost Dragon he said, "Let's get on with the plan."

There was a commotion in the saloon bar on the main deck. Captain Hardfleet had ordered all the passengers and crew apart from the stokers and the pilots and those involved in steering the boat to gather in the main saloon barroom. He stood in front of the bar flanked by a nervous-looking Tom and a slightly happier-looking Anatole Prince. The brocade on the Captain's jacket shone and the twists and scrolls in his mustachios looked more impressive than ever.

Southern gents in Planter hats, New York dudes, cowboys and gamblers, gentlemen and rogues, had all assembled in the saloon bar. The bar was the biggest enclosed space on the boat. Captain Hardfleet gave his moustache one last tug and cleared his throat before declaring in a loud voice,

"Gentlemen, you might all be asking yourselves why I've asked you to gather here this afternoon?"

There was a general murmur of agreement.

"We had been kind of a-wonderin', Cap'n!" said Wild Will Hickory. "Maybe with all this ice suddenly kickin' about, we were wonderin' if you were goin' to stand us all a cold drink!"

Hickory's words prompted a loud guffaw from the assembled men. Captain Hardfleet was not the kind of man who was renowned for standing free drinks in the boat's saloon. The laughter was quickly stifled at Hardfleet's swift reply.

"Gen'lemen, that's exactly why you're all here!"

"Well if that don't beat everything!" Buffalo Bill Croney said in a loud voice. "The Captain of a Mississippi steam packet offerin' to stand everyone a drink? That's harder to swallow than a Saguaro Cactus from Arizona and that's saying something!"

"Harder to swallow than a switch of Thornberry and

that's sayin' more!" said Wyatt Herb.

"Harder to swallow'n a-" Croney began to reply but was interrupted by the Captain.

Hardfleet held up his hands.

"Gentlemen," he said in a loud voice, "this is not merely some empty gesture of generosity on my part! I am about to stand you all a drink, that is true...but I'm not paying!"

"No surprise there!" bellowed Bill Croney.

"Who is paying then if you ain't?" asked Mr U.B. Daid looking with his squint-eyed look at the Captain.

"The young English boy, Tom here, is paying for the liquor!"

"Why if that ain't stranger than a Mississippi steam packet cap'n offerin" to buy!" guffawed Croney, "An English pup barking up a storm of liquor! Hee haw!"

"If you'll permit the young man to explain for himself?" Hardfleet said. "And kindly extend to him the courtesy of some decent American manners?"

"The Captain's right," said Wild Will Hickory. "Let's give the boy a hearin'. Besides, Buffalo Bill, all your joshin' means we might miss out on a free slug of strong drink!"

Tom stepped forward, "Thank You, Cap'n Hardfleet and thank you, gentlemen, for giving me the opportunity to offer you a...a slug of liquor, if I have the phrase right."

Undrone had woken up and was translating away inside Tom's ear.

"Why-you're the self-same young whippersnapper that Bargefly pulled on deck as a stowaway! Claimed to have been touring the Southern states with a theatre company?" Hickory said.

"That's right, sir!"

"The same youngster that saved us from having to drink our rye whisky as warm as a cup of coffee?"

"Yes, sir!"

"The same youngster that has been supplying this very saloon bar with ice these last several hours?"

"Yes, sir."

"Young 'un," Hickory announced. "No further introduction required. The floor is yours!"

Tom stepped forward and gestured towards Anatole Prince.

"Gentlemen, I'd like to introduce to you, Monsieur Anatole Prince, citizen of France. M'sieur Prince is about to pour each and every one of you a glass of his very special drink. It's a kind of spirit called absinthe!"

Anatole held up a bottle of the translucent, green, slick liquid which he had placed along with several cases of the same on top of the bar counter.

"Finest spirit in the whole world!" the Frenchman said with pride.

"All I ask is that you do the following," Tom said. "Form a line and come forward one at a time. Take a glass of absinthe from M'sieur Prince. Walk to this side table and place your glass under the statue."

As he said this, Tom stepped over to a side table that had been set up next to the bar. With a flourish he removed a large silk napkin to reveal a large statue of a dragon in creamy-white jade.

"Holding your glass under the statue, say these words in a loud voice: 'I have not stolen any goods from the English boy, Tom Wolfe. I am an honest, truthful traveller on the PS Velocity'. Then step over to the other side of the barroom. Don't drink your absinthe until I tell you when you'll all be given free ice to savour the drink properly!"

"Why all that mumbo-jumbo about not stealing any of your goods, young 'un?" Hickory asked.

"Because," replied Tom in a cool, even tone. "Earlier today someone on board stole a valuable bundle of my goods. The jade dragon is no ordinary trinket. It's a magic stone carving. It cannot abide dishonesty, criminality or felony. If any thief tells a lie while standing within three feet of the jade statue, its colour changes. Instead of the white stone you see before you now, it will glow bright red!" Tom paused then said. "If you'd like to form a line, gentlemen?"

A disgruntled murmur rumbled through the barroom. Tom heard the grumbles.

"You can knock me into a cocked hat!"

"The darned scalawag!"

"He's takin' on like a pure Algerine!"

"Accusin' us all of thievery!"

"It's enough to make a man a little wrathy!"

"Ain't he a caution though?"

"A caution or a coot?"

"Let's exfluncticate the varmint!"

Just when things were about to get out of hand, Wild Will Hickory cleared his throat, stepped forward again and said, "Gentlemen, gentlemen! I can see how your self-respect might be offended by what the young 'un is proposing!"

A murmur of agreement greeted Hickory's words. "But think about this. You *are* being offered a free drink. And only a guilty man has something to fear from the dragon...which if I may remind you is a piece of stone...and seems to rely on Magic as its modus operandi?" Hickory winked as he said the word 'Magic', "I think we should behave like gents and accept this offer of a free drink!"

The murmur of agreement swelled into a general chorus.

Tom could see that the tide was with him and stepped forward.

"Gentlemen if you'd like to form a line... The experiment will be carried out with the lights dimmed. Captain, could you arrange for the blinds to be closed as well as all the curtains, please?"

Cowboys, businessmen and cardsharps formed a queue in the gloom. Tom and Anatole Prince placed a wide-brimmed tumbler in the hand of each man in the queue. Wild Will Hickory was first to step into line and accepted his glass of spirits graciously. After saying "thanks", he walked in front of the jade statue and said in clear, ringing tones, "I am an honest man. I have not stolen any goods from the English boy, Tom Wolfe."

There was a pause while the crowd of men stared in the dim, half-light at the white, jade statue. It appeared to smoulder in the dark, as if it held a strange, unearthly glow. But the colour didn't flicker and it remained steadfastly white.

Buffalo Bill Croney was next. As Captain Hardfleet peered into the gloom he realised that he couldn't tell who was in the queue. The only reason that he knew Croney had been the second man to stand in front of the statue was that he let rip with a loud, "Yee-hah!" after saying, "I have not stolen any goods from the English boy, Tom Wolfe."

Some of the men in the line declared their honesty in a firm, strident voice. Others boomed. Some were shrill and piercing while others thundered their honesty and decency in voices that sounded throughout the bar and across the Mississippi river to reach the distant shore. There were others who muttered or whispered their innocence as if embarrassed by the whole thing. As each man passed in front of the jade statue, it remained obstinately white, signalling "In the clear" to each and every man, never once flicking its colour to the bright red "Stop" sign.

Time dragged slowly by as the line of men made its way up to the counter and then away again. At last, Cap'n Hardfleet announced to the darkened room, "Well, that's it young 'un. Every man has taken a drink and proposed your strange toast. The stone dragon hasn't even threatened to change colour. Not once. Not a flick. Not a flicker. You'll just have to resign yourself to your goods being gone forever!"

"Not quite, cap'n!" Tom said brightly. "If you could arrange for the return of daylight?"

Looking slightly puzzled, the Captain gave the command. The blinds opened, curtains were drawn back and the oil lamps were turned up to full. Clear, bright light splashed into the barroom.

"I don't see, youngster -!" the Captain began to speak, but Tom interrupted him.

"Gentlemen!" Tom said in a very loud, confident voice that hid just how nervous he really was. "I wasn't entirely honest with you."

An angry buzzing began once more in the saloon.

"This is not a magic jade dragon!"

The buzzing turned to laughter.

"You now all have a glass of the finest absinthe in your hand -" There was a cheer. "We are about to celebrate good, American plain-dealing by raising our glasses in a toast...to American honesty-" there was another cheer – "So please wait for the toast before drinking and allow me to give you all some ice and water to enjoy the drink properly!" – More cheering broke out.

Tom paused and glanced around the room before continuing.

"Most of you will not be aware that absinthe is a drink that is clear, see-through green in its pure state. When you add water, however, it turns milky. When each of you gentlemen approached the green dragon in the dark I added a splash of water to your glass. Every innocent man in this room will be holding a glass of opaque, milky, light-green liquor. The guilty man...the man who stole my goods will be holding a glass of clear, translucent green fluid. Raise your glasses, gentlemen!"

There was a moment of hesitation, of astonishment.

"Raise them, gentlemen!" Captain Hardfleet repeated the command.

"Raise them, gents!" said Wild Will Hickory, lifting a glass of milky-green absinthe and water in the air with one hand and producing an 1851 Colt Navy pistol in the other which he levelled at the room. "Let's see the guilty man!"

All round the room, hands and glasses were raised. All milky green. Then there was a commotion from the back of the room.

"Here he is! By the line of Crabtree! We have the varmint!" Buffalo Bill Crony and Wyatt Herb along with two other men were grappling with U.B. Daid.

"He was jest about to pour his liquor in yonder palm pot when I spied him and grabbed his arm!"

Daid's left arm was pinioned behind his back. Crony held Daid's other arm in a fierce grip, with his hand still clutching a shot glass from which he had spilled a quantity of liquor. The glass remained half-full of clear, see-through, green absinthe.

"Here's our guilty man, cap'n!" Tom said. "Fearing the legend of the magic stone dragon, Mr Daid hung back and then didn't join the line. He is the only man who did not approach the jade stone, fearing that it might glow red. He didn't come near the stone dragon and so failed to get any water added to his glass. The clear liquor in his glass is proof that he feared his crime would be found out. Do you think you could be so good as to arrange a search of his belongings?"

"You taking the word of this young English whippersnapper over that of a Rocky Mountains gen'leman?" Daid snapped.

He struggled again when silence met his words but Crony and Herb only tightened their grip. Wild Will Hickory stepped forward and relieved Daid of his revolvers and then took the glass of absinthe from his grasp and held it up to the light.

"Pure and green and see-through clear as a bucket of sea water! As pure as emerald!" Hickory intoned solemnly.

Captain Hardfleet and another officer returned from Daid's quarters with his belongings. The Captain flung open a broad canvas bag and from it, the handles tied with a broad cotton neckerchief, Tom's leather pouch and its contents, Antique Greek gold pieces and whittled yew darts, spilled out onto the saloon floor.

"Here's the proof!" said Hardfleet reading the old

Gothic script that Snow had ice-etched into the leather pouch, 'This money bag belongs to Tom Wolfe, Prince of the Misty Isles'"

"'Prince of the Misty Isles'?" The Captain repeated. He had ended his words with a question.

"It was a part I was playing at the time. People in the audience who thought I'd done quite well had the money bag made for me as a token of their appreciation," Tom explained, thinking *I am becoming too good at this lying Mullarkey for my own good.* Then for Snow's benefit he thought, *How did you know, long ago in Ancient Greece, that we'd have to personalise the money bag?*

"When you've been around Vikings as long as I have you very quickly learn the importance of being able to identify your own goods...without causing a dispute!" the dragon whispered directly into Tom's ear.

"We need a committee to provide Mr Daid with a hemp necktie!" said Buffalo Bill Crony.

"There'll be no lynchings on my boat!" Captain Hardfleet said sternly. "Mr Bargefly! Bring two men and clap this felon in irons. We'll hand him over to the proper authorities when we next put ashore!"

"Can't you at least make 'im walk the plank?" asked Crony with a plaintive voice. "Me 'n' the boys was just hoping for some entertainment!"

Hardfleet stared Crony down with a stony gaze and the crewmen bundled Daid out of the saloon with the minimum of fuss.

Tom breathed a sigh of relief.

"Gentlemen!" he said. "If you'd like to bring your drinks to the bar, there's ice and water. I'm supplying all the free ice you can drink today but after your first absinthe, which is free of charge, after that you'll have to buy second or third drinks from M'sieur Anatole Prince here!"

The young Frenchman was beaming. Burly gambling men and ramrod lean cowboys were smacking their lips as they drained their glasses of iced absinthe.

"Ain't bad at all!" came the murmur from the crowd.

"Tastes of aniseed sweeties but packs quite a punch!"

"Ain't nowhere near as bad as rattlesnake poison! I'll pay for a second bite!" said Buffalo Bill Crony which was taken to be a compliment and that was enough to fire up the crowd's enthusiasm for the Frenchman's spirit. Anatole Prince looked very relieved. Tom had agreed to pay for the first "free" round of drinks and some of the passengers were coming back for a second taste. It appeared that M. Prince was going to sell some of his stock of absinthe after all!

Tom stood to one side to avoid being swept along in the rush to the bar. He gathered up his belongings and his knapsack then tucked the jadestone dragon under his arm. He walked up to the Captain and saluted him.

"Thank you for allowing me to use the saloon bar, Cap'n!" he said.

"It was a pleasure, young 'un. No skipper likes to have a thief and a rogue on board. In a way I'm in your debt. You've solved the ice problem and uncovered a felon. The Lord only knows what a conniption there would have been if Daid had stolen from one of the 'livelier' passengers I have on board!"

"Well if you're in my debt, Cap'n Hardfleet I can wipe out that debt with one simple favour in return!"

"And what might that be, young Wolfe?"

"To be permitted to gaze at the portrait of Miss Shirley Shoretree in your stateroom?"

Tom could have sworn that a whole gangcrew of Storm Giants had broken out of Jotunheim and were arm-wrestling their way across the Captain's face, all the way down from his temples to his nose and on to his chin. It was a terrible face to see.

"Not this side of the grave, young man!" Hardfleet said and stormed off towards his cabin.

One of the reasons Tom had been picked to play fly-half for the school rugby team was his speed over five yards from a standing start. He realised it was time to demonstrate that skill and swiftly! He bolted over the solid pine planks and headed off the skipper before he left the saloon.

"Sorry about that, Cap'n!" he said. "I was forgetting my manners! How about a friendly game of darts instead?"

Hardfleet's thunderous look ebbed away. A much more kindly face peered down at the English boy.

"A friendly game of darts would round the day off just fine and dandy!" he said. "Permit me to retrieve my 'arrows' and I'll see you back in the saloon in two shakes of a Mustang's tail!"

Tom watched the Captain disappear from the saloon and then wandered over to where Anatole Prince was doing his best to keep up with passengers asking for, and more importantly, paying for refills of absinthe.

"I cannot thank you enough, Tom Wolfe!" the young Frenchman said.

"*Pas de problemo*, Anatole!" Tom said with a grin.

"Urm, 'problemo' is not really proper French," Anatole said, apologetically.

"Forget about giving that English whipper-snapper there a lesson in the finest language in the world!" someone said to Anatole. "And permit me to consume one glass of your absinthe and absorb two minutes of your time!" The speaker was a tall man wearing a top hat and tailcoat. "And tell me how much of that fine liquor you're able to sell me, monsieur!"

"And who might I have the pleasure of addressing?" Anatole asked.

"Monsieur Claude Revere, former citizen of France. Now naturalised as an American, tax-payer in the fine state of Louisiana. Resident of the beautiful city of New Orleans. Proud owner of the Crawfish and Magnolia Hotel, which happens to possess the biggest saloon bar in the whole of Louisiana. I have been interested in importing genuine French absinthe for some time, M'sieur Prince. Now tell me how much stock of this fine liquor you have aboard and then...name your price!"

The two Frenchmen retired to a corner of the bar and remained in earnest conversation for some time. Then they shook hands and Claude Revere walked away to join a party of gamblers who were playing poker at the other side of the saloon, leaving Anatole alone at the bar.

Anatole Prince turned back to face Tom. His eyes were filling up faster than a water butt in Mobile, Alabama. He struggled to control himself but then mastered his emotions and said, "This will save my family. It will save the chateau, save the estate. My mother and sisters will not starve, not be made 'omeless and I will be in a position to marry Mademoiselle Claire de Belleflorette. My honour is saved. Tom...I owe you a great debt of honour!"

Tom realised that he was gathering a troupe of people who were indebted to him. They were debts that he would never collect.

"As I said earlier, Anatole Prince, *citoyen de France*...nul pas de problemo!" Tom said with a big grin.

Anatole was about to wince but then realised that the English boy was pulling his leg

"Just one thing, young Wolfe," the Frenchman said. "You might say that it's none of my business. And given that you have saved my business, restored my fortunes and saved my family some might think it churlish of me even to pose the question, but – 'ow do you say in English – 'Curiosity killed the cat' – I have to ask you...If the jade dragon isn't magic, how were you able to make all those glasses of absinthe turn milky? As you said to the passengers, it only does that when you add water or ice."

"Simple, M'sieur Prince-"

"Please, Tom, call me Anatole...you have saved my family and my fortune. I consider you a friend!"

"OK, Anatole... but it was very simple. Very straightforward. I had a small tube which I wedged between the stone claws of the statue. The tube was hidden under the cloth on which I'd set down the dragon and it connected to a pump attached to a water bottle, again hidden under the cloth. Each time one of the passengers approached the jade dragon to express his innocence, I squirted a small amount of water into the glass. Only the thief, fearing that the jade dragon might glow red in the face of his dishonesty, stayed away from the statue. Only the thief's absinthe remained unchanged by water. The clear glass betrayed the criminal."

"Ah, the cunning Mr Daid wasn't cunning enough, eh?"

"Exactly! And now I must get back to my cabin to gather up and secure my goods," said Tom, "And I'd better be quick about it. I have an appointment at the oche with the skipper!"

"'Zee 'ockey'?" repeated the Frenchman.

"Yes, the oche," said Tom. It's the line you stand behind when throwing darts."

Tom shook hands with Anatole and then hurried back to his stateroom, stopping long enough to gather up the white jade dragon, wrapping it up in the silk cloth.

As soon as he was out of sight, he peeled open the silk cloth and a tiny, creamy-white dragonfly flew out and landed behind his ear.

A barrel-load of Thanks, Snow, he thought to himself, knowing that the dragon would be able to read his thoughts. *I couldn't have managed any of that without your help! I certainly wouldn't have been able to hit the glasses accurately with the water spout from where I was standing! Were any of the glasses difficult to reach?*

"Oh yes!" Snow whispered. "Some of them stood so far back and hesitated...there's obviously a strong criminal element on board this vessel they were worried about proclaiming their honesty as a general principle...they stood so far back I couldn't possibly have hit their glass with the water spout."

So what did you do?

"I aimed a thin flute of icy air at their glass and fired ice droplets directly inside the absinthe!"

Oh yes. Result! thought Tom.

"'Result' indeed!" whispered Snow. "Daid was the only one who didn't come anywhere near the table. Now get a move on. We have to find the lost Gods!"

And Stella, and Uncle Bernard and Rob!

"But first there's the small matter of a darts contest that you have to win!"

Inside his stateroom, Tom emptied what remained of his belongings from the wardrobe into the knapsack, checked that Undrone the bee was safe and sound and comfortable in his ear, checked the mirror and belts were safe and secure in the satchel, in short that he had cleared everything he needed from the room and then locked the door after him. He rushed back to the saloon, carrying the bag slung over his shoulder. Snow was still sitting comfortably behind one of Tom's ears.

"I've left nothing behind in the cabin," he whispered to Snow. "Everything's in the rucksack apart from Undrone who is in my ear. We can make a hasty exit if we have to!"

"Let's hope we have to!" said Snow.

This is great, thought Tom.

"What is great?" answered the dragon.

Having a miniature translator bee in my lug-hole!

"Why is that great?"

Haven't had to wash my ears in days.

16 Everyone Plays Darts

As soon as he reached the hurricane deck, Tom headed for the saloon but saw that the entrance was blocked by the burly outline of Captain Hardfleet. On hearing Tom approach he turned and held a finger to his lips.

"Wait here by the door with me, young 'un," he said quietly.

The look on Tom's face asked the question, *Why*?

"Wild Will Hickory is playing darts with Buffalo Bill Crony and that means it's highly dangerous in there presently!" the Captain explained in a whisper.

"Why is that?" asked Tom, "Because there might be gunfire when one of them loses?"

"Not quite," said the Captain. "The danger lies in the fact that though he might be a dead-eye and crackshot with a pistolero, Mr Crony is the worst hurler of a dart that the world has ever seen. How a man who can handle a Colt as though he had been born with one in his hand can then proceed to throw a dart as though it were a brass skillet...well – it plain beats me!"

As if to demonstrate the accuracy of the Captain's observations a dart flew up several feet above the dartboard and into the bright chandelier hanging from the wooden ceiling where it lodged between two lozenges of lead crystal.

"Jumpin' Jackrabbits! That's game over, Crony. We don't have any more darts left to play with. When are you going to learn to throw as well as you shoot?" asked Wild

Will Hickory aggressively. But Crony only sulked and walked over to the bar.

Captain Hardfleet strode into the saloon and positioned himself in front of the dartboard.

"If you gentlemen are vacating the oche, I'll be obliged if you'll allow me to give the young English pup here a lesson in the *Art of Arrows* as we call the sport south of the Mason-Dixon line!"

Tom stood next to Captain Hardfleet and examined the dart board. It resembled a modern board. It was roughly the same diameter. The main differences were that the board had only a centre bull's eye without an extra circle round the bull. The treble score section was missing and the double space was fan-shaped.

He took a closer look. It was made of very hard wood.

"Cobblers!" he said. "The barrel's made of oak...I'm not sure that my darts will stick!"

"You have a problem with my dart board, boy? It's made from the end of a fine, oak barrel butt, the finest board to be had in Christendom!"

"But my darts are made from seasoned yew. They won't stick in oak."

"Permit me to have a look at your arrows."

Tom handed over the magic yew darts.

"That's some mighty fine whittlin'!" Hardfleet said in admiration as he examined the darts. "You carve these, sonny?"

"No, it was my Pappy!" Tom lied. "He whittled them from some old yew that had been growing in our local churchyard for centuries. A branch fell from the tree during a storm and Pappy whittled three darts from the windfall. The wood is ancient. I wouldn't want to damage the darts, Captain Hardfleet. But I wouldn't want to play with any other set either. These are the only darts I can play with."

"Don't worry, young 'un," the Captain replied. I have a spare set of metal points which if I'm not mistaken will fit over the tips of your wooden arrows nicely.

Hardfleet produced the spare dart points and Tom was relieved to see that they did indeed fit over the yew tips like skin.

"That could have been a disaster!" Snow whispered in his ear. "You wouldn't want to play the Captain using ordinary, mortal darts. You'd only lose...and lose badly!"

Thanks for reminding me! —And the vote of confidence: Not! You don't have to rub it in, thought Tom.

"What would you like to play, Tom?" the Captain asked. Tom realised that the Captain was treating him as a serious opponent. It was the first time he had addressed him by name.

"Are you familiar with Three-Oh-One?" Tom asked.

"'Familiar'? Why I practically invented it!" Hardfleet said with a smile. "We both start with a score of three hundred and one. The total reduces by whatever score we hit with each of our three darts. No need to throw a double to start," he added. "We'll just throw and count the scores immediately. Though to finish, you need to hit a double. Nearest to the bull starts?"

The Captain threw a dart which landed just outside the bull's-eye. Tom stood at the oche, released his dart and hit the bull's-eye dead centre.

"Hmm, I can see you're going to give me a game, young Tom!"

Tom threw three bull's-eyes. The Captain did the same.

"One Hundred and Fifty scored by both players!" announced Wild Will Hickory, who had crept up quietly to watch.

Tom threw two more bull's-eyes and a nineteen.

"One hundred and nineteen!" said Hickory. "The English boy needs thirty-two or double sixteen to win."

Captain Hardfleet threw the same score.

Tom stood at the oche and aimed.

"You wouldn't want to appear too good!" Snow whispered in his ear. "They might begin to suspect something!"

-Good thinking, thought Tom and threw his next dart into the sixteen space, just missing the double.

"Sixteen scored. Double eight required!"

Tom missed the board altogether with his next dart.

"Is your Beginner's Luck deserting you, youngster?" the Captain asked with a grin.

But the grin was wiped from his face when, with his next dart, Tom skewered the double eight.

"Game to young Master Wolfe!" Hickory called out.

"Well done, Tom!" The Captain said warmly. "I can see that I'm in for some stiff competition. Best of five games – Loser starts the game?"

"Why not?" Tom replied.

"Time to try some strategy," whispered Snow. "I'd sincerely recommend that you lose the next game."

My thoughts exactly, thought Tom.

Tom promptly lost the next two games.

"Perhaps your first win was beginner's luck!" said the Captain with a broad grin, hitting the double that he needed plum in the middle.

But Tom won the fourth game to square the match.

"No beginner's luck here, cap'n!" said Hickory. "He's matching you dart for dart!"

The Captain won the fifth game easily. His face wore a broad merry grin as held out his hand to Tom.

"Well done, sonny – you threw some mean Arrows. A bit erratic at times, but when you're on form, you have one helluva an eye for the bull!"

Tom smiled at the Captain's compliment.

"Why don't we play again? Only this time let's make it Five-Oh-One and let's make it interesting."

The Captain raised an eyebrow. "'Interesting'?"

"Let's add a wager!"

"I'm not sure-" Captain Hardfleet began.

"Excuse me interrupting, Captain, but wait 'til you hear what it is!" Tom said. "I'll lay my ice machine that you can't beat me over five games of Five-Oh-One!"

There was a hush in the saloon.

"That's quite a stake!" Hardfleet murmured. "What would you like me to wager in return?"

"That you will open up any locked door on this boat for my inspection!"

"Done!" said the Captain and held out his hand.

They shook hands on the wager. Tom grinned. A handshake was a binding agreement for the gentlemen that Captained the Mississippi steam packets. Captain Hardfleet was sworn to honour the wager.

Magic Portal here I come! thought Tom.

He threw his darts with the precision of a machine and won the first game. No need to disguise the accuracy of his throwing. The Captain missed with a couple of throws and was struggling to catch up

"The youngster needs double sixteen!" yelled Wild Will Hickory.

Tom won the second game. Only one more game and he would be on his way home!

"Good darts, Tom!" the Captain said gallantly.

"Good darts my Great Aunt Mary-Lou!" said Buffalo Bill Crony. "There's something fishy going on here. Boy says he has a magic jade dragon. Produces ice out of thin air when everyone knows you need a machine the size of a small house to produce ice in this country! Now he's whupping the finest darts player south of the Mason and Dixon line without breaking sweat? Something smells odd to me." He marched over to where Tom and the Captain stood at the oche, waiting to throw.

"Permit me to interrupt your game, Cap'n. Jest for half a scratch of a possum's tail. Call it a refreshments break if you like!"

"I'm not sure-" the Captain began.

"There's something fishy about the youngster's darts!" Crony said and suddenly without any hint of what he intended to do, he had whipped all three yew darts from

Tom's hand and stood at the oche ready to throw.

-Bloody hell! thought Tom. *They're going to rumble that I'm using magic darts! What next? Captain Hardfleet is a serious competitor. I'm probably going to be made to walk the plank after all - once he finds I've been cheating! Buffalo Bill is the worst darts player in the whole of the USA. If he plays well I'm sunk! Can't you do something?*

"Sorry – there isn't time!" whispered Snow in his ear. "Get ready to run!"

Crony faced the board

"Watch this!" he said. "Double twenty!" and hurled the dart. Tom closed his eyes. He missed seeing the dart fail to strike the target altogether. It buried itself in a length of pine panelling near the bar.

"This time!" said Crony. "DOUBLE TWENTY!" he cast the dart. It executed a parabola and skewered the stuffed head of a moose that was hanging some four feet away from the dartboard.

"Dang!" he said in a voice laced with annoyance. "I was sure there was something fishy about those darts but they're just the same as any other set!"

"And your throwing is just as bad with those darts as any other set!" Wild Will Hickory chuckled.

Tom walked slowly over to the pine panel and retrieved the first dart. He then reached up and pulled the second from the brow of the moose. He felt very sick now and scared. Very scared.

-This is madness, he thought, so that Snow could read his thoughts. *Buffalo Bill should have hit the double twenty with ease. These are Loki's magic darts! If Crony can't hit a barn door with them then they can't be magic! What does this all mean?*

"I'm not sure," Snow whispered.

-If they aren't magic then he must have meant me to fail the first test with the deadly Yew Trees at Weyland's gate, or if not then, to have been ripped to shreds by the two-headed Roc! He must have meant me to die, Snow! Why?

"I have no answer for you, Tom," the dragon said

quietly. "But remember, Loki is the God of Mischief and Cunning."

-The God of Evil, you mean!

Buffalo Bill Crony returned the third dart as Tom made his way back to the oche. The darts were not magic! He was a fourteen year-old boy playing against a seasoned marksman. What was he playing at?

The Captain gave him a broad grin.

"Ready to play after Mr Crony's interlude, Tom?" Cap'n Hardfleet asked.

"Yes, sir," Tom said, his every word and gesture betraying uncertainty.

"Loser starts," said the Captain and threw a perfect score.

Tom stood with his right foot against the oche and faced the board. He threw his first dart carelessly and it failed to score. His next wasn't much better and his third flew limply to hit the twenty sector only to bounce back out and clatter onto the floor.

The Captain didn't miss.

Tom threw three more darts. Two missed the board completely. After two more rounds, the Captain won with a perfect score. The fourth game went the same way. Captain Hardfleet made perfect scores, while Tom struggled to hit the board.

"The match is tied! Two games all!" bellowed Wild Will Hickory. "Everything hinges on the final game!"

Tom mopped his brow. Sweat had broken out on his forehead. He felt very uncomfortable. What could he do?

"Can I grab a glass of iced water, Captain?" he asked.

"Certainly, Tom. Go ahead!"

"Might be the last chance you get to drink your own ice machine's product, sonny!" said Buffalo Bill. "After this next game you're going to have to ask the Cap'n for some of the glacial stuff!"

It was all going wrong.

What am I going to do, Snow? - he thought as he made his

way to the bar. *Stella, Uncle Bernard, the lost Gods... they're all depending on me and now I'm going to foul up again! It's just like being in Mr Porter's class all over again. Everything is going wrong. It's all turning sour! I'm fouling everything up!*

"That's where you're wrong!" the dragon replied in a shrill whisper. "I've been reflecting on this while you were throwing darts. Think about it...if the darts aren't magic, then they weren't magic when you threw them through the lock on Asgard. They weren't magic when you unpicked the entrance to Weyland's forge and avoided the deadly Yew trees. They weren't magic when you hit the Roc in the heart – bull's eye - and killed it stone dead. Don't you see? If they aren't magic now, they weren't magic then! You're the one with exceptional skill. Uncanny hand and eye. Tom Wolfe - you're a master darts player!"

The dragon paused.

"You must believe in yourself!" Snow said.

Tom stopped in his tracks.

Perhaps the dragon's right?

"You bet I am!" whispered Snow.

He grabbed the glass of water offered by Anatole Prince and returned to the oche.

"Loser throws first!" the Captain said and Tom stepped forward. He had a drink. Then he took a deep breath and exhaled slowly. He steadied himself exactly as he would when taking a penalty kick in rugger. He controlled his breathing. He made himself feel relaxed. He thought the word, '*Calm*', over and over again. If the darts weren't magic then he had to believe in himself. He had to remember that he had thrown darts through a lock in a gate eight feet distant and killed a two-headed Roc. He could do it! He breathed out and threw his dart. Straight and true it flew into the bull. He repeated the action, breathed calmly and thought of a little bird uncurling to leave its nest before taking its first flight. The dart soared! He hit the bull with all three darts and scored 150. A perfect score.

Captain Hardfleet began with two bulls-eyes.

"Perhaps I should freeze the bull?" Snow offered.

-No! I'm going to do this fair and square or not at all!

"There's no point in losing fair and square! We'd both end up spending the rest of our lives on a Mississippi steam boat stuck in the nineteenth century! Meanwhile, back in the twenty-first century, the entire globe is entering the Next Ice Age! You should cheat! Loki would instruct you to cheat! For the greater good!"

No! Fair and square or not at all!

The Captain hit a third bulls-eye: 150!

Captain Hardfleet and Tom matched one another, making perfect scores.

Tom stood ready to throw. The match was tied. He had to win now or Hardfleet would surely beat him with his next set of darts.

Breathe slowly and stay calm, he repeated to himself. He threw his tenth dart. Nineteen scored!

"Young Wolfe, you need double sixteen to win!"

He closed his eyes, relaxed so that all the tension went from his shoulders and arms, squinted along the dart in the direction of the board and then with a flick of his fingers and thumb sent the dart winging straight as a crossbow bolt into the double sixteen!

"Game and match to Tom Wolfe!" Wild Will shouted.

Phew! That was close! Tom thought.

"Close?" Snow whispered. "I'm going to need some of my own ice! That's how close it was. I'm over-heating!"

"Well played, Tom" said the Captain, and he twirled his capacious mustachios once before offering his hand and a generous handshake to the winner. "I had been fairly looking forward to taking command of my very own ice-making machine!" he said with a chuckle.

Some of the cowboys gathered round.

"Well done, young 'un!" said Wild Will Hickory, thumping Tom on the back. "That was eagle-eyed marksmanship and I should know. I'm a connoisseur of straight-shooting. You just beat one of the best darts players along the Mississippi. Cap'n Hardfleet's darts game is legendary in these parts!"

Tom's face was beaming. He had beaten a great American sportsman and beaten him fairly and squarely. The yew darts weren't magical. His *throwing* of the darts *was*!

*But why would Loki have lied? Why put me in danger? Did the God of Mischief hope I would **fail**? What's going on?*

"It would have been a privilege to lose to such a good player and Good Sport!" Tom said generously.

"Where did you learn to play like that, Tom?" the Captain asked. "Do you have special clubs or academies in England for youngsters with a keen interest in the Art of Arrows?"

Tom grinned. "There are such places, Cap'n, but they're in pubs and clubs and out of bounds to youngsters! No, I learned to play darts in my bedroom at home. My Uncle Bernard provided me with a board and I used to practise every other day at home."

"Only happy to be beaten by someone showing a little bit of dedication and commitment," Hardfleet said. "Well I guess it's time for you to collect on your wager. Which door would you like me to unlock, young Tom?"

"Skipper, I'd like you to open the door to the cabinet that contains the portrait of Miss Shirley Shoretree!"

Once again it looked as if a gangcrew of Storm Giants had broken out of Jotunheim and were arm-wrestling their way across the Captain's forehead, down his nose to his chin. And once again it was a terrible sight to behold.

"I said 'Not this side of the grave!' And when I said that I meant it!" The Captain's face bore witness to the terrible struggle that was taking place in his heart. "But a wager is a wager. We shook hands on it and you beat me fair and square..." he paused.

"I'd be very respectful, sir," Tom said. "I know Miss Shoretree's memory is very precious to you."

That decided it. Captain Hardfleet's face brightened and he signalled for Tom to follow him.

"I'll be along in a second, skipper!" said Tom, heaving up his knapsack after placing the yew darts in a pouch and stowing the pouch in the sack. "After all – I know the way!"

The Captain left the saloon. The reason for Tom's delay soon revealed itself. He walked over to the bar where Anatole Prince was polishing glasses between serving generous slugs of absinthe and collecting stacks of gold and silver dollar coins.

"Au Revoir, Anatole!" he said brightly. "My compliments to your family and to the lovely Miss Claire de Belleflorette. Good luck in all your ventures!"

"'Au revoir?'" said Anatole. "But I'll see you before we put into the next town on the Mississippi. I have a pile of silver dollars for you – there's gold here too!"

Tom scooped a handful of coins up from the bar.

"This will do - A fistful of dollars, Anatole! Thanks and Goodbye!"

I always wanted to say that.

"I know," said Snow. "I know."

Tom shook hands with a very puzzled Frenchman, gathered up the handful of coins and then walked over to where Wild Will Hickory was in conversation with Buffalo Bill Crony and Wyatt Herb.

"It's time to say 'Goodbye', Mr Hickory," said Tom, holding out his hand, "I'd like to thank you for helping me out of some fairly tight spots. If you hadn't stuck up for me today I'd have walked the plank, been flung overboard, clapped in irons and never recovered my goods from Mr U.B. Daid!"

"A pleasure, sonny. I always like to see a man, even a youngster such as yourself, given an even chance! Besides I knew from the outset that there was more to you than meets the eye!"

"How's that?"

"There's no theatre company called The Lord Chamberlain and Jarvis Z. Brakespeare's Touring Repertory Company!" the gunslinger winked and then said, "And there's no way you could have snuck aboard a Mississippi steamer and remained bone dry!"

"It's been a pleasure, Mr Hickory," Tom said, giving nothing away, "Let me give you a tip."

"What's that?" Hickory's eyes narrowed.

"Give up playing poker and don't go to Deadwood!"

Hickory grinned, "But I don't play poker, sonny! I think you must be confusing me with my cousin, Wild Bill Hickok. He's due in Deadwood sometime soon I believe."

Tom shook hands with the other two gunslingers and walked from the saloon and along the deck to the Captain's quarters.

With his rucksack on his back he knocked on the door and entered Cap'n Hardfleet's stateroom. The Captain was sitting where Tom had first seen him earlier that day, on a skipper's chair behind a broad mahogany desk. He rose from his chair when Tom entered the cabin. He had a bright steel key in his right hand.

"A wager is a wager, Tom," the Captain said.

Without any flourish, the Captain drew back a set of thick, red velvet curtains to reveal a large wall-mounted cabinet with wooden doors. He inserted the key and opened the doors.

Snow was whispering in his ear: "This is it! Listen. More of the riddle:

'Try the wolf with another proof.

Three quests to prove that you're the best,

On a ship, in a chest, pass each test.' This is the chest! It must be!"

With the cabinet doors open, Tom could see a large picture of a beautiful woman. The woman had bright hennaed red hair and was lying on a chaise longue. She was dressed as Cleopatra with a view of the pyramids in the background. The artist had painted himself into the scene.

The painter looked out of place. He was a lean figure wearing a green and olive harlequin costume. His face wore a strange, twisted smile. Tom knew that face. He had expected to see an oil painting but the picture was the biggest watercolour that he had ever seen. He blinked. Cleopatra's hair turned from red to blonde. The scene shifted from Egypt. A small green dragon appeared in a corner of the painting. Norse shields, javelins and wall hangings appeared on the walls and there standing in front of the Pool of Mimir was the artist, Loki, with a paint brush in one hand and a palette of water colours in the other. Cleopatra's hair was ash blonde. Her face shimmered. It wasn't Shirley Shoretree in the picture. It was Stella! Stella Cooke was lying on a long rush-covered trellis, gazing out of the painting, pleading to be rescued.

Tom struggled to control the panic that was seizing him.

"What do you see in the painting, Captain?" he asked, his voice trembling.

"What do you see, Snow?" he murmured. Too afraid to worry about what the Captain might think.

"Stella Cooke," the dragonfly whispered from behind Tom's ear.

"Astonishing, isn't she?" Hardfleet said, struggling to control his emotions. "Miss Shirley Shoretree in Alexandria, awaiting the return of Mark Antony. What beauty. Acting in Shakespeare's *Antony & Cleopatra*."

"You don't see a small green dragon here in the bottom corner of the picture?"

Careful, Tom! Snow warned. *I think Loki has painted the portrait using Mimir Water!*

"Where?" the Captain asked, mystified, wondering what the English boy was gabbling about.

"Here!" Tom yelled. He leant forward, his finger stabbing at the figure of the dragon. Stabbing straight through the surface of the picture.

The yell faded in an instant. The Captain was left alone in his cabin. The moment Tom had touched the painting, he had disappeared - rucksack and all - through the surface, as if falling vertically down into a pool of water. There was no sign of the boy. The Captain wondered how the trick had been performed. Not only had Tom the English kid gone, he had taken the painting with him. Where once the portrait of Miss Shirley Shoretree had occupied pride of place in the wooden cabinet, there was nothing, only an open view of the cabin panelling.

What in the name of 'tarnation had happened?

PART III

17 Snow And Ice

Snowflakes had been falling on New York for days. Blizzards swept in from the north and dumped small mountain ranges of snow and ice between the city's skyscrapers. The streets were long ice-jams of frosted cars, trucks and vans.

In Central Park Zoo, the cool water of the harbour seals' pool had been turned into a skating rink while the water tank in the penguins' enclosure was a jigsaw of cracked, floating ice and running water. The waterfall in the polar bear compound had been paralysed to form a thick glacial curtain. The bears were in a den, secure behind bars while Thumper and Barney worked away inside the compound. They were shovelling out snow and ice.

"This is the coldest, hardest work we've ever had to do," moaned Thumper.

"It's cold but you get warm when you work. It's only cold when you stop," said Barney.

"We'd still be working on the site, warming ourselves by a wooden fire if you hadn't yelled at the foreman," said Thumper.

"We had to stand by Bigger," said Barney. "You agreed

at the time. It was the right thing to do."

"Where did he come from?" asked Thumper freezing, like a still, chill ice statue with a full shovel of snow in his hands.

"Who?"

"The kid standin' right behind you!"

Barney stuck his shovel in the snow and turned slowly. He saw a boy dressed like someone in a black-and-white photograph from the nineteenth-century. He wore a black waistcoat under a suit jacket with tails, matching trousers and nineteenth-century Southern-style boots. He had a stovepipe hat on his head and a big satchel slung over one shoulder.

The boy shook his head, dusted some snow from his frock coat and said,

"Sorry to intrude, gentlemen, but could you tell me where I am?"

"Why you're in Central Park Zoo, kid! Didn' ja know?" said Thumper.

"Central Park. That's New York?" asked the kid.

"The very same!"

"Thanks - and this is....?"

"The Polar Bear pit!" said Thumper.

Tom Wolfe pointed to the ladder that stretched from the bottom of the pit to the top of the wall above.

"And that's the way out?"

"The one and only!" said Thumper.

"Thanks again," said Tom as he began to climb the ladder. "By the way," he added. "Is New York always this cold in winter?"

"It is," said Barney. "Only it ain't."

"Ain't what?" said Tom, pausing halfway up his climb.

"Winter. It's the middle of summer!"

Tom chuckled. He knew when someone was pulling his leg.

"Don't laugh," Snow whispered. 'I have a horrible feeling that's no joke. He's telling the truth...or thinks he is!"

Before either man could move to prevent him, Tom had climbed up the ladder, scrambled over the compound wall and left.

"Well if that don't beat everything!" said Barney.

"What? A kid appearing out of nowhere and wearing a rig like he stepped out of *Huckleberry Finn*?" said Thumper.

"Nah. Not that."

"What then?"

"Didn't you see it? That kid's an exact copy of Bigger in miniature. The same as Bigger only smaller. A little Bigger in fact."

"Speaking of which...where is the big man?"

"Due along any time," said Barney. "In fact – he's late!"

Tom had walked a little way from the Polar Bear Pit when he stopped and looked about, taking in his surroundings.

"I believe they are the two men who were working with Thor on the construction site," Snow said. He was sitting on Tom's shoulder again.

"I know," Tom replied.

"Why didn't you ask where you might find him?"

"How would I explain that I know who they are and that they know Thor?"

Tom glanced round the zoo. Ice and snow had piled up in all directions forming thick dams between trees. Icicles as long and thick as Mammoth tusks grew from branches waiting to fall on unsuspecting visitors. Drifted waves of snow had piled up against the bars of cages, lapping over the high walls of the animal compounds. Over half the cages were empty.

"Animals must have been evacuated somewhere warmer," Tom said aloud.

"It would be prudent to decide what's to be done next," said Snow. "If that workman in the bear pit was being serious and this is summer then we're in trouble - the Ice Giants? I fear we may be too late."

Tom's shoulders locked. The Ice Giants! And what about Stella? What about Uncle Bernard? What about – he remembered the lies Loki had told. Nothing made sense. He had to check what was happening at home – Now!

"We need to use the Mimir mirror again!" he interrupted his own train of thought. Then he stepped over a fence and walked through deep snow until he reached a tall and wide monkey puzzle tree. He stooped down behind the trunk hidden from view and placed the mirror down flat on the snow. Quickly he prised open the clasp

"Time to see if it still works!" Tom said, nervously.

He passed one hand over the face of the mirror, using the same gesture that he had seen Loki use over the Mimir Pool on Asgard, unaware that Snow had given him a strange look the very moment he made the gesture. The surface of the mirror shimmered and then a clear image appeared.

In the centre of the picture was Asgard once again, still ringed by its lofty curtain walls but Tom saw at once that something had changed. The centre of the main outer wall had been breached. A hole wide enough for an army to pass through had been punched through the stone. A throng of Norse warriors had formed a shield wall to cover the breach in the wall. The shield wall curved out beyond the breach and faced a marching forest of Ice Giants and Frost Giants. They made a grinding sound as they marched, like the sound of icebergs sliding onto rock. The giants resembled silver fir trees made from jagged chunks of ice. Their shields and axes, their spears and swords glinted white and silver and light blue as the waning power of the sun glinted on a thousand frosty prisms. The horde of giants advanced on Asgard and the shield wall. A hail of ice spears flew through the air. The warriors stiffened their shield arms and held firm. The ice spears splintered against the shields and then the giants charged. They pressed up against the shield wall. Warriors' axes swung and cleaved. A thousand ice chunks broke on steel but still the giants pressed. The shield wall began to buckle. A gap appeared and one of the giants rushed towards Asgard only to be cut down by a fiery blue sword.

A god had stepped into the gap and then smashed forward from the shield wall into the giants. He was as tall as Thor with a helmet that covered most of his face. His skin was white as an egret feather and his sword was a broad single-handed knight's sword of blue steel with fiery red flames licking round its blade. On top of his helmet was perched a rooster and it cackled as the God ran at the Ice giants.

Tom recognised Heimdal. He had not given up. Slashing to left and right the God hacked down a dozen Frost Giants that fell into hundreds of pieces like ice cubes at a millionaire's party. The giants turned and fled. The rooster on Heimdal's helmet cackled and sang.

Heimdal had retreated from battle only long enough to rest and regain some of his strength.

"Golden comb is merry!" said Snow. "Heimdal's rooster! Heimdal has turned them back."

The giants fled along the road but halted when Heimdal ceased his chase.

"They've withdrawn to draw breath but they haven't fled," said Snow. "As long as the rooster Golden Comb remains happy we still have time to save the day."

"And if he isn't happy?" asked Tom.

"When Golden Comb crows a lament, it is the first of three signs that Asgard is about to fall and Ragnarok, the Last Battle will commence."

Tom knew all about Ragnarock, the mythic final battle that culminated in the death of gods and giants and men, culminating in the end of all things. He shook his head and pointed to the Mimir mirror. "Looks like Frost Giants aren't completely stupid. The attack was a diversion. Look."

Two more sets of melting icy footprints had reached the Rainbow Bridge before dripping off down the bridge to Earth.

Tom studied Heimdal as the Gods' Sentry trudged wearily back to the gate. After repulsing the most recent attack, his shoulders sagged with fatigue. His sword arm hung sore and tired at his side. In horror Tom realised that Heimdal had made his last charge. He was spent. The next time the Giants attacked they would surge over him and overwhelm Asgard. Heimdal would fight to the end but he was finished. The picture of defeat could not have been more vivid and clear.

"Three giants on earth," muttered Snow with eyes closed in horror. "That explains why it is Winter-in-Summer. *Three* Frost Giants! Twelve is all it takes to start another Ice Age. Hurry! We haven't much time!"

Tom pointed to the mirror. The image had changed again.

Danelaw school. The main corridor running between classes. Stella was walking against a tide of pupils going the other way. She had a pile of books under one arm and was running to get away from a red-faced boy who was in hot pursuit. He caught up with her just as she reached the door of the language lab which should have been sanctuary and safety. The boy was much bigger than Stella and stopped her in her tracks when he clamped a big, heavy hand tight on her shoulder.

"Vamp!" Tom yelled as soon as he recognised the face. "Again! What the hell are you playin' at? Stella made it clear she doesn't want to see you!" He fastened his mouth shut and clenched his jaw in agony, watching and listening to what he saw and heard in the mirror, grinding his teeth in frustration at being so helpless.

"Let go, Vamp!" Stella yelled.

"No way!" Vamp leered. "We're playing the wag!"

"What?" said Stella.

"We're bunking off for the day! I've got my brother's car, the Porsche, just like I said I would. I'm taking you out to the coast for the afternoon and then tonight we're going to the Guildhall to see Snake Venom. Loud and proud. The finest thrash-metal-punk band in all of Europe."

Stella tried to shake her arm free.

"You pea brain!" she snapped at him. "I'm not 'bunking off' with you! I'm spending the day at school. As usual. As normal. Not wasting any time with you – you pug!"

"That's what you think!" Vamp snarled and he clenched her shoulder in a steel grip as he began to drag her away from the classroom door. Vamp was one of the biggest boys on the rugby team. Stella didn't stand a chance.

"Let go, Maxwell!" she said loudly, using his first name to try and get his attention.

Rob Saunders stepped out of the classroom and blocked Vamp's path.

"Bunking off, Vanbrugh? Rob said. "With Stella? I don't think so!"

Tom could have cheered. That's what friends were for! That's what true friends were like. They stood by one another. They stood up for one another.

"Clear off, Saunders! It's none of your business!" Vamp snarled.

"Bunking off, Vanbrugh? Might not be any of my business -"

"'Bunking off'?" said Mr Porter stepping out from the language lab door. "'Mitching'? 'Playing hookey'. 'Skiving'? All synonyms for Playing Truant. Now that is *my* business." He grabbed Vanbrugh by the elbow and twisted. "Come along with me, Vanbrugh. It's a trip to the headmaster for you, m'boy!"

"Ow! Let go! I'll complain to my father. Then you'll be in trouble!"

"Complain all you like, Maxwell," said Mr Porter. "I'm sure the head will be only too happy to listen to your little list of grievances!"

And with that Porter led the struggling Vamp along the corridor towards the Head's office.

Stella turned to Rob with a huge smile of relief.

"Thanks, Rob," she said. "That ape was hurting me. He was trying to drag me out of school. Wanted to take me to the Snake Venom concert tonight."

"Can't have that," said Saunders.

"Course not, Rob Saunders," said Stella still smiling. "You're my knight in shining armour-"

But Saunders carried on talking as if he hadn't heard Stella's words.

"Can't have that," he said. "'Cause you're going to the Snake Venom concert with me not Vamp!"

Stella frowned. "Don't be silly, Robert. I'm looking for Tom this evening. You were going to help me! And what's happened to your eyes, Rob? Are you wearing contacts?"

"What do you mean, Stella?"

"Your eyes are blue, Rob. Why have they turned green? Tinted contact lens? What's that all about? Now - LET GO OF MY ARM! You're being *stupid!*"

"No. You're the one that's being stupid, Stella," and Saunders' bright green eyes had narrowed. They were cold and reptilian. "You're right about one thing. Vanbrugh isn't taking you to any concert. *I'm* taking you to see Snake Venom. We aren't wasting any more time looking for Tom. He is lost and gone forever. Ask Locke the gardener. He'll tell you. Tom Wolfe has gone away and isn't coming back."

The mirror's image wavered and faded. Tom had to blink his eyes rapidly to keep his sight clear. He felt as if he had been punched in the stomach. What a creep! Scumbag! Traitor! That wasn't friendship.

What are you doing Saunders?

It was the worst sort of betrayal. Who could you trust? He looked up from the blank mirror. Snow's face was hard and grim.

"This is Loki's work! It must be!" Tom snapped. "We

have to hurry now. There's no time to lose. Loki has tricked us! The God of Mischief is playing a double game. Hurry! We must find Odin! I have to get Stella away from that creep!"

He looked at the dragon for advice, for help.

What should we do now?

But for once the dragon looked confused. Worse, Snow seemed lost. Tom understood: perhaps he wasn't the only one to have been duped by the God of Mischief. Snow seemed all jumbled up inside as though rattled by a jangle of competing loyalties.

"I'll speak to Barney and Thumper," said Tom. "Ask them where Thor might be right now. No time to be subtle. I'll bluff a story. Something. Anything. We must find Odin NOW! And Thor will at least know where he is."

Tom climbed back over the fence and was about to set off walking back to the Polar Bear Pit when he saw a tall man striding towards him through the snow as if it were a mere dusting of icing sugar. The man had fair hair cropped short. It was the colour of flax, burned through with lightning streaks of bright red. Tom didn't think he had ever seen anyone as big. He was the height of a fir tree and as broad as a boulder. The man looked as if an almighty sculptor had taken the biggest athlete on Planet Earth and refashioned him with the hair and wardrobe of a rock singer. It was as if the biggest player from American Football had been fused with the biggest second row forward from Rugby Union and decided to sing lead vocals for the world's biggest, loudest rock band. In spite of the strange blend of images, he looked very familiar. The man was passing the spot where Tom stood frozen to the ground.

"Stop him!" Snow hissed loudly in Tom's ear. "That's Thor!"

Without hesitating Tom stepped in front of the giant who would have walked straight through him if Tom hadn't held out one hand in front of him and yelled, "Stop!"

The giant paused in mid-stride and looked down.

"Hello, young feller!" he said in a loud and hearty voice. "You want to watch your step. I could have bowled right through you without even noticing you were there!" said the giant. "Now if you'll excuse me – I must be on my way."

And the giant took a step round where the young boy stood in the snow.

"Wait! We should talk," said Tom. "I've got useful information! You need to hear this!"

"Ah, another grifter with something to sell, eh?" said the giant. "Sorry, son. You might be selling but I'm not buying!"

"But I know who you are!"

"Really?" said Thor, amused but showing little curiosity.

"Really!" Tom insisted.

The lost God then coughed in amusement. "Really? Well I'm afraid it will have to wait. I've got to join my pals. They got sacked because they helped me so I can't let them down!" and the giant made as if to continue on his way.

"Let him go," Snow whispered. "Thor never was the brightest star in the night sky. Before he gets away, ask him to give us directions to where he is staying."

"I appreciate you need to be going about your business, sir, and that you can't tarry here," Tom said. "But I do have some very important information for you. Give me your address here in the city and I'll drop it off for you to attend to later."

Tom handed the giant a notepad and pencil.

"Ah, some free trade samples to be delivered later?" said the lost god. "What might they be? Plastic brushes? A throwaway razor set?" and with a chuckle he wrote out the address of the hostel where he was staying with Odd. He handed the pencil and notebook back to Tom and set off again. He glanced back once and said, "You'd better wrap up warm, youngster. It's unseasonably cold and set to get colder!" And with that he strode out of sight.

Tom frowned. "That just about takes the biscuit. You can lead a horse to water..."

Snow buzzed out from behind the boy's ear and landed on his shoulder.

The dragonfly shivered and breathed out slowly. The air filled with hundreds of tiny snowy parachutes of light as if someone had blown a ripe dandelion clock scattering white downy seeds gliding in a spiral. The parachutes sparkled as they touched the dragonfly and a spiral of light and smoke sizzled about Tom's shoulder. He closed his eyes to avoid being blinded by the bright light. When he opened them again he saw that a large lizard was perched on his shoulder exactly where the dragonfly had been perched.

"Snow?" he said.

"The same," answered the lizard.

"I thought you couldn't appear on earth as a dragon. It blows away our cover-"

"Look again. Look more closely!"

Tom did look again. He saw a lizard clinging to his shoulder. It was about two feet long with a triangle-shaped head and scaly skin covered in short spikes.

"You still look like a dragon to me-"

"I've borrowed the shape of a Pagona. Another name for the bearded dragon lizard!" Snow hissed. "A *lizard* – not a dragon at all. Native to Australia, found in arid desert conditions – so not my ideal cup of tea – but a popular children's pet throughout Europe and America. Common enough not to invite attention.

"Now unless you have any objections we should find the hostel, the address of which Thor has scribbled on that piece of note paper you hold in your hand.

"Lead on, young Wolfe," said Snow. "And hurry! We don't have much time if the build up of snow and ice in the zoo is anything to go by!"

The dragon lizard crouched on Tom's shoulder as he rushed along the snow-filled pathway through the zoo's winter landscape. Glass-roofed pergolas connected the main exhibit areas. The glass had buckled under the press of snow. Vines that clambered up the pergola trellises were scorched by frost and cold. Tom passed buildings that normally housed Wyoming toads, tamarin monkeys and fruit bats – all empty, the animals all taken somewhere warmer. He saw a metal-barred cage, home to a solitary black raven perched on the branch of a synthetic ash tree.

Tom felt his gaze drawn towards the great black bird with its coal-black feathers, great wings and big black beak like a Tartar's curved war-sword. The bird watched him as he dashed along the crisp snowy path with the lizard clinging to his shoulder. The raven gazed at him and locked eyes. Not friendly. Not cruel. Ageless, timeless, the eyes were big opals, dark and jet and deep.

What? he thought. What in that bird's gaze was pulling at his mind like a magnet?

"Hurry! We must hurry! There's no time to waste!" Snow shouted.

Tom had warmed up. He was impervious to the cold. He had run all the way through the park and onto the street. He had warmed up and his brain was working again.

This is all taking too long! There has to be a quicker way!

He thanked the gods – if any of them were listening – that New York's yellow cabs were still running. He ran to the nearest cab and swung open the rear door.

"Where to?" said the cabbie.

Tom gave the address.

"That's a nice lizard you got there," the cab-driver said. "But nice lizard or not I can't take you there!"

"Why not?"

"The streets are frozen solid. It's grid-lock everywhere!"

Snow sat like a coiled spring on Tom's shoulder.

"The time for disguise is done," the dragon muttered.

Snow looked at the cab-driver.

"Give us directions and hurry!" It was a loud and brusque command.

"Whatchoo say?" said the cab-driver staring at the lizard.

"I'm a ventriloquist!" said Tom. "I can throw my voice!"

The driver did as he was told and delivered directions to the hostel.

Snow glanced out of the taxi cab's frosted window. Strange towering shapes were beginning to form in the distance, somewhere out on the freezing river. The lizard pulled a sour face and then shook its head.

"The time for skulking in the shadows is over," said Snow. "Deception and disguise are quite unnecessary now!"

"Say! That's some ventriloquism routine you got there, kid!" said the cab driver, mesmerised by Snow's words.

"Open the door!" said Snow. "And tell the cabbie to step out of the car. Give him three gold dollars. And, Tom?"

"Yes!"

"Stand clear of the car. I'm going to need some room!"

Tom clambered out of the car and onto the sidewalk. The cabbie stumbled alongside him. The cab-driver was scared. They both watched as the cat-sized lizard slid from Tom's shoulder, over the roof of the car and over the other side to land out of sight on the icy road. The cabbie leaned forward to catch a glimpse of where the lizard had gone. Tom grabbed his sleeve.

"Keep back!" he yelled at the driver.

The driver snatched his sleeve away angrily.

"Let go, kid! What the hell do you think you're playing at?"

A sour look licked over the cabbie's face. Then his eyes began to dance a foxtrot as he looked through the car window.

There was light. Blue, green, silver and white light erupted like neon geysers all round the body of the car. The air rippled with dazzling light. Sky blue light. Cold light. Very cold light. Freezing cold light. It hurt the eyes. Froze eyelids together.

When Tom opened his eyes he saw two things at once. The cabbie had crouched down in the snow between him and the car. On the other side of the car, was a creature the size of a Shetland pony with light-blue and silver-white scales, a long snaking neck with a head shaped like an anvil and long sinewy, leathery wings.

"Snow!" Tom yelped.

"At your service, young Wolfe. One Snow dragon...half-size. Now climb on my back. We're taking to the skies."

Tom climbed on Snow's back and in seconds the dragon was aloft. Tom hung on for dear life.

He removed the Mimir mirror from his rucksack.

Doesn't matter if I spill some now!

He watched as the glass filled with pictures. Stella close to tears in a blazing row with Rob. He tried to grab her again and she slapped Saunders full on the cheek. Stella storming off, calling out Tom's name. Heimdal flinging Frost Giants down from the walls of Asgard. And just then, Golden Comb stopped cackling and opened its beak getting ready to crow its final lament.

"Hang on!" said Snow as they soared over city blocks. "I know where I'm going.

18 Odd's Last Game Of Chess

Odd was in the day room sitting at a plastic table. He was looking down at the chess board. Hobble sat across the table from him and reflected on Odd's last move. The centre was quiet. The heating was only switched on at night and during the day the temperature in the hostel was almost as cold as on the streets. Hobble was amused. Old man Odd didn't seem to feel the cold. Hobble nodded at the curiously-carved wooden staff that Odd had brought with him today.

"That's a nice bit of furniture," he said, indicating the staff.

"I'd hidden it out of the way," said Odd. "I feel stronger with it in my hand. Don't know why."

"Not just stronger," said Hobble. "It's improved your chess game. You're playing much better than yesterday.

"Though not that much better." Hobble moved one of his knights and then said with a smooth grin, "Check!"

Odd ran the pad of one thumb along the ash staff.

"More than a little bit better," he said and moved one of his rooks. He knocked over Hobble's knight and said, "Checkmate!"

"How in blue blazes did you do that?" asked Hobble. "You haven't come close to winning a game all these days we've been playing!"

Odd picked up his rook, holding the ash staff in his left hand and the chess piece in his right.

"Funny that they are called rooks when they resemble

castles. They should look like a rook or a crow. Or perhaps like a raven." Odd's eyes misted over and he repeated the phrase. "Like a raven..."

"You're the one that's ravin', old man," said a cold, familiar voice. Someone had been standing in the lobby by the outer door, hidden from view, watching the last move of the game.

"Ravin' mad," the cold voice added and then Odd understood why the voice had sounded familiar. Slicer stepped into the room, followed by the three street thugs who had accosted him and Bigger near the East River: Ringtone, Jay-Q and Zee-Tab.

Hobble got to his feet.

"You aren't allowed in here unless you're homeless. You'll have to come back tonight to register."

"Cool it," Slicer said and showed Hobble the switch blade. He had flicked it open when he stepped into the room.

"Permit me to introduce myself. Slicer is my name and slicing is the game. I just love slicing. Cheese, salami, ham – but nothing slices as nice as human skin!"

Hobble didn't move.

"That old fool has something that he took from me. That fancy walking stick is mine. Now get out of my way or do I have to introduce you to the Slicer?"

Still Hobble didn't move.

Odd looked the thug in the eye and said, "I took it from you because it's mine. You seized it by brute force. I was simply recovering my property," Odd said calmly.

Cruel light glinted on the blade as Slicer took another step towards Hobble.

Hobble tried to charge the young thug who was wielding the knife. He was on his feet and moving but age had the better of him and the charge became a stumble. Slicer brushed him aside and turned towards Odd.

"See - I've got a new blade? Cuts even better than the one you took. You're gonna feel like salami when it goes in the meat slicer!" he hissed and the cold blade flickered towards the old man.

"Stop!"

A teenage brat burst through the main door followed by a white pantomime horse with a long neck and strange, scaly wings.

Slicer sniggered. A kid and a circus trick? Some kind of joke?

The brat was pointing at him. Slicer turned away from the old men.

"Hmm – guess what happens to innocent passers-by who stick their noses in? Looks like I'm goin' to be practisin' my slice technique on a few more suckers today," he said with a sick, twisted grin. Slicer stepped towards the boy.

"Freeze him!" The brat yelled. And then something strange happened. The pantomime horse blew a funnel of air at him and Slicer suddenly felt cold. Very cold. He began to shiver. His teeth chattered with cold. He shivered and shivered again. He shivered uncontrollably and then he stopped shivering. He didn't shiver because he couldn't move. He couldn't move at all. He was a frozen statue of ice.

"And the other three!" Tom shouted.

But Snow didn't need instructions. The instant Slicer had been immobilised, the dragon had swivelled and Ringtone, Jay-Q and Zee-Tab found what it was like really to be 'chillin'.

Tom looked quickly round the room. He had recognised Odin at once.

The old man looked as if the dragon had blasted *him* into a deep freeze along with Slicer and the thugs.

"Quickly, Snow!" said Tom. "You have to fly Odin and me to the zoo!"

"Impossible!" said the dragon. "Even if I were full-size that would be difficult."

"Take Odin then. I'll wait here!"

"Still impossible. He might be old but he's a big man. Far heavier than he looks and far heavier than you. He's Father of the Gods for heaven's sake. Have you any idea how much gravity is involved in that? I wouldn't make it! What are you trying to do?"

"It would take too long to explain."

What could he do? He knew he had the answer. He had the remedy. He could undo all the damage but how to make it happen? Then he knew he really did have the answer.

"Mohamed and the mountain!" Tom said in a loud voice. "Or – we were in a hole but now we've stopped diggin'! Fly me to the zoo! Leave Odin!" he said. "It's urgent!"

Leaving Slicer and his fellow thugs frozen in blocks of ice, and Odd, Hobble and the other wanderers frozen in a state of profound shock, Tom dashed out into the street followed by the snow dragon. Tom climbed onto Snow's back and after two or three warm-up, or to be more accurate, cool-down, flaps of its wings, the dragon swept into the air and flew high above the ice-bound city. They were soon soaring over the zoo.

"Fly that way," Tom said and pointed to a row of cages. In one a raven perched alone on a synthetic tree.

"There!" said Tom, pointing again.

The dragon glided to earth and with a swoosh landed in a pile of deep snow. Tom saw a pile of tools lying by one of the cages. A workman had been driving wooden stakes into the ground ready to build a fence. A large post-hammer lay on top of the tools.

"I thought about the riddle in the scroll!" Tom said to Snow. "At first I couldn't unravel it. Thought it was a load of crap! Loki deceiving us. Sending us on a wild goose chase. Then I really thought about it...and at last I've got it! Listen!

" - pass each test,
And on the third, free the bird,

Release the cage, earn Odin's wage,
The bird unbind, free Odin's mind.'"

Tom picked up the hammer and ran to the cage containing the raven.

"Trust me!" he bellowed in the loudest voice he could muster. "I mean no harm! I'm here to set you free!" He swung the hammer and slammed it into the padlock that held the cage door secure. Thung! It clanged against the lock and barely dented it. He tightened Meginjore, the magic belt of strength, the belt that had increased his strength ten-fold while digging the ditch in Ancient Greece and he smote the lock three times more but still nothing happened. The lock buckled but did not break.

Oh, Stella! he thought. *What am I going to do?*

"From what you have told me about that girl," Snow said. "I think she would tell you to use your brains as well as your muscles, young man!"

Tom growled. "Crabbin' fang! You're so bloody annoying!" he growled again. Then he grinned. "So bloody annoying and so bloody right!" He stood next to the cage door.

"Come here please, Snow," he said and the dragon padded over to stand next to him.

"Purse your lips and blow the tightest, coldest, breath of freezing air possible into and over the padlock. Please."

The snow dragon practised, puffed out its cheeks like a trumpet player, licked its lips, formed them into a very tight and tiny "O" then blew a long slender javelin of icy air over the lock. Tom tightened the Belt of Power another notch. He ran at the padlock and swung the hammer with all his might. The metal lock smashed into a dozen pieces. The gate swung open.

"Munnin I presume? Odin's Memory?" he said to the big black bird. "Tom Wolfe at your service." Although he had never spoken to mythical ravens before he guessed that flowery ceremonial language might just do the trick. It was all he could do to stop himself from bowing.

"If you wish to be reunited with Odin, your Lord and Master, Odin the All-seeing, Father of Asgard – I'd suggest that you climb on my shoulder.

The raven's eyes were deep, dark pools. Tom could not fathom the intelligence that loomed in those depths. The bird made no sound. It flew from the cage and landed on the English boy's shoulder. Its claws gripped. It had a new perch.

With that Tom climbed onto Snow's back. The dragon raised its wings and swept into the air.

Slicer shook his head to free it of frost and icicles. His arms though unbearably cold could move again. The ice had melted enough for him to free his right arm and then he had deftly wielded the switch-blade to chip away the ice and broke free. Someone was going to pay for the pain he had endured. Someone was going to get hurt. Cut up real bad. Knife blade leading he stepped towards the old man with the fancy walking stick.

"This time you really are gonna' have the salami experience!" he snarled at Odd.

But at that very moment, the entrance door was flung open again and a big black bird flew into the room. With only two beats of its broad jet-black wings it powered over Slicer's head and landed on Odd's shoulder. The raven settled onto the God's arm as if finding a favourite perch that had been lost for a while. Bright burning coals lit the old man's eyes and he smiled an ancient and ageless smile. He held the ash staff in both hands. He stood up and placed his feet a yard apart.

He smiled.

"Very interesting," he said, in a quiet voice. "What a wonderful thing is memory."

Then he thrust the ash staff out in front of him, parallel to the ground, closed his eyes and croaked a guttural crow-cough of words that sounded like oak and ash branches crackling. Light and sound erupted as if a volcano had blown its top.

And Slicer flew out the front door and high up into the air. Up and up and higher and higher in a giddy parabola he flew and then suddenly down and down again, he landed with a very cold splash in the grey, cold water of the East River. He was followed by Ringtone, Jay-Q and Zee-Tab, all scooped up by an invisible hand after the old man had waved his crazy walking stick at them. Half-a-dozen elderly fishermen were standing on a stretch of antique quay that ran near the river. They had cast their lines for most of the day without a nibble. It had been so quiet and so cold that they were all on the point of nodding off. They snapped out of their half-dozing reverie when they heard a voice, very loud and very human, wailing as it sailed in a high arc over their heads, "Oh Nooooooo! Not agaaaaaaaaaaaaaaaaaaaaaaaaiin!!"

The solitary wailer hit the water with a loud splash and was followed by three more in quick succession, so close together that they issued a shriek that sounded like an hysterical choir trying desperately to scream in three-part harmony. The shriek ended in three loud splashes.

Odin peered around the room. His gaze rested on Tom and the dragon lizard. A large forefinger pointed at Tom.

"You, young Wolfe, come here and stand where I can see you. And Snow – I know who you are of course. Come here and stand beside Tom. Both of you. Here – right in front of me so I can take a good look at you. And don't move."

Odin's voice filled the large room.

"And that goes for all of you here. No one move. Be still. I have something else to do."

Odin glanced about the room. Then he peered at the wall and then he peered through the wall. His gaze pierced the wall and in one bound leapt across the city to the zoo. His one, good, all-seeing eye took in the polar bear compound, the cage with the broken lock that had jailed one of his ravens, Munnin, the raven that held his memory. Where was Munnin's companion: Huggin or Thought?

There will be time enough to attend to that, thought the Father of the Gods. *More pressing matters first!*

His gaze pierced to where a tall, broad-shouldered Bigger was striding along the path in search of his work mates. A voice that would crack rocks and make mountains shiver boomed out over the zoo.

"Thor, God of Thunder, Lightning and Storm. Stop! Remember who you are!"

Bigger or Thor, as he now knew himself to be stopped in his tracks. His face reflected a myriad hailstones of light. Memory raced back into his eyes.

Odin's eyelids closed and he looked to Asgard. He saw Heimdal locked in combat with the three Frost Giants: Rock-Smiter, Evil-Fang and Iceberg-Grinner. He saw the Guardian of the Bridge stumble and his helmet fall. He saw Evil-Fang grab a fistful of Heimdal's hair and pull his head back just as Rock-Smiter raised his club and prepared to brain Asgard's Sentry. He saw Golden Comb fill its lungs.

Once again the Father of the Gods raised the ash stick. A storm of red, yellow and blue light swept about the God of Thunder and in a breath he was transported from New York flying on a hover-course inches above the surface of the Rainbow Bridge to Asgard. He landed with both feet planted firmly on the ground, landing as a warrior should, ready on the instant for combat. Odin's eyelids closed again and he appeared to be lost in concentration like a virtuoso violinist playing a fine piece of music on a Stradivarius. Lying lost among a pile of tools, old weapons and garbage in a yard near the workshop of Weyland, the Gods' blacksmith, a large hammer rustled. A very heavy object like a war hammer looks most unusual, peculiar or eccentric even when it rustles. This one felt strange. It was more used to smiting things, to smashing and breaking things. It rustled like a badger coming out of hibernation.

If it had had arms it would have stretched them out and yawned. If it had hands it would have scratched its neck and back and yawned. But it did none of those things for this was Mjolnir, Thor's war hammer and it suddenly remembered who and what it was, snapped upright like a fence post, sprang up and balanced on the base point of the handle and then shot through the air like a missile, faster than sound, weaving round anything innocent that stood in its way, breaking and bursting through anything evil, sour or unpleasant that crossed its path and in less than a god's paired heartbeats it flung itself into Thor's outstretched right hand.

Bigger had been transformed. In place of his high visibility waistcoat and strengthened plastic builder's hat were a stout metal and leather breastplate and a simple steel cone war helmet. Thor grinned a grim grin. These were the tools that he understood. Far more than rivets and pneumatic hammers. War hammer and War helm. The grim grin settled as his jaw clenched.

Golden Comb stifled its lament just as the harsh tune was about to gush. The bird breathed quietly. The cockerel knew what was about to happen.

With the sound of a sonic boom, the God of Thunder flung himself across space and time and smashed Rock-Smiter between the eyes. The giant rolled over and said, "Ice Cold. Then Thaw. Then Cold." And then fell forward, face biting the frosted ground.

Thor's arm swung the other way and like a tennis player executing a perfect backhand, he clubbed Evil-Fang to the ground.

Iceberg-grinner had seen enough, turned tail and fled from Asgard, gobbling up the ground between the home of the gods and the Frosty Mountains of Jotunheim. The mountains now seemed a long, long way away and his knobbly knees and wobbly feet ached. He hoped to reach Flattjord and then blunder across it to the Frosty Mountains before the Thunder God could thunder-clap eyes on him.

Heimdal placed his right foot on solid land and leaned on his sword. The God of Thunder heaved a shoulder under the Sentry's arm and helped him to his feet.

"Better you had left me to perish, Thunder God," said Heimdal. "My hearing is gone. I can barely see... what manner of sentry would I be in the future?"

Thor ignored the Gods' Watchman and instead handed him a slice of apple.

"What's this?" asked Heimdal. "You think I simply need to eat my Five-a-Day and I will wield a sword again?"

"Just try it," said Thor. "It isn't just any old apple."

Heimdal bit into the slice. He felt some of the old vigour surge through his veins.

"What is it?"

"Wotan apple," said Thor.

"You didn't use to have a lisp, Thunderer," said Heimdal gruffly and with a wink before taking another bite from the apple.

"Eh?" said Thor.

But Heimdal remembered that Thor wasn't the sharpest pencil in the Asgard pencil case and instead relished the return of his own powers.

"Wotan's Golden Apples, tended to by the fair Freja, eh?" said Heimdal. Another bite from the apple and he felt energy surge and pulse in sinew and thew. He could feel his old sense of humour return. He turned his head slightly like a wartime radio operator. Slowly turning a dial, tuning into the BBC. Left a bit, left a bit. Right and then he had it. Yes - there was a Herdwick sheep in a field near Keswick and its fleece was growing. It was growing lustily. He could hear it.

When Thor saw that Heimdal was well again, he turned, hefted his hammer and began to run in the direction of Flattjord, the great plain that led to the Frosty Mountains and Jotunheim.

"Where are you going?" Heimdal asked.

Thor pointed Mjolnir towards a place on the plain where a straggling crew of Ice Giants were running to catch up with the main army.

"Hot pursuit," said Thor. "Giants to hammer!"

Heimdal shook his head. Partly to clear it and also to acknowledge that the God of Thunder had spent so long in New York he was beginning to sound like a native.

Odin's eyelids closed once again. Asgard was safe. The Frost Giants were in mad, crazy-eyed, pell-mell flight, chased by his son Thor, whose blood was up. Heimdal was rejuvenated and the Rainbow Bridge was secure. Odin opened his eye again. The first thing he saw was the boy and the Frost Dragon standing obediently in front of him, exactly as he had ordered.

The Father of the Gods began to smile.

"Thomas Wolfe," he said in a voice that resonated around the room. "You will not yet be able to understand how pleased I am to see you. More pleased than you can possibly imagine."

Tom was trying very hard not to blush with happy embarrassment. The King of the Norse Gods saying that he was very pleased to see him was a far greater compliment than the Rugger Coach telling him he had thrown a superb spin pass to the Inside Centre!

"And Snow," the Father of the Gods continued, "You have done well. I am most pleased with you too, Frost Dragon." Odin's gaze swept the room. Hobble was sitting in an armchair, his mouth opening and closing like a fish catching flies. A handful of tramps were scattered round the lounge. Odin knew them all. Couldn't see what he was looking for. And then he did.

"Have a look round this room, young Wolfe," said Odin. "Tell me when you find what I'm looking for."

Tom was puzzled.

"How do I know what to look for if you don't tell me what it is I'm lookin' for urm - sire?" he asked, adding enough respect to his tone of voice that he assumed would be right when addressing the King of the Gods. And to mask his growing impatience.

More riddles? Do they ever stop?

"Use your eyes," Odin instructed him. "And this." He pointed to his head. "Observe."

Tom stepped away and began to move slowly round the large Day Room, followed by Snow, still pony-size.

It was a big room laid out with an assortment of second-hand furniture that had all seen better days. The Day Room looked like any lounge in any hostel for society's less fortunate members, tramps and travellers who had lost their money and their way. It had threadbare sofas, armchairs with horsehair starting out of the back, one-armed armchairs, chipped coffee tables and dining chairs with rickety backs. It was a "Drop-in-Centre" and the Day Room was half empty.

Tom stopped in front of Hobble. He instantly thought of something cheeky and sarcastic to say: Does your toothpaste double as paint-stripper, sir? Not placing any strain on the city's hot water supplies are we? Do your clothes stand up in court even when you aren't wearing them?

But he didn't. He had learnt something about manners and respect for his fellow creatures since Locke the gardener had whisked him to Asgard. Besides he had seen Odin playing chess with this broken-down, old man earlier and that must count for something.

Tom bent down to where Hobble sat by the chess board and reached out his hand.

"I'm Tom Wolfe, sir and I believe you're quite a chess player."

Hobble smiled a crooked smile and shook his hand.

"I beat old Odd in ninety-nine games straight 'til today when he thumped me in eleven moves without blinking."

"A pleasure to have met you, sir," said Tom, "and I'm

sure you'll beat him again."

"He will when hell freezes over," Odin murmured to himself. Losing to a mortal at chess was only one of the returned memories from his recent bout of amnesia that he would have to work at rubbing out. He would work at it though. He had eternity to work on it.

Tom moved on from Hobble. He looked at the cheap prints and the coffee tables, the busted sofas and the stained linoleum.

One tramp sat on a chair with his feet gathered under him, asleep. Another lay curled in the same posture on another chair alongside.

There were a dozen people in the room. Most were asleep or snoozing. There was nothing to see. What had Odin meant him to do?

'Observe'? What's it mean? He looked at the shabby fixtures, the furniture and windows. Nothing. Absolutely nothing. Nothing remarkable. Nothing caught his attention.

An archway led to the kitchen. A tall tramp was standing by the archway, his bowed back echoing the curve of the arch. He was stooped as if to make himself look smaller, inconspicuous, and small. Reassuringly shrunken, like any old tramp, broken-down. Humbled. As if he wasn't a threat.

And that makes him a threat!

Tom glanced back into the room and walked towards the archway.

As he glanced back he called in the cheekiest tone he could muster, "Fancy a cuppa, Odin?"

The King of the Gods blinked at the cheeky question but before he had time to answer or rebuke the boy, Tom had reached the entrance to the kitchen and as he knew he would, caught the tall tramp, by surprise. The tall man, shocked out of his pose by the cheeky brat glanced straight at him as he approached. Tom looked into a pair of the brightest lime-and-grass-green eyes he had ever seen. He knew those eyes.

"Loki!" he blurted.

The God of Mischief and Evil, straightened his back, like a leaf unfurling in sun and rain, and drew himself up to his full height.

"Fool! Do you think I'll tarry to suffer Odin's Justice?" He was poised ready to spring away in a moment.

But Tom's reflexes – already keen - had sharpened after his escapades in Ancient Greece and Old-Time America.

"Freeze him!" he hissed to Snow and the dragon spat a plume of air on the God, freezing him on the spot. Snow continued to blow glacial blasts until an iced snowman in the shape and form of the God of Mischief stood by the entrance to the kitchen.

"Well done, young Wolfe," said Odin calmly, as though he witnessed one of his fellow gods being dipped in a deep freeze every day. "That is another test you have passed today. Now stand back while I rearrange the furniture. I think I'm going to convene what the Iceland Vikings call a Thing, sometimes called a Ding in Germany. You'll be more familiar with the term Hearing or Trial."

19 Trial Without Jury

All the tramps, with the exception of Hobble, had quit the Day Room. Tom scooped out a handful of gold coins from his knapsack. He extracted a promise from each of the knights of the road that they wouldn't buy any strong drink. Then he handed out the golden bounty.

"Have a coffee at the diner along the street. If you make for a booze parlour the lizard with the chillin' breath will find you and turn you into something you'd usually see in a glass just before whisky was poured over it."

Odin had wafted the ash staff over his head in two dramatic passes and a small tornado rearranged the furniture so that he and Tom sat facing one another on either side of the Loki ice statue in the middle of the Day Room.

"Sit back, young Wolfe," said the All-Father. "Make yourself comfortable. I have a story to tell you."

Odin pointed at the ice figure.

"As you observed, Tom: just before he tried to flee, Loki was over there under the arch by the kitchen. What prompted you to look more closely at that man in particular?" Odin asked.

"He was a tall man trying to look small," said Tom with a frown. "Lots of tall men do that. I've even seen tall boys do it at school. Bainbridge and Clarke are second row forwards in my school rugby team. They're only fourteen but Bainbridge is over six feet tall and Clarke isn't far behind. They both stand with a stoop – apart from when they're actually on the rugby field. That's different. On the pitch they stand full height, shoulders back and head held high. But at school? All the time they're just trying to look normal. Trying to be average. To blend in. Doing their best not to be outstanding. It's what everybody tries to be like at school. Don't stand out. Don't draw attention to yourself or you'll be noticed. Then you're more likely to be picked on. To be bullied."

"It's hard to believe, but even big guys get bullied. Especially if they're tall and lanky."

"How does that explain your noticing Loki?" Odin asked in a quiet voice.

"He wasn't just stooped. He was bent right over. Not just trying to look normal or average. It was as if he was trying to shrink right down inside his boots. I wasn't sure at first so I decided to catch him off guard. That was why I asked you in the cheekiest, stroppiest voice going if you wanted 'a cuppa tea'. Loki isn't used to hearing the King of the Gods used as a target for cheek. It threw him off guard and meant I could get close to him very quickly. And then I saw his eyes. I haven't seen another creature with eyes like Loki. They are greener than grass. More green than limes and emeralds. They are the colour green itself. The spirit of green."

"Very good. That was good observation and then working out a way to get close to him without scaring him off. Good tactics and clever planning. Observation. Tactics. Planning. All good detection skills." Odin said. "I shall ignore the cheek as a tactical diversion. This time." The warning was clear.

Do it again at your peril!

"Loki has been fulfilling his nature as Master of Mischief and Evil. He waited until I had set off on one of my Midgard-gadabouts. He picked his time and kidnapped the crow, Munnin. My Memory. The bird was smuggled to Earth and hidden in a cage in a zoo, in one of the biggest cities in Vinland. With my memory addled, my powers waned. All the gods began to fail. Loki cast a spell that fuddled Thor's mind. Thor forgot who he was. Heimdal became deaf and needed spectacles. The Frost Giants threatened Asgard. But I need to know 'Why?'

Loki has done some silly things and some evil things. He plays tricks and is a mischief-maker. He is capable of foul things. The gods never allow him to forget that he caused the death of Baldur as surely as if he had slain him with a knife.

But he has never done anything that would imperil his own hide. This latest trick brought Asgard to the brink of destruction. Loki himself would perish if Asgard was lost to the Ice Giants. What do you make of that, young Wolfe?"

Tom shook his head, "No idea, sir," he said. He wished Snow was dragonfly-size again so he could ask, *Is it sir or sire?* He really had no idea how to address the King of the Gods.

But Odin spoke first.

"What is your opinion of all this, Dragon?" he asked.

"Nothing occurs to me, My Lord," said Snow.

"Then it is time for Loki to speak," said Odin and he clutched the ash staff and waved it above the ice statue while humming in a strong baritone voice. It was a soft melody that rose and fell. The melody was a Spell of Warming.

The ice on Loki's head and torso thawed, melted and ran down to form a puddle on the floor. He remained frozen in a solid block of ice from his navel to his ankles.

"Wake up, Mischief-Maker," Odin said and then the baritone voice rumbled. "In normal circumstances I would wait until the accused could be transported to Gladsheim where I would sit in judgement and attend to your case along with twelve other gods. But these are not normal circumstances. Thus I declare: let The Thing begin. In other words: Court is now in session. The case of the

Gods versus Loki."

Odin looked into Loki's bright green eyes. The Father of the Gods cleared his throat and began to speak.

"It is our opinion that you, Loki, intended to murder The God of Thunder and myself.

"That you stole Munnin, my memory so that Asgard's strength would fail as my vigour failed. I would have been lost forever, or worse, either killed by some street thug with a knife or doomed to wander earth forever with my simple, giant son.

"That you struck a bargain with your cousins, the Ice Giants to divide and share Asgard and Midgard between you.

"That you also struck one or more bargains with the Lords of Chaos.

"That all your plots and schemes were intended to remove me from Asgard, clearing the way for you to assume the throne.

"What do you have to say for yourself, Mischief-Master? Why did you endanger all of Asgard and Middle-Earth?"

Loki looked like a boxer who had been hit with a haymaker picking himself up from the canvas. He shook his head to settle his scrambled brain. He cleared his throat and looked about him. From the waist down he was held in a block of ice. He couldn't move his big toe let alone take flight. He was trapped.

The God of Mischief gazed back at Odin.

"All-Father," he began with a sickly smile.

"Don't try to ingratiate yourself with me, Loki. I know who you are. I know what you have done in the past and what you are capable of doing in the present and future!"

"Lord, King of the Gods, Master. It was an innocent jape. For years you had said you wished to have an authentic time on Earth. As a real *traveller*. Not an immortal *tourist*. I simply arranged the holiday of a lifetime."

"Humour could not be more out of place, mischief-maker!" Odin interrupted. "Be advised: treat this seriously. Your life is at risk. These charges – if proved – lead only to one thing: your death."

"All-Father," Loki began again in a whining voice. "No harm was done. Indeed I knew all along that no harm would be done. I kidnapped Munnin as you said and hid the bird here on Midgard. I knew that you would weaken and that Asgard would be in danger-"

"Be warned!" Odin said sternly. "You have already condemned yourself to exile by this admission. Be careful and take heed lest you condemn yourself to die!"

"I knew that Asgard would be endangered but I also knew with the same conviction and certainty that Asgard would be saved. I knew that young Tom Wolfe would come to the rescue."

"How could you *know* that, cur?" Odin said scornfully. "He's a boy. And a mere mortal boy at that!"

Loki waited, took a deep breath and after a pause that tightened the tension in the Day Room he said carefully and in a low, even voice, "I knew because of all that I know about him. I knew because he is no *ordinary* boy. I knew because he, Thomas Storm Torsson Wolfe is the son of a god!"

"Explain yourself!" said the All-Father after sitting for what felt like half-a-lifetime in contemplation.

"A decade and a half ago or so, you and your son, Thor, were on Earth together on yet another of your interminable Midgard-gadabouts. You became separated. Thor went on a walkabout of his own. He found himself in Norway, in Oslo to be precise. He met a beautiful, young woman, a brilliant Medieval scholar from the North of England, Freya Thompson. She was attending a conference in the city. He fell in love with her. But of course if he had said that he was Thor, God of Thunder, she'd have fled in fear from a lunatic - so he introduced himself as Tor Odinson-Wolfe, a fisherman!"

Tom could not breathe. It felt as if all the air had been

vacuumed from the room. His shirt felt tight at his neck.

"Nonsense!" said Odin.

"Ah but do you *know* that it is nonsense?" said Loki coolly and he cast a look of pure defiance at the Gods' Overlord. Odin fell silent.

"Tor Odinson-Wolfe married Freya Thompson, sister of your old friend Bernard Thompson. And they both drowned when the boat on which they were sailing sank in a storm."

The frown that had settled on Odin's face had settled into a grim scowl.

"But," Loki continued, "I have never heard of a storm engulfing the God of Thunder. Thor *is* Storm, the spirit and essence of storm. How could Thor be engulfed by a storm at sea?" Loki's voice rose as he posed the question.

The scowl on Odin's face deepened.

"I don't like the turn that this story has taken," said Odin.

Loki looked down at his own fingers. He studied his long, dragon-claw-like fingernails, as if the answer lay somewhere like a speck of dirt on his fingertips.

"I am Loki, God of Mischief and Pranks. Unrivalled in the arts of shape-changing-"

"Be warned," said Odin in a voice that would have been the envy of a High Court Judge. "I do not like the way this tale is unfolding."

"I have on several occasions adopted the shape of my nephew, Thor," Loki said, the challenge in his voice out in the open now. "Often visiting Midgard at the same time that you and Thor were embarked on a Midgard-gadabout. After my nephew had met and wooed her in Oslo I then appeared to Freya Thompson in the form and shape of Thor, calling myself by the name he had used when he first met her. I for a while that included Freya Thompson's wedding night, I was Tor Odinson Wolfe! The real Tor Odinson Wolfe was in a drinking den with his cronies. He had left his wife alone on her wedding night!

"We had an exceptionally pleasant evening together," Loki murmured.

Tom was horrified. Speechless. He glanced at Odin but even the King of the Gods seemed lost for words.

"Sometime later, a year or two perhaps, I repeated the trick. It was when Freya and her husband and their baby son, young Tom Wolfe here, were returning home on a small boat after a trip to Norway. Tor or Thor to give him his correct name had repaired to the wheelhouse to share some yarns with the crew. I seized that moment to assume his shape and dawdle one more time with his wife. And I wanted to have a look at the baby. It had occurred to me: I did not know who had fathered the brat."

"How dare you slander a virtuous woman who is unable to defend her reputation? And how dare you impugn this innocent young man's fatherhood?" Odin scowled. "And how is it in any way relevant to your defence of your evil and reckless actions?"

"The woman's reputation should be unaffected. As far as she was aware on each and every occasion, she lay in bed with her husband.

"I was there when the storm brewed. I was there, comforting Freya. She was terrified. Thor thought it was all wonderful fun. I suspected at the time that he had whipped up the storm in a moment of play while he was drunk with his chums on board.

"I had the presence of mind to save the child. I clambered on deck. I then assumed the shape and form of Snaffler, the green-skinned fire dragon. I flew into the air, swooped down and plucked Tom Wolfe from his mother's arms and flew back to England. The foolish mortals on the fishing boat thought they'd seen a helicopter!

"I was unable to return in time to save anyone else. In my defence, I knew that a rescue craft was on its way," Loki paused, weighing his words carefully before continuing. "Besides," he said. "I assumed that the God of Thunder would come to his senses. I assumed the storm would abate. But perhaps he was too drunk to understand what he had unleashed.

"And how is this relevant to my defence? It is crucial to my defence," said Loki coolly. "It is why I stole Munnin and left you and Thor stranded and brain-dead on Midgard. Why Heimdal had to be weakened and Asgard in peril."

"Why?" Odin stormed.

"I had to test young Wolfe under circumstances of the most dire threat. I had to threaten Asgard and Midgard, his Uncle and his friends, the girl Stella above all. I had to find out whose son he is. I had discovered some of the old portals that have existed on Asgard and Earth since Earth and Space and Time began. Portals that opened to the Chaos that remained from The Beginning of Time, after Ymir created the Earth and Order and separated Order from Chaos. Once Wolfe passed through the first Portal, a set of challenges awaited him. The challenges would test whether he used his brain or his sinews to win. I had passed through each of the portals weeks ago when I prepared my plot and set the props in place for the tests. I engaged with Chaos and made a bargain so that young Wolfe would go through each portal and reach a pre-ordained destination in time and place. I hurled him to earth with a minimum of tools and help. I gave him Mimir water held in a mirror and a flask; Meginjoro, Thor's Belt of Strength as well as a Belt of Invisibility that he chose not to use; some yew darts that he wrongly believed to be magic and a snow dragon as aid and companion. Whose son is he? Mine or Thor's? He is the son of a god and I knew he would prevail. Knew he would save Asgard and Earth. And he did. But I had to know *whose* son is he?"

"And how would that become apparent? How would that be proved?" asked Odin, barely able to contain his anger

"By the way he solved the problems," said Loki. "Did he use his brain or the power of his arm? Did he reach for the subtle blade of reason or the hammer?"

"And your conclusion?"

"He raised the battle-hammer. Mjolnir flew in his hand. Only Thor can raise Mjolnir. The hammer only goes to Thor. He smashed the lock that held the divine raven using only an earthly hammer and the Belt of Strength. Only Thor's whelp could achieve such a feat. He threw a plain dart whittled from yew wood eight feet and hit a target the size of a small coin. A plain dart never thrown before, untested and he hit a minute target. Thor is supreme at games among the gods – only his cub could have hit that mark. I told Wolfe the dart was magic. I lied. His life depended on him hitting that target and hit it he did. A fourteen year-old boy dug more Greek earth than any commoner, nobleman or trained soldier could in the same time. Hercules would have been proud of such a feat of strength. He is Thor's son. I have proved it beyond a shadow of a doubt."

Tom's jaw froze. Not because he was astonished to learn that he was the son of the Thunder God but because he was sure that Loki was lying. How could he tell? Was it because he, Tom, was made of mischief himself and knew its scent? He was convinced that Loki was lying. Why? To cause more mischief? To continue the test? He did not know why Loki was uttering those words. Of one thing, and one thing only, Tom was certain: faced with each and every test he had used his brains. He had used brute strength rarely and sparingly. He had solved almost every tricky test using reason and imagination. Even breaking the lock that held the ravens – admittedly he had used an "earthly hammer" – he was unaware that he might be acquainted with any other sort, but he had used his knowledge of science – picked up in a school physics class to be precise - to know that super-cooled steel if cold enough, would become brittle. Every challenge had been achieved by using his brain. Why – he had even solved the final part of the riddle to find the raven and without any help!

Stella would have been proud of him. But that did not make him proud of himself.

It made him the son of Loki, God of Mischief and Evil.

Odin took a deep breath.

"A paternity test," he said, as if he were speaking private thoughts aloud. "Almost impossible to believe. Only the God of Mischief could muster as his legal defence that he put *All of Creation* at risk in order to find out if a rugby-playing school pupil was his own son or the offspring of his nephew, the Thunder God."

Loki held up a hand.

"If I may speak once more in my own defence, sire," he said.

"I am tempted to deny you the opportunity to say anything further, Mischief-Maker. Your defence already condemns you. Reckless. Reckless. Reckless. It is the first judgement of this Thing that you are already condemned to banishment. But go ahead, Loki. The floor is yours. We shall be interested to see if - in this hole that you have made - your defence involves even more use of the spade than young Wolfe's efforts in Greece!"

"I said I knew that the world of gods and men was safe because Tom is the son of a god. I merely wished to find out which god was his father. But I didn't simply cast him loose into a hell in which he could possibly have perished."

Odin raised an eyebrow at that claim.

"To use a phrase much loved of the young people of Midgard: *I was There For Him*!"

Odin snorted. "I am familiar with the phrase from some of my more recent Gadabouts: It is popular among young people. Proceed, Loki and explain to the court" – here the Lord of the Aesir indicated himself, Tom and Snow – "how you were '*There for Him*' "

"As well as the magic tools I furnished the riddle-scroll. The Norse excel at riddles – making and solving. I knew the brat would prevail.

"Finally: I can adopt the shape of the Thunder God," Loki said in brash pride. "How difficult would it be for the God of Mischief to take the form of an Undrone... or even a snow-white snow dragon, no bigger than a Shetland pony? I had already borrowed the shape of the green dragon, Snaffler to save him years ago when he was a baby. It was just as easy to imitate Snaffler's cousin, a snow dragon with a soft heart!"

"Impossible!" spluttered Snow. "I never left Tom's side!"

"But is that true, ice lizard? Was it true when the Roc attacked? Was it true when Tom cleared Augeas' stables? When you – in the form of a dragonfly - took a lunch-break? I think you'll find that the creature supporting Thor's son was a red-eyed, sometimes green-eyed dragon, with green scales – your cousin, Snaffler who has been retained by me for longer than I care to remember!"

Snow looked away. Some dragons belonged to Loki, including Snaffler. But the idea of the God of Mischief actually taking the form of a dragon? The ice dragon was confused. God law and gods lore was complicated. Better to leave this to the All-Father. He would know what was true and what was lie or mischief.

Odin shook his head again. "It's still unbelievably irresponsible. Reckless. Even by the standards of the Lord of Mischief. As for your defence: you have sullied the reputations of innocent people, some of whom are no longer here to defend themselves. You put the fate of the Universe at risk for what? To satisfy your curiosity?"

"I had to know if Wolfe is my son!" Loki said bitterly. "He is not. He is Thor's brat!"

"Your admission effectively means your plea is "Guilty. It only remains to decide – is there anything in mitigation: were your actions Evil or ill-considered. Mischief or Malice? Is this the work of the Earl of Evil or the Prince of Pranksters? Does this merit a term in prison or exile? Or does it deserve Death?" Odin tugged at his beard.

Odin continued to speak as if he were a High Court Judge.

"It will be our contention that this matter of testing to find out Tom's fatherhood is at worst a cover story. A lie...or at best...a hedged wager. A survival plan for Loki in the event that his attempt to usurp my throne should fail.

Loki tried to speak but the King of the Gods said, "Silence! We have heard enough. You are guilty of all charges. It only remains to pass sentence." Odin looked at Tom Wolfe and the snow dragon. They were exhausted.

"But first we should pause for refreshment."

Tom's eyes darted round the room, unable to settle on anyone or anything. Loki, God of Mischief, was claiming that all the calamity unleashed, the chaos, confusion and destruction, not to mention the killing of young gods and Ice Giants, had been set in train as a test to find out -

To find out whether Loki or Thor is my old man?

What a choice! A muscle-bound idiot or a criminal craftsman of cunning and guile!

Tom felt as though he was about to throw up. It was one thing having a nice-but-dim dead guy looking out from family photos at you. A big, burly and pleasant, honest fisherman-cum-steeplejack who was your Dad. It was something else to have this instead -

Now that's all been torn up. What am I left with? A powerful god who can summon storms and defeat Ice Giants with a single blow of his hammer but who is a complete idiot with a brain the size of a pea?

Or a god with a brain the size of a planet who can shift his shape into that of a dragon or a gardener, who is a byword for pranks and japes...and who is also a murderer. A killer, infamous in myth and legend.

Tom suddenly realised – of course! – that he could trust nothing that Loki had said to him. Nothing at all! The darts weren't magic. He could have lost his life at any time: he had relied on the things that Loki had supplied and they were phony goods.

Odin looked at Tom, deep in thought. The Father of the Gods stroked his beard.

"Tom, shall we adjourn and fetch cups from the kitchen? I am thirsty. Court work is thirsty work. I have a flask of mead. Let us bring two cups and then I can pass sentence."

Odin looked down at Snow.

"Strengthen the ice on Loki, please, dragon," he instructed and Snow breathed over Loki's legs adding another glacial layer.

"And keep an eye on that scoundrel! Shout if he so much as sneezes...which would come as no surprise given that he is half-encased in ice."

Tom stood up and followed the All-Father as he made his way through to the kitchen.

"It is time that you tried the drink of the gods, young man," Odin said cheerfully. "Now we have confirmation that your father is Thor. It is a day to celebrate. I have a new grandson or a grand-nephew- that is true whether Loki is right or wrong. Remember the Mischief-Maker is my half-brother too. Either way, I am your grandfather or your great uncle." Odin hesitated. Something troubled the King of the Gods. "Though we may need to look more closely into the proofs that Loki cites about your parentage. Is Thor really your father? That is the question!"

Tom said nothing. He believed he had the answer to that question and even found time to consider whether or not Odin was testing him. It was obvious that Loki's so-called proofs added up to a lie. Thor was not his father! He was almost sure of it. He was fed up with it all. Fed up with being tested. It was like exam season at school: one test after another after another until you never wanted to see another examination again for as long as you drew breath. He looked at the flask that Odin had produced. He wondered when would be the right time to tell the King of the Gods that he was too young to try strong drink, even if it was the Drink of the Gods. Fourteen-year-old athletes did not sup mead.

Meanwhile in the Day Room, Loki slyly moved one arm and an eyebrow. That was all it took.

Snow was about to cry out a warning but stifled the yell on finding another dragon sharing the Day Room.

"Snaffler!" Snow hissed but the Fire Dragon pursed its lips in the signal for Silence recognised by all speaking creatures.

The ice began to sizzle on the red hot dragon's limbs. It sizzled, melted and flooded to the floor in puddles or sprayed into the air as steam. Clouds formed in the Day Room.

Odin and Tom rushed back in time to see two dragons, one white as snow and another green as grass square up to one another. They barely had time to understand what their eyes had absorbed when the green dragon lifted its wings and rose in the air. It blasted the window to smithereens with one fiery breath and flew out and away soaring towards the New York skyline. Odin was about to signal for Snow to follow when he saw the green dragon return to the street outside. It had landed on the sidewalk. The God leapt to the window in time to see the Loki-dragon burst through the door of the diner where Tom had earlier sent the tramps.

Inside the diner people scattered. They had seen the paper-and-wire dragons assembled in China Town to celebrate the arrival of the New Year. The dragons were bright, colourful and Fun. They were lit by fiery lanterns. They had never seen one of those dragons smash its way into a diner before. The creature had burst through the main door and slid to a halt on the tiled floor.

Odin, Tom and Snow were in pursuit. The diner had been set out to resemble the restaurant of a Mississippi paddle boat and many of the fittings had been salvaged from an old steamer languishing in a breaker's yard in Memphis. A large full-length portrait in water colour was suspended from one wall. It depicted Stella Cooke in the pose of a beautiful actress and vaudeville singer from pre-Civil War America. The pose looked remarkably like a famous depiction of Shirley Shoretree dressed to play Cleopatra, sitting on a recliner with a view of the gardens of Alexandria in the background. The green dragon did not hesitate. The very moment that Odin appeared in the diner, the Loki-dragon dipped its head, plunged into the surface of the portrait and disappeared from sight. The portrait rippled and the image changed subtly. Stella's face was replaced by that of Shirley Shoretree.

Odin was stymied. He could not risk plunging into the portal. Even the Father of the Gods had to negotiate Chaos with Care. Loki had spent weeks, months even, striking bargains with the Lords of Chaos to ensure safe passage. Odin did not have the privilege of time.

Tom was at his side. Odin placed a hand on his shoulder and began to steer him back towards the hostel. Mute, Tom walked ahead of the God. Silence dominated the diner. Several tramps sat in stunned silence not quite able to believe what they had seen.

At the door Odin stopped and turned so that he could address the room.

"Let this be a lesson," the grand baritone voice boomed out. "No more drink! And no more stupefying substances. You don't chase the dragon. As you've seen: it ends with the dragon chasing you."

And he walked back to the hostel with the young English boy.

Back in the Day Room the Father of the Aesir took his place on the high-backed chair again.

"Well, Snow?" he said, bluntly.

The dragon was embarrassed.

"I'm sorry, sire. I regret what happened but I was taken by surprise. I have never seen any god change shape as swiftly as Loki. In the blink of an eye he transformed himself to appear as a replica of my cousin, Snaffler. He's a fire-breather, Snaffler, and the temperature of his scales is enough to melt ice."

Odin was generous. "Don't be too harsh on yourself, dragon," he said. "Loki is a wily creature. His craft and cunning know no equal... unless we take the case of Thor's young son here." said Odin indicating Tom.

Danelaw's Fly-Half hung his head. He did not feel good about any of this. He was feeling sick.

Odin stood up from the high-backed chair.

"Come here, young Wolfe," the God said. He placed a strong hand on Tom's shoulder. You've had a lot to digest today. It will take time for everything to percolate through that fine brain of yours. Listen to me. Take time. Reflect. Think of your family, your friends. Uncle Bernard, Stella, Rob. You'd like to see them again?"

Tom looked up and his face brightened.

"I'd suggest that you'd rather see them sooner than later?"

Tom was about to say with a soup-spoon's serving of sarcasm, "No I'd rather hang around in frozen New York with an old geezer and a bunch of tramps and drunks!" but just as the words formed in his mind he stopped. He remembered some of the trouble that cheek, sarcasm and pranks had landed him in and he thought twice.

"I'd love to go home, sire," he said in a dull, sober voice.

Odin pondered, lost in thought for a time.

"I have to return to Asgard," he said at length. "I have much to attend to, not least reining in Thor and preventing him from destroying every last man and jack of the Frost Giants. I shall bring him to heel and have him return to Midgard. There are at least three Ice Giants loose and causing havoc on Earth. After he has caught them all I'll arrange for him to come and visit you. Perhaps he could visit Danelaw school in time for your next home game. Rugby isn't the Thunder God's bag you understand. He's more of an ice Hockey Jock, Highland Games, Dwarfchucking Jack-the-Lad-type, that sort of thing. But you could teach him about the scrummage, drop-goals and tap tackles? In the meantime I need to get you back to where you came from and within a minute or two of when you came from!"

Odin pondered again for several long minutes and then spoke once more.

"But first a statement or two, a pronouncement, a question and a request."

Tom looked up at the God who, even though Tom was standing and Odin was sitting on a chair, was still head-and-shoulders above Tom.

"What's that, sir?"

The statements first. I can tell that you are vexed by the question, 'Who is your father?' And that you have been perplexed by Loki's claim to have helped you throughout the quests. I can assure you that isn't the case. On the contrary: while you were battling to save the earth and all it contains, including your family and friends, Loki attempted at crucial moments to distract you. Loki shape-changed and adopted the form of Rob Saunders to pester Stella. Why? To distract you from your quest, to cause you to fail. Loki posed as Maxwell Vanbrugh, again to pester Stella – all with the intention of distracting you. He told you that Time would stand still while you carried out the quests. He lied and then allowed you to see in the Mimir water that Stella was desperately anxious as was your Uncle Bernard - worried that you had been declared missing. All done to distract you. All done to make you fail!

"You were never let down by Stella and Rob. Not once did your friends fail you. Loki has found a way of moving between Asgard and Midgard without the Rainbow Bridge – that I shall have to investigate. He shape-shifted to pose as your friends and tried but failed to cause you to doubt them.

He led you to believe that the darts he had given you were magic. Not true. And pitted against the Roc, playing the steamboat Captain- failure would have caused you to lose the quest. Against the Roc – failure would have led to your death! He knew that the son of Thor would excel at games. No one throws a dart like Thor…other than his son. You raised Thor's hammer. No one is equal to that feat other than the Thunder God and his son.

"If you reflect on everything that happened, he lied to you from the very start. He told you he had made a potion that erased memory for a few days. He said that he gave the potion to me and my son, the God of Thunder. An innocent prank to liven up one of my Midgard-gadabouts. A lie! He had stolen my Memory and hidden it in a cage in New Jorvik!

He hid here in the hostel for a time, to ensure – not that my memory would return – on the contrary – he lingered here to ensure that my memory would remain lost.

He told you that my absence from Asgard caused the gods' powers to fail. Nonsense! The gods' powers do not depend on my being present in Asgard. Their power failed because Loki cast a spell on Freja and erased part of her memory. She failed to provide the gods with life-giving apples that she collects from the goddess Idunn. Heimdal's powers returned the instant he bit on the fruit of Idunn's tree.

"Be assured – these are not the actions of a concerned father. These are the actions of a murderous god trying to destroy the offspring of a rival and a possible obstacle to his own desire to wear the crown of Asgard one day. The plan's sole intention was to deliver him the throne.

"He would have been happy if you had been destroyed. I am uncertain of what grander plot Loki had attempted to weave but your destruction was undoubtedly part of it. He had satisfied himself that you were the Thunder God's son when you wielded Mjolnir as if were merely an earth-bound sledge hammer. Discount those worries about Loki having sired you. Thor is your father. I'm sure of it."

But Tom was not.

"After the statements, a pronouncement and finally a question and a request all rolled together!" Odin said. He paused briefly then looked at Tom.

"The pronouncement: it is the verdict of this Thing that the God of Mischief is guilty of putting the entire world of the gods and mortals in peril. By way of punishment, I hereby banish Loki from Asgard until he has made amends and made reparations to all that have been damaged by his mischief. The nature of those reparations shall be determined at a future Thing.

"Now for the request. I'd wish to offer you a job, Tom Wolfe," said Odin. "Part-time of course. You have to complete your studies on Midgard, at that illustrious academy of wisdom and learning that styles itself, 'Danelaw High'. Not much point in winning a scholarship to one of the most exclusive private schools in the north of England if you don't go on to win some of the glittering prizes!"

Tom's ears pricked up – was that a sneer from the Father of the Gods? Did he dislike private schools?

"A job, sire?"

"Part-time. Think of it as being like a paper round or working in a shop on Saturday mornings – only better rewarded.

"What sort of job, sire?"

"Detective. Asgard's own private detective."

"The Gods' Detective?" Tom wondered. "Gods' Sleuth?"

"One might put it like that," Odin replied with an inscrutable look of solemnity.

"I'd really like to go home, sire!"

"That can be arranged directly," Odin said, "But tell me that you will think about it. You will consider acting as Asgard's detective? It would be a part-time role only."

"I'll think about it," Tom agreed.

A typhoon of blue, red and yellow enveloped Tom. He felt

his feet lose contact with gravity and then he was in the air. And then he wasn't in the air or in gravity or in time. He was flying faster than a jet aeroplane inches above a bright, broad rainbow.

20 Danelaw High

Tom thought that he had been cast directly into the waters of the Mimir pool. He was back in the classroom, hovering above Mr Porter and the rest of the pupils, invisible – like a ghost. Looking down he could even see himself, his old self, the stroppy teenager, cocky, cheeky and a royal pain in the ...neck. Unseen by his classmates, he looked down on the past.

Tom knew that he wouldn't be able to explain to Porter what had happened without landing in more trouble but he was determined to try.

"The gardener just blasted a thick bunch of nettles at the edge of the playing field using a flame gun, sir!" Tom said. "That's why I accidentally shouted out the word."

"I've had enough of this," said Porter. "For disruptive behaviour and lying in class, Wolfe, you can take yourself off to see the headmaster."

Tom was astonished. He hadn't done anything that deserved being sent to the head. For a moment he was speechless.

His best pals tried to help but the teacher pointed to the door.

"Out, Wolfe – you know where to go."

Tom got to his feet and hurried out. He had stormed along the corridor.

The main corridor ran for what seemed like miles through the middle of the school.

The fountain of colour he had been travelling in was evaporating. The classroom scene from the past was dissolving beneath his feet. Still hovering, he glided through walls and then the colourful light-and-mist show dissolved and Tom found himself standing in the school corridor. He was dazed. He swayed unsteadily on his feet.

"Red, orange, yellow, green, blue, indigo, violet," he said. But the typhoon of coloured light had faded like May frost and he put his hand on one of the panelled corridor walls to steady himself.

Stella appeared, reached out and grabbed his forearm.

"Are you OK, Tom? You don't look well!"

Tom's eyes opened like saucers. They were big enough and bright enough to illuminate a Zebra Crossing.

"Stella! You look great! I've got so much to tell you!"

"I know!" Stella said brightly.

"But I mean it. I have! Knife fights, Greek Princesses, cleaning the Augean stables, Snow dragons-!"

Tom stopped in mid-sentence. He remembered.

"What about my Uncle Bernard? Has he been worried?"

"What are you wittering about?" Stella was surprised. "Are you trying to wind me up? It's barely an hour since we had lunch with him!" She gave him a strange look. "This isn't one of your practical jokes is it?"

"No!" Tom yelled. "And what about that scumbag Vanbrugh trying to get you to go out with him?" he blurted.

Stella took a step back surprised. "What are you blathering about, Tom?" she asked. "What about Vanbrugh?"

That stern and fierce look that he knew only too well was on Stella's face. She gripped his hand tightly and began to pull him along the corridor.

"Come on, Tom," she said. "Forget about Vamp. And forget about this stupid wind-up. It's just to stop me dragging you up there, isn't it? Come on!" You've still got time to make it."

"Make what?" Tom said.

"The head's office. I don't know where you've been dithering in the corridor but it's less than a minute since

Porter sent you out of class. If you hurry to the office now no one will notice you've been idling!"

Tom was baffled.

"But wait!" he said in a loud voice.

"No time to wait!" Stella insisted and because it was Stella, Tom allowed himself to be dragged along the corridor and shoved towards the stairs.

"Go on!" Stella insisted. "Go now and no one will question where you've been!"

The headmaster's office was up a flight of stairs at the far end of the corridor. Stella stood at the bottom of the stairs and waved her arms ushering him towards the headmaster's door. Tom, too hurried and confused to wonder about what was going on and what had happened to Time and Events and Everything You Could Possibly Think Of... ran up the stairs. A set of double doors lay at the top of the first flight of stairs. Tom swung through the doors. Out of sight of Stella he reached into his rucksack and took out the Mimir mirror. He opened it and passed his hand over the glass. Odin's face appeared.

"All-Father - what happened?" asked Tom.

"I used some of the Old Magic to send you back to when and where you came from, give or take a moment or two!"

"So Stella, my uncle-"

"Everything the same as if you'd never been away. No anxiety, no fright and no missing Tom."

"But what about Augeas' stables, Apollonia, Wild Bill Hickory and Anatole Prince, Citizen of France?"

"Oh that all happened," said Odin. "Everything that happened when you passed through the portals happened. Ancient Greece, the old Mississippi. Hobble, Slicer in New Jorvik, in a modern day Ice Age — that all happened. It's where you are now that remains untouched. For Stella, for Bernard, for Danelaw High - it will all be as if you had never been away !"

"How?" said Tom, lamely.

"I put a U-bend in Space and Time," said Odin. "It's one of the advantages of being the Father of the Gods." He described fixing a paradox of Space and Time as if it were a problem of plumbing.

"Now you need to go and see your headmaster or the U-bend will block up and you'll knock Time out of kilter."

Tom hesitated.

"Go on!" said Odin, sounding just like an angry, elderly grandparent. "Don't make me come down there!" Tom snapped the mirror shut, turned quickly, walked up the last of the stairs and knocked on the headmaster's door. Tom peered back down over his shoulder through the glass in the double doors and could just make out Stella. She was still standing at the bottom of the staircase. She had not seen a thing.

"Come!" yelled an unmistakable baritone voice in the dull steel tone of command.

Tom pushed open the door and entered.

"Mr Porter sent me to see you, sir," Tom said to Mr Ashe, the Headmaster. Ashie, as he was affectionately known to all the pupils, swivelled round in his Captain's chair. He was a big old man with an eye patch. He had lost an eye during the War. No one had ever been able to prove beyond reasonable doubt which war had been Ashie's war. Most favoured the Falklands Conflict when he would have been a very young man. Others said it was Desert Storm while those who were particularly unkind suggested the Boer campaign of 1901.

Ashie had a large head, the head of a general and his face was a criss-crossed maze of trenches and battle lines. Tom was apprehensive. What was his punishment to be? Would he be banned from playing rugby for the school?

Please give me detention and five hundred lines instead! Ashie fixed him with his one good eye and his great bushy eyebrows beetled over his brow. The Head didn't look grim as he usually did just before meting out punishment. He looked positively jovial. His face - Tom would have sworn it – was beaming.

"Ah yes, young Wolfe, young Torsson Wolfe. I asked Mr Porter to send you along. I have been reading through some of your recent reports."

Tom looked down. This was ominous! A pile of school reports lay open on Ashie's desk.

"Thomas Torsson Wolfe. Middle name: Storm. Should have been *Mischief*."

"Sir?"

"You see - I have a job I'd like you to do. Who better to find a thief than a prankster?"

"A job, sir?" Tom asked bewildered.

"Yes, a job. Think of it as being like a paper round or a Saturday morning job in a shop. We don't want to interfere with your studies!"

Ashie paused. Tom's bewilderment was complete.

"Some valuable property has gone missing recently in very suspicious circumstances, young Wolfe. I'd like to ask you to act as the school detective."

"'School detective'?" Tom parroted, slack-jawed, not certain that he could believe what his ears were telling him.

"Just between ourselves, of course," said Mr Ashe with a conspiratorial smile and what might almost have passed for a wink. Tom opened his own eyes wide and looked at the headmaster again. Did he remind him of someone?

THE END

Peter Maley was born in Northumberland and lives in the Scottish Borders.

His first efforts in print were cartoon stories drawn on old newspaper when he was a child. He has been writing ever since.

If you enjoyed this, please feel free to write a review on Amazon. You can post your review on the same page where you bought *The Lost Gods*.

The Lost Gods is also available from Amazon as a Kindle book.

Look out for new titles by Peter Maley, also to be published by Cherry House Publishing, see:

www.cherryhousepublishing.co.uk

Coming Soon: Volume Two of *The Adventures of Tom Wolfe*